The
Seventh
Etching

Judith K. White

iUniverse, Inc.
Bloomington

The Seventh Etching

iUniverse books may be ordered through booksellers or by contacting:

iUniverse
1663 Liberty Drive
Bloomington, IN 47403
www.iuniverse.com
1-800-Authors (1-800-288-4677)

Because of the dynamic nature of the Internet, any web addresses or links contained in this book may have changed since publication and may no longer be valid. The views expressed in this work are solely those of the author and do not necessarily reflect the views of the publisher, and the publisher hereby disclaims any responsibility for them.

Any people depicted in stock imagery provided by Thinkstock are models, and such images are being used for illustrative purposes only.

Certain stock imagery © Thinkstock.

ISBN: 978-1-4759-0811-4 (sc)
ISBN: 978-1-4759-0812-1 (hc)
ISBN: 978-1-4759-0813-8 (e)

Library of Congress Control Number: 2012905743

Printed in the United States of America

iUniverse rev. date: 4/25/2012

Dedication

THIS BOOK IS DEDICATED TO
THE THOUSANDS OF ORPHANS
WHO FOR FOUR CENTURIES
PASSED THROUGH THE
AMSTERDAM CITY ORPHANAGE
AND TO
THE STAFF WHO CARED FOR THEM.

Prologue

onkey brain. That is his affliction. Creatures arrive from every direction and insist that he give them life. A black lion stands on its hind feet, large front paws reaching forward ready to grab. A horned one-eyed reptile gazes with a menace that won't let go. A wizard with horizontal hair focuses his tiny eyes on the end of a long nose so sharp it could cut a slice of morning cheese.

After two rushed days of drawing, painting, cutting, and rolling the heavy presses back and forth, Nicolaas tries desperately to ban the haunting images that drive him. 'Oh for a vision to calm my spirit and soothe my aching body,' he thinks. 'Surely I can conjure up some comforting design, some calming figure from some source.'

And then there it is. His mother. Her long dark skirt on wide hips. The mussed faded white apron. The cap tight around her face. Her usual expression – straight, thin lips, grim and determined. The full sleeves of her blouse rolled up above the elbows. Her arms covered in suds, she massages the shoulders of her husband. Father, looking remarkably like his son – blond, blue-eyed and muscular. Sitting in the wooden laundry tub. His back to her, head bent forward, the tips of his long, straight hair touching the surface of the water, hiding his face. His powerful chest exposed, glistening.

No. Wait. This couple is young, playful. The girl pulls the young man's head against her belly, reaches down, cups her hand under his chin, pulls his head backwards, bites his lip. The man reaches up toward the woman's turban, unwinds it slowly, tosses it in the water. Her thick hair cascades.

Lying on his narrow, wooden bed, hoping for a few hours of deep sleep, Nicolaas moves one hand instinctively toward his groin. To unbuckle and unbutton, though – that would require the work of both hands. His breathing slows. He collapses. His inky fingers rest on his breeches. His dreams continue without him.

Nicolaas was only a child when he discovered his talent for drawing. At first he drew maps, using a piece of cooled charcoal and some cast-off paper, copying from books his father printed. Far-away places intrigued him. He added his own imagined landscapes, forests and mountains with wild beasts, rivers with fanciful fish. He felt a tug, a longing to walk along the Amstel all the way to its source, then back again to where it empties into the harbor. What might he see and smell along the way? Later he was drawn to the taverns.

The spiciness of tobacco, the sweat, the raucous behavior. A group of men gathers at a round table. A blond waif keeps their tankards full and gets a pinch for her effort. The men are alternately silent and then explosive, patting each other on the back one moment, then suddenly arguing – even exchanging threats. It's about games, he realizes. Games for money. Games using cards.

Nicolaas had found a calling. He tried his hand at designing and selling, first a deck with a king's crown, then another with the symbol of the city of Amsterdam, a red pole with three vertical black X's. When he showed these works to his father, his father sliced them into little pieces and threw them in the fire. His father told him gambling was the work of the devil and he forbade him to draw ever again.

But Nicolaas persisted in secret. His success encouraged him to experiment. His designs became more complex – snarling lion heads, docile unicorns, and wily serpents. Now eighteen, self-taught and determined, he had only recently turned to making increasingly bawdy and lucrative etchings for which merchants, physicians, and tradesmen often paid a good price. It bothered him not a whit that such transactions were illegal, given that he had never apprenticed with a licensed artist and was therefore not a member of the body that governed the sale of works of art – the Guild of Sint Lucas.

His father's plan for Nicolaas's life could not be clearer. He would inherit the print shop, live in the rooms behind and above it as his father had, marry a strong Dutch woman, go to church every Sunday, obey God. The list went on. The new sign, "Stradwijk and Son," now hung outside the shop's front door. Yet the Amstel River continued to beckon.

Finding a comfortable sleeping position was becoming even more difficult because of a damned neighborhood cat. Or was it the family cat? Had he brought it in before he fell exhausted into bed? The mewing was outside, but was coming closer and more insistent. Dogs were beginning to chorus with the cat. If it was his own cat, tomorrow he would have to endure the complaints and prying of his neighbor, Mrs. Van Heel. But he could not rouse himself to respond to the increasingly insistent pleas.

When the mewing became shrill and angry, then very close, the sound jolted Nicolaas awake. Could the cat – or something else or somebody – be hurt? He grabbed a bedpost and lifted himself up off the mattress, wincing from his complaining body. His sleeping chamber was directly above the print shop and hung out over the narrow, dirt alleyway below. He opened a shutter onto sky, earth, houses, and cat all blended together in the ink-black night. He heard, but could not see, the startled fluttering of a pigeon above his head.

The neighborhood dogs sounded really alarmed now. Nicolaas ran down the narrow wooden stairs, through the kitchen in the back, through the print shop in the front, and unbolted the main door of the dwelling. The cool air comforted his sore, bare shoulders. He peered out, hoping the cat would have heard the door open and slink in, but no cat appeared. He stepped out and down onto the first step and nearly kicked over a basket. As he shed his sleepiness, he realized that the mewing - more like howling now - was coming from that basket. He picked up the basket and, swaying it side to side with irritation, carried it to the kitchen, placed it on the table, lit a candle, and held the candle over it. A tiny human creature, red-faced and furious, was silenced momentarily by the sudden firelight. When the light did not result in instant satisfaction of its hunger, however, the creature recommenced its wailing.

Nicolaas's first impulse was to go knocking on doors, looking for a wet nurse. But how many people might he awaken before he found one? And if he did, would she be willing to rouse herself in the middle of the night for this foundling? There was something else stopping him. Why had someone left this child on his doorstep? Perhaps they would come back for it momentarily?

The infant had exhausted itself with crying and was dozing with its tiny mouth turned down dejectedly. Soft, self-pitying sobs escaped, but its expression seemed to warn, "I may be momentarily defeated, but I will soon return and with all the force of my being, I will demand to be fed."

Nicolaas grabbed a bucket and a rope. He went out to the courtyard, picked up his father's one nanny goat, brought it into the kitchen, tied it to the table, and began milking. Soon there was a good mugful of fresh, hot milk in the bucket. How to get the milk into the baby's mouth, he wondered. He looked around the spare kitchen and grabbed a rag. He twisted a corner of the rag into a cone shape and soaked it in the milk. He held the dripping corner over the baby until its mouth was dotted with white droplets. Aware of nourishment nearby, the baby woke, opened its mouth, and began screeching again.

Nicolaas coaxed the thin wet twist of rag between the tiny lips and watched the grateful creature suck it nearly dry. When Nicolaas removed the rag from the baby's mouth in order to soak it again in milk, the baby became furious, its impatient cries of betrayal filling the room. After many tries, Nicolaas learned to move more quickly. Eventually the infant learned that it could trust the gauzy nipple to reappear after a few seconds, offering the sustenance it craved.

When the baby was satisfied, Nicolaas saw that the milk had dribbled down the baby's chin into the creases of its neck and soaked the top of its shirt. When he lifted the baby out of the basket, holding it for the first time, the baby's head swung dangerously loose before it occurred to Nicolaas to support it. He reached one arm under the baby, cradling it close and, with his free hand, removed all its clothing, every bit of it damp.

He saw that the umbilical cord had only recently fallen off, leaving a not-yet-healed opening. The penis and scrotum looked too miniature to be real. He caressed the toes and fingernails, the dimpled elbows, and the downy hair. This baby was only days old, he realized. He brought the baby's face against his and felt the softness of its cheek. He laid it down on his knees and moved the candle closer to get a good look at its face. With its belly temporarily full, the infant was content now, eyes wide, curious, searching. Nicolaas brushed away a surprisingly hearty tear that had settled in the dent in the middle of the baby's chin. When the baby circled its fist around Nicolaas's ink-stained finger, Nicolaas experienced a rushing, seizing tenderness. The sensation was so unexpected and filled him with such awe, he felt dizzy. He thought he might weep.

He became concerned that this treasure not be chilled and, gingerly carrying the baby in one arm, picked up the candle and went to fetch the shirt he had thrown off while working in the print shop. The print shop was in disarray. Before his father returned in a few hours, he would have to put every item back in place, refill ink cartons, wipe every surface clean, and hide the cards and the etchings, erasing every bit of evidence that he had used it.

When he returned to the kitchen, light was just beginning to enter through the window. In the drab space, a small bit of color caught Nicholaas's eye. Fastened to the baby's cast-off wool coverlet was half a playing card cut at a jagged angle like a puzzle piece. A demon-like snake with a long forked tongue, large human eyes, and thick black lashes stared threateningly at those who took their chances with the Lord's judgment.

As the sun rose over the city, reaching toward the low huts of the poor and the high, gabled homes of the wealthy, stretching over the sails of the ships in the harbor and tapping the steeple of New Church on Dam Square, Nicolaas Stradwijk sat embracing a foundling wrapped in his inky shirt, and staring at half a playing card from a deck that he himself had designed and printed one year earlier.

PART I:
Nelleke

Introduction

$\mathfrak{N}$elleke resisted sleep. Always. So much to ponder. Too many questions. Puzzling memories. Songs to hum. There was one thing that worked. Just as she finally became drowsy, she rolled over to curl around the sturdy body of her toddler brother.

But tonight, just like every night for the past month, she did not find Jacob's comforting, soft warmth. She did not breathe in his little boy mustiness. Instead, rolling to her side, finally closing her eyes, she encountered Marja's feet, sweaty under wool stockings. That big toe with its untrimmed nail protruding through that same hole woke her once again with a heartbreaking jolt.

She could not climb in with Isabela either and fall asleep to her soothing lullabies. The Housemother was firm. "Nelleke, that is your bed – the big one over there with Marja and the other two little girls. You sleep there. Every night." And to Isabela, the Housemother insisted, "Nelleke must learn now. She must adjust."

Nelleke was weary with her own tears and her longing for Jacob. 'Can he sleep without me?' she kept wondering. 'Does he miss me too?'

Since she was forbidden from sleeping with Isabela, she decided to pretend she could hear Isabela's voice, singing in her funny language.

As Nelleke tried to imitate Isabela's songs, she allowed herself a few light caresses on the raised wrinkly mark that covered the top of her hand. "Do I have to tie your hands behind your back? You stop touching that, Nelleke," the Housemother had said repeatedly. "God is trying to heal it. You must help Him by leaving it alone."

But she couldn't leave it alone. It changed every day. She began to really explore it now, imagining in the dark that she could see where the mark ended and her normal skin began. At first it was so painful she could only scream. It looked scary and foreign, like a giant red tick stuck there. Then it got puffy and orangey. Next it turned yellow. It itched. Isabela had reassured: "*Sana, sana, colita de rana. Si no sanas hoy, sanarás mañana.*"

"In Dutch. What does it mean in Dutch?" Nelleke always demanded. Isabela would struggle to translate. Sometimes the words would come out twisted and make Nelleke laugh.

"Get well. Get well, little frog tail. If you don't today better get, then tomorrow you will."

Isabela had explained about baby frogs, but Nelleke knew something about tadpoles. Once, at the farm, she had waded into the pond trying to catch a whole family of them. They flitted so fast. She just wanted to grab one, to hold it for a moment. But when she reached for it, she slipped under the water. Uncle Johannes had to come fish her out.

If she must remain in this bed, at least she could hear Isabela's sweet voice in her head: "The tadpoles have tails, you see, but every day the tail gets smaller until one day the tail is all gone. That means the tadpole is now a big, grownup frog. It hops. It doesn't need its tail any more. And that is exactly what will happen to your burn, Nelleke. Every day it will get better and a little smaller until there's no burn left. *Sana. Sana. Colita de rana.*"

That was what happened. Sort of. Now it was a white blotch. Now it looked like an oversized drop of curdled cream, a splat with uneven edges. But it would never go away, the doctor said. It would always be there. It would always remind her of her first night in this place.

Chapter One
Last Morning/First Night

N elleke loved the sound of the cock crowing. It meant light. It meant morning. Always the first awake, she leaped up that day, slipped on her wooden shoes, and ran outside to the privy. Her pet goose waited for her and greeted her with a loud honk that roused the rest of the family. Nelleke opened the lid of a barrel and tossed him a fistful of grain. While the goose pecked at his morning meal, she gently caressed his white feathers and spoke to him softly.

"Some people eat geese. I won't eat you, Langenek. Never. Ever. Even when I'm 'one hundred years old,' I'm gonna still feed you every single day."

A lavender butterfly flew in front of her, almost landing in the yellow ringlet that fell out of her white cap down the middle of her forehead between her large, alert eyes. She laughed and chased the delicate flapping color to the edge of the pond, then watched it continue over the water where she could not follow. Even though she was still lured by the pond's mysteries, she would no longer touch it even with the toes of her shoes. The memory of the pond's frightening, sharp taste was still strong. She began to gag as if that taste were again filling her nostrils and throat, smothering her. For those few moments last summer she had felt like a lost fish caught and dragged down by green slime.

Another honk from Langenek reminded her that the amount of grain her small fist could hold was never enough for him. She ran back to the barrel where the goose stood stretching out its neck toward her, demanding. She reached into the barrel with both hands

1

and simultaneously threw out two more fistfuls, one way in front of Langenek, the other behind him, then amused herself watching him search.

'One hundred years old,' she thought, and then ran inside, calling.

"Aunt Griet. Aunt Griet. How old was your mother when she died?"

Griet was sitting up in bed trying to coach her infant toward her breast. Beginning with the first feeding every day, this was a mother/child struggle that had begun ten months before. Frans did not root like other babies or like piglets or kittens or lambs for that matter. He fussed and complained. He showed little enthusiasm for porridge and mashed berries either, even mixed with honey. In contrast to his robust, ravenous two-year-old cousin, Jacob, Frans was thin. He seemed to have no muscle strength in either arms or legs. And now Griet was pregnant again.

"Aunt Griet. How old was your mother when she died? She was my grandmother and I want to know."

"I don't know, Nelleke. Around twenty-five probably," Griet answered just as Frans finally latched on.

"How old was <u>my</u> mother? The same age?"

"I think so."

"Around twenty-five then?"

"Get Jacob dressed, Nelleke, please."

"Well, she had dark eyes. I know that much. Eyes like mine. I have her eyes. That's what people say. So does Jacob."

Frans broke off from the weak sucking and turned his head toward his lively cousin. With her constant motion and chatter, she was always more interesting to him than anything else.

"Look, Nelleke. You're distracting him again. Get Jacob dressed, I told you."

Nelleke knelt down beside Aunt Griet and Uncle Johannes's tall bed. Then she poked her head underneath the bed into the space where she and Jacob slept. Stretching out her arm, she felt a little boy leg, a leg she loved for its sturdiness and for the warmth it gave off during the cold winter nights. She reached inside the wool stocking covering that leg and moved her fingers down to the bottom of the foot. Jacob pulled away, rolled out from under the opposite side of the bed, and ran teasingly away from his sister, round and round the one large room the family shared. Twirling the stocking, Nelleke ran too. When she caught Jacob

2

and delighted him with insistent tickles on the bottom of that one bare foot, their joint giggles filled the room.

Aunt Griet propped Frans between pillows and began readying breakfast – ale and plain bread. Nelleke pushed open the shutter, letting in some welcome light. She could see Uncle Johannes in the barn milking their two remaining cows and pouring the milk into large earthen jugs for transport. They could no longer spare any milk for butter or cheese for themselves she had heard him say. He took every drop to the market to be sold.

The early autumn air was cool, but Nelleke would never let a few shivers keep her inside. She banged the house door behind her and began balancing on the long wooden planks that led to the barn. Uncle Johannes had put them there to make a path through the mud last spring, but the planks had sunk in places. Nelleke enjoyed seeing how far she could stretch her legs in order to step only on the wood, avoiding the dirt.

She stepped inside the barn with its familiar mixed odors of hay, fresh milk, sweaty cow, and cow poop. Uncle Johannes said to call it by its name, manure. He had already cleaned the barn, but the odors lingered. Nelleke passed rows of empty stalls until she came to where Uncle Johannes sat on a stool with his face against a cow's side, pulling rhythmically on its teats.

"May I taste the milk, Uncle Johannes? Just a little bit?"

"Just a little bit, Nelleke. In a minute."

Nelleke walked over to the piles of hay. In the farthest corner, she gave several exploratory kicks before she located her secret sack. Recently, she had noticed that an animal had been chewing on it. She gave the sack a hard kick before she felt assured that no mouse or rat was using her sack for breakfast feed. Only then could she play her favorite game. She closed her eyes and reached deep into the sack, feeling the stones inside. She chose one, felt its size and weight, turned it over in her palm and tried to picture it.

She guessed that the stone she held was the flat white one with the gray stripes in the shape of a cross. It was the one she had found before, turned up by Uncle Johannes's plow in the center of a field maybe one year ago. She pulled her hand out of the sack.

"I was right, Uncle Johannes. I guessed it. See?" she said, running to show him. "This is the one."

"How many do you have now, Nelleke?"

"Twelve. Want me to count them for you?"

"No, that's okay. I believe you."

Uncle Johannes had taught her to count, but he was too busy to listen to her counting them every day.

"Do you think I'll ever get a hundred in my collection Uncle Johannes? Is a hundred the highest number in the world?"

"Just about."

Uncle Johannes moved the stool and bucket over to the second cow and began milking.

Nelleke sat down in the hay and poured out the sack's contents on the barn floor. Recently, since people had learned that she collected stones, they had been giving them to her. Her favorites were the ones Mrs. Kist gave her last Sunday after church.

"Here, Nelleke, I found these for you," she said as she tucked them into Nelleke's palm. Three clear, rounded stones, each the size of the tip of her thumb. At first they looked exactly alike, but now Nelleke could tell one from the other. One was slightly flatter. One had a jagged side. One had a tiny blue dot.

"What shall I name the sister stones, Uncle Johannes?"

"Up to you."

"I know. How about Liesje, Femke, and Antje?"

"Nelleke, breakfast," Aunt Griet called.

Nelleke returned all the stones to the bag, twisted the top, and tucked it back into its hiding place. She used to play with the stones inside on the floor of the house. But she often forgot to pick them up even when Aunt Griet reminded her that Frans and Jacob might eat one and choke. One day Aunt Griet swept all the stones outside along with dust, dried apple peels, and dead spiders. Nelleke had to rescue them one by one. Now she kept them tucked away and protected with a layer of hay on top.

Usually, before Aunt Griet could find tasks for her niece, Nelleke would try to escape into the yard, the barn, down by the pond – anywhere she could explore and search for bugs, snakes, and dead birds. Every day she watched as her uncle loaded the mare he shared with a neighbor. He would tie down the milk jugs and begin the walk to town.

On Sundays Nelleke went to the church at the edge of the town, but she had never been to the market in the center plaza. She would bombard Uncle Johannes with questions: "Do they sell pretty skirts?

4

Do you ever see books? Does anyone there play the violin? Can I go? Please, Uncle?"

At twenty-three, Johannes had become sullen. He and his neighbors thought that they had saved the land forever from the water threats. The dikes were built, patched, and regularly reinforced. The recently improved windmills drained the polders efficiently at first. Yet after three weeks of constant rain, they had been powerless. Johannes struggled to hold onto his former vision of grazing cattle, freshly painted buildings, and a contented wife surrounded by rosy children. He had intended to raise his wife's niece and nephew along with his own. Now he felt he was abandoning his family role.

Today Uncle Johannes did not load up the mare. He borrowed another neighbor's wagon and lined up the jugs in it. He hooked the mare up to the wagon.

"Why are you taking the wagon, Uncle Johannes? Are you going to buy something special for us? Bring us back something big that fills the whole wagon? Please, Uncle. A surprise? Will you?"

Aunt Griet called, "Stop pestering Uncle Johannes, Nelleke. Come inside." Nelleke walked slowly, kicking pebbles, picking up sticks, and throwing them. She was sure that some unpleasant task awaited her. Scrub the floor. Hang up the wet clothes. Change the squirmy, smelly baby.

Yet here was the surprise: When Nelleke arrived at the door, Aunt Griet was holding Nelleke's Sunday clothes. This wasn't a church day. Why did Aunt Griet look so sad? She might have been crying.

"You're going with your uncle today. Come here. I'll help you dress."

"Just me? Now who died?"

"No one has died, Nelleke. You're just going with your uncle, that's all."

"To town? To the market? I know. Maybe we're going to visit Mrs. Kist.

She'll give us snacks, I bet. Am I starting school? Will I learn to read?"

"No, Nelleke. Stop this mindless guessing. Please. Turn around while I tie your apron. Put your cap on straight. Go now."

Nelleke whooped and leaped right out of her shoes, sending them clattering against each other. She picked them up and ran in her stockings out to where her uncle was waiting.

Only later did she realize that she had never said good-bye to Jacob.

* * *

Nelleke kept moving up and down, rocking side by side on the seat beside her uncle.

"When will we get to the market, Uncle Johannes?"

"Never, if you don't sit still. Stop it, Nelleke. You'll tip us right over."

"I bet you'll buy flour. Maybe you'll buy Aunt Griet some lace. Maybe we can find a toy for Jacob. Maybe . . ."

"I'm buying nothing. I'm selling the milk. That's all."

"Can we at least buy Aunt Griet some cheese?"

Johannes gave the horse a little lick of the whip.

Nelleke waved vigorously to every neighbor they passed. She remembered when their fields looked like lakes. There were still puddles or thick mud in many places. Finally, she saw her church, then houses close together, then another church right in the center of town, then an open plaza.

"Stay here in the wagon, Nelleke. I'll be right back."

Nelleke stood up, held onto the side of the wagon and watched her uncle leave with the heavy milk jugs. He walked along the canal and then disappeared around a corner.

A ragged man with a dirt-smeared, caved-in face walked by the wagon, mumbling. Nelleke was frightened. When the man was gone, she climbed down off the wagon and went looking for Uncle Johannes. She set off in the direction where she saw him round the corner.

But she was quickly distracted. There was so much noise. Chickens squawking. Children whining. Others running. Parents calling. Vendors shouting. She stopped at a fabric stall. Bolt after bolt of solid-colored cloth: black, brown, gray, and one exquisite red. Wouldn't she love it if Aunt Griet would make her a new Sunday dress! And ready-made aprons. Some just her size. So white and clean. With a full-length apron like that her new dress would never get dirty. Caps, too, trimmed in dainty lace.

Suddenly, the stench of raw meat overwhelmed her. In the next stall, there was a family of butchers – husband, wife, and son all with red-streaked aprons, hacking at a side of pork. The pig's head hung at the front of the stall. The head was an enticement to all who passed by and a promise that the pork was fresh. Nelleke held her nose and rushed by, trying to escape the blood odors. She noticed that all three members of the family had what looked like permanent rust stains under their fingernails, on their hands, even on their arms.

The pungent smell of the herring stalls was more pleasant. A customer removed his hat, tipped back his head and, holding the raw herring by the tail, lowered the slimy, salty fish down his throat, then took a long slurp of beer and let out a contented belch.

Nelleke ran on, but stopped at a frame stall. Wooden frames of all sizes. Most were empty, but a few had paintings in them. She gazed at one in particular. It was a little girl, perhaps a year younger than Nelleke, about five. The child was concentrating on the knitting in her lap. In a small cart beside her was a chubby infant. They were in a field beside a lake. That could be me and my brother, she thought. Except that Nelleke could never sit still long enough to knit. The child in the painting was so calm. How long did she have to sit there, she wondered, to be painted like that?

"Little girl. Little girl. Here." A stout woman in a fruit stall was holding out to her a big, red apple. "Thank you, Ma'am, but I have no money," Nelleke said, looking back and forth between the smiling vendor and the juicy offering.

"Never you mind, child. If you want it, it's yours."

"Thank you." Nelleke smiled her gap smile. Her two front teeth were missing. When they had become quite loose and were hanging, Uncle Johannes gave them a final tug. "Best not to swallow these," he said. Nelleke added the teeth to her secret pouch in the barn. New teeth were just beginning to peek through. She reached for the apple and, using her side teeth, took the biggest bite she could.

With sweet crunchy apple filling her mouth, Nelleke continued to wander more deeply into the labyrinth of vendors. By the time an hour had passed, she was holding in her small fist an orange flower with a broken stem, two crispy string beans, and a whirligig. Shiny apple juice stained her chin. Her apron was covered with wet soapy spots from the bubbles game a chubby little boy had shared with her. Some of the bubbles had splashed on her cap, too, and on the flaxen curls that spilled out of the cap.

"Is that a violin, Sir? It's so big."

"It's called a gamba, child," said the instrument dealer. "The notes are lower than a violin's. Listen."

The vendor plucked one of the strings. The deep, vibrating sound sent a thrill through Nelleke.

"Do it again."

The musician plucked out a quick melody, showing off all the strings. The tune made Nelleke think of the frogs in the pond.

"Here, you try it."

Nelleke stretched her small finger toward a thick string, intently anticipating the sound she was about to produce. Before she could reach the instrument, though, someone tucked her finger into her fist and pulled her hand back.

"Nelleke, I've been looking for you for a long time. I told you to stay in that wagon."

Chapter Two
The Aunts Decide

Already, Griet regretted the decision. She and Johannes had discussed it for months. The idea first came to her after the waters had receded enough for them to come down out of the attic. Two weeks up there with three children and the only animals they had been able to save: five chickens, one goose, and two cows. A whole herd gone. Some days people rowed by and threw up a bit of bread. Other days Johannes grabbed the rope outside the attic's only window. Slowly moving one hand, then one foot, then the other hand, then the other foot, he descended into their small rowboat and paddled away looking for food.

It took weeks longer for the land to dry. Their once promising farm was in ruins. They could no longer afford laborers. Johannes had to care for the animals, till the soil, rebuild the barn, and keep the boat repaired. He also worked with the other farmers to continue to drain the land and build more dikes and windmills. And, of course, he went every day to the market. The milk from the two cows brought in needed cash.

Household help was now out of the question. Griet alone ground the grain, baked the bread, made the candles, even combined herbs in an attempt to build strength, soothe sore muscles, and cure headaches. Gone were the days when Griet could enjoy a quiet moment at her lace making or read favorite books to the children.

Griet and Johannes were barely twenty when they married. They had so many plans for building up the farm that Griet's father left for her. Now at twenty-two, she was pregnant again and exhausted. Her first born, Frans, was only ten months old.

He was sickly and fretful. He couldn't even sit up yet. He wanted his mother to hold him every waking minute. She could not rid herself of the fear she lived with during her first pregnancy. Her own mother had died giving birth to her. Would this be her fate too? Would she die young, leaving her husband with all these children to raise?

Her nephew, Jacob, was a solid toddler, good natured, and bright, adoring of the sister who doted on him. But he was only two. He required constant supervision.

And Nelleke! Her niece had no interest in helping with the baby or with housework. She disobeyed. She wandered. She asked endless questions. And the child barely slept! They set a strict bed time for her, but she would just lie awake, talking and singing to herself. It was her voice they heard as they fell asleep and her voice they heard when they woke.

It was the pond incident that convinced them they must make a change. Only by chance, Griet glanced out the open doorway and saw a corner of Nelleke's sinking bonnet. If she hadn't seen it at that moment? If Johannes had not been nearby repairing the tool shed? They most certainly would have lost her.

Griet rocked her fretful infant and patted her spreading stomach. What awaited these children? Would Frans live? Would the baby be healthier than its older brother? It was so difficult raising children with no family nearby. Griet's family had not suffered the fate of many families that lost everyone to the plague. Yet some of them had died young, anyway.

Griet's father, Hendrik Stradwijk outlived both his wives, but the losses made him bitter and strict. His printing business thrived, but it was hard, physical work. He purchased the farm to escape to on weekends. He lived long enough to see his fourth grandchild, and first granddaughter, Nelleke, become a lively, curious, talkative three-year-old. The only surviving child of Hendrik's first marriage, Elsbeth, lived in Amsterdam with her merchant husband, twin boys, age nine, and ten-year-old, Willem. It was extremely unusual for twins to survive, yet both of Elsbeth's twins were thriving.

Griet and her brother, Nicolaas, Nelleke's father, were born to Hendrik's second wife.

When Nelleke's mother, Rona, died giving birth to Jacob, and Nicolaas was inexplicably murdered six months later, the two sisters together made a decision about their orphaned niece and nephew. Or perhaps Elsbeth made the decision. Griet always deferred to her strong-minded older sister. Griet was newly married and had no children yet. She and Johannes had inherited a large, promising farm. Griet should be the one to raise Nelleke and Jacob.

Elsbeth had a reasonably comfortable life, three strong sons, and an attentive, respected husband. She did not want an unruly niece in her home, leading her children into trouble. Perhaps even bringing disaster. She offered to send additional money, but she refused to take any responsibility for Nelleke. "Her people can put a pox on you, you know. Just look, Griet. Both her parents dead. The flood. Your losses. Your sick baby. If I let that child into my home, we'd have the plague at our door in no time." Griet knew that her niece was no witch, but she could not argue with the self-satisfied, suspicious Elsbeth. The only other option was the City Orphanage in Amsterdam.

They sent the papers. Both of Nelleke's paternal grandparents and her father were *poorters* – Amsterdam citizens. Nelleke's parents, Nicolaas and Rona, were married in the *Nieuwe Kerk*. Nelleke herself was baptized there. All was in order. However, they made the decision to leave blank the spaces "Mother's Family Name." "Date of birth." "Place of birth." They did not want to prejudice the Regents against Nelleke or risk a rejection. In any case, they didn't even have all of that information. It wasn't recorded anywhere.

The usually contented Jacob was growing impatient. "Nel. Nel," he had been calling all day. He banged on the door, wanting to go out, wanting to find her. He reached toward the window, demanding that Griet hold him up so he could look out.

When Griet looked toward the window, she saw the flowers on the ledge. Just yesterday Nelleke had come running in with two large bouquets of wildflowers. "Look, Aunt Griet. I found Queen Anne's lace, heather, daisies, dandelions." Somehow, she knew all their names. "These are for you, Aunt Griet. Aren't they beautiful? All for you."

Chapter Three
Breakdown

After they had resumed their trek and had been bumping along for about three-quarters of an hour, the right side of the wagon collapsed, sending Nelleke sliding downward. The sudden crack and weight shift alarmed the horse who bolted forward. Fortunately, he couldn't move fast, dragging a one-wheeled vehicle.

"What happened, Uncle Johannes? What broke? Can you fix it? I wanna see." Johannes lifted Nelleke down from the wagon.

The upper half of the wheel was suspended in mid air. Shards of wood from the lower half covered the ground. The sun was hidden behind the thick trees. They were alone on the rutted road. They could hear no animal or people sounds.

Nelleke covered the beginnings of fear with chatter and giggling. "The wheel's so lopsided. Uncle Johannes, remember last week? I kicked a leg loose from the table? Everything on the table crashed. The hot porridge nearly burned my leg. The serving dish clanged and rolled. It was Aunt Griet's best pewter plate, wasn't it? That leg of mutton was so greasy. It slid all the way across the floor. And a pitcher full of beer!" Nelleke giggled.

"Yes, Nelleke, I remember."

They began walking to seek help. Nelleke, faced with Johannes's silence in response to her bombardment of questions, entertained herself. She stopped to count on her fingers how many butterflies she had seen. She imitated rabbits. She tried hopping backwards. She chased a chipmunk into the woods.

Hoping she would not lag far behind, Johannes put his head down and kept walking. So it was Nelleke who first spotted the smoke.

"Look, Uncle. There must be a house up there." Leaving the road, they followed a path, came to a pond, a field full of haystacks and then a farmhouse whose sharply pitched, triangular roof ended in a tall brick chimney. Baskets of all sizes littered the yard. An overturned wheelbarrow lay on its side next to a stack of rusty barrels. A large hog, mud sticking to its left side, tried to reach them, but was stopped by a rope tying him to a fence post. Cabbages were piled high on a front step leading to an open door from which floated the inviting scent of fresh bread and burning peat.

The house's few windows were shuttered. A sunburned, bow-legged man and a large-hipped woman cradling an infant in her arms emerged from the cottage's dark interior and greeted them hesitatingly. Once Johannes explained their dilemma, the farmer offered to walk back to the wagon with him to investigate the problem. His wife offered to watch Nelleke and sat next to the cabbage pile to nurse her baby. A boy of seven or eight came running from the side of the house, using a stick to guide a rolling hoop. When he saw Nelleke, he stopped and stared. The hoop kept going and scattered the chickens.

"Who are you?" he asked, with a mixture of suspicion and curiosity. The straight blond hair hanging to his shoulders looked like the haystacks they had just walked through.

"Dirck, this is Nelleke," his mother explained. "She's visiting us for a little while."

Dirck stood motionless for a long moment, studying what seemed to him like an apparition. He decided that Nelleke was an angel who had appeared on his doorstep. Then, partially recovered and hoping to keep the angel from flying away, he hoisted up his jacket and reached into the back pocket of his oversized pants. "Wanna play marbles?"

Dirck squatted, picked up a stick, and drew a circle in the dirt. This was a new game for Nelleke. Squatting beside him, she was oblivious to the thick dust that soon covered the hem of her skirt. While she watched the large marble shoot off from Dirck's thumb and crash into the smaller ones, she listened to his steady monologue. "Go, crasher. Hit it. Oh, no, don't turn that way. The blue one, you. Go." And then to Nelleke, "Here. This is yours. You like it?"

Nelleke gazed at the little ball Dirck had placed in her upturned palm. She felt as if she were holding a round, smooth scoop of sky.

The mother went inside to put the sleeping baby in its cradle.

"I bet I know where there's some raspberries," Dirck said. "Wanna find 'em?"

Dirck and Nelleke were bouncing down a path, each holding wooden buckets, when an arrow zoomed by and stuck in a tree just over their heads.

"Sebastiaan," Dirck yelled. "Do I look like a pigeon to you?"

Another boy, a head taller than Dirck but with the same straw hair, emerged from the woods. "No, but she sure does."

"Leave her alone. Don't you go near her." Dirck bonked Sebastiaan over the head with his bucket. Sebastiaan tried to whack Dirck with his bow. They scrambled and fell to the ground, hitting each other with their fists, pulling each other's hair, ripping each other's shirts.

With trees all around, there wasn't much room for a fight much less a spectator. The boys were soon covered in leaves and twigs. They looked like one large, misshapen log rolling back and forth on the forest floor.

Nelleke stepped backwards away from the battling boys and stepped on something squishy. It was a fat pigeon with an arrow running right through its body, lengthwise. She bent down closer. Blood was running from its wounds and it was still warm, but it wasn't breathing.

Sebastiaan noticed Nelleke reaching out to his most recent catch. He disengaged himself from Dirck and ran over to her.

"Hey, don't touch that. It's mine." Sebastiaan snatched the bird, and placed it in a bulging hunting bag. Patting the bag as he hung it over his shoulder, he said, "I got five of 'em in there. We're gonna eat good tonight. You too, if ya want. And it's me you'll be sayin' thanks to. This little brother of mine's not allowed to hunt with bows and arrows. Are ya, Dirck?" the older brother asked mockingly.

Dirck sat up and rubbed the bump on the back of his head. Stunned from his brother's blows, he stood and brushed himself off. That girl with the large, dark eyes was still there. She held a bucket in both hands and was swinging it gently side to side in front of her in a mesmerizing motion.

Having exerted his superior position over both younger children, Sebastiaan softened. "Hey, I know where you're goin' with those buckets. I'm comin' too."

Dirck agreed reluctantly. Unless he was willing to chance another physical battle, he had no choice.

Hours later, under a low-hanging sun, the children approached the house, buoyed by new-found friendship. Thumping out rhythms on a drum, Sebastiaan took the lead. Nelleke followed, blowing on a tin whistle. Dirck was left with the heavy, but triumphant task of pushing a wheelbarrow loaded with bucketsful of berries. The procession woke the baby.

At the moment they arrived, the mother was balancing her infant on her hip and stirring sugar into hot porridge in a pot suspended over the fire. She served each child a portion in a wooden bowl and dropped some raspberries on top.

Nelleke stirred slowly, watching the juice swirl, leaving mysterious red trails in the smooth white. "Ma'am, will there be enough for my uncle, do you think? Or shall I save him some of mine?"

"What a dear niece you are, Nelleke. The pot is full. Don't worry. My husband will have that wheel fixed any time now. We'll serve you a good evening meal and send you on your way home."

While the mother skinned and boiled pigeons for a flavorful soup, Sebastiaan showed Nelleke and Dirck how to climb up and check out the starling catcher. It hung just below the gutter.

Starling parents were raising three babies in there. Sebastiaan explained that as soon as the babies were big enough to leave the nest, just when they were plump and juicy, but not quite ready to fly away, he would grab them, roast them, and eat them with bread. They were almost ready.

"Here," he said, removing a protesting bird that just fit in his palm. "You can have this one for a snack." The bird's frightened chirping ended abruptly. Sebastiaan had broken its neck with his thumb. Nelleke accepted the limp gift and put it in the pocket of her apron.

The wagon repaired, Nelleke and Uncle Johannes climbed back into it, saying their thank you's and good-bye's. Dirck chased after the wagon until he was overcome with dust in his mouth and eyes. He turned back to find his family still in the same positions where he had left them. They looked downcast. Did they miss her already, as he did? The father had just told them about Nelleke's fate. She was not returning home. Johannes had other plans for her. "Had I known, I woulda kept her right here with us," said the mother. She held her baby tighter and placed an arm around her breathless Dirck.

Nelleke held onto the side of the wagon, watching and waving until the family became five small specks. "I have so many stories to tell Aunt

Griet, Uncle Johannes. I'll stay up all night and never get tired. I'll just talk and talk." Then she lay down and fell asleep.

Flashes of their one afternoon together came to the three children throughout their growing up years:

- The red berry juice that brightened Nelleke's tongue and lips.

- The tanned fists she held out to Dirck. "Which one?" she asked. Dirck tapped the left one. She opened her hand. Empty. Dirck tapped the right one. She opened her right fist. A tiny ladybug sauntered along the crease in her palm and moseyed up to the tip of her thumb. It perched there a moment and flew away.

- Sebastiaan biting down on a beetle that had gotten to a berry before he did. He gagged, coughed it up, and thrust his whole head into the stream to rid himself of the squirming, crunchy insect.

- Dirck climbing the ladder in the barn to find the instruments in a covered box. Sebastiaan removed the ladder and wouldn't replace it until Dirck promised Sebastiaan that he could be the one to play the drum and lead the procession. When Dirck climbed down, he whispered to Nelleke, "I don't care. I want to walk behind you anyway. I like to watch your curls bounce. Can I touch them?"

In a spontaneous, generous gesture, Sebastiaan had offered the starling to Nelleke. He expected that she would take it home. Her aunt would roast it up, put it between two pieces of bread and smear some mustard on it. Nelleke might think of him as she enjoyed the tasty treat. He never knew that within hours the dead starling tucked into Nelleke's pocket would play a role in a series of incidents culminating in a painful accident, an accident that would cause Nelleke anguish, pain, and disfigurement.

Chapter Four
Turtle and Bath

"You arrived just in time, Sir. We close the city gates in one minute, half past nine." It had been drizzling for half an hour. Nelleke was dozing under a blanket in the wagon. The sound of the heavy gate slamming woke her. She sat up and saw the soldiers bolting the gate. One of them secured the enormous key to his belt beside his sword.

"What are you doing with that giant key?" Nelleke asked. "Is that wall yours?"

"No, Miss. That's the city wall. I'm taking the key to Town Hall," the guard told her. "To the mayor. He locks it up in a special cupboard for the night. When the sun comes up, another guard gets the key from the mayor and opens the gate again. Until tomorrow morning, no one goes out, no one comes in. I hope you've got a place to spend the night."

Other soldiers remained by the city wall, patrolling with torches and lanterns. Nelleke saw dozens of huts built into the wall, roaming pigs, flocks of geese. There were small, haphazard vegetable gardens and dilapidated windmills.

"Uncle Johannes," she yelled. "Where are we? What are we doing here? Where are we going to sleep? Look at that goose, Uncle Johannes. Doesn't he look just like Langenek?" Johannes drove on.

It began to rain harder. Nelleke amused herself with her whirligig. A gust of wind twirled the pinwheel playfully for a moment and then tore it out of her hand. She stood up and grabbed at the rapidly turning flags. The whirligig flew all by itself for a full minute. It hovered over a canal, fell, and was gone.

They passed more and more houses, all very close together. There was a strong odor of wood burning, of peat, and of horse manure. They turned and followed a path along another canal. Nelleke reached under the blanket for the forlorn orange flower and buried her nose in it. Nothing helped to block the stench of animal and human waste, of the sickening smell rising from the piled-up garbage in the canals.

This was certainly not the farm. It was not the village.

They passed a large warehouse. The smells coming from that building were so sweet, so foreign, and so welcome, that Nelleke was overcome with gratitude. The intriguing fragrances seemed to lift the building off the ground. They also raised Nelleke's spirits. And they shook some memories loose.

"It's Amsterdam, isn't it Uncle Johannes? I know it is. Church bells rang a few streets away. "This is where I was born. Jacob too. I know those bells."

* * *

"You say you're expected? Awful late, ain't ya? What's the name? I'll have to wake up the Housemother. She won't be too happy."

The gatekeeper at the children's wing spoke to them through a barred opening in the heavy door and then trudged off. Nelleke could no longer be contained. She was out of the wagon, trying to find answers to the questions that Johannes refused to answer.

"Look, Uncle Johannes, up there above the door. I see one, two, three four girls, four boys, and a bird. It's a dove, I think." And then turning her attention to an enclosed metal basket on a pole: "What's this? Some kind of offering box? Nelleke wiggled her fingers through the slot. You drop coins in here. Is this a church?"

The gatekeeper returned and unlocked the door for them. He said nothing, but he took charge of the horse and wagon and opened the gate.

They crossed a treeless, bricked courtyard and entered a long, three-story building, dark and silent. Did anyone live here? Ghosts, maybe? The Housemother was waiting.

Johannes finally spoke. "I expected to arrive much earlier. Had to repair a broken wheel. The roads are so full of ruts still. I hope we didn't waken you."

"Well, you're here now," said the Housemother. "We have checked all of your information. The child's credentials are strong. She's a third-generation Amsterdammer. Without that, of course, we would have to send you to some other, less desirable place."

Johannes swallowed hard. Griet had been emphatic: "If, for any reason, the city orphanage won't take her, bring her back." This was the best.

Nelleke had been exploring the simply furnished room. She stopped when she heard the word, "orphanage." Wasn't that a place for children whose parents had died?

Her parents had died. But she had an aunt and uncle to care for her. She had Jacob, her brother. She became aware of her pounding heart and returned to stand next to her uncle.

"We'll take charge now, sir. We find it's best if you don't linger," said the Housemother, gesturing toward the door.

Johannes realized that he was holding Nelleke's hand. He looked stunned. For a moment he didn't move. Then he bent down, embraced Nelleke quickly, and left.

Nelleke ran to the door. "Uncle, Uncle Johannes, where are you going?" she yelled after him. "Come back. I don't want to stay here. Not all by myself."

The Housemother pulled her away from the door. "This is your new home, Nelleke. You will sleep here tonight and many nights. You are not alone. There are lots of children here – two hundred of them."

A servant appeared with a bowl of warm milk for Nelleke. Nelleke knocked the bowl out of her hands, ran to the door again, and began pounding her small fists against it. "Uncle Johannes. Come back. Please come back. Come get me. Don't leave me here."

The servant shrugged and began cleaning the spilled milk. The Housemother took advantage of the incident to instruct Nelleke. "Little girl, you are not permitted to behave in that manner. Tell Maria you are sorry."

Nelleke turned and began pounding on the Housemother's stomach. "I will not. I am not sorry. Let me go! Let me out of here!"

19

The Housemother tried to protect herself and restrain Nelleke's flailing arms. "Stop that this instant, little girl. What kind of demon child are you? Maria, you better wake Isabela."

* * *

Isabela had often been awakened in the night to attend to a wakeful child in her care, but the housemother had never before summoned her to leave her sleeping charges behind. When Maria shook her shoulder, she knew she needed to respond quickly. She was halfway down the stairs when she realized that she was holding her rosary. Perhaps because of her skill with children or her own known losses, or even because of her beauty, Housemother tolerated Isabela's Catholic beliefs. She certainly could not flaunt them, however. She usually kept the rosary hidden under her pillow. Had she reached for it earlier seeking comfort in its familiarity and solidity? She ran back upstairs and returned the rosary to its place.

A moment later, disheveled and squinting, dressed in ankle-length white nightshirt and cap, Isabela stepped into the room. The housemother raised a critical eyebrow at the young woman as she glanced at Isabela's bare feet and cap askew, the long raven locks escaping in all directions. When Isabela saw a child collapsed against the outer door, sobbing, she understood at once why she had been summoned. She would not leave this child to return upstairs and tidy herself.

Nelleke was stooped, hugging her knees, resting her head on her arms, her back to the room. Although her posture would seem to reject everything behind her, when she heard the patter of Isabela's feet, her curiosity led her to turn slightly and peek with one dark eye.

In spite of the obvious, Housemother explained, "A new arrival. Check her head and get her to bed. Give her a good clipping if necessary. Nelleke's her name. Nelleke, this is your Big Sister, Isabela."

"I don't have a sister," Nelleke yelled through her sobs without turning around again. "I have a brother." Nelleke curled up even tighter against the door, her arms covering her streaked face. Isabela sat down on the floor next to Nelleke. Without touching her or speaking to her, she began to sing softly.

"Tortuga, tu colita, dónde está?
Tortuga, tu cabeza, dónde está?

Yo quiero ver la carita.
Sal de tu caparazón."

Nelleke looked up. Her lower lip continued to tremble. The tears continued to fall, but she had to know: "Can you sing that in my language?"

"I'll try. It's about a child who finds a turtle. All she can see, though, is its shell.

She really wants to see its face, so she sings – oh, it won't rhyme right in Dutch. But here it is:

"Turtle, your tail, where is it?
Turtle, your head, where is it?
I just want to see your little face,
So come on, come out of your shell."

"So the child coaxes the turtle some more, he pops out his head, and he says, 'Boo!'"

Just as Isabela said the word, "Boo!" she tickled Nelleke ever so lightly under her arms.

Nelleke had stopped crying, but she wasn't ready to respond to games. She spoke with a quivery voice and a down-turned mouth, "How big is the turtle?"

"I'd say…about this big." Isabela made a circle with her hands.

"This big?" asked Nelleke. "About the same size as a bowl you eat porridge from?"

"That's exactly right. Just that size."

"How big is the child? Is it a girl or a boy?"

"A girl. How big? Well, let's see. Stand up a minute."

Nelleke stopped crying and stood up, both tentative and expectant. Isabela rose to her knees, facing Nelleke. She placed her hands on the floor on either side of Nelleke and raised them very slowly. Once her hands were level with the top of Nelleke's head, she rested her hand very lightly on Nelleke's damp cap.

"The little girl is just about . . . yes, just about exactly your height."

"Does she find frogs too? I'll bet she chases geese."

"You're right. She finds lots of animals. And she talks to them," said Isabela, taking Nelleke's hand. Then, making animal noises, "Gobble,

gobble, meow, honk, neigh," she guided Nelleke into a small room with a fireplace next to the kitchen.

"Maria, heat some water for washing, please."

"Oh, Miss, you're not going to immerse the poor child in the tub, are you?" asked the maid.

Isabela understood Maria's concern, but she didn't share it. Dutch housewives were judged on the orderliness of their homes and the cleanliness of their floors. Over and over they scrubbed their floors until there was not a speck of dirt. The orphanage floors were spotless too. Yet they wore the same clothes for several days. Mornings they splashed some water on their faces, but they rarely bathed. Isabela found this puzzling. For a country that was built on water, they were awfully suspicious of it. Did they fear that bathing a child would make it ill?

Although she had been in the orphanage only four months, Isabela's ability to soothe upset children was already legendary. Therefore, Maria did as Isabela instructed her. She brought water to the pot over the fire, heated it, and poured it into a wood tub.

Isabela continued to sing softly as she helped Nelleke out of her damp, stained travel clothes and lifted her into the water. Nelleke stood in the tub, the water reaching just below her knees.

"You talk funny," Nelleke said.

"I'm not from here. I'm from another country. It's called Spain. I lived in a big house with my mother and my aunts."

"I have aunts – Aunt Griet and Aunt Elsbeth. Did you have lots of toys?"

While Maria entertained Nelleke with descriptions of her home, she motioned for her to sit down. Now the warm water reached Nelleke's chest.

"Oh, yes. Dolls from many countries. A doll house too."

"Spain. Is that far? Does your mother miss you? Do your aunts want you back?"

"Spain is quite far. I've written to my aunts. They know I'm safe. My mother is dead now, though."

"So is mine. She died so I could have Jacob."

When Nelleke pronounced her brother's name, a sound from deep in her belly rose up, stabbed her chest, and popped out. It sounded like a loud hiccup combined with a single sob. It was such a helpless, sudden, and strange sound that it startled both Nelleke and Isabela. Isabela took both of Nelleke's hands in hers. They looked at each other across the water. For a moment they both thought that the other might laugh. The sound was just that unexpected and bizarre.

Isabela grabbed a wooden top that a child had abandoned on the floor nearby and placed it in Nelleke's hands.

"Look. Isn't this pretty?"

There was a mischievous cat face painted on one side of the top. The cat's whiskers spread out and became decorative lines that met on the top's opposite side. The cat had one raised eyebrow over a large eye. The other eye was closed. It was impossible to twirl the top in water. Nelleke kept trying to push it under, but it would shoot right back up, wink at her, and go bobbing around and around in circles.

Nelleke liked the feel of the smooth wood and the rounded knob on top that was painted as a slanted hat for the cat. She became so relaxed that she did not protest when Isabela poured water over her head. She tried to imitate Isabela's Spanish rhymes and, of course, to get her to say them in a way she could understand.

"Water, water, here and there.
Water, water, everywhere.
We can sail in the water
and mix it with ink."

Nelleke cupped some water in her hands and raised it to her mouth.

"But this is not to drink," Isabela said, finishing the impromptu rhyme, shaking her head, and covering Nelleke's hands. Nelleke opened her hands and let the water splash back into the tub.

While Nelleke made faces at the winking cat, Isabela began her scalp inspection, carefully parting each strand. She had to look so carefully, but yes, there were a few – those ugly miniature gray eggs stuck fast to a piece of hair. Isabela crushed each egg with her thumbnails, pulled them off, and buried them in a dish of molasses. Then she combed and combed.

Finally, she lifted Nelleke out and wrapped her in a cloth. She moved her closer to the fire so she wouldn't get a chill. Isabela reached around Nelleke and dried her carefully. This was a healthy, fleshy little child whose skin did not have the pinkish hue of most Dutch children. Even her little round belly had a beige brown color – more like Isabela's skin tone. She had small lavender bruises on her bottom and legs and a light green bruise on her right hip. "From the wagon ride, I'll bet," Nelleke explained and she told Isabela about the broken wheel, her new friends, the raspberries, the ladybug, and the pigeon soup.

Her hair was Dutch yellow, but not the usual straight. It hung in full ringlets down to her shoulders. It would be a shame to have to cut off those curls. The lice Isabela had seen could not be called an infestation, Isabela thought, absent mindedly scratching her own head. No, the golden locks would stay for now, flowing freely at night, tucked up in a cap during the day.

But it was her eyes that distinguished Nelleke most from other Dutch children. Nearly black. Large. Dark lashes. Even through the sorrow, confusion, and fatigue, Isabela could see their intelligence and their curiosity.

Isabela held Nelleke close to her for a moment and then dressed her in the night clothes Maria had provided. Warm stockings, an undergarment, and a gown that was too large. The sleeves hung down and the hem dragged on the floor. Isabela rolled up the sleeves and tied the lower fabric of the gown in a large knot on one side so that Nelleke could walk. Finally, she tied an apron over the gown.

Now Nelleke was receptive to Maria's offer of warm milk. She swallowed it gratefully, and used the few final drops to soften a piece of hard bread.

Chapter Five
Bed. Straw. Mishap.

he Housemother had long since joined the Housefather in their quarters. Maria and all of the servants had gone to bed. Isabela explained that everyone was asleep, so they must move very quietly. Nelleke would sleep in a bed with three other little girls, Marja next to her, then Wilhelmina, and Bernadien on the far side.

"There are rows of large beds for the children and a few beds for the Big Sisters like me. I sleep in the same room. I won't be far away. I'll show you."

While Isabela was busy putting out the fire, Nelleke remembered the starling. She could not leave the poor thing behind. She went over to her pile of dirty clothes, reached into the apron pocket, removed the starling, and dropped it in the pocket of the clean apron she was wearing. It was completely cold now and stiff, but its young feathers were still soft. She almost showed it to Isabela, but decided to keep it a secret. It was so small that she could hide it inside her fist. Only the tiny beak poked out a little.

Their shadows followed close behind as Nelleke and Isabela moved through the house to the light of Isabela's candle. Isabela tucked Nelleke into bed, kissed her goodnight, and sat with her until she fell asleep. The night watchman's voice came through the window: "Midnight in Amsterdam. All's well."

Two hours later, Nelleke was awakened by an animal landing lightly on her stomach. Alarmed, she sat right up, ready to knock off whatever it was. From the light of the oil lantern hung in the hall, Nelleke could see that it was a small yellow cat, probably a kitchen cat curious about the newcomer. She lay back down and immediately named the cat Straw.

Straw stepped up to her face, sniffed her ears and neck, turned around, walked down her body, and curled up on her abdomen. The sudden pressure made her need to go to the privy – urgently. Where, though?

Isabela had taken her somewhere before tucking her in and given her other instructions, but she had been too drowsy to pay attention. The place was so large. She moved the cat to one side and pushed back the coverlet. She walked over to Isabela's bed and whispered her name once. Then again. Isabela groaned and turned her back. She was fast asleep.

Nelleke took the covered, slow-burning candle from the table beside Isabela and walked past the rows of sleeping children. When she stepped into the openness of the hallway, the candle blew out. She dragged a chair over and positioned it under the hallway lamp. Then she climbed up, reached on tiptoe, lowered Isabela's candle inside the lamp and held it there until the candle was able to shed some light on its own again. When she separated the candle from the oil lantern, however, the flame flickered and died. She lit the candle a second time, and climbed down off the chair.

Now she remembered. The privy was in a courtyard at the bottom of the steps. She walked down the steps carrying the candle. There was a row of dozens of wooden shoes just inside the door. She slipped into a pair and, using all her strength, she pushed open the door. Immediately, the cold air enveloped her. The candle seemed to panic for a moment, but recovered. The rain had stopped, but the bricks were slippery.

She found the privy shed. The smell was bad enough she could have found it without candle light. She remembered now more clearly. There were four low seats all in a row. She worked open the door of the shed. Three small rats ran up to the rafters, through an opening, and onto the roof. Nelleke didn't like rats. No one did. But she had seen many. These seemed to be gone for now. In her drowsy, confused state, her only thought was, "Aren't they lucky? They get to play with their brothers and sisters all night long."

She placed the candle on the ground. It was difficult to untie the knot on her nightdress, but she managed to do it and to pull the oversized garment up high enough to keep it clean while she sat.

Then she reversed the long trek: close the privy door, walk across the courtyard, open the orphanage door, remove the shoes, start up the stairs. She couldn't tie the nightdress back into a knot, so it trailed behind her. When she nearly tripped, she gathered it up as best she could in one hand while holding the candle in the other.

She was halfway up the stairs, when Straw appeared on the landing at the top. There was something in his mouth. A rat? A mouse? No, it had feathers. It was her starling! Straw had found it in her bed. "Straw," she hissed, as she shook the candle at him. "Give me my baby starling. Sebastiaan gave it to me."

Straw bounded down the stairs, escaping to enjoy his easy prey. Nelleke dropped the hem of her gown and tried to grab him as he ran past her. She lost her balance and tumbled in the near dark, rolling over and over, screaming out.

When she landed she continued to scream. Except for one deaf mute, every child and every Big Sister in the children's wing was awakened. Some just sat up in bed, frightened. Others ran to investigate, following the shrieking. When Nelleke looked up, she saw scores of sleepy, stunned faces staring down at her. Boys and girls in all sizes, ages four to ten, in the hallway, on the landing, on the stairs, gathered around her – all staring at her.

Isabela worked her way through the group to Nelleke's side. Nelleke tried to tell what had just happened, but the words came out in bursts and gasps: Straw . . . Starling . . . . Mine." No one knew anything about Straw or a starling. They thought she was hallucinating. They took her to the infirmary and woke up the doctor.

The doctor examined her limbs and determined that she had no broken bones. But she continued to scream and the words became clearer. "My hand! My hand! It hurts. It hurts." She had been holding the pained hand protectively with her other hand and no one had seen it. The doctor discovered the wax. The candle flame had gone out as soon as she began to fall, but the tipped-over candleholder had spilled hot wax all over the top of her hand. The transparent wax had to be cut in pieces and pried off.

Chapter Six
Johannes Reacts

arly next morning Johannes knocked once again at the massive oak gate of the orphanage. He was delivering something he had forgotten the previous night – a wooden box in which Griet had carefully packed all of Nelleke's belongings. The guard admitted him to the courtyard and then Maria admitted him to the orderly reception room. He began to explain he simply wanted to drop off the box and be on his way. However, when Maria recognized him, she interrupted him and left the room abruptly.

Johannes could smell fish frying. He placed the box on a long table. He was tempted to simply leave it there and go. He didn't want to take still more time talking to anyone. They had said last night all the papers were in order.

The Housemother had discouraged him from lingering. "We will take over now," she said yesterday evening. Surely the staff was busy with their charges at this moment. He could hear young voices coming from the back rooms of the orphanage. Excited chatter. Someone whining. Someone crying. Occasionally one adult male voice followed by child laughter. Nelleke was in there somewhere having a good breakfast, he thought. She's probably already made lots of friends.

He reviewed more good reasons for bringing her here. She would be educated. Hadn't she been begging to go to school? With the nearest school miles away from the farm and Griet now too busy to teach her, it had not been possible to start her on her letters. She deserved to learn, didn't she?

Johannes knew that Nelleke missed the music that had surrounded her when she was with her mother's troupe. She could even play simple four-note tunes on her tiny violin. Unlike in their isolated region, there were many talented musicians in the city. Concerts. Performances. Perhaps she would be given the opportunity to advance?

He and Griet trusted this place. The orphanage was endowed by city funds and well run by the Regents, members of Amsterdam's select wealthy class. They met weekly and oversaw every aspect of the orphanage – finances, building maintenance and repairs, staffing, menus, quality of education, health care.

There were several other possibilities in the city, but Griet would never allow Nelleke to be placed in one of those. They were set up for the city's poorest children, many of them foundlings and children of recent immigrants. This orphanage, the only civic orphanage in the city, was already over 100 years old. It was reserved for the children of Amsterdam citizens only – families with enough means to pay a hearty annual tax. Two years ago, before Johannes and Griet left Amsterdam with Nelleke and Jacob to live on the farm, an ambitious expansion and renovation of the orphanage had begun on the very site where Johannes now stood. They had watched workers lay the foundation. Last year there had been a ceremony to celebrate the completion of this new facility. The burgomasters, the town council, and many dignitaries had attended. Now there were three buildings, one for young children of both sexes. Orphans between 12 and 18 lived in two other buildings with separate courtyards separated by gender. It was located in the very heart of the city and yet with its own school, medical care, bakery, and brewery, the orphanage was an enclosed self-sufficient world.

Perhaps most important of all, Johannes thought, there was a rigid daily schedule, something that would help bring discipline to a child whose whereabouts he and Griet had difficulty keeping track of. He shuddered as he remembered the terrifying time he had dragged a sodden Nelleke from the pond. Desperate for a breath of air, coughing and spitting up the brackish water, she was still clutching the butterfly net she used to catch tadpoles.

* * *

Looking more haggard and worn than she had the previous night and less confidently in charge, the Housemother stepped into the room and sank into a chair.

"I have some upsetting news, I'm afraid, Mr. Verhoeven. Please sit down."

Johannes imagined himself returning home, already a day late, groping for the words to tell Griet . . . what? That the orphanage couldn't keep Nelleke after all? That she was too rowdy, disobedient, and uncontrollable? That she had contracted a terrible disease? That she had died suddenly?

Pressing his fists toward each other in front of his chest, he leaned forward and waited anxiously to hear what the Housemother had to say.

"The entire children's wing has been in an uproar caused by your niece. We all got very little sleep last night. It appears that Nelleke got out of bed some time in the night and lit a candle. Fire sources are kept out of range of the children, of course. We don't yet understand how she did it. We also find it highly unusual that a child would go wandering through the building alone at that hour."

"She fell down the stairs, dripping hot candle wax on her hand. We had to wake the doctor and the wound is being treated. The Big Sister we assigned to her is one of our most capable assistants. We do not hold Isabela responsible. She has insisted on being by Nelleke's side since the incident."

During the Housemother's report Johannes had begun to tap his knuckles against each other, in a noisy gesture that was beginning to annoy her. "But how is the child, Mrs. Heijn? Is she in pain? Is she disfigured?" asked Johannes, with increasing agitation.

"She is resting now. Isabela is quite capable at soothing upset children. Let me emphasize that the burn is confined to her hand only. It is a surface wound. No other part of her body was harmed and she has no broken bones. The doctor thinks she will probably have a scar, however."

Johannes dropped his fists into his lap and began palming the tops of his thighs. "May I see her?"

"No, Mr. Verhoeven. As I told you yesterday evening, we have found that it is confusing for a child to be visited too soon by the person who put her in our hands. She has suffered a trauma. We want to facilitate her adjustment here, to move her as quickly as possible into our daily routines. I assure you that she is receiving excellent care."

The Housemother stood up, indicating that the discussion was over. She walked to the door that led to the courtyard and opened it, waiting for Johannes to exit. She was relieved this first telling of the incident was over. News of it was spreading among the staff. It would soon reach the outer community. She had to answer to the Regents. She must portray herself and the orphanage in the best light possible. It was unlikely that this uncle would visit soon again, but the child had Amsterdam relatives. Surely they would want to observe the child once they knew of her accident.

As he walked by her, somewhat dazed, the Housemother unexpectedly laid a hand lightly on his arm.

"You have other family members nearby, do you not? Ordinarily outside visitors are welcomed only on Sunday afternoons. I will ask the doctor about making an exception in this case. Nelleke will remain in our infirmary until the doctor feels that she can return to the children's wing. She is being treated in an area separate from sick children. It might cheer her to see someone she knows."

Johannes had spent the previous night at the home of his sister-in-law, Elsbeth. Elsbeth was suspicious of Nelleke, even believing her to be the cause of Johannes's and Griet's recent bad luck. Elsbeth had never trusted Nelleke's exotic mother and resented the way Rona lured Nicolaas away from his responsibilities. With Nicolaas gone for long periods, the increased burden of the family printing business on their aging father caused his death, she was sure.

If Johannes could convince Elsbeth to check in on Nelleke, though, and report to them, there would be something positive to add to what he dreaded having to tell Griet. Revisiting Elsbeth meant that there was one more task to complete before Johannes could return home to all the chores that awaited him at the farm. Griet was surely becoming worried by now.

"Yes," said Johannes. "I will speak with my sister-in-law."

He looked back at the wooden box he had placed on the table. It contained all of Nelleke's worldly belongings. It seemed insignificant now.

The Housemother responded to his glance and nodded toward the box.

"Maria tells me you have brought part of Nelleke's inheritance. We will inventory the contents and store it for her. We will take good care of it and return it to her whenever she leaves here. Good day, Mr. Verhoeven."

Chapter Seven
Sick Room

⟨⟩

The first thing Nelleke saw when she awoke was the window across from her. There was a wooden building very close by and, above that, gray clouds. She could tell from the light it was much later than her usual waking time. Why did she sleep so late? Where was she anyway? She turned her head and saw Isabela asleep in a chair next to her. Then last night's memories rushed at her and mixed with earlier memories.

She rode a horse once all by herself. She wasn't supposed to. The horse's owner, Symon, a neighbor boy, was distracted for a moment and the horse took off before he could mount behind Nelleke. Her familiar world sped up. Fields, bushes, trees, and flowers hurried by. Not easily frightened by any animal, she held on tight with her hands, arms, and legs. The horse's mane blew up and tickled her nose. The ride lasted perhaps three minutes. The horse slowed as it approached a stream and became more interested in drinking than running. Symon caught up and took charge. Thinking about that brief ride always brought back to Nelleke a wonderful exhilaration.

There was no exhilaration in today's jumble of memories. She couldn't arrange them in any order that made sense. Again, there were animals – two of them, - no - more than two, counting the rats. She had stayed on that horse and was unhurt. Last night, though, she had fallen, down, down, going bump on each stair.

She was lying on her back now. Her body felt heavy. Her head hurt. She became aware of prickly pain on the top of her left hand.

33

Slowly, almost dreamily, she lifted the hand above her head. Its redness reminded her of the raw meat she had seen hanging in the market stalls yesterday. Cold drops fell on her face. The hand was wet. It had been soaking in cold water. Once the air hit it, it began to throb. She let it drop back in the bowl at her side and experienced some relief.

The splash startled Isabela awake.

"*Tortuguita. Hijita. Mi amor,*" Isabela said. "How you feel today? You scare us so much."

Nelleke tried to answer. For the first time since she said her first two words ("skinny dog") in Romany at age seven months, Nelleke could not talk. Her tongue was thick, her eyes were droopy. She almost dozed again, but some of the familiar Nelleke was returning. Her curiosity would not let her sleep.

"Dear child, my little turtle, the doctor gave you hops from the brewery last night. It help you sleep, no? But I see that you are sailor in a tavern. I told doctor. No more hops. Anise water, please. It will calm my pretty girl, with no more tipsy. You want breakfast now, yes?"

Isabela motioned for Tanneke, the sick room assistant, to bring food from the kitchen. Dr. Voerman, his arms full of packages, returned from a consultation with his colleague at the apothecary. He stopped briefly by Nelleke's bed.

"I'm pleased to see you awake, Nelleke. My friend, Mr. Koppel, has given me bandages and medicines to make you feel better. I'll be right back."

Nelleke turned to Isabela.

"I'm ready to go home now. Aunt Griet will be mad if I stay away too long."

"Nelita, my sweet child. You're going to live with us for awhile."

"I have to feed Langenek," said Nelleke, tears starting to form. "Jacob misses me."

"I know he does. Let's write a note to your brother. To Aunt Griet too."

"I can't write."

"Not yet. You'll learn, though. I don't write well in Dutch either. I'll learn with you. In the meantime, you tell the Schoolmaster what you want to say in your letter. Here's your breakfast."

Tanneke placed a platter next to Nelleke. Isabela helped her sit up. When loud rumbles from her stomach filled the narrow room, she looked at Isabela to see if she had done something wrong. Apparently a growling stomach was not impolite. Isabela was grinning reassuredly.

For the first time since she had arrived, Nelleke smiled. Isabela was jarred momentarily by the open mouth. The gap from Nelleke's four missing front teeth marred the little girl's beauty that Isabela had so admired since she first saw the child huddling and weeping.

"Is that butter? For the bread?"

Nelleke had not enjoyed a butter treat since the flood.

"Can I put some butter on the peas too? Is that fish for me? What's that?" Nelleke asked pointing to some round, pale orange, wrinkly pieces on her wooden plate."

Isabela and Tanneke, who had taken turns sitting with Nelleke so that she was never left alone, were amused and relieved by the sudden burst of questions. They exchanged a smile.

"Those are dried apricots. Sent especially for you from the cook," Tanneke explained.

Once she had finished breakfast, Dr. Voerman stood by her bedside to get a good look at the injury. When he removed her hand from the cold water, the painful throbbing intensified. She tried to pull her hand away and lower it back into the bowl.

"No, child," he told her. "I must examine your hand in order to decide on the best way to make it better."

Dr. Voerman's vision was not perfect. He bent so close that his whiskers brushed the tender, raw spot. It felt like fingernails scraping. Nelleke began to howl. This time she succeeded in freeing her hand from his grasp. She buried it under the covers. "Go away," she screamed. "Don't touch me. Don't touch me."

All the confusion and fear of the past day began to overwhelm her. She had been so delighted to follow Uncle Johannes when she thought he was taking her to the market. Instead he had left her here in this strange place. Why did Aunt Griet allow Uncle Johannes to abandon her? Did Aunt Griet really want her here? And Jacob! Whenever she thought of his smile, she couldn't bear it. She was inconsolable now.

"I WANT TO GO HOME!" she cried as she pounded her legs on the bed.

Isabela and Tanneke rushed to her side. Isabela held her and murmured to her softly.

Tanneke ran to the kitchen to see what treats she could find.

The doctor was embarrassed and dismayed. How could he treat her without winning her cooperation and confidence? Isabela suggested that he return in fifteen minutes. The doctor glanced back anxiously as he left the room. Isabela placed Nelleke's hand gently back in the cold water. So far that seemed to be the best way to lessen her pain. She sang the healing Spanish song five times. "*Sana, sana, colita de rana. Si no sanas hoy, sanarás mañana.*"

Tanneke arrived with seven cherries. 'They're very sweet." she told Nelleke. "I tried one."

"I know what," Isabela suggested. "We'll let the doctor finish the treatment. It won't take long. Then we can share the cherries. Let's count them."

"NO," said Nelleke between sobs. "I DON'T WANT CHERRIES. I DON'T WANT TO COUNT CHERRIES."

Eventually, Isabela's voice and caresses calmed Nelleke to the point where she convinced her to drink some saffron water. By the time the doctor returned, the mild sedative had taken effect. The beard was tucked into his collar. Isabela continued to hold Nelleke tight, kiss and sooth her. Tanneke held the hand steady. The doctor sprinkled the wound with a cool mixture of myrrh and aloe. Then he wrapped it in a clean bandage. By the time he was finished, Nelleke was sleeping in Isabela's arms.

By evening Nelleke had eaten the seven cherries plus two more meals. The doctor had wrapped her hand in a tightly woven fabric – four times. "It's important," he explained, "to keep the bandage very clean." Always fearful that another outburst would jeopardize the treatment, he sought Isabela's help in relaxing Nelleke before attempting to secure the cloth. He squinted, but he would not get too close again.

"Nelleke, shall I tell you a story?" Isabela asked, weary herself and ready for sleep.

"Oh, yes, please. Is there a turtle in the story? A little girl?"

"A duck. A lonely duck. But first, you and I must have a serious talk."

Isabela took Nelleke's healthy hand in both of hers and looked directly in her eyes.

Nelleke gulped. She had no idea what Isabela was going to say, but she knew that she must pay attention.

"No more walking around at night without me. Agreed?"

"Yes."

"If you need to go the bathroom, you know what to do now. Right?"

"I don't go to the courtyard."

"Definitely not. That's for daytime."

"I use the little pot under the bed."

"Right. You won't forget?"

"Can I hear the story now?"

"Okay. Once upon a time there was an island."

"What's an island?"

"It's land with water all around it."

"I don't like that much water."

* * *

Two days after Nelleke's accident, the entire orphanage knew about her. The story became embellished with each telling.

"Her clothes caught on fire. Her hair got singed. She'll lose her fingers. Her arm turned black. Her hand is going to fall off."

Sympathy and concern for the child, whom few had met, began to reach Nelleke. Soon everyone was using Isabela's name for her – Nelita. A loyal, but demanding Regentess, Mrs. Comfrij, sent notice that she would visit shortly to investigate the incident and see the child for herself.

The Housemother paid a visit to both the older boys' and older girls' houses, explaining her view of the accident, excusing herself from blame, and asking for some sort of contribution to the child to keep her amused.

On Tuesday Nelita received three rolls of lace from the older girls. They made it themselves and often sold the lace in town. They wanted her to have something pretty to look at and feel. In their note, they offered to sew the lace onto her Sunday cap – later when she was well enough to go to church.

The Schoolmaster came for a visit. He brought a slate and taught Nelleke how to make the letter "L."

"Draw a straight pole with a foot," the Schoolmaster, explained, demonstrating.

Nelleke was pleased. She practiced.

The burn still stung. When the bandage was being changed, she could see that it had become puffy. It looked like a small, smooth red pillow.

"That's a blister," Dr. Voerman explained. "The blister is good. It's protecting the area below the burn. Just don't touch it."

On Wednesday, the older boys sent her a wooden spoon. Using scrap wood, they made it especially for her in their carpentry class. They carved the letter "N" on the handle.

The cook sent cabbage soup with bits of lamb.

The Schoolmaster taught her a new letter.

"Draw a pole with a foot; place a flat cap on its head; halfway down the pole, give it a small shelf. That's an "E.""

By the time the Regentess arrived, the Housemother felt reasonably certain that her reputation was salvaged.

"Nelleke, dear," the Housemother said in the sweetest tones she could muster, "this is Mrs. Comfrij. She visits us here at the orphanage from time to time."

Nelleke had never seen anyone dressed so lavishly. She wanted to touch the layers of fabrics, the delicate lace collar; the white blouse with embroidered sleeves under the long blue vest that covered her hips, the gray silky skirt that came to her ankles. Nelleke studied Mrs. Comfrij from the silver circles dangling from her ears to the velvet shoes on her pampered feet.

Mrs. Comfrij conferred with the doctor, Tanneke, and Isabela. Satisfied that the child was receiving good care, she sat with Nelleke and showed her the package that she had brought.

"Do you want to open it yourself, child? Can you do it with one hand?"

"Oh, yes. I can do anything with my good hand. I can even make two letters. The Schoolmaster showed me."

Resting her injured hand on the bed beside her, Nelleke deftly used the other to unwrap the layers of paper. Tucked inside was a pair of thin light brown leather slip-ons, lined, with decorative slits near the toes.

"To keep your feet warm while you're healing," Mrs. Comfrij said. "Shall we see how they fit?" The Regentess pulled back the bottom of the blanket and glided Nelleke's feet into the light-weight slippers.

"They're soft," Nelleke said. She lifted her feet into the air to admire them and tapped the slippers together.

On Thursday, Mrs. Comfrij sent a second gift – a china plate decorated with tulips. "To make your food taste better, so you'll get well soon," she wrote.

The Schoolmaster asked, "Do you know this letter, Nelleke? Draw two poles side by side. Then connect them with a slanted pole from the top of this one to the bottom of the other."

"I know it," said Nelleke. "See, it's on the handle of the wooden spoon. It's my letter. What's it called? I want to try it."

A gooey, yellow substance was oozing from the wound. The pain was less constant now.

"Look, Doctor. My hand is crying," Nelleke said.

"It's all right, child," said Dr. Voerman, summoning every ounce of tenderness to rub ointment on it. It's getting rid of something that's not helping."

Nelleke turned her head away from the sharp smell of the dark salve.

On Friday Nelleke emerged from bed and looked out the window. She had heard children's voices all week. Now she could see them in the courtyard. Most were running around, chasing each other. Some of the girls were jumping rope. A few boys were throwing a ball. The Big Sisters gathered in clusters, chatting, occasionally comforting a fallen child or settling a dispute. Two small girls were sitting close together on a bench. They were holding hands, but not talking. Would she ever be well enough to join them? Did she want to?

The doctor came to change the bandage and found her straining forward, her nose almost touching the glass.

"You'll be out there playing soon, Nelleke. You're a very strong little girl."

Dr. Voerman had once seen poison spread from a burn and incapacitate large parts of a patient's body. He was relieved that Little Nell's wound was healing quickly. He didn't know it, but Nelleke's strength was due in part to the many hours she had spent living outdoors with her mother's family and later wandering in the fresh air on her aunt's farm. The soak and scrub that Isabela gave her hours before the accident helped too. But the doctor remained vigilant.

Mr. De Vries said, "Are you ready for a difficult letter, Nelleke? Draw the pole. Find a point halfway down the pole. From that point draw matching twigs – one up, one down. Like this."

Nelleke tried the "K," but it was hard. She couldn't make the twigs match. One always came out longer than the other. Sometimes she forgot to look for the halfway point. She didn't know where to stop the twigs. They covered the whole slate.

"Pretty good, Nelleke. You'll get better. "K" demands practice. But I have a surprise for you. It's kind of a riddle."

"I love riddles," said Nelleke, offering one herself. "What is lighter than a feather but it's harder to hold?"

"My goodness. I can't think. A leaf?"

"Maybe. That's a good guess, Schoolmaster."

Nelleke inhaled loudly, puffing up her chest for several seconds. Then she let the air out with a loud push.

"That was a hint," she told him.

"What's lighter than a feather but harder to hold?" he puzzled.

"Your breath," Nelleke laughed.

"I see. That's a good one. Can I tell you my riddle now?"

"Yes, please."

"There are seven letters in your name. You have learned only four letters. Yet you can write your whole name. How is that possible?"

"Write my name for me. I'll figure it out."

"N E L L E K E. Nelleke."

"There's the 'L' with its foot. TWO of them. There's the 'E' with its flat cap. One, two, THREE of them. That's a lot. There's the 'N' at the beginning. And the 'K.' I can't make that one very well. I know all the letters, though. Isabela! Tanneke! Dr. Voerman! I can read my name!"

Chapter Eight
Best Visit of All

When the housekeeper opened the door five days ago and Willem saw Johannes standing on the threshold, he could tell immediately how distraught his uncle was. He had said good-bye only a short time ago and here he was pounding on the door again.

Since then, Willem asked his mother every day if he could visit Nelleke at the orphanage. Even though she was four years younger and a girl, he had always been drawn to this cousin. He could go by himself, he told her. Now that he knew Nelleke was there, he walked by the orphanage every day on his way home from school. He couldn't see over the high walls, but he could hear children playing. He stopped and listened to see if he could distinguish her voice, but there was too much noise.

Although he hadn't seen her for two years, he remembered her clearly. Her inventiveness drew him out of his dreaminess. Her infectious energy got him moving. Her constant questions left him in a state of wonder. She used to pull him into the garden to climb trees. She poked her head in every room. Then when she knew his house better than he did, she challenged him to games of "Hide and Seek." He could never find her and she would jump out laughing from some niche she had created. At age four, she had been so small, she could fit into a cupboard, tuck herself behind a chair, or disappear behind a heavy curtain.

For years Elsbeth had been barren. She had been miserable without a child and fearful that Rutger would leave her. Then God sent her an angel. Willem may have been an abandoned infant – a foundling – his parents may be unknown, but he was a blessing. Not only was he a sweet, intelligent child, but he loosened her womb. The twins were conceived less than a year after she accepted Willem as her own.

Willem's younger twin brothers were boisterous and loud. They did everything together, made demands, and usually got their way. Willem, on the other hand, spent many quiet hours just wondering who he was. He wove elaborate fantasies about his "real" parents. Sometimes they were royalty, sometimes bandits. He had discovered a ledge under the roof just big enough to sit on cross legged. He snuck out there at night, studying the heavens, searching for answers. The playing card was the most intriguing mystery.

Nelleke's father had been his favorite uncle. Uncle Nicolaas visited often and seemed much more interested in Willem than in the twins. Uncle Nicolaas taught him to draw when he could barely hold a piece of charcoal. He taught him to skate when he was only four.

It was The Story, though, that he loved best. His mother and father didn't like the story much. They never uttered the word, "Foundling." He heard it occasionally spoken in whispers by the servants. His life began, his parents thought, when Uncle Nicolaas brought him to their house. His father had even worn the paternity bonnet-crown for two weeks, just like a father whose wife had just given birth. Willem's father recently modeled this very headdress for him. Fitting tightly at the base with pointed crown-like shapes, it rose up high over his father's head, ending in a small tassel at the peak. Willem's arrival had turned this merchant into a father king overnight. His parents posted a paper and lace birth announcement on their door. They feasted and partied. They loved him, he knew. He was theirs. But when he was alone with his uncle, he would always ask.

"Tell about when you found me, Uncle Nicolaas."

Uncle Nicolaas told the story differently every time. Sometimes he left out parts. Other times he added something brand new. He was vague about the playing card.

Now, with Uncle Nicolaas gone, Willem didn't know if he would ever really learn the truth. But he wanted to see his cousin. She was hurt. He couldn't bear to think about that.

On Saturday, Elsbeth relented. She knew she was seriously shirking her duty to her niece and Griet would be anxious and angry with her. She really could not stand the wild Gypsy child. If Willem wanted to go, though, why not? She would send a honey cake with him and be done with the matter. Then maybe he would forget about her.

"*Waddelen* really wanted to get off that island. He could see all the other ducks across that long expanse of water. They were chasing each other, quacking, and laughing. But it was far. How could he reach them?" recounted Isabela, continuing the story she had been telling all week.

"*Waddelen* needs a bridge. Can he build one?" Nelleke suggested.

"You have another visitor, Nelita," Tanneke announced.

Whenever Nelleke heard those words, she thought it must be Jacob. She was sure that he would burst into the room on his sturdy, chubby legs, run to her, and leap on her bed.

For a moment, it <u>was</u> Jacob. Two people seemed to have grabbed hold of him, though. One under the arms. One by the ankles. They had pulled and pulled until this Jacob was stretched out, lanky and awkward. Then she recognized the hesitant ten-year-old. They used to play together when she lived in Amsterdam. He was always nice to her. It was her cousin, Willem.

Nelleke was sitting on the edge of her bed, wearing a night dress (one that fit her this time), dangling her feet in the new slippers. Seeing her blond curls and the nearly black eyes with the thick lashes, Willem felt the familiar awe. He couldn't even say, "Hello." Immediately, though, she drew him into her world.

"Is that Willem? Come here. I can write my name."

She was paler than he remembered, and thinner. The bandage was smaller than he had feared, but when she hopped off the bed and ran to him, she held the arm with the wounded hand tight against her leg to keep it from jiggling.

"What are you carrying?" she wanted to know.

Willem had thought and thought about what he might give her. He went through all his belongings. He counted his coins. What could he buy? She's six years old. What would please her?

He couldn't decide so, in the end, he grabbed two familiar items from his room.

First he held out his mother's offering.

"From your Aunt Elsbeth," he said.

As Nelleke reached for the smallest of Willem's packages, she became aware of the enticing smells emanating from it. She pressed her nose against the thin cloth surrounding the loaf shape, grateful for its warmth and for replacing the medicinal odors that had surrounded her all week. These were the same delicious mysterious smells that had engulfed her briefly as she entered Amsterdam less than a week ago.

She held the package up to Willem's shy nose and called over her Big Sister.

"Isabela, you smell too."

"Mmmmm. Cinnamon and cloves, I think." Isabella speculated. "Probably some nutmeg. My father often brought us spices."

Forgetting that it hurt to move the fingers on her injured left hand, Nelleke began eagerly unwrapping the package.

"It's a honey cake," Willem said.

Tanneke cut slices and served them on Nelleke's new china plate with the painted tulips. The four of them had an impromptu tea party.

Nelleke was beginning to remember. She had family in Amsterdam. She was only four when she left here and hadn't thought about them much.

"I'd like to learn to make honey cake," she declared. "Will Aunt Elsbeth show me how?"

"And I brought you these too," was Willem's answer.

He put down the large, awkward, heavy package and unrolled the smaller one – a large, thick piece of parchment.

Nelleke glanced at the lines and swirls on the parchment. The words were towns, she knew. The meandering open lines were rivers. There were large empty spaces that were probably lakes or seas.

"It's a map," she pronounced decidedly, taking more honey cake.

"Your father gave it to me. He drew it. I watched him."

"He was always drawing maps. If the troupe got lost? He'd tell us where to go."

"He gave me this too," said Willem, patting the largest item. "It's too small for me now."

Willem set the sturdy wooden stool on its three legs.

"How clever. It's just the right height and size for you, Nelita," said Isabela, lifting Nelleke onto the small triangular seat. Her feet reached the floor.

"When it's cold. When the canals freeze. When you're well. I'll take you for a ride on this stool," Willem promised. "I'll show you how it works."

When the last cake crumb had been nibbled from fingers, Isabela and Tanneke went into the next room to clean up the plate and forks.

Willem leaned toward Nelleke and almost whispered.

"Do you know the story?"

For Willem there was only one story. He never fully understood it. He hadn't heard it for a long time. The parts he knew were always in his thoughts.

"My Story," Willem said. "About when your father found me and took me to your Aunt Elsbeth. Did your father ever tell you anything about the playing card – the one cut in half?"

"I know a story," Nelleke said. "About a duck. Waddelen."

And she told it from beginning to end.

Chapter Nine
Show Me

$\curvearrowright$

fter caring for Nelleke for two weeks in the Infirmary and rubbing lanolin onto the healing burn several times a day, Dr. Voerman felt certain that Nelleke was sufficiently cured to join the other children. Isabela promised to continue to give the little girl a dose of rosehip syrup every day.

The Housemother decided that Sunday morning would be a good time to introduce Nelleke to some of the routines. She had visited the Infirmary only once when she guided Mrs. Comfrij, the visiting Regentess, to the wounded child's bedside. This morning the Housemother appeared in the Infirmary early and shook both Isabela and Nelleke by the shoulders.

"Wake up, girls. You're returning to the children's wing today. The others are already dressed and having their breakfast. Please join them right away."

Holding a basket over her arm, the Housemother gathered up Nelleke's gifts.

The gifts had been Nelleke's friends and major diversion during her weeks of isolation. She had held them and studied them. She had poked her nose into the deep bowl of the spoon, taking deep breaths of the freshly hewn wood. She had held the cool smooth plate against her sometimes feverish cheek. When no one was looking she had flipped her tongue back and forth over the raised part of the china where the tulips were painted on. The gifts gave her hope that the people in this

46

large, plain house – all those people she hadn't yet met – were generous and caring. Their gifts had helped her heal.

Groggily, Nelleke watched as the Housemother wrapped in cloth her lace, spoon, slippers, and china plate. Into the same basket went the map her father had drawn.

She was excited about being able to play with the other children. The word "breakfast" made her salivate. She thought that perhaps she could smell – what? Buttermilk? Fresh cheese? Sausage? She slipped out of bed and reached toward the basket.

"I'll carry these, Ma'am. Mother."

"You won't need them where you're going, Nelleke. Orphans aren't allowed individual belongings here. You're all treated equally. I'll keep them for you."

The Housemother gathered up the one remaining gift, the three-legged stool, too large for the basket, and moved quickly toward the door.

Fully awake now, Nelleke yelled after her.

"Those are my things, Ma'am. You can't have them."

The Housemother stopped. For a long moment, Nelleke and Isabela saw only her back, rigidly still. The two of them moved close together. Then the Housemother put down the basket and the stool, turned around, and returned to the pair.

Glaring down at Nelleke, she said, "Yelling at your mother. Disagreeing with her. Those are not acceptable behaviors in this house. Do you understand me, little girl?"

Turning to Isabela, she said, "See that the child is under control before bringing her to breakfast. But if you don't hurry, you'll both miss church."

She moved quickly through the Infirmary again, picked up the basket and stool, and disappeared.

Nelleke began to wail. Tanneke came running. Dr. Voerman too. She was no longer in physical pain, though. She was mad. She had been violated and robbed. She became aware that what she felt for the large, imperious woman who controlled her life was something she had never felt before. Worse than unfriendly. Far stronger than dislike. It was solid, tense, and ugly like a gray, misshapen rock pressing from inside her belly, trying to get out. "I HATE HER," said Nelleke looking up at the trio of concerned adults circling her. Naming the emotion gave her no release. Saying the word out loud only hardened the rock and made her hate herself too.

During the past week as the uniforms were released from the laundry and placed in the large armoire in the hallway, Isabela had been selecting the best pieces for Nelleke's return – the newest, the best fitting.

Now here she was, dressed in the standard orphan uniform in Amsterdam colors.

A basic white under blouse with a narrow lace collar showed at the neck of the full-length flared dress gathered at the waist. The left side of the dress was solid red, the right side black.

Snug black wool sleeves reaching to her wrists shielded Nelleke from the autumn winds that whipped over the nearby waterfront called "Het IJ," an inlet of the Ijselmeer and Amsterdam's harbour. A flowing full-length white apron covered the dress from chest to ankles and hooked in back. Isabela wound Nelleke's hair into a bun and covered it with a white, folded, tight-fitting cloth. The cap was held in place with two round brass pins on top – or it should be if Isabela could make her be still long enough.

"*Nelita mia*, you are a child. You are not a bunny rabbit. *Por favor.* We're almost finished. No more wiggle. I cannot fasten bonnet pins on a bobbing head."

Isabela held Nelleke at arm's length, stopping her motion for a seconds-long inspection before they descended the stairs to join the others for breakfast. In front the white head cloth parted over Nelleke's forehead. Partway up her scalp, the blond curls attempted to burst out of the small tight open space. Her dark eyes peered out impatiently underneath.

Isabela was dressed in the same uniform with two changes. The older girls, whether orphans, servants, or attendants, wore half aprons and thick white folded shawls covering their shoulders. The shawls formed a "V" in front and in back, ending in a sharp point at the cinched waist. Because today was church day, Isabela had gratefully shed the plain weekday headcovering. Sunday's was thinner and more delicate, her black hair visible through it. The metal pins were cut in a lacey pattern and hung over her temples. Isabela felt buoyed by the hint of glamour these pins gave her. Not quite as daring as earrings, the pins were the closest thing to jewelry any girl in the orphanage was permitted to wear.

Every Sunday when she attached them to the sides of her head covering, she thought of the jewelry in the Chinese box with the gold lettering – the one in her bedroom in Spain on the shelf above her bed. It was in that box she kept heirlooms like her grandmother's ivory brooch and mother's gold wedding band. It was her safe box for her pearl and shell bracelet. She should have left it there. Now that bracelet was lost. Oh, the shipwreck! Her father! She had no time to think about that now.

Isabela glanced at her faint reflection in the window pane. She was becoming impatient to escape the confines of the orphanage, to be off on a Sunday sojourn through the city.

"No skipping. No hopping. You must descend slowly. You must be a lady," insisted Isabela with a firm grip to Nelleke's healthy hand. The two descended the wooden stairs – the site of Nelleke's mishap – and moved toward the sound of children babbling and to the smell of roasted meat mixed with white beans.

Throughout her nearly seven years, Nelleke lived as much outdoors as in. The forests, fields, streams, and ponds were her habitat. The animals, wild and domestic, were her teachers and companions. She explored her world with all her senses, holding a tickly butterfly in her palm, following an ant parade to its hill home, picking and sorting flowers by scent, color, and pattern.

While traveling with her mother's troupe, she often fell asleep around a campfire, sometimes on a blanket, sometimes in loving arms, always with music being played around her. Later, at the farm, her days were filled with the lure of changing seasons and smells.

Nothing in Nelleke's life had prepared her for the scene in front of her now. There were two hundred children dressed precisely alike. The girls seemed like puppets in a theater, each one identical to Nelleke herself in size and shape as well as costume. The little boys differed, not in the color of their uniforms that were also half red and half black, but because they wore pants and jackets. Only their brass buttons added a tiny touch of variety.

The children were arranged on benches at long wooden tables. The walls were bare. Gray light attempted to reach in through the row of windows on one side. Two servants poured each child a mug of light beer from a large pitcher. Two others went up and down the rows holding the handles of a large straw basket. They stopped every few steps to reach into the basket and place slices of bread on shared plates.

Nelleke caught a glimpse of the only object that stood out in the monotonous sameness – a massive, mahogany chair with strong, carved, inviting arms. "Could that chair be for me?" she wondered, waiting to make an entrance. "Am I a princess?" "Will they curtsy to me?"

As the children began noticing the pair in the dining room doorway, the jabbering became quieter and then stopped abruptly. There were several moments of complete silence as all the small heads turned to look at them. Then murmurs began – "Is she that new girl?" "It's the one who burned herself." "They cut off her hand, didn't they?"

The murmurs grew until the usual sounds of chatter and clatter, munching, drinking, and spills again filled the space.

If all the eyes on her were terrifying, if their comments made Nelleke feel freakish, it was the children's indifference that hurt most. Beginning to realize that, far from being a princess, she was just one more among that mass of anonymous children, Nelleke pulled loose from Isabela and ran from the room. She was dressed like them. She was one of them. They had no parents. She had no parents. What did the Housemother call them? Orphans. She ran down the corridor she had just passed through, almost gliding on the shiny black and white tiles. She ran through the reception room. She shoved with all her strength on the heavy outside door, startling the bored guard. She ran and ran across the bricks. A bonnet pin came loose. The cap sagged to one side. The sickening odors from canals she couldn't see reached her. A wall stopped her. Hearing familiar steps behind her, she turned around and buried her face in Isabela's apron.

"I am not an orphan. I am <u>not</u> an orphan." Nelleke repeated every few seconds between sobs. Isabela held the child against her. They stood clinging to one another in the middle of the courtyard, rocking gently. Soon there were tears in Isabela's eyes too. Only sixteen, having lost her own parents in the past year, and far from home, she desperately needed a day away from the orphanage herself. Since Nelleke's arrival two weeks ago, the child had absorbed all of her attention.

Isabela adored this child, but she needed time to think about her own situation. In place of a pampered life as a Captain's daughter, she was now employed and earning her own keep. Instead of living in a sleepy hill town tucked above a harbor in Spain, she was part of a large, loud, bustling Dutch harbor city with people from all over the world.

What awaited her in Spain? Luxury, yes. And two maiden aunts who doted on her. What else? An arranged marriage. A life much like her mother's. Did she want to go back? Could she if she wanted to? Spain and the Southern Provinces had been locked in a war her entire life. She had barely made it here alive after the shipwreck.

What was that proverb the Housefather sometimes quoted? "You take care of today. God will take care of tomorrow?"

The door to the orphanage opened. The Housemother called across the courtyard.

"Isabela, bring the child in here. The children are lined up. You'll be late."

The children were leaving for the Calvinist *Nieuwe Kerk* soon, but that was not where Isabela worshipped. Forty years ago throughout the entire country, Catholic churches had been banned. Priests and nuns were run out of town. Their churches were vandalized. Now Catholics were tolerated, but they were still not permitted to have their own churches. They met in homes. Some Dutch Catholics had remodeled their attics into chapels, or added extra rooms. It was to one of these hidden spaces that Isabela went every Sunday.

Isabela re-arranged Nelleke's cap and patted the tear stains. As she half carried and half pulled the reluctant child back toward the building, she made up a song:

> "*I know a little girl named Bernadien.*
> *She's the funniest child you've ever seen.*
> *She raises one brow and rolls one eye.*
> *Tell her to stop and her guilt she'll deny.*
> *She's proper she'll say*
> *But when you turn away,*
> *She'll raise the other brow*
>   *and stick out her tongue.*
> *Now my little song of Bernadien is done.*"

When they stepped inside, the Housemother took Nelleke's arm and pushed her in line. "You certainly won't remember, Nelleke," she said, but the church we're going to is where your father and mother registered your birth. You were baptized there too. I expect you to behave yourself in the *Nieuwe Kerk*.

Isabela interfered one more time before abandoning her charge for the day.

"Mother, I think Nelleke should be paired with one of her bedmates."

Isabela walked with Nelleke down the row of orphans. Red. Black. Red. Black.

Only the eyes – all watching her – came in different colors.

"Hello, Bernadien. Will you hold Nelleke's hand, please?" Isabela asked.

Bernadien stuck her chin up and looked at Nelleke. Then she said what 200 orphans wanted to say.

"Show me your hand."

Nelleke held out both hands. Bernadien lifted her left brow and held it up while she inspected the hands, looked at Nelleke, then at Isabela, back at Nelleke's hands again.

"See," Nelleke said, "This hand has a star on top. When it fell to earth, it hit so hard that it became a little twisted and lopsided. The points aren't even any more. It bounced off the earth first very high, then lower and lower with each bounce and landed on my hand. Now it has a new home."

Nelleke reached her hand up as high as she could and shook it up and down.

"If I hold it up toward the sky at night, it waves to its twinkling friends. 'I'm down here, everyone. I live with Nelleke now.'"

"It's not a star at all. It's a scar. It's ugly," Bernadien said, reaching for the normal hand. "I'll hold this one."

"Are you standing up straight? Are you facing forward? Is the line crooked? It better not be." The Housemother barked. The children shuffled tighter into their places.

She asked one of the Big Sisters to lead. She placed herself behind the two little girls she considered to be the least likely to behave. When the group passed through town, everyone would know who they were. Discipline and comportment were important.

It assuaged wealthy Amsterdammers' mild guilt to see the orphans healthy and well cared for. It also comforted them. Plague and disaster could threaten even the most comfortable families.

Isabela kissed Bernadien and Nelleke. "I'll see you at bedtime," she said and she left.

Chapter Ten
Genuflect and Shipwreck

Clutching her white prayer book with gold lettering, Isabela rushed out the orphanage gate, turned right onto narrow St. Luciensteeg and crossed the Kalverstraat. The bridge over the Rokin was raised to allow a small vessel to pass under it. After this delay, Isabela traversed the lowered bridge and walked straight to the city's inner brick wall. She turned left and followed a path just inside the city, weaving in and out among the dilapidated wooden huts, avoiding the scavenging animals and their mess. The wall towered above her and was so thick there was a path on top where sheep and goats grazed and townsfolk strolled. "Some day," she thought, "I will walk the entire wall to see what lies beyond it. I will look west toward England and south toward Spain." She said a silent, sad thank you to her father. Because of the map-reading lessons he gave her onboard ship, she had a clear idea of where she was on the earth at this moment.

Isabela's father had been a ship's Captain. For nine months out of every year his ship was in service to the Spanish navy. In the early years he sailed with a crew of cooks and bakers, delivering meals and bread to officers. When the wars with Holland were most intense, his ship also carried extra ammunition.

During the middle years of the eighty years of fighting, his ship was enlisted to transport medical crews. In the heat of battle, his small, versatile, easily maneuvered ship appeared quickly alongside a battleship that had raised its red "Wounded" flag. Through the fog and gun smoke, the crew scrambled aboard with bandages, remedies, and whisky.

There were always some sailors they could revive and save. If necessary, they were prepared to amputate. They wrapped the dead in the remaining torn pieces of their own uniforms, stripped them of swords, guns, and ammunition, crossed themselves, and tossed the bodies overboard.

Isabela saw her father only three months a year. During his away months, she sat with her mother and aunts. Together they sewed, read, told stories, and recited poetry. Sometimes they passed the time singing. Occasionally Isabela would wander into the kitchen to chat with the cooks, help them knead the bread or turn the spit over the fire.

Isabela was the only child among them and Tia Anacleta was the only one of the three adult sisters who left the house. Tia Lucia never recovered from losing her soldier fiancé. Seeing young men in the streets jostling and shouting, so full of life, only saddened her further. She taught Isabela mournful tunes for the harpsichord.

Isabela's mother was delicate. Isabela brought her cold fruit drinks or hot gin, depending on the nature of her current malady. She opened the drapes wide or shut them tight following her mother's mood. For days Isabela's world was her mother's bedroom. She patted her mother's dear, pale face with scented cloths, gently brushed her hair, stroked her feet. Once in awhile she was free to accompany Tia Anacleta to visit friends, shop at the market, or linger at the dock.

Her favorite activity was sharing the many gifts her father had brought her through the years: Dolls. A bracelet with alternating pearls and small shells. Hair ornaments. A toy windmill. Isabela would arrange the gifts around her and ask, even though she knew, "And this one, Tia Lucia, where did Father get this one?" "What is this made of, Tia Anacleta?" "Mamma, hold this against your ear. Can you hear the sea roaring?"

It was the books she enjoyed the most. She had seven in Spanish. Two in French. One in English. Her mother and aunts helped with the French and English. But there was also a Dutch book that no one could decipher. Isabela studied the illustrations and tried to pronounce the strange names of people and places: Geert, Elsje, Muiden, Weesp, Utrecht. She memorized the name of the printer on the inside page: Hendrik Stradwijk and Son, Amsterdam. Never had she ever imagined that she might actually one day live in that city.

Then from the docks would come the excited shouts she always listened for: "La Fortuna sighted! La Fortuna returning! La Fortuna docking!" When those words reached her home's courtyard, she would run free, all alone, straight to the ship. She bolted so quickly that no servant, no aunt, not even her mother had time to catch her, to tidy her up, to place a hat on her head or to restrain her.

Isabela would arrive out of breath, hair swinging, lifting her skirts, nearly tripping, anticipating her father's thrilled smile when she emerged from the gathered crowd. She would push her way to the ship's off-ramp and there he would be. She always expected to throw herself into his arms. Instead she always stopped, unanticipated shyness nearly filling her with panic.

Her hesitancy was short lived. Within moments, her father scooped her up, twirled her around and around, held her tight, put her down, and looked at her. Then, becoming mockingly formal, he would doff his hat, bow low, and say with exaggerated slowness, "Señorita Isabela, I believe. And how is the lovely young lady? Grown, I believe. More beautiful, certainly." Then teasingly, "And hoping for a present from the Captain, is she?"

The last time they performed this yearly ritual, Isabela's step was slower. The Captain did not twirl her. Perhaps she had become too tall? She saw his sad face and felt his arms around her. They both wept. Someone had told him the news the moment he stepped off the ship. Her mother had died two weeks earlier, calling her husband's name. Isabela was fifteen.

Clinging to each other's hands, they climbed the hill to their home. For the first time in all the years she had been dashing to greet her father, Isabela didn't give a thought to what gifts he might have brought.

Over the years, the Captain had often returned with paintings. "There was an explosion of art in Holland," he told his family. All the newly rich merchants wanted themselves immortalized on canvas. Sometimes alone with symbols of their profession. Sometimes with their families, wives, and daughters dressed in the latest fashion.

But the baker, the tiller, the forger, even the farmer – they were all collectors. The Captain had seen paintings adorning the churches and the tavern walls as well. Traders rowed out to the ships docked in Dutch harbors and beyond, anxious to sell their wares, beautiful works of art included.

This time her father brought a self-portrait by an Amsterdam artist. At first Isabela was disappointed in this gift. Perhaps it was just that in her mourning, nothing would please her. With his large nose, his thin curls, the unkempt moustache, and his strange hat, the painter was far from handsome. She turned the painting toward the wall.

Gradually, though, she began to study the painting and she always saw something new. The casual strokes on his dark cloak. The glimpse of white shirt at his throat. The way he looked directly at her with his small, dark eyes. Where was the light coming from? It lit up his beret, one side of his face, his earlobe, the book he was reading. "Was that the Bible? Or a forbidden book perhaps?" she asked herself.

This artist was not trying to make himself appealing. Wrinkles and sagging jowls. Pock marks on his nose. Isabela began to respect him. He was so honest. He became increasingly real to her as if he might say something any moment that would amuse her.

For the next few months, Isabela begged and cajoled, "Take me with you this time, Father. They say that the fighting has subsided, that it's not as dangerous as it once was. In all these years, Father, you were wounded only twice, and you healed quickly. I can cook. I can bandage. I know something about herbs and healing. I want to care for you, Father – on the ship. I want to see some of the places you've always told us about. I want to be with you. Don't leave me here, Father, please."

Until two days before his scheduled departure, her father was adamant. "Absolutely not, dear daughter. Stop making these demands. Your place is here in your home."

The stern words belied the Captain's thoughts, however. Although there were always those who believed a woman aboard was bad luck, there was some precedent for it. Certainly no woman was climbing the masts or wiping down the deck, but he had seen one wife accompany her Captain husband, and a sister with her navigator brother.

Those women had a calming influence, he noticed. The men softened their language. The ship felt less rough, less temporary, almost at times like a home. It was true that the battles had stopped for now. There was talk of a peace treaty. So, in spite of his doubts, the Captain of the Fortuna looked at his precious child, thought about leaving her behind, and agreed to take her. Just this once. He knew that, once married to Diego, her life would again be constricted. She was certainly his child. She too felt the lure of the unexplored. He wanted to share with her some of the adventure that remained for him forever fascinating.

Then it was the Aunts' turn to grieve and argue and fret as they helped Isabela choose the few items to pack: two changes of linen, her mother's most cherished tea cup, five books, the pearl bracelet, and the self-portrait by the Amsterdam artist that had by now become a favorite possession. The painter would keep her company.

* * *

Isabela stopped to admire the magnificence of the *Oude Kerk* and marveled at what the Schoolmaster had told her, that construction began more than three hundred years ago, and that it had miraculously survived two fires that reduced the area around it to ashes. Knowing her father was a ship's captain, the Schoolmaster informed her that the church was originally dedicated to St. Nicolaas, the patron saint of seamen. She shuddered, remembering his descriptions of the violent looting and destruction that took place there. Calvinists drove out the Catholic nuns, monks, and priests and made the church their own. Some day perhaps she would feel brave enough to enter the church's alien territory and view the three stained glass windows in the Lady Chapel.

Nearly running now, she hurried on and abruptly turned left into a narrow alley. Looking to the left and right and seeing no one, she gave the secret knock: one long followed by three short, for Father, Son, and Holy Ghost. The door opened. As she stepped inside, she reached up her left sleeve, pulled out her black mantilla, and placed it over her head. Falling forward, it nearly obscured her face. The mantilla and prayer book were one of many items shipped to her via England by her aunts. The Housemother stored most of the items, of course, but allowed her to use the mantilla on Sundays.

The mistress of the house opened and shut the door quickly and greeted her with a kiss on each cheek. With soft organ music beckoning her and becoming louder with every step, Isabela mounted two flights of stairs before entering the makeshift sanctuary. She had arrived at Our Lord in the Attic. Making the sign of the cross on her chest, she genuflected at the edge of a bench in the back and sat down, then kneeled, bowed her head, crossed herself again, and said a quick prayer.

The service had already begun. About one hundred people were crowded into the space, sitting on wooden benches and on crude chairs along the sides of the room. A few smiled at the young woman dressed in the red and black orphan uniform. Most kept a reverent face forward, eyes on the crucifix and the religious paintings. When the small organ stopped, the priest appeared and began the Mass.

Isabela had been to church nearly every Sunday of her life. The familiar phrases in Latin comforted her. The language's cadences enveloped her, creating a calm protected space. She took a deep breath. The child chatter and demands of the past six months faded. She felt her shoulders, head, and neck relax.

The calm was short lived, however. Closing her eyes she pondered once again the events that had brought her to this city, her role in the shipwreck, her guilt.

* * *

The plan was to return Isabela to Spain in four months. She would actually be on the ship for only one month total. The other three months she would stay with the Captain's dear friends, Mr. and Mrs. Hatterbrook, in London. In addition, he would give up the hazardous work of providing medical care to battleships. To transform the vessel into a cargo ship took weeks of construction, though. He also had to find crew suitable for the new tasks and train a new first mate.

Finally the ship was ready, loaded with raw timber for a shipbuilding center in England. Isabela's aunts rarely left the house and they did not come to the pier to see her off. Knowing they were grieving, disapproving, and alarmed was upsetting to Isabela, even frightening. But as she watched her small coastal town become smaller and smaller, her sense of excitement returned. "All hands about ship. Prepare to set a course," her father had shouted. "Man your stations." She was onboard. She was sailing – sailing for Norwich, England!

For days Isabela was so ill she could only lean over the deck or lie limply in her father's quarters, the space that was hers for this journey. The Captain slept in the tiny office that adjoined it. Her meals were served in her chamber; she was not allowed to mix with the crew. Once she adjusted to the constant motion, she passed her time reading, writing to her aunts, studying English and, when he was free, conversing with her father, her only companion.

Early in the journey, her father spoke with her seriously in his formal way. It was the first time she could remember feeling like an adult in his presence. His mood was melancholy.

"My dearest Isabela. There are those, including your aunts, and members of this very crew, who think I am foolish to take you with me on this trip. They feel I have no right to expose you to possible danger. Although this new crew is untested, throughout my career I've always had a close, loyal team of seamen. We've fought off every potential disaster. Many others have not been so fortunate. Should the ship be imperiled, I want you to know of the plans I have made on your behalf."

"Yes, Father. Thank you, Father. I only want to be with you, Father."

"This is most difficult to say to you, my child, but as Captain my first loyalty must be to the ship and the crew. I am responsible for the cargo and the men. In order to command from them the strength, respect, and discipline required at sea, in order to avoid the insubordination that can result in tragedy, the men must believe at all times that I, as their leader, will make wise decisions on their behalf. They have families too. I must do everything in my power to bring them home safely."

"As for your security, I am entrusting you with a secret that you must reveal to no one unless it becomes necessary for you to leave this vessel. I had a small rowboat built for you and a hidden space carved out for its safekeeping. Spain is behind us. We will pass by or moor in two additional countries on this voyage: France and England. As we approach each country, I will give orders to Jules, and then George, natives of those two countries, to abandon ship, take you with them, and do whatever is necessary to get you ashore. I will confer with each as we pass from one territorial water to another, so that it will be clear who is responsible. When we sail in and out of Norwich, we will be across from Amsterdam. Therefore, once we are near Norwich, I will ask Cornelius to follow that same command, should we stray somehow into Holland's territorial waters. I will point out each man to you and show you on the map where we are every night so that you know who to turn to should I be indisposed. I will also reveal to you the camouflaged trap door that leads to the rowboat they would use to take you to safety. Depending on our location, only one of the men will be authorized to abandon this ship and take you with him.

"I understand, Father," said Isabela as she stood up and put her arm around her father's slumped shoulders. He almost looked as if he were praying. "I, too, will obey the Captain's orders, Father," she said in a mock military voice.

The Captain lifted his head and smiled at his daughter. She had grown into a lovely young woman, gracious, intelligent, and brave.

He thanked God for her and for the chance to share this journey with her.

Jules, George, and Cornelius. Her would-be saviors. Isabela was not introduced to them, she did not converse with them, but she could soon distinguish them from the others. Short, stocky, yellow-haired Cornelius was the Dutchman. Because he climbed the masts faster and more assuredly than anyone else, he was most often seen aloft. With the superior view the high location afforded, he would call down to the others, "Ship ahoy. Royal English vessel starboard. School of dolphins approaching. Veer to port."

George, the Englishman, long-legged and bare-headed, always wore striped shirts that fit tight across his narrow chest. During her brief forays on deck, many of the sailors, including both George and Cornelius, acknowledged Isabela with a nod and continued their work.

The Frenchman, Jules, did not nod casually. He stared. At first she was dismayed, unnerved, even shocked by the relentless brown eyes under bushy brows. She turned, looked out over the sea, adjusted her skirts, and hid behind her parasol. Yet she could not resist the temptation to check back and see if his gaze was still upon her. Yes, there he was, the black cap thrown back, the profusion of curly chest hair spilling out of the open front of his blousy white shirt with its flapping full sleeves and dark stains under the arms.

His regard might have mocked her confusion. He might have sneered at her naïveté and innocence. He might have scorned her feminine presence in the rough, male environment. He did not. He simply beheld her, steadily, consistently. She came to enjoy his contemplation of her, even to count on it, to look forward to it. Pretending to find the endless sea fascinating, she kept her back to him. She could feel his gaze burning through the parasol, right through her layers of garments. The heat began in the small of her back and crept up her spine. It teased the back of her neck and spread to her shoulders, down her arms all the way to her fingertips. If, by chance, Jules was below deck during her evening promenade on her father's arm, she felt acute disappointment. She imagined him swinging in his hammock, smoking his pipe, silent.

It was the evening conversations with her father, though, that were the most fulfilling part of the trip. He spoke about his childhood, the friendships he had forged with both his countrymen and citizens of all walks of life in many countries. He told tales of his near escapes administering medical care among the battleships. For him, this was the most leisurely trip he had ever experienced. For her it was an opportunity to get to know her Pappa.

The ship stopped briefly for supplies in a small French port. Disembarking and walking the narrow, dirt streets on her father's arm, Isabela was amused by the barefoot children who crowded around her. "*Bonjour, Mademoiselle. Comme vous êtes jolie, Mademoiselle. Voulez-vous du pain?*" She found that her aunt's tutoring enabled her to read some of the shop signs: *Tailleur. Livres. Vin. Fromage.*

She caught site of Jules ahead of them. Less serious and intense than on the ship, he chatted with the vendors, lifted a toddler high, kissed a small girl on both cheeks, and jauntily tore off and chewed pieces of the baguette he carried under his arm. Up ahead, Jules lingered at a stall in front of which a pretty, pink-cheeked maid distributed cheese samples and directed people to her mother's well-stocked shelves. When Jules helped himself to several bite-size pieces, he said something that made the girl giggle. Isabela turned her head away and walked by, clutching her father's arm tighter.

Three days later, a graceful gull flew out to meet them. When Isabela held up a crust of hard bread, it swooped and bit down on it, almost taking a finger with it. The gull squawked and came near her repeatedly, but she did not dare feed it again. Still, the friendly bird – or was it just a hopeful beggar? – accompanied them to shore. It was twilight when they arrived in Norwich waters. As the ship glided into place, Isabela felt protected and welcomed by two bright moons. One in the sky. The other reflected in the water. Although occupied with the demands of mooring the ship, the Captain took a moment to point out to Isabela the spire of the cathedral. That meant they were not far from the town center where tomorrow she would meet the family who would host her throughout the summer.

And what a lively summer it was! The Hatterbrook's oldest daughter was married and had a family of her own, but she lived nearby and visited with her small children almost daily. The four younger Hatterbrooks – three girls and a boy – were all two years apart in age, 12, 14, 16, and 18. Mornings there were studies with a tutor. Afternoons were spent visiting friends, strolling, boating, picnicking, playing croquet. Evenings there were concerts and parties, some casual and spontaneous, some lavish. As an only child from a quiet, secluded household, Isabela thrived on all the activity.

While her father was off delivering the timber, loading goods for the return trip, and readying the ship, she turned sixteen. Her father had left money with the family with the request that they celebrate the occasion in any way they thought appropriate. To prepare for the surprise event, the Hatterbrook sisters had a dress made for her and brought her to the hatter who made her a yellow straw bonnet covered with flowers and flowing ribbons. When the family sang to her and brought out special treats and gifts, she was stunned, but pleased to find herself the center of attention.

Two days later, her father arrived. When they were alone, he gave his daughter a kiss and spoke to her seriously.

"Have you enjoyed your escapades with the Hatterbrooks, my dear?"

"Oh, yes, Father," she answered breathlessly. "I do believe I could be happy living here forever."

"I hope you will always remember this summer as an adventure, as an opportunity for you to see part of the world that lies outside our little village, but my darling Isabela…."

The Captain looked down for a long moment. Then he raised his head and looked directly at her.

"Now that you are sixteen, it is time to think about adult concerns. It is my responsibility as your father to see that you are well cared for always. As you know, my friend Captain Miguel de Vega and I made a pledge to each other – that you and his son, Diego, would one day marry. That day is upon us, my dear. The De Vegas and your aunts are making wedding preparations as we speak. Upon our return to Spain, you will become Diego's bride and move into his family home."

"But, Father, I barely know that young man!" Isabela cried out in disbelief.

There was only one other wealthy family in Isabela's village of fishermen. Miguel de Vega – who lived on the opposite side of town – was also a sea captain at one time, but since his left leg suffered a serious injury, he ran the business from home and no longer sailed. The two Captains, once rivals, became close friends after the accident. When Isabela was born, Captain De Vega's son, Diego, was three years old. The two Captains made a pact that their children would one day marry, uniting the two families and securing for their joined progeny their combined wealth.

Isabela grew up knowing that she was betrothed. It took a long while for her to even understand what the word meant and she rarely thought of it. Although the Captains visited one another – usually sharing a smoke and sailing stories in a local tavern, the families never socialized with one another. The two wives could not abide each other's company. Isabela's mother was furious about the arrangement – made without her consent, even without consulting her. It was simply not mentioned in their house.

Isabela had seen Diego twice in her life. Once when she was seven when her father took her to the De Vega home for a lavish party to celebrate their only son's first decade of life. Stiffly dressed in a full-length gown and uncomfortable shoes, and overwhelmed by the number of people, the music, the platters piled high with meats and sweets, Isabela clung to her father and asked when they could return home to the quiet of her calm, studious, poetry-writing, crocheting, household. The second time was when her father insisted on taking her to join the De Vega family when Diego set off on his first sea voyage at age fourteen. A crowd gathered, waving banners, cheering, and applauding as the slender young man mounted the plank and stood on deck. Although Isabela suspected he was really frightened, he raised his chin up, saluted the onlookers unsmilingly, and appeared cocky and quite certain he could conquer any challenge. Diego did not acknowledge his mother, who wept profusely and insisted on staying until the ship was out of sight. Captain De Vega finally took his wife's elbow and, leaning on the cane that accompanied him everywhere, led her home.

All her life Isabela had watched how her mother fell into a state of quiet, sustained sadness every time her father set sail, finding little solace in Isabela's presence or from her two maiden sisters. Is that the kind of life she would have as Diego's wife?

"It's true and unfortunate that we did not socialize with the De Vega family as you were growing up, Isabela. The lad has shown promise as a seaman, however, and will be a good provider, I'm certain. The wealth of both our families – the two most prominent families in our village – will be combined. You will always be well cared for."

"But, Father . . . ," Isabela began without knowing how to put into words her feelings of shock and betrayal.

"Ready your belongings for the journey, Isabela, and prepare to bid farewell to the Hatterbrooks."

* * *

STRENGTH. RESPECT. DISCIPLINE. The words stood at attention in a line at the top of the page and began marching down it like orderly soldiers. A crash broke the words apart and sent them leaping. "All hands down," her captain father said to the scattered letters. "Stand fast." The letters rearranged themselves and landed back on the paper. Isabela could not make sense of the scrambled words now. They looked like the words in the Dutch children's book her father gave her years ago.

A persistent, staccato hammering attacked the book's binding, beating it apart and separating the pages that flew in every direction and disappeared. Now the book's cover became enveloped in blackness and was no longer visible.

Isabela pulled the pillow over her head and tried to redirect this alarming dream. The narrow bed was bolted to the floor. The mattress sat deep inside it. But the ship was rocking so violently that the pillow would not remain in place.

She was becoming anxious and impatient when a thunderclap woke her fully and sent her leaping out of bed. Instinctively, she groped in the dark for her warmest shawl and gathered it around her nightdress. Now she could hear howling wind, trampling feet, banging. She barely had time to note that a fierce, beating rain was demanding entry, when a man burst into her chamber. She clutched her arms across her chest, and gripped her own shoulders in terror. No man was allowed near her and certainly not in her private quarters. When he held up the lantern he was holding, she saw it was Cornelius. But he, too, looked terror stricken.

"Where is my father?" she demanded, straining to see beyond Cornelius into the adjoining office where her father usually slept.

Cornelius avoided her question and yelled something unintelligible, drowned out by a second, louder burst of thunder. Now she was fully aware of the terrible rocking of the ship. She tried to hold onto the stabilizing bars attached to the outside wall, but the ship's jerking hurled her toward Cornelius.

Grabbing her arm, he yelled once more. "Come with me." As she was being dragged out of her private space, wearing only her nightdress and shawl, she grabbed her parasol. White, ruffled, and beribboned, it had shielded her from the sun during her limited strolls on deck. Perhaps it would protect her now from the torrents she could hear striking every wooden plank. Or would she use it as a weapon, she wondered.

Her father's bed was tousled and empty. She nearly tripped on the twisted quilt that lay half on the bed, half on the floor. Outside now, it seemed to her as if every crewman was shouting simultaneously amid the clanging and banging. A single, rocking lantern shed small hints of light on a nightmare. The sails were in shreds. Parts of the masts that had supported them stuck jaggedly into the sky. Others lay in pieces on the deck. One sailor lay motionless, pinned under a heavy bar. Another was hanging upside down, entangled in the ropes, writhing. She heard an angry voice near her but could not see the speaker. "What'd I tell ya? A woman on board is always BAD LUCK." Out of the darkness, her father appeared in front of her, frantic and desperate. "Cornelius will take you ashore, my darling child. He knows about the hidden space." Then he was gone, calling out orders that were heard by no one.

Cornelius pulled her across the undulating deck, her shoeless, stockinged feet sloshing in water halfway up her legs. While Cornelius opened the secret hatch and lowered the rowboat, she held the useless parasol over her head, trying to keep from falling and sliding. Amid the deafening thunder and crashing noises as the ship broke apart, there were more angry shouts. Isabela could make out the shadows of a brawl. The small rowboat had been discovered. Disobeying her father, the men were rushing toward it, shoving each other away. One knocked another in the angry water. One man socked two others in the stomach. One fell and did not move. The other slid across the deck, more like a river now, and fell overboard. Cornelius was no longer by her side.

Suddenly she felt a man's arm around her waist lifting her upward. Her right arm became pinned against his body. The wind ripped the parasol out of her left hand. Dangling, held in a forceful embrace, she went rigid. Attempting to kick this man would have been laughable. Screams would never be heard.

When a jagged bolt lit up the sky, she recognized the smooth tanned chin and moustache. Jules's face was coming closer. She could barely see them, but she knew those eyes were more intense, sure, and direct than at any time on this trip. His face was so near hers now she could feel the tip of his nose against her cheek. Then his lips were on hers, lightly for a moment, then harder, but not rough, pushing until both their icy mouths opened to each other. She had not stopped shivering since Cornelius had barged in and dragged her into the open – shivering from the cold, the knife-pointed rain, the fear, the confusion. Now the trembling moved inward. All of her was electrified, quivering, and fluttering helplessly. For a moment she was lost in the salty, hot, soft moistness of Jules's mouth. When Jules straightened, he did not loosen his hold on her. Carrying her in his arms, he took four long strides and lowered her into the small rowboat, barely large enough for two. She caught a glimpse of his right arm, hanging and motionless. Blood ran down it, mixed with the rain, and dripped into the boat.

Cornelius was waiting for her, oars ready to move quickly far away from the disappearing ship. Isabela sat where Jules placed her and held tight to the boat's sides. As soon as she was settled, Jules gazed at her for one last second, then dove, his head down, the left arm that had just embraced her aimed at the thrashing waves, and the injured arm dangling as if it were no longer part of his body. Fighting the furious waters, a sailor swam up and grabbed the side of the tiny boat, nearly tipping it over. Cornelius gave the man a sharp, vicious kick in the jaw and he disappeared back into the raging sea.

Within minutes, the sounds softened. Isabela could soon hear only the ship's bell ringing wildly and tunelessly, crying out for help that did not come, and then muffled in mid-clang. In the fog she thought she saw the hearty lantern float for a moment. Then it too disappeared.

Cornelius rowed. The boat rode high on wave after wave and dropped back down hard. Isabela was sloshed with every jostle and became so thoroughly soaked, she felt more like a fish than a girl. She loosened her grip, stood and tried to put one leg over the boat's side. The sea bottom beckoned. Her father was there. The ship was there. Jules was there. It would be calm. She would no longer feel the iciness, the nausea, the desperation. She began to pull herself up, ready to plunge. Then, in the dark, she felt a human touch. Not warm, not patient, not sympathetic, it pulled her back down into the boat and jolted her back into life. Two hands grabbed hers and wrapped them around a wooden bucket. Two hands guided hers down to the floor of the boat, scooped up water, lifted up the bucket, and threw the water overboard. "Bail," Cornelius screamed. She was alive. She had a task. She repeated the motions until every muscle ached. She uttered the words until she was hoarse and her lips were covered with thick icy salt. "Bucket down. Fill. Lift up. Empty. Bucket down. Fill. Lift up. Empty."

* * *

The kiss. Yes, it was a kiss. Not just a moment of calm and tenderness amidst chaos, though. Not just a good-bye. The kiss was both a command and a promise. "Stay alive. Struggle as much and as long as you must. You are just beginning to understand what life is about." Would Diego kiss her often? What would happen to her if she were never again kissed? Was that why her mother was so sad? With no kisses for nine months every year of her married life? Was that why Tia Lucia never left the house? To be kissed and then to lose one's fiancé? Was Tia Lucia unwilling to risk that pain again? Was that why Tia Anacleta was the only happy one of the three sisters? Because she had never been kissed? Because she was an innocent? She didn't know? She didn't mourn and pout and feel a miserable longing?

Isabela was innocent no longer. The kiss was her favorite memory. Not just of the happy moments of that disastrous voyage. No, she had to admit it to herself. It was her favorite memory ever. She wanted more. She wanted to be kissed again – like that and not like that. How could she find a man to kiss her when she lived in an orphanage with only women and children? How could she return to Spain? To Diego? Did she really want to? The questions taunted her. She knew it now. Day and night, memories of the kiss drove her.

"Our Father who art in Heaven," the Priest began. Isabela had known the Lord's Prayer since she was a small child. With head bowed and eyes closed, she repeated it in unison with the rest of the congregation. "Hallowed be Thy name. Thy Kingdom come. Thy will be done on earth as it is in Heaven." When it was her turn to be administered the sacraments, Isabela rose and moved down the center aisle toward the priest. Kneeling at his feet, mumbling, "Forgive me, Father, for I have sinned," and adding her lip print to the many invisible others pressed fleetingly onto the backs of his delicate fingers, she opened her mouth to receive the holy bread he placed on her tongue. "Take. Eat," the priest said. "This is the body of Christ. Given for your sins. Given that you might have life. And that you might have it more abundantly."

Chapter Eleven
Church

Step. Step. Across the courtyard. March. March. March. The guard opened the gate. The orphan parade exited. St.-Luciensteeg, a narrow street bustling even on a Sunday morning, gave hints of the larger streets beyond. Dogs running or fighting. Piles of baskets with a large cloth hiding their contents. A child, pulled along by a parent, trying to stop and stare at the orphans. The orphan line had to go around a horse that was stopped in the middle of the cobblestone street. Attached to the horse was a two-wheel cart filled with barrels. Every time the horse lifted a hoof or shook its head, the barrels realigned themselves with a loud clatter.

March. March. Right turn. Stand up straight. Left onto the Kalverstraat. Families. Wide lace collars. White cuffs from wrist to elbow. Large-brimmed black hats. Babies in mothers' arms. Toddlers on fathers' shoulders. Now the church bells were becoming very clear. Everyone hurried toward the clanging sound.

Skip. Skip.

"No skipping," said the Housemother.

Step. Step.

When they reached the open square space of the Dam, Nelleke gasped at all the ships – dozens of them right in the center of the town, lining both sides of the river. Their imposing beige sails stood taller than some of the surrounding buildings. Rising even higher were the flapping flags in dozens of different colors and designs. She began to count them silently, but couldn't get beyond fifteen. There were a lot more than six flags, though. Would the Schoolmaster teach her the next number?

It took all her developing self-discipline not to run to the ships, to hop on board, to explore and ask questions. Where did they come from? Where were they going? Did people live on them? The self-control dissipated, though, when she saw a flock of seagulls cleaning up the fallen bits left behind by the fish sellers. She dropped Bernadien's hand and chased them, joy and power filling her, running across the open plaza, seeing the white and gray birds flap and fly and protest.

Too soon, fingers clinched her elbow and yanked her back into line.

"You stay with the group, you wicked child. You think you're a princess? You can do whatever you want? Because you were in the sick room for two weeks and had visitors who gave you gifts?"

The word "gifts" coming from the Housemother's twisted mouth drove away all the exhilaration of the brief break away. Would she ever again see the lovely things – <u>her</u> things – that the Housemother had taken that morning?

"You will learn to obey the rules now. Do you hear me?"

"Yes, Ma'am."

"Yes, MOTHER. As long as I am in charge of your care, YOU CALL ME MOTHER."

"Yes, Ma'am."

"Yes, MOTHER!"

"Yes, Mother."

The Housemother put Nelleke back in line beside Bernadien, and continued walking directly behind the two little girls.

Bernadien took Nelleke's hand again. When she squeezed it, Nelleke glanced at her. Almost imperceptibly, Bernadien nodded backward twice toward the watchful Housemother. Then, keeping her head rigid and her gaze forward, she rolled her eyes. Nelleke suppressed a giggle and pursed her lips in a secret smile that only Bernadien knew was there.

As they approached the *Nieuwe Kerk* on the far side of the Dam, Nelleke could see by the door someone playing tunes on a battered violin. His face was red. His whiskers grew in every direction. His crumpled hat was on the ground. It held a few coins. The slow, melancholy music caught her attention. As the orphans came closer, the violin player moved his fingers higher and higher up the strings, vibrating more intensely on each note. The melody went from sorrowful to grieving.

Nelleke was almost beside the player before she noticed his size. He was scarcely taller than she was, with stubby legs, an adult face, and thick hands.

Now face to face with him, she lifted her voice above the powerful music. "Are you a man or a boy?" she asked.

"He's a dwarf," Bernadien whispered to her.

By the time the group began filing through the huge arched doors, the instrument was wailing. The Housemother shoved them both ahead.

Nelleke called back to him over her shoulder, "I can play the violin too, Mister." She was propelled forward. She was inside. Immediately there was a hush. The outside noises, the violin music, even the sound of the bells, could have been in a different town. The orphans sat on benches in the elevated gallery reserved for them. The long sermon began. Nelleke could see the head and shoulders of the preacher sticking up in the box that seemed to grow like a sideways mushroom stuck on the wall. He was so far away that even if she followed her impulse to stand on the bench and wave at him, he probably wouldn't notice her. She leaned forward and looked down to the raised platform to study his face. If she squinted, her sharp eyes detected a wrinkled forehead under a skull cap covering what was probably a bald head. Layers of thick garments broadened his shoulders. His head seemed to be supported by a collar – round, broad, stiff, white, and thickly ruffled. "If he lost that ruff, would his head roll off?" she wondered. His grey beard covered the collar in front and hung below it. The collar rose on the sides to graze his ears and continued to rise, covering his whole neck in back. "Was that Jesus maybe?" Nelleke wondered. Jesus said, "Let the little children come unto me." If that preacher was Jesus, maybe she could run up to him and tell him how much she missed her little brother. He would understand and take her home.

The preacher's voice rose, fell, threatened, and cajoled. Nelleke grasped little of his message. With the Housemother beside her, alert to every twitch and forbidding even the most hushed whisper, Nelleke kept her head rigid, but turned her eyes in every direction, exploring the high, airy spaces that seemed to stretch to Heaven. "Was God up there in the rafters? Were Mamma and Pappa up there with him? Could they see her here? Would they know that she was a good girl, sitting here quietly on Sunday morning?" Nelleke felt awed by the white columns and arches and the expanse of large gray tile floor leading to the imposing alter. Before long she was remembering the humble, village church she attended with Aunt Griet or Uncle Johannes. They took turns so that one of them could stay home with the younger two children. Hoping to discourage any heathen tendencies she may have inherited, they tried to find the time to take Nelleke to church every Sunday. The minister there spoke more lovingly than this one. When he saw her, he would place a gentle hand on her shoulder, or take one of her hands in both of his large, warm ones.

"How is our Nelleke today?" he would ask.

Warmth and familiarity were absent in the grand setting of the *Nieuwe Kerk.*

She missed leaning against Uncle Johannes's strong arm when she became drowsy. The psalms were set to music and sung by all. She wished that Aunt Griet were there to share a battered hymnbook with. Nelleke loved holding her side of that book even though she couldn't read yet. The little church had only two such books. Most of the congregation memorized the words.

Here, though, she saw only strangers, families sitting together, and then rows of red and black uniforms. "I am not like them," she insisted to herself. "I do not want to be an orphan." Tears formed and trickled down her cheeks. Her nose ran. She became her own mother cat. She ran her tongue over her face as far as it would reach in every direction, enjoying salt and gooeyness. Flashes of Jacob running to her whenever she returned from church increased the flow. Jacob hugging her knees, wanting to be held, wanting her to play. She sniffled. The Housemother gave her a stern look.

* * *

In a sea of red and black, hundreds of orphans poured from the dark church into the large plaza. They arranged themselves in the straight lines required of them and began their return walk. The Housemother believed that rumbling tummies would drive the orphans straight back after services without incident. She placed Nelleke's hand in Bernadien's and followed close behind them for a short while. Halfway across the Dam, she left the orphans to do an errand, placing a Big Sister in charge of the unpredictable pair. Experiencing the world beyond orphanage walls meant that this Big Sister had a rare opportunity to assess the city's youths, however. Every time she saw a young man walking toward the group or leaning against a building or showing off with companions, she had seconds to decide if she should lower her eyes demurely or make the bolder choice and attempt eye contact.

Bernadien amused herself and the orphans around her by yelling out a sermon quote. A tap on the shoulder from the Big Sister did little to discourage Bernadien's rebellious behavior. "Debauchery!" she yelled at startled passersby. "Drunkenness! Indulgence!" she said, trying to imitate the preacher's voice. Nelleke soon joined in, at first using the same words and imitating Bernadien imitating the preacher. Then she remembered some words herself and the deep threatening voice that said them.

"Revelry! Iniquity!" she threw out in a mock base, enjoying the momentary surprise and shock the words caused. Mothers glared and hugged their children closer. The two girls giggled and readied their verbal assault for the next unsuspecting Amsterdammer.

Neither child had any sense of the meaning of the words, but it became a game to see who could solicit the strongest reaction. "Indulgence!" shouted Bernadien.

Nelleke tired of the game and immersed herself in the scene. The bright crowded plaza was a feast to be explored. She first noticed the many stately folks whose well-made, if plain, garb identified them as Amsterdam's merchant class. They began to climb into long, open wooden wagons. The men helped the women and children to seats and climbed up after them, as strong horses pulled them to their elegant homes along the canals. Horses. It was the first time Nelleke had seen a live animal since Straw had sent her bumping and burning down the stairs. She stepped out from the orphan line and reached out to pet a large, muscled horse the color of dark ale, but then stopped, wondering if, like so many of the new rules she didn't understand, it might be impertinent to touch the possession of this wealthy family.

She studied the family to see if she had offended them. Two boys were already seated. Two brothers like Sebastiaan and Dirck, only so clean. Their perfectly cut hair formed a straight line just above their brows, under the bill of their matching caps placed straight on their heads. Their trousers, in the same fabric as their jackets, stopped right at their ankles. Their polished leather boots shone. The father was scarcely taller than the boys. He was holding the elbow of the mother, a young woman like Nelleke's mother had been, but smaller and paler. The father guided the mother up the stairs leading to the wagon. The mother noticed Nelleke, smiled, and reached out her hand to caress Nelleke's cheek. The gentle touch from the soft leather glove, and the woman's sad eyes drew Nelleke to the woman.

"Catherina," she whispered.

"Nelleke. I had a family once. But my mother died. Then my father too. Now I just have Jacob. He's my brother. I'm going back to the farm soon. My aunt and uncle are there. I'm just visiting the orphanage." Nelleke began her life story confidently, but her voice faltered when she added, "I'm just there for a little while."

The mother was seated now, but continued to smile slightly and nod slowly, with a sweet, sympathetic expression. The father gave the signal and the horse took off. Bernadien dragged Nelleke back into the orphan line.

Poorer folk moved aside to let the wagons pass. They lingered on the Dam to gossip and see the sights. A man strolled by, beating a large drum strapped to his shoulders. His son followed him, playing a flute. Four defiant men straddled barrels and set up a card game. Sailors sauntered. Women circulated, selling mugs of beer. Other women attempted to entice the sailors and card players to their rooms behind the taverns. Civil guards kept a careful eye. A beggar hovered over a chafing dish warming his hands. The knapsack at his feet was mounted over a long, thin stick. His soiled hat was as tall as his face was long.

Where was that tantalizing smell coming from? Nelleke searched the busy Dam for its source. Her nose led her eyes to a trail of smoke rising from a flat grill. A crowd was gathered around a heavy-set woman grilling pancakes. A child clung to her skirts with one hand and held one of her wares in the other. The child managed to take one bite before a small brown dog wrenched it from him and ate it all in one swallow. The child cried out and was quickly silenced with another pancake. The busy mother continued to pour batter on the grill, turn the flat, round sweets, serve them, and pocket her earnings.

The orphans marched on. Straight down the Kalverstraat. Right on St. Luciensteeg. The orphanage guard heard them coming and opened the gate. Nelleke made one last accusation. "Avaricious!" she yelled. Bernadien giggled her approval. The city was shut out. The orphans were home. The noonday meal awaited them. They rushed to the dining hall.

The hours in church trying not to squirm, sandwiched between two brisk walks in the fresh air, combined with the fact that she had eaten no breakfast, left Nelleke ravenous.

The mushed vegetables, the thick slices of bread, the round pieces of meat in front of her – she was nearly drooling with anticipation. She scooted over the first bench and reached toward the food.

Just as her fingers touched the edge of the platter, a servant scooped her up, lifted her back over the bench, and placed her three benches down with Bernadien and two other little girls. She looked longingly at the platter on this table too, but became aware that everyone else was standing quietly, eyes on the podium at the far end of the room. One of the orphanage's older girls was standing there, apparently expecting silence. Nelleke cast another glance at the full platter and stood with the others. The older girl opened the heavy book and read haltingly.

"O Lord my God, in Thee do I trust; save me from all them that persecute me, and deliver me . . . Lest he tear my soul like a lion . . . ."

"I'd love a pet lion," thought Nelleke. "I wonder what I should feed him."

"Oh let the wickedness of the wicked . . . ."

"Wicked." Nelleke glanced guiltily at the Housemother – at "Mother," as she had been instructed to call her. This 'Mother' seems to think I'm wicked. Does that mean God thinks so too?"

"God is angry with the wicked every day," continued the reader.

"'I knew it," thought Nelleke. "I am wicked. God hates me."

"He hath also prepared for him the instruments of death; he ordaineth his arrows against the persecutors."

"Death? Arrows? Will God send an arrow through me like Sebastiaan did with the pigeon?"

"I will sing praise to the name of the Lord most high."

"Well if He's so high up, maybe He can't reach me. Maybe He stays in the church rafters."

The reader closed the Bible. The children scrambled over the benches. The food competition began. There was no time to examine what she was eating or savor a flavor. Nelleke quickly realized that she would have to gulp the food down to get her share. She ate off a large platter shared with her three bedmates.

Vague, confused, frail Marja picked slowly at the food. Hendrikje ate systematically and steadily from each pile. She heard nothing. She said nothing. Bernadien hissed and pointed, "Nelleke, look over there. In the corner." Nelleke turned and studied the corner, but she saw nothing interesting there. When she turned back to the platter, Bernadien wrinkled up her nose at Nelleke. She was chewing a sausage. Another one dangled from her fist. The platter was empty.

PART II:
The Collectors

Chapter Twelve
Rituals

As Jos Broekhof approached the door to his third-floor study, he adroitly removed the key from the ring fastened to his belt. Closing his eyes, he rolled the key back and forth on his palm, ran his fingertips down its slender metal rod, and fondled its rectangular shape. The key's sharp teeth pressed into the soft pillow of his thumb. After squeezing the key in his fist for a moment, he opened his eyes, slid it gently into the small opening, and slowly turned it, listening for the crisp, satisfying click of the obedient bolt. Sanctuary. He was inside. The world was locked out.

Once the key was snapped back onto the domestic side of the ring, in position between the keys to the kitchen storeroom and the dining room china cabinet, Broekhof crossed to the large windows of the room's outer wall. Even alone, he attempted to elongate the lengths of each stride.

The street was abandoned at this hour and quiet, save for the voice of the night crier —still too faint to decipher. Unable to commit to a single direction, the autumn winds blew the inky canal waters to one side and back again. The bouncy light from several front-door candles danced with the water's motion.

Across the canal, Broekhof could see hints of more light inside his neighbors' homes. He imagined a servant hanging a heavy pot on the chimney, an oldest son preparing his Latin assignment, perhaps a couple chatting in bed before blowing out the lamp and making love, he thought with jealousy and resentment.

Crossing his arms, rocking back on his heels, and smirking slightly, he comforted himself by studying the house directly in front of his. Dark, abandoned. The fool. Christoffel Mennes had risked everything – his business, his home, his family…for what? A tulip bulb. Admiral. Viceroy. Queen of Night. Seductive names. Surely. Purple. White. Black no less. Intriguing colors. Yes. "But even the possibility of selling for one hundred times the purchase price would never tempt me," Broekhof thought. "As long as people were willing to spend thirty percent of their income to purchase flour for their daily bread, what could be more secure than grain? A grain merchant I have always been. A grain merchant I will always be."

"Steadfast, my Jos," he had once overheard his wife say to her sister as she was showing off the new velvet drapes in the front parlor. "Out of the house every day at 8:00, home with the family at 5:00, up in his study after supper every night working on the books. In bed by 10:00. I always know where he is. I always know what he's doing."

"Half past nine and all's well," yelled out the familiar bored, singsong voice as it passed below. For Broekhof, that was the signal to leave his contemplation at the window and continue his nightly ritual. As he turned back toward the center of the room, the wind blew open one of the uppermost shutters. Startled by the bang and irritated by the interruption, Broekhof walked to a corner and grabbed the window pole. He was less angry at having to perform the menial task of reaching up and fastening the window than he was humiliated at having to drag over a chair to stand on in order to reach it. There was probably no other home owner on the Heerengracht who needed such support.

The window shut tight, Broekhof jumped off the chair, resisting the momentary undignified pleasure that the child-like leap gave him, and approached his desk – the large wooden, oak desk that dominated this third-floor study. Every time he caressed its smooth carving, whenever he admired its breadth and its shine, he remembered seeing it dangling, one solid curved leg visible beneath the heavy carpet that surrounded it, the pulley draped over the hook, bringing it up, up, closer, closer, and finally through the large window – inside, intact.

Before continuing the ritual, he grabbed a quill pen, dipped it in ink, and wrote in his notebook: "Remind C to check fastener on shutter." As he wrote the brief note, he admired his fastidiousness. The date at the top of each page. Domestic matters written in block letters. Business notes in script. Urgent notes in large letters. In the margins, the initials of the person to be contacted.

With the notebook back in his jacket pocket, Broekhof gave his full attention to the room's only visible work of art, a large painting, covering the entire section of a wall that protruded out from under the eaves. "So that the light can reach it," he had told Myriam when he had first showed it to her, having chosen an afternoon hour when he knew the sun would indeed fix itself on the painting. "I had a section of the wall built out that way in order to enhance the painting's effect." "And so it does, my dear," she said, admiring her husband's cleverness and artistic taste. But the painting was actually something cheap and insignificant that Jos had picked up at an auction. It was camouflage.

He lifted the painting from the wall and placed it upright next to the outcropping, exposing two tall wooden doors side by side. Breathing deeply, deliberately forcing his shoulders to relax, he stretched out his short arms, grasped both door handles, and dramatically opened both doors simultaneously, revealing a cupboard with eight shelves. Reaching inside, he picked up one by one, seven identical ornate silver frames and arranged them face down in order on the oak desk. There was one word on the back of each. *Maandag. Dinsdag. Woensdag. Donderdag. Vrijdag. Zaterdag. Zondag.* Ah, Zondag. Sunday. Today. Broekhof leaned back in his chair and sighed deeply. There was no way to prepare himself for the disappointment, the loss, the longing he would feel momentarily. He leaned forward, bent over Sunday's frame, gripped it with both hands, and turned it to the front side.

This is the way every week ended for Broekhof. He shook the frame. He punched his fist back and forth through the empty space. The set was still incomplete. The series was still unconsummated. As a punishment for his desperation and his shame, he gazed into the nothingness, allowed it to consume him, to force out all other thoughts. Five minutes. Ten minutes. Thirty. Holding the frame in both hands, imagining what could be there, what was supposed to be there. Regretting the 300 guilders he had paid – not once, but twice – in order to fill that frame.

"Jos, dear, surely you've finished the books by now." His wife's weary voice broke his reverie. Her knock pulled him into the present. "Soon, Myriam. Go back to bed, dear. I'll be there shortly."

He had no intention of joining her soon, however. The ritual was not yet complete. This is where he belonged, here among his beloved etchings. Besides, there was nothing drawing him to the conjugal bed.

Ten years ago when their wedding guests were absorbed in drink and dancing, Myriam and Jos snuck away up to the room he had prepared for them – this very room on the third floor when the house belonged to Jos's parents. At his cousin's wedding a month earlier, when the guests discovered that the newlyweds had escaped, the most drunken among them gathered outside the room, shouting, singing bawdy ditties, and demanding to be let in. When their pleas were met with silence, they barged in, startling the poor couple. They gathered round the bed and continued their merrymaking. When one of them tried to jump into bed next to the young bride, the groom leaped up. The crowd could not have been more delighted seeing him naked, ranting and furious. But it was the new wife's tears, that eventually shamed the unwanted visitors and sent them scurrying.

Jos took precautions. He would never want to subject his sweet Myriam, barely seventeen years old, to such wanton behavior on the very night he had looked forward to for months. It was then – just before the wedding – that he had the lock installed – the same lock he now used to protect his solitary self and his secrets. Jos had imagined a long seduction of his virgin bride, a night of tenderness and reassurance before she would finally agree. Instead he was somewhat taken aback when Myriam displayed no hesitation or timidity. She was as eager as he was, it seemed. And she giggled – oh, did she giggle. The sound began lightly – apparently from amusement. Then a gasp or two, followed by higher-range giggles – from surprise he wondered? If he attempted to relax her and slow down, she would shake her head vigorously, giggling all the while. The sounds deepened and became louder as her pleasure intensified, ending in prolonged shrieking laughter. She continued to be a full participant in their mutual pleasure throughout her pregnancies and recovered from them quickly.

Yet, almost immediately after Catherina's death, a time when Jos felt they needed shared tender closeness more than any time in their marriage, Myriam announced that she was through with "that nonsense." Four pregnancies, one miscarriage, three live births, their only daughter dead four months ago at age three. She had two healthy boys now. She would never again allow him to get close enough to put her at risk, she told him.

Attempts to woo her back were fruitless. He tried gentleness, light caresses, gifts. Not a particularly clever man, he experimented with humor and wit. He even made an effort to impress her by writing poetry: "My darling, when I look into your eyes, I sink as if into an abyss – a heavenly abyss that is smooth and sweet. My darling, when you speak, I hear the wind. I hear bells. My darling, when I sniff your scent, . . . " Jos read his own words aloud, trying to sound seductive. Myriam merely turned over in their shared bed cupboard and, with her back to him, fell asleep. He ended up reading the final lines to himself and feeling utterly foolish. "When I sniff your scent, I am transported to the world's most exquisite garden where flowers bloom as far as the eye can behold."

Meanwhile, the multitudes of harlots in the city seemed to know instinctively that he had a frigid wife. The way they sauntered up to him, caressing their own breasts, patting him on the cheek, describing their services in detail. He could not bear it. To spend money on such a woman. Perhaps contract a disease. Perhaps be identified by a neighbor or colleague as he walked arm in arm with her. He was Jos Broekhof, second-generation wealthy grain merchant, upstanding citizen, Regent of the city orphanage. He would not succumb. He would not.

Broekhof returned Sunday's frame to its place on the desk. He stood, walked to the cupboard, and stooped to lift the heavy book from the bottom, the eighth, shelf. He opened the cover and read in his own careful, flowing script the title he had given this journal, "Straddle Series: Quest for the Seventh Etching." Impatient, he flipped through bunches of pages at once, catching glimpses of words from months of entries: "soapsuds," "shoulder," "lick," "thighs." He found the entry he sought and began to read, slowly, carefully, sure that this time a clue would reveal itself.

10 October in the year of our Lord 1639

Last night I gave Stradwijk the payment for the final etching –- 300 guilders, enough to provide some Dutch families five years worth of their daily bread. He assured me it was complete, that Mennes' bid had been lower than mine, that he would return with the work within the half hour. I settled in with a third gin at The Thirsty Bull, anticipating his return. Soon I would possess all seven of these magnificent etchings. I told myself at first they were an investment, sure to double or triple in value in today's demanding art climate. Gradually I'm realizing I may never be able to part with them.

Stradwijk never arrived. Curfew hour was approaching. The guards were authorized to arrest anyone found on the streets after 10:00 at night. No matter how pressing my business or engaging a conversation, I had never taken the risk of humiliating my family in that way. Would I now? Would I inquire? Go searching for this artist? For MY etching? No, I would not. Not tonight. Stradwijk had faithfully delivered the previous six etchings. There must be some explanation.

The following day, a public post gave this report: 'The body of Nicolaas Stradwijk, age 26, of Stradwijk & Son was found partly submerged in the Singel Canal last night at approximately half past nine. The apparent victim of robbery and murder, Mr. Stradwijk had a deep knife wound in his neck. His pockets were turned inside out. His money bag was ripped off his shoulder and emptied. However, when his socks and shoes were removed at police headquarters, 300 guilders rolled onto the floor. There is speculation that Mr. Stradwijk, a man of modest means, may have been involved in a scheme of some sort.

I set off immediately for the guard station and explained to them that the money belonged to me – payment for an etching of Mr. Stradwijk's that was never delivered. The guards laughed heartily, saying I was already the fourth person to claim the money belonged to them for one reason or another. Did I have a receipt? Were there witnesses to the transaction? Wasn't that a large sum to pay to a young, obscure artist?

I further explained that I had purchased six previous etchings and that this was the final and most valuable piece in the series. Fine, they said, bring the other six and we'll see if that proves anything. I left, realizing that neither my marriage nor my reputation would withstand the public revelation of the nature of my collection.

Was the etching in Stradwijk's possession at the time of his murder? Is that what the murderer was really after? Stradwijk had told me that Jos's neighbor Mennes had seen the etching and made a bid. Perhaps Mennes did not know that it was part of a series I owned, but admired the single etching in its own right. Or perhaps he did know about the existence of the other six etchings and was plotting – still plotting –- to acquire them. Could Mennes be involved somehow in this murder? Ambitious, yes. Risk-taking, yes. Scheming, perhaps. But capable of authorizing murder?

Chapter Thirteen
Quest Begins

Jos closed the journal and returned it to its hiding place in the cupboard. He did not need to read the journal once again to remember the months of false leads, of hopes that lead to one dead end after another, of his frequent descents into despair.

* * *

When he failed to convince the guards that the 300 guilders was his, he set out for Stradwijk and Son. Down one winding path after another, each more narrow than the last, the dust from the unpaved streets collecting on his boots, lighting the bottoms of his trousers, it seemed his short legs would never get him there. And finally there it was in front of him, a worn, tilted sign announcing the print shop. He leapt up the steps, sure that his precious etching was only a few feet from where he stood. He would merely convince whomever he found there that he was the legitimate owner of the seventh etching, that he had given Nicolaas 300 guilders for it only minutes before his death. Another, cruder sign was nailed to the front door. "Closed until further notice." Jos pounded on the door and called. This was also Nicolaas's home. Did he have a wife? Children? They must be there. No one answered his knock or his entreaties. The only response was complete silence.

The next-door neighbor stuck her head out her window. "What you lookin' for, Mister? That shop's closed. Old man dead two years now. Young one murdered they say, found dead in a canal. It's that Gypsy curse, I tell ya. Never should have run off with that woman. Livin' in the woods like that. Rustlin' her skirts. Dancin' in the town. Provocative is what it was. His father never recovered from the shame."

'Gypsy woman?' Jos thought. 'Perhaps she has my etching. But she'll surely sell it at the first opportunity.'

"Where can I find the Gypsy, Ma'am?"

"Oh, she been gone and buried – years now. Had one child – lively little thing - wild, blond curls stickin' outta her bonnet. Big black eyes. But the second one . . . she died givin' birth to that one. A boy."

'So there were heirs. The artist's possessions could be with his offspring.'

"Who is caring for the children, Ma'am? Are they with a relative nearby perhaps?"

"Not really sure, Mister. Those children have two aunts. One of them must have taken them in. What's it to you, anyway? You don't look like a friend of the family."

"I was a customer. I had a business arrangement with Mister Stradwijk."

"I hope you don't mean you bought those playing cards of his. His father found those things once, tore them in pieces, threw them right in the fire. Wild. Crazy pictures. Scare ya to death. But he kept on. Sold them for a pretty guilder in the taverns, I hear."

It took every bit of patience Jos could muster to continue to listen to this neighbor's drawn-out, slow-spoken gossip. 'Clues,' he kept saying to himself. 'Clues. She might reveal something.' Eventually she did. One of the aunts lived not far from the Damrak – Elsbeth van Randen was her name. "Had one boy – some say he was a foundling. She was well up in years, had celebrated a dozen years of marriage. I say celebrated, but what's a man and woman got to celebrate if she was barren, I'd like to know? Not a single pregnancy that whole time. Soon as that one boy come along, wouldn't you know, she up and gives birth to two more boys – twins they were."

And so, having secured the name and vicinity of the aunt's home, Jos set off for the Damrak. A few steps and he turned around abruptly. The woman was still leaning out of her window, watching him walk away. "You have been very helpful, Mrs. _____," Jos said with a small nod. "Mrs. Van Heel." "Mrs. Van Heel, I wish you well." And Jos was off again.

Heading for the Damrak, he repeated to himself what little he knew about the woman he now sought, whose cooperation he so needed. Her name: Elsbeth van Randen. Daughter of a deceased printer. Marital status: married – to a patient man, no doubt. A sister – somewhere. A deceased brother. Three sons. How old? He didn't know. Husband's profession? No idea. Her nature? Generous or suspicious? Talkative or silent type? He wished he had not been in such a hurry to escape Mrs. Van Heel.

He stopped twice to ask passersby if they knew the location of the home of Mrs. Van Randen. The first mumbled "Sorry," and kept walking. The second looked him over and gave him directions. "Two streets over on the Singel. You'll know it. It's the smallest house on that street. You'll probably know you're approaching it. Lots of racket from those twins – all day long."

A suspicious thought seized Jos. With three sons and a modest house, Mrs. Van Randen could use the money from selling the works Nicolaas left behind. In fact, she probably already had sold the etching. Or perhaps, not knowing what it was worth and catching a glimpse of it, she was horrified, disgusted. Perhaps she destroyed it immediately, before her husband or children could see it. Jealousy now is what Jos felt. This woman had actually seen the etching and did not appreciate it; whereas Jos, who grasped and admired her brother's talent and creativity, had actually never set eyes on the seventh etching.

A running, laughing child nearly knocked Jos in the stomach. As he was preparing to reprimand the child, a second running child, identical in appearance to the first, passed him on his other side, threatening his balance. With the help of his walking stick, Jos righted himself and mustered some dignity as he continued his strut. It occurred to him that these were the rowdy twins Mrs. Van Heel had referred to. When he looked up, he was indeed standing in front of the smallest house visible on either side of the Singel.

A stout, weary woman who could have been the boys' grandmother stood on the stoop looking to the left and right. Then she yelled. "Dirck? Otto? Come back here immediately. If I don't see your faces in front of me by the time I count to ten, believe you me, you will be mighty sorry. Willem, go get those brothers of yours."

An older child appeared behind his mother. Willem did not seem to have his brothers' robust energy nor their tendencies to disregard both their mother and anyone else in their path. Slender, peeking out shyly for a moment at Jos from behind the woman's skirts, he was apparently also quite obedient and polite. He descended the stairs, nodded at Jos with a "Good day, Sir," and set off determinedly.

As the woman turned to re-enter the house, apparently believing that the task of tracking down her twins was in good hands, Jos called to her, "Excuse me, Ma'am. Might you be Mrs. Van Randen?"

The woman looked down at Jos and answered guardedly, "That is my name, yes, and you are?"

"Jos Broekhof, at your service, Mrs. Van Randen. I was a business acquaintance of your brother, Nicolaas. I extend to you my sincerest condolences."

"I don't think you came here just to give me your condolences, Sir. What is it you want?"

Standing a mere three steps below this imperious woman put Jos at a disadvantage.

He had been in such a hurry to move ahead on the information Mrs. Van Heel had given him that he did not have a plan for approaching this sister of Nicolaas.

"I understand, Mrs. Van Randen, that your brother was the father of two children. I wish to extend my condolences to them as well."

"Well, they're not here. They're with my sister in Ouderkerk."

"I see. Mrs. Van Randen, I realize that you may not have been particularly knowledgeable about the various aspects of your brother's business, but . . . ."

"I knew enough, Sir. I knew that all that map printing led him to no good. He grabbed up those maps and ran off with that Gypsy woman to wander the earth. Abandoned my elderly father. Killed my father having to do all that heavy work alone. I knew all I wanted to know."

"Perhaps you also knew that Nicolaas's talents extended beyond map making. He also labored at etchings and sold them."

"Never saw an etching of Nicolaas's. Never wanted to. Still don't want to. Good day, Sir."

Jos stood for a moment staring at the door that had just slammed shut, fighting an acute sense of disappointment and creeping self disgust. Yet another plan quickly began forming in his mind. Another sister. The children were with her. They must have cleaned out the shop and the house and taken the children and all their belongings and inheritance, such as it was.

Still leaning on his walking stick at the bottom of Elsbeth van Randen's stairs, he heard a child call out, "Whoever gets to the kitchen first, gets the first bite of honeycake!" The twins nearly knocked him down again before they leaped up the stairs and ran into the house, pushing and shoving each other.

Willem then approached the stairs, walking unhurriedly and again greeting Jos.

"How do you do, young man. I see you've found a good way to round up your brothers and bring them home."

"They always respond to promises of treats, Sir," Willem responded.

"Permit me to introduce myself. Jos Broekhof. I was a business associate of your Uncle – Nicolaas."

Willem's eyes brightened and then saddened.

"I am sorry for your loss. Did you know your uncle well?"

"Oh, yes, Sir. Whenever he was in town, he visited. He brought me presents."

"What sort of presents?"

"Oh, things he made. Or things he found on his travels. A horse he drew. A top to play with – lots of colors. A bubble dish and pipe. I still have them all. And several maps. He even invited me to go with him on a trip. Of course, my mother and father refused."

"And your cousins? Your Uncle Nicolaas's children?"

Again the boy's face lit up, a brief smile breaking through his usual serious expression.

"Nelleke," Willem said almost reverently, sitting down on the middle stair. She is a few years younger than me. Our favorite game was hide and seek. Because she was small – and clever – I could never find her. She would stay so still in the same place without making a sound and then, when I yelled out that I had given up, she would leap out and startle me screaming 'Willem, here I am. Your turn to hide.' Once she disappeared for so long that we all had to go looking for her. She had fallen asleep in the bottom of the kitchen cupboard. She had arranged sacks of flour in front, so she was not visible when anyone opened the cupboard door. We had looked there several times, but not seen her."

"And you? Where did you hide?"

"Oh, it didn't matter. She always found me right away. She once told me she could smell me."

"So, do you still see your cousin?"

Poor Willem's emotions were always so apparent, it seemed. Dejectedly, he explained that Nelleke and her baby brother, Jacob, lived with his Aunt Griet now. The cousins couldn't live with his family because they already had three boys, whereas Aunt Griet was newly married and had no children at the time.

"In Ouderkerk?"

"Yes, that's right. Do you know it? I would love to go there."

"I do know it and I plan to visit soon."

"My mother would never let me visit. Good day, Sir. If you see Nelleke, please tell her that her cousin Willem misses her."

Chapter fourteen
Ouderkerk

No more hapless, impromptu searches, Jos vowed. This time, he would summon all his organizational skill, his resources, his wisdom. He would arrive fully prepared. He would at last locate his precious etching. First he sent Karel ahead to quietly investigate and report back while Jos carefully recorded everything Karel told him:

Griet Verhoeven, born Stradwijk. 20 years old. The second child of Marja and Hendrik Stradwijk. Younger sister of Nicolaas Stradwijk. Younger, half-sister of Elsbeth van Randen. Husband Johannes Verhoeven. Married two years. The couple met through his mother and her father, who had become friends when Hendrik purchased a small, rural property to escape to after his second wife, Griet's mother, died. Johannes and his widowed mother owned a working farm that abutted Hendrik's property. Upon the death of his mother, Johannes became the sole owner of that farm. Griet inherited her father's land.

When Johannes and Griet married they combined the two neighboring properties. The first year of their marriage, they worked hard and did well, raising cows, chickens, and ducks. Griet's kitchen window looked out on a pond well stocked with fish. A field of wild flowers – blues, violets, yellows – stretched down to the river where the shade of one large tree beckoned. Occasionally, Griet grabbed her slate and strolled down to the river to sit under that tree, drawing perhaps, or reading one of the few books her mother left behind.

Raised mostly in the city, Griet had become somewhat accustomed to rural life but, while it had been a carefree weekend experience when her father was alive, it now became an exhausting responsibility, working from dawn to dusk, milking, feeding, cleaning, making cheese, taking eggs to market, cooking, maintaining their modest home.

Johannes cared for the animals, kept the barn clean, made repairs, slaughtered and prepared meat for sale. He had recently added a second floor to their home – doubling their space in anticipation of the children they both hoped for. Within a year they had three children living with them. There was their weak and sickly son, Frans, plus the children they agreed to raise, after Rona died giving birth to Jacob and Nicolaas was inexplicably murdered. Griet loved these children, but the lively Nelleke, who at age six might have been capable of helping Griet, always found a way to escape her assigned chores. Her face was perpetually smeared from digging in the earth where she delightedly searched for stones, buried shells, and insects.

Jacob had just learned to walk and would howl loudly when he was not allowed to follow his beloved sister outside. Griet had to keep watch that Jacob did not eat the multitude of small stones, ants, and spiders that Nelleke brought inside to show Griet. Although Griet repeatedly forbade Nelleke to bring her treasures into the house, and at least initially cleaned the child's face and hands multiple times per day, Nelleke was too determined and curious to obey, Griet too timid and fatigued to discipline her. Nelleke's explorations took her farther – to the neighbors, to the river, to the pond. She made friends with all the animals, naming them, and weeping when one was chosen for slaughter, refusing to eat the flesh of one of her "pets." Griet glanced longingly at the river, but her many responsibilities prevented her from finding refuge there.

Then several serious floods threatened their plans. The first carried away the grain they needed for their own bread and for feeding their stock. The second was worse, carrying off some of the animals, drowning others. They, the remaining animals, and Griet's niece and nephew, were forced to move to the second floor for a week, taking with them whatever belongings they could carry up the ladder. Neighbors came by in primitive boats and lifted up food for them through the only outside window.

Jos was convinced that this struggling young family would happily sell him the etching. If he could not convince them he had already purchased it, he was prepared to offer 300 guilders to buy it a second time. He and Karel took off with their driver, stopping only once to refresh themselves with a beer and leg of lamb.

When they stopped in front of the Verhoeven property, a small girl came running up to them. Barefoot and without a bonnet, a smudge across her pretty nose, she greeted the men briefly and then petted the horses gently – first one, then the other, whispering into their ears.

"The horses are thirsty, Sir," she said. "Shall I bring them water?" For a moment Jos was diverted from his errand, so attracted was he by the child's direct look coming from large dark eyes surrounded by black eye lashes.

"That is very nice of you, young lady. If you will show our driver the water source, he will care for the horses."

"You are from the city, aren't you? the child asked. "From Amsterdam? I was born there. Now I live with my aunt and uncle."

"How nice that you can live on this lovely farm. The city is crowded, you may remember, noisy and dirty." Even as he said these words, Jos felt assaulted by the strong manure odors that seemed to surround him.

"I liked it. I was going to go to school there, but here the school is too far away and Aunt Griet needs help all the time. Can you teach me to read, Sir? Would you like to see my seashell collection? I dug the shells up myself. They were buried right there," she said, pointing to a spot by the cottage door. "Do you know what that means? Once upon a time, the sea was right here. It covered all the land. It keeps trying to come back. I wonder what it would be like to live under the sea, don't you?"

"Nelleke, stop badgering the gentlemen," Griet called from the doorway, holding a squirmy Jacob in her arms. "Please show the driver where he can water the horses." Jos noted that this young woman did not resemble her older half-sister in any way. She was slight, even fragile perhaps. Jos observed with relief that she had a pleasant demeanor, that she appeared approachable.

"I assume, gentlemen, that you are here to speak to me. My neighbors and the villagers say someone has been inquiring about me."

"How right you are, Mrs. Verhoeven. I was a business associate of your late brother's. I admired his work and I give you my sincere condolences."

"Would you care for a beer and a bit of bread and cheese, gentlemen? My husband will return from the market shortly."

Jos was delighted. So far, his interaction with this young woman was allowing him to follow the new strategy he had outlined for himself in his notebook: First Rule: Demonstrate patience. Take your time.

"Very thoughtful of you, Mrs. Verhoeven. We accept."

Griet led the way into her humble home and to a corner of the dingy single first-floor room that served as a kitchen, placed Jacob on the floor with a toy top, and motioned them toward a worn wooden table and stools.

As she poured the beer and cut two generous portions of bread and cheese, she asked, "Do tell me the latest news from the city. I never get to go there any more. Life here is so busy, especially since Nicolaas's death and the arrival of the children."

Jos believed himself to be an expert on the city, but he wasn't sure what sort of news would please Griet. Business? Ship arrivals? Fashion? Art? Perhaps a discussion on art would bring him more quickly to the purpose of his visit. No, not yet. Follow the strategy. Rule two: Engage the young woman in conversation. Get to know her. "What do you miss most about Amsterdam, Mrs. Verhoeven?"

Griet thought for a moment as she grabbed the sticks on her churn and began turning them round and round. Her arms scarcely looked strong enough to turn milk to butter.

"The art," she said. Art everywhere. In the wealthiest homes. In the alehouses, they say. In the offices of those tall bustling warehouses. Even in the humblest of establishments. Our neighborhood baker, for instance, had a lovely still-life on the wall. An original too. I admired it every day. Very simple, really. Against a black cloth a white basket on its side. Full of ripe, red cherries that spilled over into a low, pale-blue bowl and onto the table. The cherries were so real looking, I felt I knew exactly how it would feel to bite down on one. I could nearly taste the sweet juice. As a child, I wanted to reach into the painting, grab the basket's handle, and run off with it. Are you a collector, Mr. Broekhof?"

So the topic was to be art after all. Jos was delighted.

"Perhaps you are familiar with the twin paintings of women reading letters they have just received, Mrs. Verhoeven? One appears to contain good news. The other, judging by the woman's countenance and the way she tears up the letter, the opposite. Charming juxtaposition. My wife keeps them above her writing desk. But the artist who has recently made the most news is Rembrandt van Rijn."

"Tell me about him. Does he do religious paintings? Portraits?"

"He can do anything – and in such an authentic way that you feel you are there in the room with the subject, that at any moment the subject – often Rembrandt himself – will turn to you and begin to converse with you just as you and I are doing. Most recently he completed a group portrait – *The Anatomy Lesson of Professor Tulp*. The group consists of some of the most illustrious men in the city; including, of course, Professor Tulp himself. The painting hangs in one of the guild halls."

"Oh, I should love to see it one day."

'Careful, Jos. Strategy Rule Three: Listen. Charm.'

"Does Madame draw perhaps?"

"Oh, I fear my leisurely drawing days are over, but I do so enjoy seeing drawings by others."

Nelleke had been playing with Jacob while studying the men's clothes, their expressions, the way Mr. Broekhof often stretched himself as if he wished to bump his head on the ceiling.

"I miss Amsterdam too," the child said suddenly. "I miss my mother. My father." And then sadly, with a tremble of her lower lip, she added, "I miss everyone. She picked up the toddler, kissed him, and carried him to Jos, although Jacob was more than half her size. Did you meet my brother? His name is Jacob."

Jos had just reached out to caress the toddler's cheek, when everyone suddenly turned to the sound of clomping. Someone was approaching from the back of the house. A young man in work clothes, muscular, slightly stooped, with a sunburned nose, ducked and entered. Surprised to see a crowd around his table in the middle of the day, Johannes nodded, removed his hat and wooden clogs, and shook hands with the men as they introduced themselves.

"These gentlemen have come all the way from Amsterdam to talk with us," Griet explained to her husband, "although I have not yet learned the purpose of their visit."

So, Griet had her own strategy. In spite of the curiosity she must have been experiencing, she diverted them with conversation until her husband returned. Or perhaps Elsbeth had alerted her as to the nature of his quest? That would have given them time to hide the etching, to have sold it even.

Jos tried to remain calm. 'Deep breath,' he reminded himself. 'Continue strategy.' Now that the husband had arrived, he would have to begin again. 'Follow your own rules. Rule one. Rule two. Rule three.'

"Quite a large piece of land you have here, Mr. Verhoeven. Must keep you very busy."

"Indeed it does," remarked Johannes. He sat at the table and, relieving Nelleke of her heavy burden, placed Jacob on his knee. Johannes then took some time arranging small pieces of bread for Jacob, spread butter on several thick slices for himself, and drank his beer.

"So, you raise ducks, I see," Jos attempted.

"Yes, sir. Ducks, chickens, cows."

"And you've got quite a few of each."

"Six ducks now. About twelve chickens. Four cows."

It was not going to be easy to bring the subject back to art. Jos could see that.

Or to any topic.

Johannes drained his glass and reached for the pitcher. He slowly filled the mugs of Jos and Karel, then his own. Then he turned to look at them.

"I doubt that city gentlemen such as yourselves are particularly interested in the daily life of those of us who work close to the earth. You surely had a reason for riding out into the country today and ending up at our place. I wish to learn the nature of your errand."

Jos was taken aback by Johannes's direct question. Johannes, too, had a strategy apparently and it was destroying Jos's attempts to implement his own.

"Perhaps you are aware that, in addition to assisting his father to run a print shop, your brother-in-law was an artist, Mr. Verhoeven?"

"If it's those maps he made, those are for his children, Mr. Broekhof."

"I understand he took great pleasure in sharing the map drawings with his children."

"Yes, Pappa showed me rivers, oceans, other countries with names like Spain, France, English," Nelleke piped up.

"England," Griet corrected.

"England. He drew animals on them. Tigers. Lions. Elephants. He took them with us when we lived with Mamma, Opa and Oma, and all the others in the forests. But he gave some to me, to Jacob, and to Willem. Would you like to see them?"

"By the way, Miss Nelleke, I met your cousin Willem. He asked me, if I saw you, to tell you he misses you."

Nelleke hung her head and smiled slightly. For once, she seemed to have no verbal reaction.

Johannes put his arm around Nelleke to stop her from running to her memory box.

"Let's find out why the gentlemen are here first, Nelleke."

"Thank you, Mr. Verhoeven. Yes. Nicolaas Stradwijk made more than maps."

"Playing cards. Yes, we know about those," Johannes said with the slightest raising of his thick, blond left eyebrow.

"He also made some excellent etchings. In one case, a set of seven. I purchased all of them. However, I possess only six. Just before he died, I paid him 300 guilders for the seventh. He returned to his shop to fetch it while I waited, but he never returned with it. I was alarmed."

"Because you were afraid he had absconded with your money?"

"I admit to disappointment. But no. That would not have been in character."

I was alarmed for his safety. The following day I learned of…" Jos glanced at Nelleke, who was listening carefully.

"Pappa died. I know that," she said, in the uncanny way she seemed to have of reading others' thoughts.

"So you are here in an attempt to complete your collection."

"Yes. You have stated my purpose exactly."

"I have seen none of Nicolaas's etchings. Perhaps, though, you could describe the missing one for me?"

Jos reddened and swallowed loudly. He looked away.

Karel spoke for the first time. "The subject of the etching is not appropriate for a family gathering, Sir."

"I see, gentlemen. I think we have nothing more to discuss." Johannes moved toward the front door of the cottage.

"Mr. Verhoeven," said Jos. Standing and swerving slightly from the beers, he attempted to regain his composure and pull himself up to an imagined height. "Should you find the work at any time, I am prepared to pay 100 guilders for it."

Johannes turned. "100 guilders? Didn't you say it was worth 300?"

"Very well. 300 guilders then. I will wait while you search for it."

"Mr. Broekhof, I assure you that the etching is not in this house."

Since the arrival of her husband, Griet had said little. She had no idea what was in the etching, but she could see how important it was to this man.

"We will inform the new manager of Stradwijk & Son of your quest, Sir," Griet offered. "Perhaps he is better informed than we about Nicolaas's work and what happened to it. It will be dark in a few hours. Have a pleasant journey."

The two men shook hands with Johannes and tipped their hats at Nelleke and Griet.

"Thank you, Ma'am, for the nourishment. Good day."

Chapter Fifteen
Purchased Anew

Jos sat with the manager of his firm, Timotheus de Nes. The figures for the past three months, Timotheus was telling him, indicated that, in spite of the fact that the city continues to grow in population and that one would think there would be more demand for their grain than ever, sales were down by 5%.

"What's going on, De Nes?" Jos demanded. His father had founded and built up this business. It had grown to be the largest grain distributor in the city. How could it be losing sales? That 5% represented thousands of guilders.

"You may recall, Sir, that the Van Deventer firm was founded only two years ago. Its location in an industrial area filling up with new businesses and just on the outskirts of many newly constructed homes gives it advantages. What's more, Van Deventer is innovative. It is no longer necessary for bakers and housewives and maids to go to them for their purchases. They deliver, Sir. Customers like this convenience."

"But Van Deventer has the added expense of paying for carts, for drivers."

"True, but some customers are willing to pay extra for the delivery. In addition to the growing sales, those fees are another source of income for the firm. Van Deventer is also diversifying. They do not rely entirely on the wheat imported from the Baltics. They negotiate with farmers to pick up rye and hops in their rawest form and bring it to their site for processing. This saves farmers the time they were previously spending on deliveries and frees them to concentrate on growing and harvesting other crops or on the multiple demands of any farm. The farmers are willing to bargain for this arrangement."

"Do what you have to do, De Nes." But by the next report, I want to see that we've recaptured that 5%, if not surpassed it."

"I will need your authorization to purchase small delivery carts for use within the city, Sir, and large wagons for traveling to the farms for pick up. I will need to invest in new equipment for processing."

"Expenses. Expenses. If all that will build up our business again to where it belongs, so be it. Recapture the market, De Nes."

Jos dismissed Timotheus and grabbed his hat. Before placing it on his head, he noticed how dusty it appeared, that the wool was wearing out on one side of the brim. Time to purchase one of those broad-brimmed felt hats that everyone was wearing these days. And why not one with a tall feather?

Meanwhile, he could barely concentrate on his business or on his appearance. Hendrik Stradwijk and Son had a manager. The print shop was operating. Somewhere in a dark corner, closed off in a neglected cupboard – that was where his etching was. Nicolaas was probably killed before he could even make it back to the shop to pick up the etching. It was still there. It had been there all this time. He was sure of it. Of course, the manager may have discovered it. May have even sold it, not realizing its value, not knowing that a customer had already paid for it.

As planned, he met Karel outside the Amsterdam Gin Factory. Together they set out on foot for the print shop. After one block, however, he saw coming toward him a figure he most wanted to avoid.

Mennes. Christoffel Mennes. His former neighbor. Now engaging in who knows what activities – legal or illegal – in order to rebuild his fortune. Too late to cross over to the other side of the canal. Christoffel was accompanied by his man, De Bruin, who carried a wrapped package of some kind, Jos noticed. Square. About the same size as each of his six etchings when framed. That weasel. That crook. That thief. Mennes had found the seventh etching. He had purchased it for a small amount of money. He would claim that a famous artist had made it. He would then sell it for ten times what he had paid. And Jos would lose it forever... unless he was willing to meet Mennes's price.

As they were almost within speaking distance, De Bruin handed over the package to Mennes, who held it with both hands in front of him as if tantalizing Jos.

"Meneer Broekhof," Mennes began. "How are you? The granary business continues to flourish, I assume. Such that you are free to take a mid-morning stroll around our illustrious city?"

Mennes had spies everywhere. Did he know somehow that Jos's firm's revenues were down? Was he taunting him? But Jos didn't care. He was focused on the package that Mennes held tight, tucked under his arm. Besides, he could quickly put Mennes in his place.

"Good day, Mr. Mennes. I see that your finances are making a comeback such that you can make expensive purchases. For a new home on the Heerengracht? A lavish new office? Or is this for resale perhaps?" Jos asked, gesturing toward the package.

"None of the above, Sir. At least for now I intend to simply enjoy being the new owner of a tantalizing etching by an as yet little known artist."

"So it WAS his etching," Jos thought. Mennes must have found out that Jos was searching for it. That rascal found it first. He was going to ransom it, but first he would gloat. He would make Jos wait.

"Tantalizing, you say, Sir? What might the subject matter of such an etching be then? Certainly not religious."

"Correct, Mr. Broekhof. Not a religious etching. Something more… human, let us say."

"Human. That is a rather broad category. What aspect of humanness does the work treat? I've seen several paintings by a young Jan Steen. Families and friends enjoying a night of drinking and eating, music and merriment. Are you referring to that sort of scene? Too complicated to capture in an etching, I imagine."

"Indeed. This etching deals with a smaller, but common human activity. Only two people are depicted. And now if you'll excuse us, Mr. Broekhof, Mr. De Bruin and I have business to attend to."

Panic grabbed Jos's throat as he imagined his beloved etching disappearing down the street, sold to an unknown buyer, stored in a dank cellar, hung in a dark corridor, or worse – destroyed, discarded.

"Is that by any chance the Stradwijk seal I see on the package you're holding, Mr. Mennes? I was actually on my way to the former Stradwijk and Son to inquire about an etching myself. May I invite you to The Hungry Lion for an ale or two, gentlemen? Perhaps you can advise me."

"You have keen eyesight, Mr. Broekhof. The package does bear the Stradwijk seal. The print shop is again operating and still under the

same name. One of the former assistants is now managing the place. Legally it belongs to the Stradwijk heirs."

An image of the eager little farm child and her adoring brother leaped into his mind, but Jos would deal with the repercussions of that news later. For now, he felt torn. Should he continue his afternoon quest and go directly to the shop as he had planned before this encounter? No. There existed a strong possibility that his etching was at this moment less than an arm's length away from him, tucked possessively under the elbow of his despicable former neighbor. He must not let Mennes escape.

In as warm and inviting manner as he could muster, Jos gestured for Mennes and his man to continue toward the tavern. Once there, Jos settled the group into a corner and ordered a pitcher of the best house ale and a plate of oysters. He winced as Mennes placed the package on a stool and placed his coat over it. It was unsettling to no longer have the package within his sight. He must be watchful that Mennes did not pull any magic disappearing trick. He had no idea where Mennes lived or what he now did for a living. Should he not be able to negotiate a deal this very afternoon... Mennes was a quick and clever adversary, however, and after a long slurp from his mug, he was the first to speak.

"So, Mr. Broekhof, you were on your way to the print shop to inquire about an etching yourself. Interesting co-incidence, might I add. What exactly were you looking for? Something for the lady of the house, perhaps? The manager has some lovely still-lifes – fruit, flowers and such that appeal to the feminine sensibility. Another of a child – a misbehaving child, quite amusing. Or were you thinking of something more manly, perhaps, an investment for your home study or your office? A conversation piece when potential clients come calling? I have become somewhat of a connoisseur. Much to the benefit of both sides, buyers and sellers alike are taking advantage of my expertise. If you tell me exactly what you are looking for, I could do the searching for you, save you the time."

'Hire Mennes? A horrific prospect,' thought Jos. 'Yet if it brought about the desired result?' But first he must learn more about... must in fact somehow see for himself the etching that lay tantalizingly close on the stool between them.

"Interesting prospect, Mennes. Thank you for offering your services. I shall ponder that possibility. Meanwhile, I suggest we begin with the etching you have in your possession at this moment. May I see it?"

"I am truly sorry, Mr. Broekhof. That is not possible. The etching was purchased for a client of mine. I've already had it framed, as well as wrapped and packaged to his instructions. I was on my way to deliver it and in fact, were it not for your friendly offer of refreshment, it would be in his hands – or perhaps already hung on the wall of his establishment."

"And what establishment might that be?"

"My client runs a public bathhouse. He wanted an etching whose subject matter reflects the services he offers."

Mennes' casual description seized Jos's heart. He could not keep himself from glancing at Karel, who was fully aware of and had frequently supported Jos's long search. 'Was Jos asking him to somehow steal the package?' Karel wondered. Surely that was impossible, given that it was buried under Mennes' heavy wool coat, in full view of the four men. In any case, he was not willing to become a thief in order to fulfill his master's obsession.

Karel did nod ever so slightly, however, with enough ambiguity and in such a way that Jos was free to interpret any way he wished: 'Sounds promising? Grab it and run? Keep talking? Get more information? Demand to see the etching? Make an offer?'

Mennes noticed the glance, which, combined with Jos's new-found friendliness, made him think he might be able to push a far better deal than the one he had made with the public bathhouse owner. Meanwhile, Mennes remained relaxed, reached for the last oyster, drained his mug, then rose and reached out his hand to Jos.

"A most enjoyable interlude, Mr. Broekhof. I must continue on with my delivery."

Jos motioned for Mennes to sit back down, and quickly ordered another pitcher.

"Bread and herring for all too, please," he told the serving girl.

When Mennes was again enjoying the free repast, Jos asked, "An etching whose subject matter reflects the services of a bathhouse owner, you say, Christoffel. Can you be more specific?"

"I am well aware of your stature in the community, Mr. Broekhof. You are a wealthy and respected merchant. You serve as a Regent for the city orphanage. It's said you never miss a Sunday church service. I cannot imagine you would find this etching a tasteful addition to your own superb collection of paintings and artworks - if that is indeed what you are thinking. I can tell you that it depicts a man and a woman –

mostly unclothed – in a tub of water, engaged, in the act, if you will. Enjoying themselves immensely, I might add."

"Thank you for your compliments as to my standing and ethics, Christoffel. It is not for myself that I inquire as to the nature of the etching, but for a colleague who collects works such as you describe. How much, may I ask, is your bathhouse owner paying for the work?"

"That is a private matter, I'm afraid. I protect my dealings with my clients and do not reveal the financial details."

"I respect such confidentiality, Christoffel. If I were to make an offer, on the part of my colleague – who shall remain unnamed, of course – I understand that, you would have to sell the item in question for an amount significantly higher than what the client has promised to pay you."

"That is correct, Sir. Spoken like the true businessman I know you to be. Let us then get to the point. The client ordered the etching to be delivered no later than today because it is to be part of an expansion celebration. He has added a new room – and has advertised it as a private space, decorated with blue and white tiles from China and drawings from various minor artists – drawings that you and I would label 'bawdy' and not suitable for display in our homes or offices. Disappointing this client, however, or worse, not concluding my part of my understanding with him, presents risks for me. It could sour our relationship and destroy our mutual trust. Such an act could have repercussions with other current and future clients as well. In order to compensate me for the loss of an excellent client, I would need to sell the etching to your colleague for 150 guilders. I would also need to collect those funds today."

Seeing Jos's hesitation at the large sum, Mennes added., "I will offer this. I could keep my client at bay for a day or two – tell him that the etching is not quite finished. I would apologize. Explain it was beyond my control. He will not be happy as the celebration is tonight and this etching was to be the centerpiece of his new collection. But for every day that I must wait for your colleague's decision, I must add to the price another 20 guilders."

"150 guilders," said Jos, finding it hard to believe that he would even consider paying such a sum – a full half of what he had already paid for the same item. "I think that for that amount, and because I am taking the chance that my friend will appreciate the gesture and pay for it, I must see the etching."

"Again, I must repeat, Mr. Broekhof. My client was very specific about the frame, wrapping, and packaging. The shop manager took a great deal of time to meet his demands. I cannot possibly unwrap and rewrap in anything resembling a professional manner. I do not have the tools or skills. Should you refuse to purchase, I do not have the time to return to the shop to have it rewrapped and repackaged."

Taking one more long slug of his beer as he stood up and began removing his coat from the stool, Mennes said, "Obviously, we are unable to come to an agreement. De Bruin, let us be off."

Jos stood and put a hand on Mennes' arm, removed the coat from his grasp and placed it, gently, even lovingly, over the package.

"I am certain from your description that my colleague will purchase the etching, Mr. Mennes, Sir. Please give me a moment to speak with my man here. He will fetch the money quickly and return."

Jos motioned for Karel to follow him to the front door of the tavern and step outside. He instructed Karel to retrieve 150 guilders from the safe of his home study and return with the money immediately.

At the same time, Mennes gave instructions to his assistant. As Jos returned to the table, he passed De Bruin, who was on his way out. Jos noticed with relief that the man was empty handed. He was not absconding with the package as Jos feared.

Jos rejoined Mennes to discover that he had ordered brandywine plus plates of mutton and turnips for them both. "To celebrate our exchange," Mennes said between mouthfuls.

Karel returned shortly. The exchange was made. Karel and Jos bid Mennes good afternoon and left with the package.

Chapter Sixteen
Contents Revealed

$\mathcal{I}$t was already too late to return to the office. Arriving home at his usual time, the reassuring odors of a well-scrubbed house, delicious dinner, and writing ink met Jos as he opened the door. Karel helped him with his hat, coat and boots. "Did he have time to mount the stairs to his study and take a peek at his new, beloved acquisition?" he asked himself. No. Now that it was his, he felt complete. He would enjoy it on his own later when the house was quiet. For now, he would dedicate himself to his family. Karel took charge of the package.

His sons were bent over their desks completing their lessons. He kissed them and glanced at their work. Samuel seemed to be writing out Latin verb forms. Daniel was doing some sort of mathematical calculation. Not an outstanding student in his day, Jos was satisfied that his boys were applying themselves and advancing at the expensive private school he had carefully chosen for them. Anna was in the kitchen using a large wooden ladle to stir a milky, steaming liquid in a large pot. Peeking over the pot, Jos saw bits of ham, onions, beets, carrots. There would be a hearty soup tonight. She greeted him and handed him his evening gin.

And Myriam? He found her setting the table, wearing a fresh clean bonnet and apron. She took pleasure in the preparation and anticipation of the evening's sit-down ritual for supper. Rather than keeping their most beautiful table settings stored in the glass cabinet for guests, Jos had an agreement with Myriam that once a week she could use them for a family dinner. Here she was carefully arranging the imported porcelain bowls, the silver, the goblets.

Yet Jos noticed that every evening she was moving more slowly at these tasks, even stopping for periods, staring into space. He understood the problem because he too felt it. Where once there was little girl chatter and laughter and so many questions – "Mamma, what is this? What color is that? Can I taste the soup? When will Pappa come home?" – there was now silence. The pleasure Myriam used to derive from this time in her day seemed to lessen continually as it reminded her of how her daughter used to happily skip around the table, accompany her mother from kitchen to cabinet to table and back again, how eagerly she followed her mother's instructions, how gleefully and gingerly she placed fresh flowers one by one in the vase each evening.

It was also Catherina's job to call her brothers to the table, an assignment she relished since she was not allowed to interfere with their lessons until that moment. "Samuel, supper time! Daniel, come to table!" she would call out with authority in her high, little-girl voice.

Even though it saddened her further, Myriam thought often of Catherina's last days. The final evening before Catherina suddenly fell ill, Myriam had allowed the eager three-year-old to carry one bowl from the cabinet all by herself for the first time. Catherina knew the story of the bowl's origins, of how her Pappa had carefully chosen the most beautiful pieces from a newly arrived ship and presented them lovingly to her mother. Her Pappa had once brought her over to a window and shown her that the bowl was very thin. When he took her hand and placed it under the porcelain, she could see two of her fingers right through it.

Catherina would stare at the designs on the lustrous bowl for long periods, entranced by the blue and white colors, yet never see or understand it all. "Look, Mamma, a bald man sitting on the ground smoking a pipe. He forgot to put on his shirt. Another man in a cap. Playing an instrument maybe? This one is dressed – in a long robe. There are men and women in a garden. And children too, Mamma – children crossing a bridge over a river. Are there lots of children in China?"

That night for the first time, after much begging, Catherina was thrilled that her mother allowed the child to move the bowl from the cupboard to the table. There she was holding it in her two small hands, balancing both herself and the object carefully, taking light, tiny steps toward the table. Then she reached up and placed it on the table's edge – the only place she could reach. Myriam quickly moved it to a safer position closer to the middle of the table, but Catherina did not notice. She was too busy rejoicing. "I did it. I did it," she chanted, jumping in circles in rhythm to her words. "I carried the bowl, Mamma. I did not drop it. I did it. I did it."

Then, just hours later, the sudden fever. Frantically calling the doctor. The bloodletting she suffered. Her savage, desperate attempts to breathe. Calling out. "Mamma. Pappa." Their hopelessness. Their despair. The doctor, giving up, reminding them that many children died suddenly. It could be a variation of the plague, a weakness she carried within her, something else they did not understand, he explained. He was sorry. They should thank God for the time they had with her and replace her with another child.

But Myriam refused to even consider another child. Catherina could never be replaced, and she could never again risk putting herself through the misery, the life-long misery of loss.

Three months later, after this evening's meal - a somber one, as their sons were no substitutes for the lively and amusing presence of their sister, Myriam ushered the boys to bed and Jos retired to his study at last.

As instructed, Karel had locked the package in the cupboard beside the other etchings.

With an enormous sense of anticipation and with his heart racing, Jos cut the string that held the package together and carefully unwrapped it, exposing the back of his precious purchase. With the set now complete, he would carefully write out the word *zondag* – "Sunday" – on the back and place it in the frame that matched the other six – that frame that had lain empty and waiting for these many months. But first to view it. Jos pulled off the remaining protective cloth, took a deep breath, and slowly turned the work over so that he could observe it fully from the front. Immediately, he was struck by a sense of horror, betrayal, anger, and disgust. He was indeed holding a scene of a partially clothed couple in a bath, engaged in an intimate act. Yet this was not the work of Nicolaas Stradwijk. It was a cheap, hastily completed portrayal of a similar theme. It contained none of the precision, the eroticism, the teasing, the delight of the six etchings Jos so admired. This was mechanical, ordinary. The couple could be any couple. They were not a poor imitation of the original couple. They did not even resemble them. Jos ripped his new possession from its cheap wooden frame, tore it into pieces and threw it into the fireplace. In a fit of acute self-loathing and loss, he pounded his forehead on his desk, locked the cupboard, abandoned his study behind him, and sought comfort in his sleep chamber.

Myriam, however, was in the position she had assumed since Catherina's death – against the wall, on her side, her back to Jos. Sometimes her eyes were open, sometimes closed, but always she was unresponsive, engaging in neither conversation nor affection.

Chapter Seventeen
Return to Stradwijk and Son

The following day, after a quick check-in at his office, Jos set off on his original destination – the print shop of Hendrik Stradwijk and Son. He should have kept going yesterday and never let himself be seduced into stopping and dealing with that despicable Mennes. Yet Jos had to admit to himself that Mennes had not lied to him. He had told him what the package contained. He never identified the artist. He certainly had tricked him into paying an exorbitant amount of money for a piece of trash, but Jos had succumbed to his own eagerness, his own lack of control, his own folly. Now Jos determined that he would never again allow himself to be manipulated. He would continue the quest, but cautiously, wisely.

The sign had been freshly painted and set straight. The door and window of the shop were open and Jos walked inside. Two heavy, wooden printing presses took up most of the space. Solid wooden letters were arranged neatly in their own container, waiting to be lined up by hand to spell out the next message. Neat rows of freshly printed pages hung on lines just below the ceiling.

The manager, sleeves rolled up above his elbows, a large ink-stained apron covering his chest and reaching below his knees, dealt pleasantly with two customers. One paid for a stack of flyers announcing a new theater production. The other picked up a large poster warning Amsterdammers that any infringement of curfew hours would be met with fines and possibly incarceration. Just as Jos was about to begin querying the manager, a third customer arrived. Jos stepped aside until this customer's business was concluded. He must speak with the manager in private.

Finally Jos introduced himself and explained his predicament. Had the manager, who had assisted in the shop for many years while Hendrik and then Nicolaas ran it, ever seen the etchings as Jos described them? As a matter of fact, the manager had seen them – once briefly. Nicolaas showed them to him – six of them all at once – and told him he had an admiring buyer who wanted the full set and who had paid him an enormous sum for it. The manager never saw the seventh etching. Yet, given the progression of the activity in the first six, he could see it in his head, he said. Based on his imaginings, and with limited skill, the manager then tried his hand at producing an etching with similar content.

The manager climbed a ladder, opened a cupboard and descended with a pile of etchings all on the same theme, all crude: the women with oversized, misshapen, repulsive breasts and buttocks; the man leering, one hand on his member, lifting the woman's skirts in some, placing his head under her skirts in others.

"Apparently," the manager explained, in a business-like tone, "this theme is very popular with a certain segment of the population. One client – a Mr. Mennes – actually purchased two of them in one day – only yesterday in fact."

"And how much do they sell for, Sir?" Jos asked, dreading the answer.

"Ten guilders, Sir. If you like I can wrap up as many of them as you like."

Jos could not even answer. Mennes had made a profit of 140 guilders on the inferior, wretched etching he sold to Jos, and then sent his man to purchase a second one just like it to deliver to the bath house owner, probably making a tidy profit on that one as well.

Gathering his wits momentarily, Jos implored the manager to comb every inch of the shop and home where he now lived. He promised that for the genuine completion of the set, he would pay 200 guilders. In spite of the attractive offer, the manager was not reassuring.

"When Nicolaas was murdered, the family quickly cleared out everything from both the shop and the family rooms behind them. What little there was they took with them – to save for Nicolaas's children – their "memory box" – they called it. I find it most unlikely that such an etching would have found its way into that box."

"My offer stands. Good day, Sir," Jos said dejectedly as he stepped out of the shop.

Two weeks passed. Jos refused to allow himself to look at his etchings or to reread the journal. He forced himself to concentrate on his business, his family responsibilities, his duties in the community. As Regent of the City Orphanage, he was required to attend the opening of the theater season. The night's profits were set aside for the orphanage and would help support the orphanage's growing numbers. It was to be a lavish evening with the most prominent Amsterdam citizens attending. Jos pleaded with Myriam to accompany him. It would be an amusing evening – an opportunity for her to forget her sadness. She could have a new elaborate dress made, purchase a new hat, gloves, shawl, stockings, shoes. She would wear the jewelry inherited from his mother. She would look lovely.

"Please go by yourself, dear Jos," Myriam repeated every time he raised the issue. "As long as I am in this mournful state, I have no desire to partake in such an outing. I cannot."

Although he so would have preferred to have his beloved Myriam at his side, Jos put on his best chemise, the broad laced collar and voluminous sleeves with broad embroidered cuffs visible through slashes in his vest, grabbed his shiniest cane, his freshest gloves and tallest hat, and set out, determined to enjoy the evening.

Chapter Eighteen
A Master's Opinion

With many of Amsterdam's most illustrious residents in attendance and with the proceeds donated to the City Orphanage, the theater evening had been a success. The amusing performance offered Jos a momentary diversion. The elegant attendees reminded him that to remain a member of the wealthy class into which he was born, he must continually be vigilant and diligent. His comportment must remain beyond reproach.

The following week Jos exercised the necessary discipline to concentrate on his business, to "modernize" it in the words of his right-hand man, Timotheus de Nes. De Nes had ordered the carts, hired the delivery drivers and was making forays into the countryside to negotiate with farmers – direct pick-up and transportation of rye and hops in exchange for paying them a lower price.

What De Nes was finding, however, was that the farmers closest to the city had already signed exclusive agreements with Van Deventer. In order to benefit from the new model, he needed to go farther afield and the farther he went from Amsterdam, the higher the costs to the company. Still De Nes was confident that Broekhof could recapture some of the 5% loss of the previous year.

On Wednesday of that week, Karel had met Jos at the end of the day as he exited his office. Had Jos heard of a certain artist who was being paid large sums for his portraits – portraits so life-like, you felt the subject would begin speaking to you at any moment? Karel asked. Born and trained in Leiden, the artist had moved to Amsterdam, married the niece of the well-known art dealer, Van Uylenburgh, and purchased a large home on the Sint Anthoniebreestraat. His bizarre collections alone were worth a visit – skulls, armor, feathers, antique statues, specimens of land and sea animals, shadow puppets, death masks, pistols, shields, hundreds of books.

Portraits might be his mainstay but, with the same acute vision, he painted, drew, and etched all subjects: still-lives, biblical, landscape, animal, human. Karel suggested that a visit to this gifted man might somehow fulfill Jos's need to complete the Straddle Series.

Curious, Jos set out the following Monday with Karel to the Breestraat. Although not as grand and stately as the canal houses, including the Broekhof home, this structure was indeed impressive – all three floors of it. Built to capture as much natural light as possible, to provide workspace for himself and his pupils, with welcoming first-floor client space for the business of buying and selling his and others' works, it also housed the painter's growing family.

A housekeeper met them at the door and led them up a narrow, winding staircase toward the large second-floor studio. The closer they came to the studio, the more Jos's eyes and nose stung. By the time they entered the studio, he was sneezing profusely. A quick look around the large space revealed the sources of the caustic odors: peat burning in stoves placed at either end of the large room; knives, brushes, and cleansing tools of every size soaking in pungent oils; powders of every color arranged on shelves; palettes and smocks tossed in corners.

Several smooth, copper sheets were propped against the walls. Four easels were arranged around the room, each accompanied by a three-legged stool. Pieces of chalk, stray paint brushes, panels and canvases were strewn haphazardly. A Bible lay open on a table surrounded by more artist paraphernalia.

Four pupils gathered attentively around the master as he demonstrated the proper ingredients and measurements for concocting a deep red paint. By the looks on their eager faces and the cleanliness of their frocks, Jos concluded that this was a fresh crop of students. Every ambitious young artist desired to apprentice here, it seemed. The tuition fees they were willing to pay provided the master with a steady income – in addition to the portraits and other works his skill commanded. Even those pupils who were eventually accepted into the guild and chose to continue to apprentice with this masterful artist paid for that honor.

The artist nodded in Jos's direction, continued his lecture for a few more minutes, and then left the group to give his attention to the visitors.

"Gentlemen," the artist said extending his oily hand. "How can I be of service?"

Jos felt the small focused eyes on him. It was as if this man could see not only every blemish of Jos's skin and every speck of dust on his clothing, but could also discern his deepest thoughts and perceive his character flaws. It seemed to Jos that after only a few moments of studying him, the artist was capable of painting a likeness that would capture Jos's pride, the constant embarrassment his small stature caused him, his fears, his desires . . . and, yes, the obsession that drove him here.

The artist led them down the stairs to the two front rooms where he conducted business with clients. He showed them a variety of works. Portraits of prominent men whom Jos recognized. Portraits of married couples – husband and wife in separate frames. Sleek black frames, austere with a narrow molding. Whole families too – one painted in a Roman-looking courtyard. Husband. Wife. Two girls. One boy. A dog. Another boy, apart from the group, pale, in faded clothing. Jos swallowed hard, thinking of his lost Catherina. He had seen this before. Families never forgot their deceased children and included them in portraits.

Then there were the biblical paintings. "The Raising of the Cross." "The Descent from the Cross." The light illuminating Christ's body. The agony. The gentleness. The courage. So it was true what they said. This artist is a genius.

That women fascinated this artist was obvious. He showed them a folder of drawings. The Pancake Woman. Mother Nursing Her Child. And another – totally charming. A woman in a large-brimmed hat, looking directly at the viewer, smiling slightly, mildly amused, resting her face in one hand, holding a flower in the other.

When Jos lingered longer in front of that particular drawing, the artist explained. "My wife, Saskia – three days after we were betrothed."

"Many of these works have been commissioned and will be delivered soon to my patrons. A few are for sale, however. What did you have in mind, gentlemen?"

Jos looked around the open room nervously. It had three doors. One leading to a second reception parlor. One leading to the staircase they had just descended and beyond the stairs to the back of the house from which came sounds of household activity. The third to the front door through which they had entered. "Is there somewhere we could speak in private, Sir?"

The artist led Jos and Karel to a tiny room tucked under the stairs and closed the door. There was a desk covered with piles of papers that spilled onto the floor – legal documents of some sort, it appeared. The artist sat behind the desk and cleared a stack so that he could see his visitors. He stood up again, disappeared and brought two stools into the room. Kicking debris into the corners he placed the stools on the other side of the desk. Jos and Karel sat down on the uneven, uncomfortable seats.

"There is something we wish to share with you, Sir," Jos began. "We respectfully request your expert opinion."

Karel had been guarding a large satchel, holding it close and resting it on his knees. With a nod from Jos, Karel set the satchel on the floor, reached into it and one-by-one held up the six etchings for the artist's viewing and returned them to the satchel.

Jos had intended to study the artist's reaction, but he could not refrain from regarding his beloved possessions himself. After returning the sixth etching, Karel stopped and returned the heavy satchel to his lap, his arms around it.

"May I see that last one again?" the artist asked.

Before handing it over, Karel looked for guidance to Jos who nodded acquiescence.

The artist held it in both hands and studied it for a short while.

"Who did these?" he asked.

"A relative unknown. Nicolaas Stradwijk."

Without taking his eyes off the etching, the artist asked. "I see that each is marked 1/1. Is it true that only one copy has been made of this series?"

"Stradwijk assured me that was the case. I have no reason to believe otherwise."

Handing #6 back to Karel, the artist gestured for another.

Karel reached into the satchel and handed him #5.

After a brief look, the artist made an offer. "I'll give you 300 guilders for the series."

"Oh, but they are not for sale, Sir."

"360 guilders." That's 60 guilders for each of the six.

"I'm sorry."

"420. I can sell them for twice that. I'll split the difference with you."

'420 guilders then for his share,' Jos figured. 'Obviously, this man knows quality. He also knows the market.' Few men in the Dutch Republic could afford 420 guilders when an average house cost 500. He would have to break up the set, sell each individually. If Jos signed an agreement, the paper would become lost in the morass of documents surrounding him, but he believed he would see the money – probably quickly.

But earning money from the sale of his etchings? That was not the purpose of this visit.

"There is a seventh etching," Jos explained.

"A seventh? I see. One for each day of the week. Clever."

The artist gestured for another etching and took it from Karel. #4

"Ah, yes," he said, noticing the writing on the back for the first time. "Thursday. Don't hold out on me, Sir. Where is the seventh etching? Assuming it flows naturally to complete this scene and is of similar quality, adding it to my purchase will, of course, raise the price I pay and the amount I receive from a resale. Naturally I must see it first."

"The seventh etching is lost, Sir. I paid Stradwijk for it. He agreed to return immediately with the etching. Sometime between our meeting and his planned return, he was murdered. The motive was apparently not robbery, or perhaps the robber was a petty, inexperienced thief. The exact amount I had given him was found on his body. The murder has not been solved. The etching has not been found. I have spent considerable time searching for it."

"This is my request, Sir," Jos continued. "Would you, as perhaps Amsterdam's most admired artist, produce the seventh etching – the culmination of this scene, as you say, in the style of the previous six?"

The master's face became red. He scowled. His jowls shook. He stood abruptly and towered over the seated men, his small eyes regarding them with disdain, his large nose and lips pulled back as if he were a wolf about to attack. Jos, tottering on the low, uneven stool in the small space, felt trapped. When he leaned sideways seeking escape from the sudden fury that filled the room, he tipped over and was forced to grab the edge of the desk to bring himself upright.

Had he insulted the artist by his use of the word "perhaps," Jos worried. Might outright flattery have been more effective? Obviously he had again bungled a situation and lost another opportunity to complete the set.

Pushing by the two men, the artist shoved open the door. From the hallway, he hissed back at his visitors in a livid, scornful, scolding tone, "Rembrandt does not imitate the style of an unknown hack, gentlemen. If you wish to sell the six, my offer stands. Now if you'll excuse me, I have many projects to complete – my own."

Moments later, the housekeeper arrived and led them to the front door.

"Good day, Sirs." She curtsied.

Chapter Nineteen
Delayed

T he sun pushed through the heavy drapes that surrounded the raised bed and crawled across the coverlet, landing on Broekhof's closed eyelids, trembling with resistance. When the sun won the struggle, lifting him up into the day, he saw that the bedclothes on Myriam's side were in disarray. He pulled back the bed curtains and grabbed his pocket watch from the bed stand. Dismay woke him fully. De Nes's plans to modernize had involved many expenses, but little results. It was now nine in the morning, the very hour he was to meet Lukas van Hutten, the chief grain distributor from the Baltics. A clever, mutually-satisfying arrangement with Mr. Van Hutten, would allow The Broekhof Company to outbid Mr. Van Deventer, build up its customer base, expand throughout the Republic, gradually dominate the market, increase the price it charged for its product, and possibly nearly double his yearly profits. Or at least so Mr. De Nes believed.

It had now been two months since his unproductive visit to Rembrandt. With no more clues or new possible directions, Jos had suspended his search. But he had not forgotten his beloved seventh etching. Last night he had fallen back into severe mourning and longing. Reviewing the many failed quests had demoralized him. He had dragged himself to bed only hours ago.

Refusing the three wooden steps that connected bed and floor, he slid off the bed and landed on the heavy, brass key ring he had removed from around his waist and placed there quietly only hours earlier. Disturbed by the sight of his keys splayed in all directions, he bent to pick them up, letting out a gasp when his back objected to the strain of stretching over his belly. He clipped the keys in place on his belt, pulled his trousers on over the nightshirt that doubled as a day shirt, and buttoned the vest that came to his knees.

Having rushed to the kitchen for a quick bite of honey cake, he found Anna with her feet propped up, sipping ale. In all the years Anna had worked for his family, he could not remember ever seeing Anna relaxing in such a casual manner. Along with the house, he had inherited Anna from his father. While continuing to fulfill her household duties, she cared for Jos's mother throughout his mother's long illness. After Jos married, Anna adjusted well to a new, young mistress. Had she walked the boys to school? Wasn't there wash to be done? Bread to bake? Were there no errands to run?

Rushed, impatient, Jos cast a quick look in Anna's direction. Throughout her decades-long service to his family, he made sure that St. Nicolaas gave her a generous gift each December. He also gave her a small raise each New Year. Had she aged, grown stout, even lazy, while he wasn't paying attention? Was she sick? "Make a note," he said to himself. "Block letters. Domestic matter. Question Anna on her health and attitude."

"Bread and ale for you, Sir," Anna said, pulling herself to a standing position, curtsying slightly, and gesturing to the tray awaiting him. She sat again and continued to sip her ale, gazing out the window to the courtyard, where he was relieved to see she had done some minimal work that morning. There was laundry hung and drying.

After this gulp of a breakfast, he nearly ran through the center hallway that led directly to the front door. He glanced to his left into the empty dining room. The door to the family parlor on his right was closed. Toward the front/canal side of the house, the corridor separated the music room from the greeting parlor.

Propped against the oak front door were a bucket and broom. Although his wife – like most Dutch wives of every class – maintained a spotless home, often joining her only female house servant in the daily scrubbing, he was accustomed to seeing only the results of their efforts. He nearly spit up his ale at the odor and sight of grayblack water oozing from a pile of rags toward his shined leather shoes with the gold buckles. He would have to step carefully on the black-and-white tile floor in order not to slip in the muck. He must remember to make another note (block letters - domestic matter) to instruct Myriam to speak to Anna about leaving this mess unattended.

Where was Myriam at this hour? Why had she not awakened him, knowing his daily schedule? He retreated back down the hallway, opened the family parlor door, and found her in her private alcove, leaning over her narrow, pale-yellow writing desk. Her hair hung below her morning cap, some of it stuck under the collar of her beige linen blouse, some resting outside the collar, so that her white neck was visible in patches. He could see the edges of her red leather notebook in front of her, her favorite long-handled quill pen moving slowly and delicately across the page.

A pleasant fragrance rose from the crushed rose petals in a basket at her elbow. Blotters, envelopes, and sealing wax were arranged on either side of her. Her feet were propped up under her desk on her favorite foot warmer. Her letter-writing manual, Puget de la Serre's *Secrétaire à la Mode*, was propped open on a shelf above her desk, below a Dirck Hals painting of a woman seated contentedly before a calm seascape, a letter flapping gently in her hand. Lately, he realized, this is where Myriam always sat, writing, writing. That *Secrétaire* book had become her Bible and Puget de la Serre her God. He had assumed these were letters to her sister. Could she be corresponding with others as well? People he didn't even know? He made a mental note to enter in his notebook – later when he wasn't so harried (domestic issue), a reminder to question her later.

"Myriam. Good-bye, Dear. I'm quite late. I'm afraid I must rush out." Myriam gently rocked the blotter back and forth on her composition, reached into the basket by her side, picked up a handful of rose petals, and delicately pinched and sprinkled them over the page. Jos noticed her shoulders relax as she completed the ritual. He approached her and put his arm around her.

"Myriam, did you hear me?"

Myriam closed the notebook and slowly turned her head, looking up at him in that vacant way she had now.

"Myriam, why did you not wake me? I am late for an important meeting."

Myriam's blurred stare moved from his eyes to a point above them. She reached up and caressed his forehead in gentle, circular motions, from his hairline to his nose.

"What is it, for God's sake?" he said, stepping back into the hallway to observe himself in the mirror. Seeing his reflected face was always a welcome antidote to the rejection he felt toward the rest of his body – his small stature, the feet that pointed outward. There were the eyebrows Myriam once found attractive – now a 2/3-1/3 mix of black and gray, he calculated. Thick, but not overpowering, they drew attention to the large, dark eyes underneath them. His dark moustache was trim. His beard ended fashionably in a point below his chin. But what was that above his brows? Into the flesh on his forehead was imprinted a vertical curlicue design. He must have fallen asleep over the empty frame last night. He had intended to purchase a new hat today – one of those large-brimmed beaver ones seen on the proud heads of many of Amsterdam's most fashionably dressed merchants. That hat would have covered the unwanted, odd imprint in his skin, but he would have to wear his current smaller hat instead and hope that the cool air would return his forehead to its normal state.

Back at the front door, Karel was edging the broom and bucket aside, touching them as little as possible. This was women's work, quite below the duties of a manservant. He helped Broekhof into his outer coat and handed him his scarf, hat, gloves, and satchel. Turning his nose away, Karel pushed the rags aside with his foot and opened the door for Jos while handing him a note folded awkwardly down to the size of a stuiver. "This was delivered this morning, Sir."

Broekhof hoped it was a message from Lukas van Hutten saying he too would be delayed. He had to remove his gloves in order to unfold the thick paper. There was no "Dear, Sir." No "Dear Mr. Broekhof." There was no signature. Just five words in a rushed script: "We have what you seek."

"We have what you seek?" Could it be that his long dream of completing the set was coming true? That the discreet inquiries, recently more like pleadings, were getting results? But who, then, was it who had knowledge of his precious, unseen etching? Or perhaps even possessed it? And how much would he be willing to pay (a third time) to obtain it for himself?

Jos Broekhof descended the five stone steps leading to the street. The boatman who usually rowed him to his place of business on the Geldersekade must have given up and left to seek other customers. He would have to go on foot.

Rounding the first corner he saw coming toward him his former neighbor. Mennes was wearing that outlandish full-length, tightly woven dark wool overcoat from his days of opulence. Even in the most punishing weather, he wore it unbuttoned, boasting its lush fur lining. Jos noticed with a mixture of disdain and satisfaction that the hem was frayed and caked with mud. And the nerve of the man, trouncing around his former quarter as if he still belonged here. Jos had heard that Mennes had sent his wife and children to live in Rotterdam with her parents and was trying to re-establish his former wealth and position here in Amsterdam. They had not spoken since the etching debacle. Jos nearly choked on the sudden loathing that engulfed him.

"Mr. Broekhof. Good day, Sir." Was that a smirk? Jos had been too humiliated to confront Mennes after he took advantage of Jos's eagerness. In fact, going over that afternoon's conversation many times in his mind, he had to admit some admiration for the way Mennes had closed the sale patiently, without lying outright.

The confidence and familiarity in Mennes's greeting irritated Jos further.

"Mr. Mennes," Jos said, with a slight nod, continuing on as quickly as his short legs would carry him across the cobblestones without actually running.

Following close behind Cristoffel Mennes was that servant, Egbert de Bruin, who had remained loyal to Mennes throughout the tulip debacle. Mr. De Bruin pulled a small wooden cart behind him. On the cart was a cone-shaped object, wrapped in cloth, about the height of two barrels. Although he certainly had no interest in their affairs, Jos could not control the urge to glance backward at the pair. At the moment they turned the corner heading in the direction Jos had just come from, Egbert de Bruin turned to steady the cart. He noticed Jos looking back over his shoulder and nodded. Jos was forced to nod at De Bruin in return. In that moment he noticed the tip of the cone exposed above the covering. Adding a touch of jollity to the street's staid wooden and brick structures and gray stones, it beckoned with a deep forest green.

Jos became aware that his head was aching. Instead of taking the usual steadying boat ride that gave him the opportunity to review the day's agenda, he would have to move through the noisy, pushing throngs. Already he could hear the drummers and the shouts of the herring sellers. He tightened his grip on his satchel to ward off beggars and thieves. He would avoid Dam Square, taking the long way through winding side streets, passing the shops of shoemakers, glass blowers, tailors, and weavers. The streets were made narrower by the profusion of products hanging outward from the open windows – harnesses, brooms, locks in all sizes, bolts of cloth. It seemed that while he had slept away the morning, the entire world had been producing, trading, making money, becoming richer. The city's energy suddenly exhausted him.

Relief and satisfaction engulfed him, though, when he eventually saw the large sign ahead – commanding, freshly painted, assertive, confident: The Broekhof Company – the sign his father had originally hung and which his manager maintained. Wagon-loads of grain were returning from the weighing house. Wholesale buyers were leaving with large sacks of flour. The smaller, retail area was bustling. The investment he had made in well-trained, loyal managers was paying off. When he had a moment, he must make a note to consider praising them, perhaps to raise their pay. He avoided the warehouse for now by climbing the steep outside stairs that led directly to his second-floor offices, counting each step in rhythm with the ringing of the city bell. Eleven o'clock. At the top of the staircase a pair of blasé, pea-green eyes glanced at him and then through him. After this non-greeting, one of the granary's many gray cats yawned and returned to its morning toilette, meticulously licking off each paw the remains of its rodent breakfast.

Broekhof was an unforgivable two hours late. Lukas van Hutten had left a message:

"Dear Mr. Broekhof:

After waiting most of an hour with no communication from you, I am taking my business elsewhere.

Kind regards,
Mr. Lukas van Hutten
Van Hutten Distributors"

Chapter Twenty
Dwarf Song

efusing to give up yet on the deal, Jos Broekhof skipped back
down the stairs and headed for the most likely place to find
Van Hutten – the city's largest tavern, The Lion's Mane, where
thousands of guilders exchanged hands daily in back rooms, a handshake
closed the deal, and successful exchanges were celebrated immediately
on site.

Adjusting to the tavern's din after the sunlight outside, Jos looked
around for Van Hutten. When he didn't see him, he set off to explore
the Sailor's Delight, The Lombard, The Golden Sail – all without the
result he hoped for. Discouraged, hungry, and thirsty, he made one more
attempt at the lowly "The Knowing Eye." Still no Van Hutten.

Instead, he caught sight of that irritating blind dwarf, Rudolf, his
gray cap pulled down over his ears, accentuating his child-size face. Not
surprisingly, the only available seat in the place was at Rudolf's table.
Broekhof sat down quietly without greeting Rudolf, but the alert man
recognized both his step and his voice when he ordered ale.

"Mr. Jos Broekhof, I believe, Sir. Is it not, Sir? And may I request that
I be included in your order, Sir? Thirsty, I am. Performing does that.
And may I perform for you, Sir? A musical piece perhaps? A song? A
story? A poem, Sir? What do you say?"

Jos found Rudolf's violin playing passable, although sometimes it
seemed deliberately screechy. Perhaps the coins fell more quickly into
his cup if the music alienated, the sooner to stop the sound. But he

was already singing one of those rambling, insinuating songs whose meaning seemed vaguely relevant to the listener but just out of reach.

His voice was surprisingly deep, however, and commanding. Their table was soon surrounded by a group of attentive listeners.

"There once was a young lass
just turned 15 years.
Little did she know this
was the start of many tears.
Ja ja ja, hidy ho hidy ho. ja, ja, ja, hidy ho.
Alone in the world, no parent, no friend.
She made her living at the Village Mile Inn.
Serving beer and serving gin.
But saying "no" to serving up sin."

The inebriated group guffawed knowingly. Rudolf, encouraged, continued on in an insinuating near whisper. The crowd quieted and moved closer in order to follow the story.

"Ja Ja Ja hidy hey. Hidy hey. Ya, ya, ya, hidy hey.
One night a young artist
on a corner bench.
Observed the drunkards tease the sweet wench.
They'd drop their mugs, make
her pick 'em up, then lift her skirts
with their walking sticks.
Ja ja ja Hidy ho, hidy hick Ja ja ja hidy hick.
I'll care for her m'self says the lad
with circling arm.
' Elsje come with me.'
Hidy ho. Hidy ho
And to her tiny room off they did go.
Three months later there's Elsje.
A pleadin'. 'Leave those cards
And take me to my weddin'.'
For I your wife am meant to be.'
'There'll be no wedding,' says the young man.
'I love another. I'm traveling far.
Off I go. Away today.'

He pulled himself from Elsje's grasp and
left her weeping, the helpless lass,
with one hand on her belly, her secret nest.
'Revenge I'll surely seek thinks she
once this tiny critter exits me.'
Ja ja ja. No no no hidy ho and ja ja ja hidy he.
Revenge she sought. Revenge she got.
Five years later her artist love lay
stabbed and drowned in the . . . ."

His audience growing, coins clinking into his cup, Rudolf was warming up when the subject of the song, Elsje herself, emerged from the kitchen with a plate of hot oysters. Catching the ditty's final lines, she banged down the plate on a nearby table, picked up the pewter cup next to Rudolf and turned it upside down over him, sending his coins bouncing in all directions over the tiled floor. Then she whacked him with it on top of the head.

"Stop that story making, you devil dwarf. And don't you ever use the word revenge in my place. I'll send my man after you. Then you'll know what revenge is."

The dwarf pressed his stubby thumb against his cheek and stool, knelt, and began feeling the floor for coins.

Head down, he mumbled, "Don't that man o' yours know revenge now Elsje? Ain't he just the perfect revenger, though?"

"I said, 'No such talk.' You're as much a gossipmonger as those fishwives on the Dam. Get out of my establishment, you ugly man. Blind and you think you know everything."

No longer the dainty helpless lass in the impromptu song, Elsje lifted up the dwarf and placed him outside the door of the Knowing Eye. She almost threw the violin after him, but controlled herself and placed it on his lap instead. Her young sons, arriving from school for their midday meal, nearly tripped over the small, seated figure.

Jos, however, had been drawn by the song. Why did Rudolf decide to tell that particular story in his presence? Did it relate to Jos in some way? Did Elsje have her revenge? Was there really a child? Who was the artist?

Jos paid for his beer and exited the tavern, pressing a coin into Rudolf's dirty palm.

"Good entertainment, Rudolf. What do you say you and I step over to the Lion's Mane and you complete the tale? Quietly, this time. Just for my ears."

"Delighted, Mr. Broekhof. It'll cost ya, though. Two more coins. A beer and a plate of oysters. Elsje threw me out before I could taste hers. Lead the way, Sir."

* * *

Having spent the afternoon and many more coins to hear the rest of the dwarf's story, Jos gave up on his quest to find Lukas van Hutten. He had bragged to his managers for weeks about the possibility of an alliance. Now he could not bear returning to the office and admitting to those same managers his probable defeat. The managers were likely aware that Van Hutten had waited for him in vain that morning and left disgruntled. Instead Jos sought the solace of home. It had been months, perhaps years, since he had returned home before 4:00 in the afternoon. He had left late that morning. Why not round out the day with an early return? The symmetry of that decision heartened him. The boat ride home relaxed him and gave him needed time to order both his notebook and his thoughts. He looked forward to a good meal and an evening writing a new entry in his Strad journal, contemplating the additional details of the dwarf's story.

As he opened his front door and slipped out of his black leather boots with the gold buckles, carefully arranging them on the designated tile, he noted with satisfaction that the day's cleaning had been completed. No more stinking canal water oozing off filthy rags. The black-and-white tile floors shone. The welcoming smells of Anna's mutton stew promised comfort and order.

His home seemed unusually cold, however. Checking on the main fireplace, he noticed that Anna apparently had neglected to perform the daily chore of carting out ashes and replenishing the wood. Yesterday's embers lay black and scattered. There were no new logs in sight. Anna and Myriam were well aware of his desire to return home each day to a welcoming fire in the chimney. He must speak to Myriam about this neglectful behavior.

Then he became aware of bumping sounds, grunting, and bursts of yelping. His two sons, prone and holding tightly to one another, rolled out the parlor door and down the corridor to where he was standing.

Only 15 months apart, they resembled each other so closely that Jos could not immediately identify which was which.

"Sir!," the one on the bottom said.

"What about him?" The one on top said, taking advantage of his brother's distraction to bop him on the head, grab him, and begin rolling him back up the corridor.

"Pappa!," the older son said again, for now Jos could see that one was indeed nine-year-old, Samuel. "You're here."

"Get up this instant," Jos told the boys. "Greet your father properly."

The boys stood up and sheepishly shook their father's hand.

"Good afternoon, Sir," said the older one.

"Good evening, Father," said the younger one. When, Jos wondered, had Daniel become the taller of the two? The stronger? The more dominant? Samuel looked weak beside his robust younger brother.

"Where is your mother?" he asked.

"In the usual place," the boys answered together.

"I'm sure you have school assignments," Jos told them. I expect you to be completing your lessons at this hour, not behaving like rowdy bear cubs."

"Yes, Sir," said the older.

"Yes, Father," said the younger.

"In the usual place" could only mean that Myriam was back at her writing desk, Jos assumed. Could she possibly have been sitting there the entire day? He hung up his coat and hat, stepped into his slippers, and went straight to her special alcove, determined to learn about the nature of her letters and the identity of her correspondents. No matter how she explained them, he would certainly chide her for this unproductive pastime.

But Myriam was not in her alcove. Her writing desk was neatly arranged, but her ornate wooden chair with its embroidered cushion was tucked under the desk. There was something that made the scene seem empty. The twin paintings by Dirck Hals no longer hung above the desk. He had delighted in giving them to her just two months after Catherina's death as a way of distracting her and contributing to this special space of hers. He had also taken great pride in his artistic choice and business prowess. Perhaps he could not afford 500 guilders to have his portrait painted by that Rembrandt, yet he was certain these less costly purchases were a wise, far-sighted investment. The twin paintings contrasted the emotions of two different women's experiences with letters they have just opened. In the one on the left, a woman sits beside a calm sea, dreaming contentedly, a letter flapping gently in her hand. In the companion piece another woman sits on a cliff, so distraught by the contents of her letter that she is tearing it to pieces and throwing the shreds out over rough seas.

Jos now recalled that during his rushed encounter with Myriam that morning, only the calm painting hung above her desk. Now both were gone. She must have moved them to another part of the house. Jos felt dismayed. They had seemed perfect in this location above her writing desk. Myriam's taste in art and décor was sometimes questionable.

Jos sought out his sons again and found them in the kitchen, laughing with Anna and enjoying tall glasses of fresh milk.

"What? Still not applying yourself to your studies? Your mother isn't there."

"Isn't there? She's always there."

"Well, she isn't there now. Where is your mother?"

Daniel, grabbing and chewing bits of bread, went to the kitchen door, opened it, and pointed outside. "There, Sir. Where she always is."

Soon after his marriage ten years earlier, Jos inherited this property, a double lot that now included the three-level home on fashionable Heerengracht with the horse stable and stable boy quarters at some distance behind it. In between the two structures lay the garden, the most heavily used part of which was an extension of the kitchen. Water was gathered there from the cistern. Clothes were washed daily and hung to dry. Chickens roamed freely.

The formal dining room overlooked the carefully kept green space beside the kitchen garden, but a high wall hid the garden's domestic unsightliness. Jos had left the remaining garden space untended, instructing the gardener to pull up weeds several times a year, but to leave the low trees, bushes, and wild flowers in their natural state.

The sun had fallen behind the west side of the house, casting the entire garden in shadow. Jos's business dealings and, if he were to be honest with himself, his many, fruitless attempts to locate the prized etching, had so occupied him that it had been a long time since he had returned home before dark. On weekends he did not venture beyond the near, formal part of the garden whose original design he had once carefully supervised.

Now as he opened the rear door of his home, he could see that the far side of it was transformed. A partially hidden curved brick path drew him forward. Several of the taller trees he treasured had been removed. Rocks outlined a large section. Filling that space were carved stone animal statues – rabbits, frogs, turtles, bear cubs, alternating with bushes and flowering shrubs. The brick walk split in two directions. The odor of fresh earth drew Jos to the left side of the walkway that abruptly ended at three small pine trees whose cone shape and deep green tips seemed familiar to Jos. The loose dirt around the center one indicated that the pine had recently been planted there. With dismay, Jos realized that this pine was the very object Mennes and De Bruin had been pulling on their cart that morning. They had been heading for his house then? How dare they! With their cheerfully deceptive greetings! He retraced his steps and followed the right side of the path.

The bricks' dampness seeped unpleasantly through his slippers. A sharp metallic odor irritated his nose. It was at the end of the right side that he saw Myriam, still dressed as he had left her that morning, but wrapped in a shawl, on her knees at the base of a bronze statue of a life-size child angel. She was tending to a vine trailing dark orange butterfly-like flowers at the statue's base. Every few seconds, she lifted her head to gaze lovingly at the angel.

"What are you doing, Myriam?" Jos called as he began walking toward her. "What is all this? Where did you get it? Did that Mennes take advantage of you? How much did you pay him?"

The smallest activity so absorbed her, that it was impossible to startle Myriam these days. Slowly she removed her adoring study of the angel and turned her head to respond to her husband. The vagueness of her look reminded him of the cat in his office that morning. Indifference from a cat was disappointing, perhaps even amusing, but that same expression on the face of a beloved was piercingly hurtful and rejecting. Myriam gathered the beige wool shawl tight around herself, leaving black marks on both sides of it where her dirt-covered hands touched it. Jos saw that she was trembling and bent to help her stand.

"It's a memorial garden," she said. "To Catherina. I wanted it full of life, Jos. And with color year-round. Just today I had the third pine installed – one for every year she lived. Unlike our child, the pines will thrive, Jos. They will outlive us. Mr. Mennes is supplying me with special soil treated with nutrients. The garden will be forever lush he says and will remind us of Catherina's beauty. He's found the perfect statues for me. Isn't it wond . . ."

Tears began flowing from Myriam's eyes. As Jos put an arm around her and led her back to the house, Myriam wiped her tears on her soiled shawl and he calculated the loss of the twin paintings. Worth probably 20% more than he had paid for them two years ago, the charming originals were sure to double in price in another ten years. The investment would have yielded enough to purchase a new pair of fine horses every year, or a country house to escape to on weekends or, if Rudolf's story were true, for the ransom on his beloved, captive seventh etching which he had named, sight-unseen "Consummation Sunday."

PART III:
Home

Chapter Twenty-one
Cinnamon and Cloves

"Folly is the only thing that delays youth," recited a familiar voice.

"Only with age does wisdom come," responded fifty little girls.

The Bible passage had been read. The children were settled down to a morning meal of bread, cheese, and buttermilk. Although they were instructed to eat quietly and calmly, the volume of chatter and twittering rose and then fell as the little girls watched two of the older orphan boys assist Housefather move through the room and settle into his carved, oak breakfast chair. Once he was settled, the boys promptly left and returned to their quarters on the other side of the courtyard.

"Father. Father. Good morning, Father," some of the children shouted out.

Two of the youngest girls cried "Pappa!," abandoned their places, slid off their benches and approached the Housefather, at first patting his wrinkled, motionless hands resting on the strong arms of the sturdy chair, then climbing up on his frail knees. One put her arms around his neck. A third child approached him from the back and began playing with his hair. Another ventured a kiss on his wrinkled cheek.

"After the rain, the sun will shine," pronounced Housefather.

"The sun rises for free," chimed the children.

These girls had memorized the Housefather's favorite sayings, but they could not remember a time when he was employed as a wise, but strict Schoolmaster at the orphanage. For two decades he guided his multi-level students through their ABC's, warned them about overturning the writing ink as he arranged a goose feather in their small fingers, helped them count out their numbers on the abacus, and read them a daily psalm – all with an eye for preparing them for a future productive life outside the institution.

For the past five years, however, since a bad fall, he could barely stand on his own for more than a minute. He took pleasure in seeing the children each morning, but he knew none of their names, did not take note that they began their day freshly dressed, was ignorant of the effort they exerted to contain their energy in order to meet society's expectations of decorum and behavior.

For the children, Housefather was the only man, besides the current Schoolmaster, with whom they had any regular contact. They did not see him as disabled, but as a figure of benign authority, albeit a confused and unpredictable one. Because he never objected, perhaps wasn't even aware of their close physical presence, and even though he did not reciprocate, they took advantage of the opportunity to express affection. Some of them never knew their own grandfathers, fathers, uncles. Here was a male figure, however unresponsive, whom they could touch, sniff, behold.

For his part, the Housefather apparently felt a lingering responsibility to educate. This desire manifested itself in bursts of proverbs spoken with surprising force, given that he no longer had the ability to converse.

"The world is turned upside down."

"Leave at least one egg in the nest."

"Nobody can predict the future."

When Housefather bellowed "To lead each other around by the nose," Bernadien grabbed and twisted Wilhelmina's nose, startling her and making her cry. A few others – the most bold or the meanest – followed her example.

"Big fish eat little fish," he bellowed.

Isabela stood up and began trying to soothe, settle and comfort.

"As patient as a lamb," yelled Housefather, adding to the din.

"All good things come to an . . . ."

Housemother entered the room and angrily shooed the children away from her inert husband. They leaped away from Housefather and scattered back to their seats. Silence fell over the room as the children took a last few swallows of buttermilk.

As she did at every meal, Housemother covered her husband with a large napkin, tucking it into his collar and stretching it out over his legs. Then she fed him small spoonfuls of gray, liquidy porridge. He continued to attempt to spout his proverbs, but Housemother hushed him and dabbed at his spittle.

With only whispers all around now, Isabela sat back down at the long wooden breakfast table. She looked out the large windows – opened slightly for the first time in six months – and gazed at the row of trees along the canal. She could not recall her first experience of the canals. She was unconscious when Cornelius sought help to carry her from the wharf on the IJ to his family's home on the outskirts of the city. The United Provinces and Spain continued to fight a long, protracted, bitter war. Spaniards were not welcome. In order to protect her, Cornelius told his family that she was from England and that her name was Isabelle.

Cornelius recovered from the ordeal quickly and soon found a position on a ship bound for England, leaving Isabela in the care of his mother, father, and sister.

For a month, his kin cared for the feverish, delirious young woman as she sometimes mumbled, sometimes cried out, and occasionally sang phrases in at least two languages they did not understand. Once she seemed to have recovered, they shared with her whatever food they could. When she was strong enough to walk, she insisted on helping them with chores and began picking up Dutch phrases. They had neither the space nor the means to keep her, however, and brought her to the city orphanage.

Because she was not the offspring of Amsterdam citizens and was already sixteen, the institution could not keep her there as an orphan. However, Housemother recognized in Isabela a combination of grace and intelligence that would be useful. In addition, she reasoned, since Isabela appeared to have few options, her gratitude should make her a malleable servant. One Big Sister had just left to marry and needed to be replaced. Housemother offered Isabela the Big Sister position and she accepted. The fact that she was from Spain made no difference inside the orphanage walls, but on the rare occasions she was in the city, she introduced herself as Isabelle. The position provided shelter, plentiful and nutritious sustenance, a uniform, a small stipend, and serious responsibilities. As an only child and now an orphan herself, Isabela adored her group of little sisters.

Even so, she longed for England where she had spent an exciting summer with the Hatterbrook daughters and cousins on almost daily outings to visit friends in the city, to evening parties and theater productions, for picnics in parks, lush gardens and horseback riding. They had delighted in dressing her in the latest English fashions – bonnets, dresses, shoes, and boots – all of it now at the bottom of the sea. Having learned of the shipwreck and her survival, they wrote her often, urging her to return to them, to live with them.

Isabela also thought of her aunts whose letters were full of anxiety, who pleaded with her to come home and live the life her father had planned for her. For whatever reasons, so far Isabela resisted both of these possibilities. Certainly the sojourn in England had been delightful, but something held her here. Perhaps, she thought, that particular something was purpose or meaning or even fulfillment at some level – something satisfying that fed her soul in a way that all the frantic socializing in England did not.

As for returning home, that would mean a very constricted life with a man whom she hardly knew and would probably rarely see. One day the previous week she realized with a shock that it was her seventeenth birthday. With so many living in the orphanage, birthdays were not acknowledged or celebrated. "Should I be thinking about marriage and children now?" she wondered.

Then there was the city where she now lived and which she hardly knew. What secrets and delights might there be beyond these walls – something other than the daily life in this institution and the once-a-week walk to Our Lady of the Attic and back? Would she ever know?

She could smell the freshness of new growth. Leaves were beginning to appear. Across the canal she could perceive red and yellow tulips in window boxes. The bright colors made her want to leap through the window and run through the city.

Instead she would follow the daily routine. Soon she would lead her girls to their classrooms and return upstairs to tidy up their room, mend and prepare their clothes, sort their bonnets, take their soiled aprons to the laundress. When those chores were complete, she would then join them in their classroom to assist the Schoolmaster.

After a lunch of white beans, salted bacon with carrots or cabbage, bread, and, if they were lucky, a shared apple, she would supervise the children's outdoor play. Even outdoors, children were expected to be calm and quiet. Marbles were acceptable and were played on a raised, flat surface, since the stones in the ground were too uneven for that delicate game. Jump rope too, with its rhymes and songs, was fine for girls, but when Nelleke once found a hoop and stick left behind by a visitor and began to explore it, the outdoor supervisors took it away. "This is a boy's game," they said.

Then they would head back inside where the smallest would nap while the older ones would work at their sewing, embroidery, and lace making. After a light evening meal of rice porridge and more bread and cheese, it was time for more Bible reading, after which the children would beg her for a story in her less-than-perfect Dutch and a lullaby in Spanish.

As if reading her escape thoughts, Head Cook approached Isabela and said quietly, "We're nearly out of butter. We need some for the rest of the week. Ella is sick in bed today. I've spoken to Housemother and she agreed I could ask you to run to the butter market to fetch some."

"Line up, Katje, Wilhelmina, Nelleke, Marja. You too, Bernadien. Move along," said Isabela. But Nelleke had overheard Cook's request. After Isabela greeted the Schoolmaster and gave her girls a little pat, pushing them into the schoolroom, Nelleke held back and grabbed Isabela's sleeve. "PLEASE, take me with you, Isabela," she whispered fiercely. "I'll be good. I'll do anything you say. Please, please, please. Say yes. Say yes."

"No, darling child, you belong in the classroom. I'll be gone only a short while." Yet, even as she said the words, she knew she could not resist the child's pleading eyes, her need to explore beyond the orphanage walls matching Isabela's own. And wouldn't the outing be richer and more fun with Nelleke's lively companionship?

Isabela rarely asked the Housemother for any favors and now, after asking Nelleke to wait calmly in the corridor, she approached the rigid woman with some fear. She found Housemother in her office nook, distracted, preparing a report for the Regents. After explaining that Nelleke was ahead of her classmates in nearly all subjects and promising they would return quickly, Isabela was surprised to win her approval for the brief joint outing.

Returning to the hallway where Nelleke waited with her eyes closed tightly and her palms pressed together in dramatic prayer pose, Isabela warned, "Housemother has made a decision. Do you promise that you will neither shout nor leap up and down, nor run to Mother and kiss her when I tell you? Can you be calm?" Nelleke opened her eyes, but she closed them again, interwove her fingers and raised them to her forehead.

"Yes," she said tightening up her face, bracing herself for possible disappointment.

"Very well, then. Let us fetch our shawls and slip away quietly." Isabela kneeled down and took Nelleke's hands in hers.

"But first, these are the rules. We will hold hands the entire time we are out in the town. If my little Nelleke wanders away, her Big Sister, Isabela, will find her and bring her directly back to the orphanage and continue on the errand alone. One more rule. Outside the walls of the orphanage, my name is Isabelle. Outside I am not from Spain. I am from England. Can you remember to call me Isabelle?" Nelleke reached for Isabela's hand and sauntered up until she was right up against her Big Sister. "Of course, Isabelle, and I will not leave your side," she said, smiling coyly.

They stepped into a glorious day. Still cool, but unusually sunny. In eight months, except for the march to and from church every Sunday, Nelleke had been outside the orphanage only once, when Willem took her skating. She remembered that day with longing and confusion. Why had Willem never returned to visit with her?

Isabela decided to skip the butter market and buy butter at the Damrak instead. Surely there must be some butter for sale there and there was so much more to see. Both girls were immediately captivated by the crush of people. Soldiers, wealthy merchants with their servants, beggars, small boys running after wood hoops with sticks. Two live goats. Ships. Sailors. Flowers of every hue. Sides of beef and mutton strung up, dripping fresh blood. Maids weighed down with their daily purchases. Babies strapped to mothers' bodies.

A young soldier tipped his hat. "Good day, lovely ladies," he said. Isabela could sense Nelleke preparing one of her chirpy responses, ready to chatter away at the young man. She gave Nelleke's hand a tug and kept moving.

"We don't know that man," Isabela instructed. "We don't talk to strange men."

And the noise! Sellers trying to outdo each other with their cries: "Fish, mutton, eggs, cream, tools, paintings, etchings. Apples. Sausages. Hot teas. Croquery. Delicate porcelain. "Just arrived this morning on the The White Lion. "China's finest dishes for your household. Limited supply. Get them before your neighbor does." Carvings. Felt hats. Rugs.

There was the pancake woman, calling out "Get your pancakes here. Hot and tasty." A bright green-and-red parrot in a cage over her stall repeated in his crackly voice, "Hot and tasty. Hot and tasty."

Suddenly, Nelleke stopped. She sniffed the air. Above the odors of the cooking oil, the raw meat, the rolls of fabric, and the manure, she caught a whiff of something foreign. It was the same unusual smell she noticed going by a warehouse as she entered Amsterdam months ago, bumping along in the back of Uncle Johannes's wagon in the rain.

"Isabela, what is that smell? I want to know the name of it."

"Isabelle," Isabela corrected. "Which smell?" Isabela asked, tugging Nelleke toward the butter stalls.

"I'll find where it's coming from. I think it's over there. Isabela, please come with me. It will only take a minute."

Now it was Nelleke who tugged on Isabela. Nelleke lost the scent several times, but ultimately ended up at a table covered with small, open sacks, each filled with a mound of small, dark-brown objects or fine powders. Nelleke began putting her face into each bag and breathing deeply.

"Are these for smoking?" she asked the couple behind the table, thinking of a man she had glimpsed leaning against an outside tavern wall earlier, blowing smoke out his nose after drawing it in from his long-stemmed pipe. "Or do you eat them?"

"Sometimes they are laced with tobacco," said the kindly wife. "But they are also used for medicines, made into teas and added to sweets. You don't eat them alone. They're called spices."

The woman reached into the sacks and arranged three samples in her own outstretched hand: a thin, jagged brown stick; a much smaller harder black stick that resembled a nail and had a tiny burst bud on the end; and a brown, smooth nut. "Cinnamon, nutmeg, and a clove," she said, pointing. Then she repeated the names, as she reached for Nelleke's hand and arranged them one by one in Nelleke's palm. "Cinnamon. Nutmeg. Clove."

"I love these," Nelleke said, picking up each one and sniffing it. "Thank you." Can I eat them?"

"You can't really eat them alone. They need to be ground or soaked or cracked, but you can suck on the clove if you wish. Here take another one." The woman gave Isabela and Nelleke each a clove which they gingerly placed on their tongues. It stung a little, but it was intriguing.

Nelleke bit down on it lightly, but controlled the urge to chew, wanting to prolong the taste and the mild sting.

There was a long line for the butter. When it was their turn, they made the transaction quickly. Isabela placed the butter packet in her satchel and they headed back slowly to the orphanage.

Suddenly, Nelleke was jolted by the feeling of warm fur moving against her ankles. In a most unladylike gesture, she lifted up her ankle-length skirt and nearly tripped over a small white dog. Freed from its momentary shelter, and sensing a potential playmate in Nelleke, the dog took off running. Then it doubled back and ran off again as if to invite her to follow. When the dog found its apparent master, it began yipping and leaping, even chasing its own tail round and round with excitement and frustration.

To the puppy, it must have looked as if its master was in the sky. The man stood on one of the wide paths on top of the brick wall that surrounded the city. Nelleke could no longer be held back. She chased after the puppy and yelled up to its master. "He's so happy to see you. Is he yours?" Nelleke picked up the wiggly dog and took two steps up the steep slope. Her small legs could not negotiate the bank. Reluctantly, she patted the puppy's head one more time, but he leaped from her arms and ran rapidly up the slope.

"It's okay, Runt. You found me. Thanks to this lovely child. What is your name, little girl?" the man called down.

A panting Isabela arrived just then, put her arm around Nelleke, and squeezed her shoulders to convey the reminder that she was not to speak with a strange man. Nelleke understood the gesture, but could not resist saying and pointing, "I want to go up there."

In their unique ankle-length dresses, fitted at the waist, red on one side, black on the other; triangular white shawls tied neatly and symmetrically across the bodice and tucked into their skirts; clean white bonnets covering their heads and ears; hair gathered in a cloth-covered knot at the nape of the neck, the girls were recognized by everyone. "Oh, do come up," the young man said, "You can reach the orphanage from this side. I'll show you."

Having grown up with a frail mother and two maiden aunts and with her Captain father away for months at a time, it was not until after her mother died and she was a passenger on her father's ship that Isabela, then sixteen, had first had an opportunity to observe the opposite sex. Although she was not allowed to mix with them, she had two months to study them surreptitiously from a short distance. Probably the presence of the Captain's young daughter tempered their behavior and language. Yet Isabela was often shocked by how raucous their laughter could be, how reckless they sometimes behaved, climbing rapidly up the mast and swinging from it. One Spaniard even slung one leg over the mast and hung upside down, rocking with the waves, trying to keep her attention.

A few dared to tip their caps to her, sometimes with a wink, sometimes with a hint of a mocking smile. One regarded her with what appeared to be studied respect, as if he believed his serious visage gave him an excuse for a lingering look. Yet there had been others who seemed mild, gentle. And then, of course, there were her heroes – Jules, who while seriously injured had rescued her, and Cornelius, who fought fierce wind and seas and brought her to this land.

The young man above her now on the city wall, stroking his returned pet, talking to it as if it were a child, had curious, amused eyes that peered down on her. Set back on his head was a smashed gray cap tilted casually as if to deny that it was actually made of the finest imported felt. His wrinkled silk shirt with blousy sleeves gave off the same ambiguous message. The woolen trousers were well pressed and fitted, yet the leather boots, once shiny, appeared to have been mud-splattered for months. They also had strange-shaped splashes of color on them. She quickly suppressed the thought of what his small moustache and trim beard might feel like against her cheek.

"Pieter Hals," the man said with a small nod as he stooped to place his dog on the ground. It took Isabela a moment to realize that he was offering her his hand, not as a greeting, but in order to help her reach the top of the brick wall. The gesture and the thought of touching him left her shaken. Nelleke, however, did not hesitate. She raced up, grabbed the hand, jumped onto the path, and took off running after the dog again. Isabela had no choice but to follow, although she climbed up on her own without the aid of the proffered hand.

Instantly the city's frenetic movement, noise, and odors were behind them. Beyond the city wall were fields, trees, streams, farmhouses. The cottages, smothered with straw, their walls slanting in different directions, looked as if they had been dropped haphazardly from the sky and suffered a shock upon landing. The cows and sheep grazed calmly. The only object in motion was also the largest. Four large blades moved round together against the sky on top of a clay mound with a little door. Even with Nelleke running away, Isabela stood and gaped for a moment.

"Beautiful, isn't it?" Pieter tried again.

"Like a painting," she couldn't help responding.

"Exactly."

Then Isabela noticed a mother duck confidently leading her ducklings across a pond on the farm in the distance.

"Excuse me," Isabela said, pulling herself away from the tranquil scene and looking down the path for her charge.

But Nelleke had not gone far. She had followed the puppy to a group of three seated men and had stopped there as the puppy turned and ran back to its master.

"Look, Isabela. I mean, look, Isabelle," Nelleke yelled to her, as if she had discovered a great treasure. "They're drawing."

Isabela thought artists painted only indoors in their studios, but hadn't she already noticed how picturesque the scene was stretched out beyond the city? Of course, an artist would want to try to capture it. Nelleke was chatting with one of the artists who seemed to be the teacher. His unruly reddish curls stuck out from under his cap in all directions and reached to his shoulders. His face was pink, his nose pinker still and large. He had the beginning of lines on his forehead, under his eyes, and on the sides of that large nose. There was something very familiar about his face, yet Isabela was sure she had never met this man before. He held a board on one knee and a piece of charcoal in his smeared fingers. Suddenly the teacher gave out a loud guffaw and Nelleke joined her girlish laughter to his.

"I asked him if he could draw a cow swimming," Nelleke explained to Isabela as she arrived on the scene. "He thought that was funny. But look," she said, pointing to his canvas, "there is my cow, trying to stay above the water. She was so scared," she added sadly.

"Can you draw these too?" Nelleke asked, opening her fist and revealing the spices.

"Cinnamon, nutmeg, and clove? Here you go." Before she could blink, it was if the sweaty spices in her hand had jumped onto the canvas. The quick drawing matched them exactly and now the artist was drawing her little palm holding them as well.

"How do you do that so fast?" Nelleke asked the teacher.

The teacher swung around and looked at her with great concentration. She felt his eyes move from her hair to her eyes, her mouth, her clothes.

Although the gaze was very intense and she didn't understand why he was looking at her like that, it was not accusing or scary.

"Fast?" he said as his eyes completed the tour. "You'll see fast. Turn around and close your eyes until I tell you."

Nelleke played the game, although it was very hard to keep still. She could hear charcoal moving over the canvas.

Isabela was watching everything, however. Once she saw that Nelleke was safe and was more or less behaving herself, she could not pull herself away from the portrait coming alive as she watched.

"OK," the master said, "open your eyes and turn around." And when Nelleke did open her eyes and turn around, she was staring at herself, her tight white cap with the golden curls spilling out, her dark, intelligent eyes, her bitty nose and mouth, her orphan costume, her white apron with the pockets. The outstretched palm with the spices had been incorporated into the drawing. Her likeness was smiling and seemed to be sharing with the viewer what she had been given in the market just minutes ago. The struggling cow swam by in the background, as alarmed as ever.

"That's me!" Nelleke cried out in amazement.

"It's you," said the teacher, "and you know what? I'm working on a very large painting of the City Guards' Headquarters right over there," he said, pointing down toward the Amstel River. I would like to draw you into that painting. You'll be like a little firefly lighting up the night. Is that all right with you? And if the orphanage will let you," he said, turning to Isabela, "I'll invite you both to view the finished work." "That is very kind of you, Sir. We would be pleased to be your guests. We must return now, Nelleke."

"May I accompany you? Nelleke? Isabela/Isabelle?" asked Pieter. Isabela was shocked to hear Pieter Hals pronounce her dual first names, but then remembered that Nelleke had used the names several times. Apparently he had noted it and felt comfortable using them without a formal introduction.

Isabela looked around hesitantly. Although the talent of this teacher was extraordinary, she could not be sure he or his pupil, if that's what Pieter was, was trustworthy. Then she noticed the canvas propped up against the empty stool. That must be Pieter's. On it was the outline of the large, turning object she had noticed when she first looked beyond the wall. "Of course," she realized now, seeing it up close. "A windmill. We have lots of those in Spain too." The young man had also sketched his dog, Runt, and had skillfully captured the animal's friendliness and zest. There was a child carrying a bucket who leaned over to greet the dog. Isabela felt she could see the dog's tail wagging happily back and forth right there on the canvas, looking up at the child, hoping to play, just as it had with Nelleke. It was an enchanting sketch.

"Yes, that would be very nice of you," she said, not quite believing her boldness.

"Rembrandt van Rijn," said the master, adding his signature to the lower right corner. When he completed the sketch by drawing a tiny caterpillar on Nelleke's shoe, she began leaping up and down. "How did you know I love caterpillars?"

"I'll finish this up and send it to you, Nelleke. How would that be?"

"Oh, yes, please, Mr. Rembrandt van Rijn," Nelleke answered delightedly.

"I'll be happy to deliver it," added Pieter quickly as he began to lead the girls back to the orphanage.

Pieter led the girls along the promenade through a part of the city they had never seen. Graceful linden trees lined the canals, swaying, as if to welcome them to the neighborhood. Here the way down was not a slippery slope, but a set of recently swept stairs. This time Isabela accepted Pieter's offer of a steady hand. The commercial bustle seemed far away. Instead they walked past multi-storied, brick, gabled homes – one after another more elegant than the next, showing their best as if lined up for a competition. Isabela was so enchanted by the houses, so involved in wondering about the families inside and also so distracted by Pieter's long easy gait beside her, that she did not notice for a moment that Nelleke had again slipped away.

"Come see," Nelleke called, bringing Isabela abruptly back to her duty. "The shadows." You can see the trees in the water." Nelleke was standing with her toes lined up with the edge of the street, bending over, peering down into the canal. Isabela gasped. If she returned to the orphanage with a child soaked in brine and filth, they would dismiss her. Where would she go? Isabela was paralyzed, afraid to approach the little girl for fear that any motion would send her plunging.

Stealthfully, Pieter took four large steps, grabbed Nelleke around the waist, and set her down next to Isabela. Isabela bent down and put her arms around the child. "You must never go so close to the canals, Nelleke. You might fall in. You might get sick." Then, with tears springing into her eyes, she added, "You might drown."

"I threw my cinnamon, my nutmeg, and my cloves in the water, Isabela/Isabelle. They sank. They're all gone," Nelleke answered. The three continued walking, Nelleke's hand held extra tight in Isabela's.

Pieter stopped in front of one of the widest homes they had seen. Its windows gleamed. The shutters were freshly painted. The threesome stepped back as water came tumbling down its façade. Two maids were washing down the outside walls with sprays from special syringes made for this purpose. The spray reached all the way to the roof. The girls looked up and up to the house's pointed top. The wide entrance consisted of two doors side by side with a large brass knocker in the shape of a man's hand. A man stopped his pushcart by the front door. Pieter called to the man.

"Here you go, Henry," Pieter said, handing the man a few coins. Pieter reached into one of the cart's baskets, chose three buns and shared them with Isabela and Nelleke. Nelleke sniffed hers before sinking her new permanent teeth into the warm, soft bread. "Isabela," she cried, chewing, "I taste cinnamon."

"Thank you, Mr. Hals," the pushcart man said before he climbed the stairs and lifted the heavy brass knocker. A maid responded, accepted the package he offered, paid him, and noticed the group a few feet away.

"Pieter," the maid called, affectionately. "Aren't you supposed to be working with the master? Out gallivanting with pretty girls instead, eh? Will we see you for dinner tonight?"

"I'm delivering my new friends back home, Adriana, after which I shall return to the master's studio. Doesn't a young artist get a break once in a while? Would I miss one of your meals? I'll be home tonight. Now get back to work yourself, Miss," Pieter added playfully.

"That's YOUR house?" Nelleke asked.

"That's my family home, yes. Where I was born. Where I grew up. Where I'll continue to live, in fact, until I've been accepted into the artist guild and established myself – after my studies with the master are complete."

Five minutes later, Pieter brought the girls to the orphanage door. They had approached it from a direction that was entirely new to them and they were surprised it was so close to Pieter's neighborhood.

Turning to Isabela, he looked her directly in the eye, studying her features and said, "I should like to paint your portrait. Would you be willing to sit for me?"

Momentarily breathless from his direct gaze and at the thought of seeing the young man again, Isabela, said, "I would have to speak with Housemother about that, Mr. Hals. Thank you for delivering us safely."

After allowing Nelleke to bend down and give Runt a goodbye pat, Isabela took Nelleke's arm and moved her toward the gatekeeper. With dismay, she realized that she had ignored the bells ringing out the hour. She was concerned that their simple butter errand had taken far too long. With a final nod to Pieter and a brief smile, she pulled Nelleke past the gatekeeper and into the courtyard. Before she entered the building, she heard Pieter call his dog and then whistle a tune. Was he still standing on the other side of the gate out in the street? Isabela had a bizarre thought – or was it a wish – that the next time she had an occasion to exit the orphanage, even if it were two weeks hence, she would find Pieter there, holding Runt and still whistling.

They could see the last few orphans crossing over from the school side to the living side of the courtyard. The church bells rang out the hour and this time Isabela counted. Was it possible that lunch was being served already? Isabella told Nelleke to join the group while she delivered the butter to the kitchen. On her way to the kitchen to complete her errand, she had to pass by Housemother's office.

Isabela, still wearing her outdoor shawl, rushed by the Housemother's open door, but Housemother looked up, saw her, frowned, and reached for her timepiece. Isabela kept going, but feared that there would be consequences for the stolen hours.

Chapter Twenty-two
Housemother and Regents

athalie Heijn had work that earned her respect and a modicum of stature. With the position came a comfortable one-room apartment and three meals a day for both her and her disabled husband. None of this was easy to come by in 1630s Amsterdam where occupations for women were mostly limited to tavern girls, fish sellers, and prostitutes.

Many women would have been grateful, but Nathalie Heijn was bitter. At twenty she had married the orphanage Schoolmaster who was double her age, and set about turning his bachelor quarters into a home. Like all good Dutch housewives, regardless of their level of wealth or status, she scrubbed walls, floors, and windowsills daily. Although her husband's duties included supervising children in the dining hall so that cooking was not one of her wifely chores, she made sure that he awoke each morning to a cup of hot tea and honey, that his clothes were tidy and comfortable, and that his timepiece was set to the correct time.

Soon she was bored. She began joining her husband in the dining hall. Early in her marriage she was actually somewhat affectionate with the youngest children, holding them on her lap and calling them "poor motherless things." When that too became boring, she asked the Regents if there were tasks they could assign her about the grounds. They put her in charge of the laundry where she earned a small stipend as well as a reputation for efficiency and exactitude.

When the orphanage was enlarged just in time for a surge of new residents, the Regents advanced her to Kitchen Supervisor for the

Children's Wing. Here too she applied her intelligence and energy to cutting waste and demanding from the cooks less chatter and more attention to chores.

Throughout those first five years of marriage, as her responsibilities outside her home grew and she acquired a small savings, she purchased a cradle and knitted small blankets, bonnets, and booties, certain each month that her menses would not arrive, signaling a new life growing inside her – a child, <u>her</u> child that would not be like those "poor motherless things," no, not at all like those children to whom her husband dedicated hours every day.

Mrs. Heijn's dreams of a family of her own were dashed the day the Schoolmaster's assistant came running into the kitchen. He lead her to the schoolroom where the children were gathered around her husband slumped forward in his chair, his face resting in a pool of drool on his wooden desk. Some of the children were poking him. "Schoolmaster. Schoolmaster. Wake up." Others were crying, having realized quickly that once again they had been abandoned.

Mr. Heijn survived what the doctor said was a temporary stopping of his heart but, because of the lack of blood and oxygen in his brain during that few minutes, his mind turned back in time. Mrs. Heijn did indeed have her own child now, but it existed in the body of a frail, confused, dependent adult.

The Regents gave the Heijn's apartment to the new Schoolmaster who had a wife and two children. They could have simply turned the couple out at that point. That they did not, was a tribute to both the husband who had served the orphanage for 20 years and to the wife whose handling of responsibility impressed them.

The couple was given smaller lodgings – a first-floor space next to the orphan sick room. When the Housemother of the Children's Wing left two years later, the Regents offered Mrs. Heijn that position and she accepted. Her goals were straightforward. She saw herself as a strict administrator. She valued order and fairness. She set rules. She insisted they be obeyed. She showed no favoritism. There were no exceptions.

The frequent sight of hundreds of children, none of them hers, irritated her. She no longer touched them if she could avoid it, never felt a soft cheek next to hers or the warmth of a child grateful to be held. Yet she was aware enough of her near hatred to know that, if she were to keep the position, she must see to it that others met the children's needs. She was adept at choosing sensitive young women to perform the numerous daily tasks.

By learning to balance deference with demands, Mrs. Heijn worked well with the orphanage's most important and highly paid employee, the Bookkeeper, Lucas Sterck. Every Wednesday before Sterck's lengthy financial report, Mrs. Heijn gave her weekly report to the orphanage governing body, the Regents, and introduced them personally to selected new arrivals.

The Wednesday after Nelleke left the sick room and returned to the children's wing presented challenges to Mrs. H that she had never before faced in seventeen years of reporting. Mrs. H disliked this child even more than she did the others. She was having difficulty taming the child's willfulness and independence. Nelleke's unpredictability unnerved Mrs. H. What's more the usually agreeable Isabela stubbornly took the child's side repeatedly and refused to discipline her properly.

Mrs. H made a decision. Rather than explain the child's mishap, rather than take responsibility, and risk dismissal, and even knowing that many people were aware of the accident, Mrs. H decided that if questioned, she would casually downplay the entire incident. And she would certainly not introduce Nelleke to the Regents until the child was tamed, cowed, and obedient.

Luck continued to favor her. The Regents' agenda was full that evening. Being a Regent brought prestige, but also serious responsibility – overseeing the hiring of new staff; supervising the operation of a complicated institution with an educational wing, a boy's wing, a girl's wing, plus a children's dormitory, the kitchens, the sick rooms; keeping the children fed, clothed, healthy; and eventually assuring that guidance was offered when they transitioned to adult life outside the institution. The deadline for submitting the account books to the city magistrates was approaching. That night the Regents' primary areas of focus were the bookkeeper's report on the budget and how best to invest and protect the orphans' assets.

After a few days, Nelleke's burn healed and she more or less adapted to the orphanage's daily routines and, given the need to register and help other new arrivals to settle in, the incident seemed to have faded. Yet, the star-shaped scar on Nelleke's hand was a reminder that the incident had never been fully explained.

If Mrs. Heijn were ever challenged about the incident, if she were ever accused of neglect, she would need to be sure that her account and

Isabela's were consistent. She would need Isabela on her side. Therefore, she did not punish Isabela's pushing the limits with the butter outing. Although her intuition told her there was more to the story, she simply accepted Isabela's apology and explanation that, as unfamiliar as she was with Amsterdam, she and Nelleke had been lost for awhile.

Besides, tomorrow, Wednesday, the regular Regents meeting day, the orphanage doctor was to make his annual report. Mrs. H was in no position to question what the doctor might say. There was Marja's recent death and that also made her nervous. In order to demonstrate proof of her continued vigilance and care, and given that Nelleke's six months at the orphanage had contributed to improved self-discipline, rather than hide the child any longer Mrs. H selected Nelleke as one of the children to present to the Regents. The Regents rarely engaged the children. They just wanted to see some of them from time to time and assure themselves that the orphanage was providing the services the children required. It could be a quick introduction and then she would usher them out.

Once Dr. Voerman had finished his report on the general health of the orphanage population, Mrs. H entered the Regents' Room moving Nelleke and three other orphans ahead of her. The other three stood awkwardly as Mrs. H. gave their names and summary.

Six Regents, dressed in severe black accentuated with white lace at their throats and wrists, sat in tall, straight-back, leather chairs around a heavy oak table in the middle of a rectangular room large enough to sleep twenty orphans, but used only by the Regents. Nearly-life-size portraits of past Regents covered the walls. In several of these, barefoot, ragged children were being presented to the Regents. Fleshy cupids, symbolizing goodness and charity, looked down from a circular mural in the ceiling. Oil lamps burned. Quill pens lay about next to glass goblets and several open bottles of wine. The Bookkeeper removed a heavy book from a cabinet and placed it on the table in front of his chair. "*Kinderboek*," the cover read. "1637-1640." The Bookkeeper sat and turned the stiff pages covered with small, fine notations until he found the heading for each of the four children. Three children hung their heads and said nothing as the Housemother introduced them and the Bookkeeper read their entries.

Nelleke looked from one Regent's face to the other, however. One man – smaller than the rest – looked familiar, but she couldn't recall where she might have seen him – at church perhaps. She perceived at once that these men had more authority than the unpleasant Housemother. Their large black hats and long beards reminded her of the grandfather in whose home she once lived – the house where Jacob was born. Although severe looking like these men, her grandfather smiled whenever he caught sight of her. He pulled her up on his lap. He encouraged her to talk to him. He listened. Her stories and her many questions amused him.

When it was Nelleke's turn, Mrs. H. placed one arm around Nelleke's shoulders and held the scarred hand inside her own. "Sirs," she said, summoning an affectionate tone, "This is Nelleke Stradwijk, age 6. The Schoolmaster reports that Nelleke is an eager learner. She is also helpful with our smallest children."

Then the bookkeeper read, "Nelleke Stradwijk, 13 October, 1639, 9:40 evening. Accompanied by uncle, Johannes Verhoeven. Raining. Child was damp and shivering." He then gave the date her parents became citizens of Amsterdam, Nelleke's birthdate, the church where she was baptized, and the date of the baptism.

Nelleke twisted and glared up at Mrs. H who tightened her grip. She wiggled forcefully, though, pulled away, and ran to the opposite side of the table. Looking directly at the Regents, her lower lip trembling, she said to the assembled group, "She took my things. My lace. My wooden spoon. My china plate with the tulips. The chair my cousin gave me." She was beginning to cry, but she was determined to list every item. "The map my Pappa drew." As she pronounced the words, "my Pappa," the losses she had endured overwhelmed her. Sobbing, but determined to communicate her distress, she finished. "My slippers too. She kept them. She won't give them back."

When she hid her head in her hands, the star-shaped scar on the beige skin she inherited from her mother stood out stark and white. Mrs. Heijn moved swiftly to Nelleke and pushed the still weeping child and the other children toward the exit door. "The children are weary and must be put to bed," she said as a way of explaining Nelleke's outburst. "Thank you, Gentlemen. Good night."

Picking up his magnifier, the Bookkeeper continued his report by describing each child's assets. For Nelleke, he said, "Among her belongings there are a violin, a Gypsy skirt, a bright-colored turban, and about a dozen rolled-up maps. The 300 guilders found on Mr. Stradwijk's body has been invested on the child's behalf and, as you know, will be returned to her with the interest earned when she exits our institution."

"Nelleke's father, Nicolaas Stradwijk, inherited Stradwijk and Son from his own father. The business continues to operate under the direction of the former manager. In addition to Nelleke there is one other heir – her brother, Jacob. At the present time, my assistant and I are working with the family to sort out these assets and guarantee that they are protected for Nelleke's benefit."

Although the child could not identify the only Regent she had previously met, Jos Broekhof certainly recognized her. What's more, he had just learned for the first time that the child's belongings which her aunt and uncle refused to search months earlier when he visited them in Ouderkerk were at this very moment in storage only a short distance down the hall. As a Regent, he could request access to those belongings, although that would be unusual and he would have to give the Bookkeeper an explanation for wanting to see them. What's more, if he were to find his precious missing etching in those belongings, what then? He could certainly not steal it away, even though he had paid for it. Nor could he offer to purchase it. The risk to his reputation would be too dangerous.

Nelleke was the same child, he now realized, who had broken away from the marching orphans last fall and run toward his carriage. Since she was wearing the austere orphan uniform, he did not recognize her as the barefoot, little farm child he had met earlier half a day's journey away. Myriam had seemed momentarily smitten with her – or perhaps just confused seeing her beauty and thinking of Catherina. In any case, Jos wanted to keep the focus on Nelleke and find out all he could.

"Thank you for the excellent report, Doctor Voerman," Jos began, stretching himself up to his full height. "Although it is lamentable that several deaths have occurred, we know that some of the orphans arrive malnourished and that even the best-cared-for child can be lost to us almost with no warning."

Surprised by the reaction in himself his own words brought about, Jos swallowed hard and nearly teared up before continuing.

"I would like to inquire about the unusual scar on the Stradwijk child's hand. Was it there when she arrived?"

The doctor explained the incident, the care administered in the sick room, the attention from the Regentesse, from Isabela, from the Housemother. The child came from a farm where she had spent much time every day outdoors. She was quite hardy. She healed quickly. Although the burn was initially painful, the staff worked to distract her.

"Was she traumatized, do you think?" Jos asked.

"Initially, certainly. But she appeared to enjoy the attention. In fact, when she returned to her regular routine, she showed off the scar to the other orphans who were curious," said the doctor.

The Bookkeeper added that steps were immediately taken after the incident to avoid such an occurrence in the future.

The head Regent cleared his throat in an attempt to move the group to other orders of business, but Jos pressed on.

"And relatives?" he asked. Does the Stradwijk child have relatives nearby? Do they visit?"

The Bookkeeper took some time to search his notes and then reported.

"Our records show that she has been visited three times by a 10-year-old cousin, Willem van Randen. It was he who brought her some of the objects the child spoke of. These were gifts he brought during her convalescence and afterwards as well. As you know, however, children have no access to their personal belongings during their stay. Obviously, the Stradwijk child laments that situation and blames Mrs. Heijn, but Mrs. Heijn is following the orphanage rules. The Van Randen child stopped visiting in the wintertime."

Jos realized he was drawing attention to himself with too many questions about this one child out of hundreds, but he could not hold back from throwing out one more.

"So she does not receive any Sunday visits then and she has not been invited out by anyone in the community?"

"There has been a non-family visitor, Mr. Broekhof. Mrs. Comfrij, the Regentesse who helped nurse Nelleke after the burn incident, visited her again after she recovered and also invited her to her home twice on a Sunday.

"Thank you, Mr. Sterck."

Chapter Twenty-three
Delivery

Pieter Hals wasted little time returning to the girls' gate at the orphanage. A few days after meeting Isabela and Nelleke, he was explaining that he had something to deliver to a young woman named Isabelle.

"I know all the young women by name, Sir, and there is no Isabelle here," said the gatekeeper. Shutting the heavy door, he said, "I suggest you try the other orphanages. Good-day."

Pieter stuck his foot out to stop the full closing of the door. "Perhaps the young lady goes by the name of Isabela, Sir?"

Still cautious, the gatekeeper reopened the door and reached for the wrapped package. "I will see that Isabela receives the package, Sir."

"Thank you," Pieter replied, holding on tightly to the package, "but I must deliver it in person. Can you summon the young lady, please?"

"What is the nature of your mission, Sir, and whom do you represent?"

"The package is a framed drawing that my master, Mr. Van Rijn, sketched of the little orphan, Nelleke. Mr. Van Rijn promised to deliver the finished product. I am a student of the artist. He asked me to complete the errand in his place. He requested that the package be delivered directly to Isabela, who is apparently in charge of Nelleke's care here."

Seeing that the gatekeeper was skeptical, Pieter added, "Perhaps you are not aware, Sir, that Mr. Rembrandt van Rijn is one of the most sought after portraitists in the city. He is paid handsomely for his work by the wealthiest Amsterdam families."

"None of these orphans has a stuiver to pay for such a portrait, Sir. I am instructed to turn away all solicitors from these gates."

Exasperated, Pieter, burst out, "The sketch is a GIFT, Sir. May I speak to someone in authority please? Where is the director of the institution?"

"Very well. I will notify Mrs. Heijn first, Sir."

"And what position does Mrs. Heijn occupy? If she is a cook that will not do."

"No, Sir, Mrs. Heijn is the Housemother for the Girl's Dormitory and I warn you, she keeps a careful eye on them."

"Not so careful, apparently," Pieter thought to himself, "since at least two of them were able to go wandering around the city recently."

"By the way, the name is Pieter Hals," Pieter yelled to the shut gate.

If this Mrs. Heijn were ignorant of Rembrandt's standing in the city, perhaps she might have heard of Pieter's uncles at least?

Standing on the narrow St. Luciensteeg Pieter tried to amuse himself by whistling, then by thinking about how he would approach a drawing of the maids who passed by carrying baskets of eggs, clutching greens or pitchers of milk or a child's hand. Mostly, though, he lost himself in thoughts of Isabela. "Should he ever be allowed to see her, would she appear as beautiful to him as she did the day he met her?" he wondered. He tried to summon her features, her expressions, her gestures, her walk. When ten minutes had passed, he pounded on the door. Another two minutes went by before the gatekeeper returned.

"Mrs. Heijn will see you shortly, Sir. I will show you to the reception area."

Pieter's artist eyes took in everything as he crossed the courtyard behind the gatekeeper. The stone he walked on, the newness of the brick buildings, the pumps for drinking water, the fenced-in play area, the overall feeling of bareness. He could hear young male voices reciting their lessons to the left of the courtyard, but there were no young women's or children's voices that he could detect.

The reception area contained a locked glass cabinet to display what Pieter supposed were gifts the orphanage had received over the years – religious sculptures, two matching silver goblets, a porcelain plate, ceramics. There were no paintings or drawings on the walls. Mrs. Heijn's tardiness in meeting him allowed him to devise a plan that could lead to his spending time in the company of the lovely Isabela.

Finally, a rather severe, unsmiling woman entered the reception room. As she introduced herself – "Nathalie Heijn, Housemother to the Girls' Dormitory. What can I do for you, Sir?" – she examined her visitor's rumpled clothing and poorly cared for boots while noting that they were made of the finest materials.

"I have the pleasure of bearing a special gift – a sketch of a most enchanting orphan by an artist who is rapidly becoming Amsterdam's most famous portraitist, Mr. Rembrandt van Rijn," Pieter said, unconsciously falling into biblical language "and what's more I have come to offer a second future gift directly to the orphanage."

"Are you certain the subject is a resident of the City Orphanage, Sir? The children in our care follow a strict routine. None of them would have had the time to sit for an artist, nor would such an arrangement have been allowed without our permission."

Pieter remembered Isabela's rush to return to the orphanage. He was naïve enough to think that she was uncomfortable in his company, but now he understood. Now he feared that if he revealed the encounter on the promenade, the two girls might be punished in some way.

"There was no sitting. Rembrandt, Mr. Van Rijn, caught sight of two orphans last week apparently out on an errand of some kind," Pieter explained. "He has a keen eye and works very quickly. He also always has his materials with him and at the time was on his way with his students, including me, to set up on the promenade for a morning of practice sketches and lessons. He is gifted at being able to reproduce a likeness quickly. It was obvious from their clothing that they live here. The master asked me to deliver the finished sketch to the older of the two. I overheard the younger one call her Isabela or Isabelle."

"Very well. I will have to see the sketch before giving it to the young lady."

"The master was explicit. "Please place the gift directly in the hands of the older orphan," he instructed. May I show it to both of you at the same time? Then you can decide whether to share it with the younger orphan for whom it is ultimately destined."

Mrs. Heijn sat rigidly. This is why she so rarely gave permission for the girls to venture forth on their own. They attracted attention that could lead to this very situation.

She did not like unpredictability, not being in control. Yet Isabela was seventeen – marriageable age. Until the war with Spain was over, she could not safely return there – even if she wanted to. Perhaps this suitor – and Mrs. H was sure that courtship was the real reason this young man was here – with his silk, leather and imported felt – would be a good match for Isabela and could benefit the orphanage in a way that would reflect positively on her leadership.

Mrs. Heijn rose and summoned a maid who was on her hands and knees scrubbing the hallway floor. "Please bring Isabela here, Grietje. She's in the school room." Then Mrs. H turned her attention to Pieter.

"You mentioned a second gift, Mr. Hals?" she inquired.

"Yes. As a student of the great Rembrandt, I am required, with his guidance, to complete a portrait on my own. I should like to ask for your permission to paint Isabela. The sitting would take place here – wherever you designate. If it meets with your satisfaction, I should then like to donate the painting – perhaps to be hung in this very entrance room, or, if it is deemed of high quality, to be sold with the proceeds benefiting your excellent work here."

Mrs. Heijn did not have time to react as Isabela arrived at that moment. She was surprised to see Pieter with the Housemother, but Pieter smiled and bowed slightly and introduced himself, setting in motion the acting out of a scene as if they were speaking for the first time. "Pieter Hals. A pleasure to meet you, Miss . . . ."

"Calderon. Isabelle Calderon," Isabela said, with a small curtsy, giving the English version of both her names – the way she pronounced them while speaking with anyone outside the orphanage.

"Mr. Hals has a sketch to deliver to us, Isabelle. Apparently the work was done rapidly when his master, Rembrandt, saw you and a little girl orphan pass by on your butter errand last week."

Isabela smiled briefly at Pieter, in recognition that he had re-invented the story of their meeting, possibly to protect her from unpleasant consequences.

"You may show us the sketch now, Mr. Hals," said Mrs. Heijn.

Pieter carefully unwrapped the package to reveal the charming duo in their neat orphan uniforms holding hands, smiling sweetly. As pleased as if he himself had executed the work, Pieter removed the sketch and held up the simple wood frame for their viewing.

Isabela could not help smiling fully now. How wonderful to see that delightful encounter skillfully portrayed once again. It was as she remembered it, but with a few additions. The frightened cow now swam by a windmill and a tree. And there was Pieter's dog, Runt, peering up at Nelleke, hoping to engage her in more active play.

"How interesting that your master was able to capture the child's over-active imagination by simply watching her pass by," Mrs. Heijn remarked, with more than a hint of suspicion.

Isabel spoke up. "It is lovely, Mr. Hals. I'm sure Nelleke will be amused by the sketch. If you will leave his address, I would personally like to send your master a note of appreciation. And thank you for taking the time to deliver it."

Pieter handed the sketch to Isabela. The light touch of his fingers on Isabela's during the exchange and the blushing on Isabela's cheeks did not escape the notice of Mrs. Heijn.

"Give it to me for safekeeping, Isabela. We will place it in storage with Nelleke's other belongings. You see, Mr. Hals, the children are not allowed access to their personal inheritance. Our staff serves as gatekeeper until such time they become adults or leave us for other reasons. The sketch will be waiting for her."

Isabela was crushed both for herself and for the artist. That Nelleke would not see the finished, framed sketch – perhaps for some time – seemed so unfair. The Housemother's decision angered her and gave her the courage to say, "I must return to my duties, Mr. Hals. I will accompany you to the gate."

The distance between the building and the gate felt much too short to the two young people who found themselves walking side by side – alone for the first time, but observed. When they arrived at the gate, Pieter took a notebook from his pocket and scribbled Rembrandt's address on it.

"If you manage to deliver the thank-you in person, Isabelle/Isabela, between the hours of 7:00 AM and 3:00 in the afternoon, I would be most pleased."

Aware of the alert gatekeeper on the other side of the closed gate, Isabela smiled, but said in a matter-of fact tone, "Goodbye, Pieter, and thank you again for the delivery."

Once again on St. Luciensteeg, Pieter felt both elated to have seen Isabela again and saddened that the visit was over so quickly. But he had managed to convince that Housemother to summon her and had come up with the offer to paint Isabela's portrait. What's more, Isabela just might appear at the studio. Surely he would see her again soon.

Meanwhile, he would ponder the many mysteries she evoked: her Dutch was accented. Why two similar first names? Was she English? With her dark hair and eyes, could she be from Spain? Calderon. She had pronounced it with the accent on the first syllable as if it were English, but had she said it with an accent on the last syllable, it would surely be a Spanish last name. With her bearing and poise, she might be from a wealthy, educated family. But why, then, was she working in the orphanage? Was she herself an orphan? How did she end up in this city in that place?

Chapter Twenty-four
Elsje

aving spent several hours the night before recording the dwarf's story in his Strad Journal – the first entry in several months – and knowing he could not give his business the concentration it required without first pursuing that story's implications, Jos dressed quickly, skipped breakfast, and headed for The Knowing Eye. This time, although perhaps unwise if Elsje's husband were the criminal Rudolf said he was, Jos did not ask Karel to accompany him. He wished to reassure the couple, not intimidate or accuse them. He wanted them on his side.

Even at that early hour, a dozen men were playing cards and drinking. Rather than make a scene, Jos decided to go around the tavern and approach it from the back. He picked his way around six large barrels of ale that took up most of the space in the tiny courtyard along with a privy, a few chickens, caged live pigeons, and a tub full of grease-smeared platters.

The back door was open and he could hear a woman's voice singing a ribald song. As he approached it, the smell of herring and baking bread reminded him that his stomach was empty. But he did not come here as a patron.

He knocked and stepped inside the kitchen. Elsje stopped her singing abruptly and turned from her kneading. The fragile Elsje whom Nicolaas knew had become a sturdy, self-assured woman.

When Gerard Levens walked by Elsje ten years earlier as she sat curled up and shivering in a doorway, he had just inherited a small, nonfunctioning tavern. Once a thriving family business when both his parents ran it together, the tavern's clientele drifted off after his mother died and had been completely neglected during the two years of Gerard's father's fatal illness. It was filled with trash left behind by tramps who had broken in to escape the cold and broken down the door and window frames to use as firewood for small fires which they set throughout the structure. Mice built their nests among the refuse. The dying man insisted that his teenage son finish his schooling, that Gerard fulfill his father's dream by attending the University of Leiden and becoming a scholar. He did not want him to repeat his own life serving ale to hooligans.

But the abandonment of the business combined with the medical costs of caring for the old man had bankrupted the family. With no funds to speak of, Gerard could not enter university and simultaneously care for two younger sisters. His only hope, he felt, was to re-establish the tavern as an income-producing establishment. His sisters would not set foot in the filthy site. He could not face the task alone and he could barely pay anyone to help him.

When he saw the fragile woman in the doorway, he walked right by her, thinking "There's someone who is even worse off than I am." A moment later he returned. With her head resting on her knees, she might be asleep, he thought. "Miss. Miss. Would you like some work? If you can help me, I can give you a bed to sleep in."

She lifted her head and glared up at him. He was stunned at how young she appeared, how pale her face was against her reddish-blond hair.

"I ain't no whore, Mister. Beat it, now."

He took a few steps away, but again turned back. He told her his dilemma. Again he asked for her assistance.

"I can't pay you much – not at first, but once the tavern is up and running, I can offer you more."

Elsje studied the man and stood up shakily. She nodded warily and indicated that he should lead the way and she would follow behind.

First he took her to the home he shared with his sisters. They were at school and the house was empty, but he did not invite her in. She might misinterpret such a gesture and run off.

"Wait here a moment," he said, returning soon with a bowl of last night's pork stew. Standing on the street, she drank the full bowl, hardly taking a breath between swallows. Following behind him to the tavern, she ripped the bread he had given her in her teeth, barely chewing it in her rush to fill her stomach. Walking ahead of her, turning his head around every so often to be sure she was still there, Gerard pushed a wheelbarrow with brooms and cleaning supplies.

Elsje surprised Gerard with the verve and energy she displayed, partnering with him to clean up, haul trash, and whitewash. Gerard designed and Elsje distributed notices about the re-opening of The Knowing Eye. Once customers began to return, her experience serving in a tavern also proved useful. Their business partnering turned into romance. They married and Gerard moved her into his home. The younger sisters resented Elsje, though, and looked down on her.

It was not until Elsje was pregnant with their first child that she told him that she had given birth before. She showed him the playing card. Gerard was livid that she had suffered so much before he found her. He stalked Nicolaas at times, but was never sure what exactly he would say if they met face to face.

After a few months he decided to confront Nicolaas and went to Stradwijk and Son to seek him out. Nicolaas's father told him his son had run off with a Gypsy woman and her family. "Why couldn't he have married a fine Dutch woman like his mother?" the father bemoaned. He hoped never to see Nicolaas again.

By the time Gerard's and Elsje's second boy was born, Gerard had purchased the shop next door and turned it into a home for his growing family. Elsje was relieved to be away from her spoiled, unhelpful sisters-in-law.

When her boys started school, Elsje wanted to participate in their lessons. Gerard taught Elsje to read. The boys, enjoying the role reversal, shared with her what they had learned each day.

She had a husband who cared for her, two strong sons, a business to look after. Yet every time she heard an infant cry, the sharp memory of her own firstborn gripped and saddened her. She would stop whatever she was doing and listen to the sound of her newborn's whimpering as if the child were laying in that basket right at her feet at that very moment. The most tortuous part of the memory was the fading of the baby's pleas – fainter with each step she took away from him – until the cries disappeared altogether.

"Mr. Broekhof, I believe? What can I do for you at this hour?"

Her clean bonnet hugged the still reddish-blond hair in place. Her short-sleeved blouse revealed muscled arms strong enough to drag a drunken lout out her tavern door. Sweat ran down her neck and into the space between her breasts. An apron that may have been fresh an hour ago was smeared with grease and blood.

Although Elsje suspected Jos's early appearance had something to do with the dwarf's allegations, she had her own reasons beyond shear curiosity for greeting him pleasantly, although guardedly. Her husband might return at any moment. He was a suspicious man with a temper. She wanted to hear what this Broekhof had to say, determine if he might be of use to her, and send him on his way.

"I saw you were intrigued with the imagined stories the dwarf subjected you to yesterday, Sir. If you've come here with accusations, you're a fool. Rudolf is a beggar by profession, but an entertainer at heart. The better and wilder and more fantastical his songs and stories, the more people gather round and the more coins find their way into his pockets. He has a gift for linking his malicious gossip to specific individuals, rarely using their names, but giving just enough description so that his audience surmises who he's talking about. Mischief, is what it is, Mr. Broekhof. Lies. Truth has nothing to do with it."

"Let me assure you, Madam, that I am not interested in solving any mysterious murder that took place years ago. My concern is not with the murderer or his motivation. I am here because of my business relationship with the murdered artist referred to in Rudolf's song."

"Are you referring to Mr. Nicolaas Stradwijk, Sir?"

"I am. May I explain?"

Elsje placed a small mug of ale and a plate of herring before Jos, then moved the kneading board around so that she could continue to work while facing Jos and study him as he spoke. While listening carefully, she pulled, pounded, and rolled the dough, ground cinnamon over it, sprinkled it with sugar, placed it in three large bread pans, and put the pans in the hot oven.

While he continued, she picked up the sharpest knife in the room and began preparing yesterday's herring. She would fry them up and serve them to the early customers in her front room before her husband brought a fresh batch from the fish market.

Instinctively, Jos moved his chair away from Elsje and her knife while explaining as he had so many times about the six etchings and his quest for the already paid for seventh; how he believed it was possible that, at the time of the murder, Nicolaas was returning in order to turn over his prized work to its new owner.

"I simply wish to inquire if either you or your husband ever saw the etching, saw it lying by the side of the canal perhaps that night, or later saw it in the hands of a thief who might have sold it."

"I understand what you're saying, Mr. Broekhof. You believe the dwarf's story. You believe my husband killed Nicolaas Stradwijk because of the coarse way he treated me when I was a young and vulnerable woman with no family, no home. You believe he may have taken your precious work of art, may have it still or may have sold it. Is that what you think, Mr. Broekhof?"

"I am a grain merchant, Madam, not a member of the police, not an informant. I am merely trying to complete a collection that is important to me. And I am willing to pay anyone who finds the missing and final piece of that collection. Once it is in my hands, I will ask no further questions."

"Let me tell you in no uncertain terms, then, Sir. My husband hated Nicolaas, it's true, hated him for abandoning me when I was going to have his child, for what I went through to bear that child on my own; begging, some days nearly starving, cold, for all that happened to me before I met my husband. I, however, cannot fault Nicolaas entirely. He too was very young and, as I've told my husband many times, I was never able to admit to Nicolaas that I was with child. I was too ashamed."

"But that does not mean my husband killed the man. He did not. He would never do such a thing."

"And the etching?"

"I know nothing about it. I never saw anything such as you are describing. This I can tell you. Since I see that it means so much to you that you are willing to pay for it, I will certainly ask my husband if he has seen it and we will both inquire casually among our patrons and suppliers. What I will never tell my husband is your suspicion that he was the assailant and that it was Rudolf who put that idea into your head. Who knows what he would do to either of you.

"But since you are so enthralled with Nicolaas, the artist, there is something I want more than the money you're willing to pay for such a find. I too have been searching. For ten years I have been searching. Not knowing where to turn, how I would feed my baby. I left him in the middle of the night – only hours old – on the front stoop of Stradwijk and Son. After wandering all night, my mind cleared somewhat. I realized that I had acted impulsively. Surely God would look after a young mother and her baby, but God might send me to Hell for my act. I wanted my baby back. I wanted him desperately. Just before dawn, I scurried back to that house. The basket in which I had left the child was no longer there. Frightened, hungry, and deeply ashamed that I had abandoned him, unwilling to face Nicolaas or his family, I ran away."

Elsje washed her hands in a washbowl. After shaking her hands in the air to dry them, she reached into the bodice of her dress, pulled out half a playing card, soiled and shabby, but with its magnificent drawing still intact. Elsje held it up and then gave it to Jos so he could have a closer look. A demon-like snake with a long forked tongue, one large human eye, and thick black lashes stared threateningly at those who took their chances with the Lord's judgment.

"At that time Nicolaas was designing, printing, and selling playing cards. The cards were in demand. I remember clearly what one player said one night, holding a winning deck in his hand. 'Nice cards. Beautiful, in fact. Very alluring. Mysterious.' I realized those words described my feelings for Nicolaas. A good-looking, alluring, mysterious young man who paid attention to me. One night when I was cleaning up, I found this card – separated from the pack. I kept it. Months later, just before I stole a blanket and basket for my baby, I took the knife I had used to cut the umbilical cord – yes, I gave birth alone in an alley – and cut the card in two. I left the one half in the basket with my baby. I kept the other. I learned soon after that Nicolaas had run off with a Gypsy woman. There was no child with them."

"I can't let go of the thought that whoever raised my child – if he's alive – kept the half card, perhaps even showed it to him. I look at every ten-year-old boy I pass on Amsterdam's streets, wondering if that boy could be mine – if maybe he even has the card in his pocket. All I want is to know that he's safe. If his life is good, I would leave him alone. If he's become a beggar, I would bring him home to become the older brother of my boys."

"Let's call it an information exchange, Mr. Broekhof. I remain alert for news of your etching. You look out for Nicolaas's card and for his child – my child."

Chapter Twenty-five
Doll, Hoop, Custard

fter learning about the Stradwijk orphan's friendship with the family of the Regentesse, Sofie Comfrij, Jos was alarmed. Could he compete with Mrs. Comfrij for the little free time the orphan was allowed with visitors – Sunday afternoons? Perhaps the child would worm her way into the heart of that entire family, even find a home there. Any hope he had of somehow completing his collection through Nicolaas's heir would be dashed.

Mrs. Comfrij had probably first taken an interest in the child while she was recovering from the burn accident, but had then become attached to her, he surmised. And why not? The child was beguiling and fearless. Judging by last night's outburst, she knew how to speak up for herself in adult company. Jos felt intimidated by the little girl's outspokenness, but perhaps Mrs. Comfrij found this quality appealing. Would Myriam agree to have such a child to Sunday dinner? Would the child behave herself or would she be shrill and demanding, thus destroying any hope Jos might have of future contact with her?

The Friday morning after the Regent's Wednesday meeting, Jos approached Myriam with the idea of a visit. At first he tried appealing to Myriam's sympathy, explaining the frightening and painful incident that occurred the very night she was left at the orphanage, caused no doubt by her confusion and upset at being abandoned.

"That is dreadful, Jos. But, there are hundreds of children in the orphanage who have experienced upsetting losses. Why this particular child?" she asked.

Jos was taken aback, not by the nature of the question, but by the fact that Myriam asked any question at all. He realized that since Catherina's death she had displayed no curiosity about anything. Before she could lapse back into her dreary, vacant self, Jos quickly moved on.

"Do you recall one Sunday while we were returning from church last fall, my dear? An orphan child broke away from the group and ran toward our carriage. She wanted to pet our horses. Before she was reprimanded and dragged back into line, you reached out and touched her cheek. This is this same child. Her name is Nelleke."

"I'm not sure, Jos. A little girl. Here. With us. A little girl who is not our own sweet Catherina. I'm not sure I could. It would make me too sad."

Myriam retreated to her desk and began writing a letter. Absorbed and comforted by the ritual, she dedicated to the paper, the quill pen, the ink, her slow, careful calligraphy, the sprinkled rose water, the neat folding and addressing – all the attention she no longer bestowed on her husband, sons, or household. She then summoned Anna and asked her to deliver the note.

Jos was putting on his boots when Anna passed by and out the front door, the note fluttering in her hand. Angry and suspicious, he returned to Myriam's desk, but she was no longer there. He found her in the kitchen, smiling to herself, wrapped in a warm shawl, slipping into a pair of dirt-covered gloves.

"Myriam, if you are planning to somehow find additional funds to pay that rascal Mennes for more garden objects, I must tell you that I will not allow it. If the note Anna is delivering is written to that man, I will chase after her and rip it to pieces."

Myriam looked at Jos for a moment while he squirmed and turned redder.

"My dear husband, I assure you the garden is complete now. Did I not show you the third and final small pine? I will add nothing else for now, but I will maintain it. The note was written to my sister. As you well know, we correspond several times a day."

That same evening, as Myriam headed for bed and Jos for his study, Myriam turned to him and said casually, "My sister recommended that I agree to your request, Jos."

Excited, overjoyed, disbelieving, impatient, Jos took the candle from Myriam and placed it on a hall table. Enveloping her tenderly in his arms, he covered her face, nose, and cheeks with kisses. When he held her tighter against him, moved his hand toward her buttocks and tried to kiss her mouth, she turned her head away, wiggled from him, picked up the lit candle and held it between them.

"Jos, whatever are you thinking? I've been quite clear that I am no longer interested in sharing this sort of activity with you."

"But you said your sister recommended it. I know how you rely on your older sister for advice. I am indebted to her for encouraging you to return to your wifely duty."

"Your request, Jos. The one you made this morning. You may invite the orphan child for Sunday supper. I agree to one visit. Good night."

The following Sunday, after church service, the horse-drawn carriage of the Broekhofs arrived at the main entrance to the City Orphanage on the Kalverstraat. Although there was a slight drizzle, families filled the street, strolling, apparently in no hurry to return home. As Jos helped Myriam step down onto the cobblestones, he instructed Daniel and Samuel to wait in the carriage. When Myriam tucked her arm under his, he turned to look at her. She was wearing her best lace cap. None of the usual strands of hair stuck out haphazardly. Instead they were all tucked into the cap and the hair visible above her forehead was neatly combed. Myriam was smiling, but not that usual far-away smile inspired by conversations only she could hear. This time she was smiling directly at Jos.

Myriam stopped and caressed the round top of the donation box, placed to capture the notice – and hopefully also the contributions – of generous passers-by. "May I have a coin please, Jos?" she asked. They smiled at each other as they heard the coin clink – a quick, happy sound as if the coin were greeting the community of fellow coins waiting for it. As they moved down the passageway that would take them to their guest, they passed under an archway carved with the images of boy and girl orphans in their red-and-black uniforms. When Myriam looked up and read "As you are blessed by God, comfort us out of your surplus," she allowed herself a feeling of adventure, her certainty and excitement growing with each step.

The couple gave their name to the gatekeeper who was expecting them.

Just inside the building, Housemother was explaining to one orphan that she had been invited out to Sunday dinner.

"Oh, what a happy day, Mother. To Mrs. Comfrij's? I do so adore her daughter and did you know she has three cats? Their names are . . . ."

"No, it is not Mrs. Comfrij. Mrs. Comfrij is very busy these days planning the wedding of her daughter."

"Is it Willem, then? My cousin?"

"No, Nelleke, it is not your aunt and uncle either. It's one of the Regents to whom you were introduced this week. Mr. Broekhof. He has a wife and two sons. Nelleke, do not talk all the time and do not ask lots of questions, do you hear me? If you do not behave, you will not be invited back."

Just as Nelleke opened her mouth to promise she would be good, the door opened.

When Nelleke saw the woman with the sad eyes again, she felt a stab of shyness. If Isabela were there, she would have clung to her and whispered, "I don't want to go." But Isabela was not there. Housemother did not like to be touched and she did not tolerate disobedience.

"Here is our young lady," Jos, said in a jolly tone. "Nelleke, I believe? May I introduce you to my wife, Mrs. Broekhof."

When Housemother nudged her, Nelleke, curtsied slightly and said, "Good day, Mrs. Broekhof."

Myriam nodded, smiled, and took Nelleke's hand. "We will return the child by 3:00 in the afternoon for rest, Bible reading, and evening meal, as you instructed, Mrs. Heijn."

Once Nelleke was introduced to Samuel and Daniel and settled into the carriage next to Myriam, Nelleke asked,

"May I touch your glove, please? I remember how very soft it is."

"Perhaps you would like to try it on? asked Myriam, carefully removing it.

"Oh, yes. Could I really?"

Myriam fit the glove on Nelleke's hand, trying to tuck each of her small fingers and her little thumb into the adult glove. Nelleke stroked the glove as if it were a kitten. She lifted her hand and shook it. The loose fingers that were much too long waved back and forth. When Nelleke said, "They look like puppets," both she and Myriam laughed. Still shaking the loose fingers, Nelleke turned to the boys behind her and, imitating a woman's voice, said "Good afternoon, young sirs." Everyone laughed.

The light mood continued as the family reacted with smiles and amusement to Nelleke's chatter. "Oh, look, there's a goose. I had a duck named Langenek. I had to leave him behind. I didn't even get to say good-bye. This goose is a mother. She has – one, two, three, four – ducklings."

"Goslings, I believe they're called," corrected Mrs. Broekhof.

"Goslings? Not ducklings? Goslings. What a funny word," Nelleke responded, storing it in her mind for future use.

"Mrs. Broekhof, do you know what number comes after 79? I think it's 80, but I'm not sure. Oh, there's the home of Pieter Hals. He's a student of Master Rembrandt, you know. He's painting Isabela's portrait. Isabela has sat for him twice. He would like for her to sit for him more often, but she has duties."

"Is Isabela an orphan?" Myriam asked.

"Yes, but she's a big one," Nelleke explained. "She's a Big Sister to us. She sings to us in another language."

When they arrived at their home, Jos helped Nelleke and Myriam out of the carriage.

The boys jumped out and ran to the door, anxious for some of Anna's cooking. Nelleke, suddenly lonely, watched the coachman drive away with the horses. Myriam noticed and quickly distracted her.

"Samuel and Daniel, will you show Nelleke where to leave her shoes and where to wash up? I've left two books in the parlor she might enjoy. Samuel, perhaps you could read to her while Anna and I finish preparing the meal."

Daniel helped Nelleke remove her shoes and place them on the black-and-white tile just inside the entrance. Then he led Nelleke to the wash basin and brought over the stool that had been Catherina's. Nelleke needed only one step to reach it, though, whereas his sister had needed two steps. Nelleke was older than Catherina, then, he thought. Closer to his age. Maybe she could be trusted with his toy ship.

Samuel settled Nelleke down on one of the most comfortable chairs in the family salon. Nelleke tried to remember what Housemother had told her. She sat straight in the chair and straightened her skirts, her feet together and dangling. She resisted the urge to swing them back and forth.

Samuel sat on the floor beside her and gave her a choice: Which book did she want to read first? Nelleke pointed with her scarred hand. "The cat book, please. We have a cat at the orphanage. I named him Straw. He wanted the bird in my apron pocket and made me fall down the stairs. That's how I got this scar."

"I see," said Daniel. "It's pretty on you, actually. Like a diamond."

"What's a diamond?" asked Nelleke.

"It's a jewel. The most expensive you can buy."

"What color is it?"

"It's clear, like glass, but it sparkles."

"Do you have one?"

"No. Women sometimes wear diamonds in their ears or on a necklace, but men don't."

"Will you give me one then?"

"Maybe some day. Meanwhile you have a prettily shaped one with you all the time right there on your hand."

"Samuel, I want to show Nelleke my toy sailing ship," Daniel said, bursting into the room.

"No. We're just starting to read the book," his brother replied with irritation.

"My ship is much more interesting. Don't you think so Nelleke?"

"Mother told me to read to her, Daniel. Go away. Play with the ship yourself."

"Boys," Myriam called. "Don't fight over our guest. Bring her to the table now please."

The family of four, and Nelleke, stood behind their chairs while Jos read from the Bible and said grace. With the enticing smells of the pea soup and sausage in front of her right at nose level, it was difficult for Nelleke to keep her eyes closed during the prayer. Finally, they all said "Amen," and sat down. Jos helped Myriam and Nelleke move their chairs forward.

"I like having my own bowl," said Nelleke between mouthfuls. "At the orphanage we always share. Sometimes Bernadien grabs before I have a chance."

"Here at our house, you may have your own plate, Nelleke – every time you visit," said Myriam, "and as much food as you would like."

"Sweets too?"

"I think Anna may have a surprise dessert for us. Let's wait and see."

Myriam rose to clear the soup bowls as Anna arrived with a platter of lamb, greens and carrots.

Each boy reached for a piece of bread and dipped it into the gravy. Nelleke did the same, but when she struggled with cutting the lamb, Samuel helped her cut it.

"Do you know my cousin, Willem?" Nelleke asked. "He's about your age."

"I know a Willem who has twin brothers. Is he your cousin?"

"Yes. Yes. Dirck and Otto. They are my cousins too."

"Why don't you live with them then?" asked Daniel.

Myriam shook her head at Daniel, but she did not change the subject.

Nelleke was quiet. Then she said, "My Aunt Elsbeth is too busy with three boys."

Besides, I don't think she likes me. When I was little, I used to play hiding games in her cupboards. She scolded me and called me a wild Gypsy child. Jacob and I went to live with my Aunt Griet instead. I don't know why Aunt Griet sent me away."

Myriam then spoke quickly to prevent Nelleke from slipping further into a brooding state.

"Anna, is our flan ready now?" Myriam called to the cook.

"Mmm, I taste cinnamon and cloves," Nelleke said. Savoring the taste, she ate two bowls full of the sweet gooey concoction.

As the meal ended, Samuel asked his mother if he and Daniel could play with Nelleke outside on the street. Myriam agreed, but warned them to watch her carefully.

Once outside, the boys took turns rolling their hoop. They gave Nelleke the task of counting to see which boy could keep it going the longest before it fell. They had attached metal disks to the inside of the hoop, so that it made a light jingling sound with every turn.

She soon tired of her sedentary assignment, though, and of the boys' squabbling.

"Let me try it. May I please?"

Samuel showed her how to hold the stick and where the best place was on the hoop to hit it to keep it rolling upright. The hoop was as tall as she was. He also pointed out that if she got that far, there was a cobblestone that stuck up a little from the rest. If the hoop hit that protruding cobblestone, it would bounce, roll away and fall flat. If she could guide the hoop around it, she could keep it going longer, but that would require skill.

Samuel patiently held the hoop for her and picked it up every time it fell. After many tries, she was able to keep it going for a few seconds. She was nervous about that sticking-up stone, but she never got that far. Her long skirts wrapped around her legs and tripped her, leaving her sprawled face down.

Samuel and Daniel ran to pick her up and discovered her crying, with blood flowing from her nose. Sheepishly, guiltily, they led her back into the house and into the kitchen where Anna and Myriam cleaned her up as best they could. She had a scratch under her left eye. Myriam gave her an old doll of Catherina's to hold. The painted eyes on the porcelain head stared fixedly, but the body, dressed in clothes that resembled Mrs. Broekhof's, was soft and comforting. Nelleke held it against her chest the way she had seen Aunt Griet hold Frans when he was small. "Thank you, Mrs. Broekhof. We can't keep dolls and toys at the orphanage, you know. They're in our belongings box. We only get them when we leave there."

"If you like this doll, I'll keep it for you at our house," Myriam said, kneeling down to speak directly to the upset child. "Then it will always be here for you when you visit."

"I'm sorry I fell down. I was trying to be a good girl."

"You are a good girl," Myriam assured her. "And a proper guest. We should not have let you play that rough game. The boys are older and used to playing. We'll find a better game for you next time. Would you like to visit us again?"

"Oh, yes, please. Thank you, Mrs. Broekhof."

When Nelleke spontaneously reached out to Myriam and put her head on her shoulder, Myriam was moved to tears, not only by the memories of holding her own little girl, but also by the surprise that she could feel sympathy and fondness for someone else's child.

It was time to return to the orphanage. Jos was ready to walk Nelleke back, but Myriam insisted on going with him to explain and apologize for the mishap. Nelleke walked between them, subdued and weary, still carrying the doll. When they reached the Kalverstraat gate, Nelleke again embraced Myriam and handed her the doll. "Good-bye, Mrs. Broekhof," she said shyly. "Mr. Broekhof."

As the three of them passed through the gate, Isabela was waiting. Nelleke ran to her and began chattering about her day. The Broekhofs went in the direction of the Housemother's office.

Chapter Twenty-six
Overnight

"**M**rs. Broekhof. I'm ready to go back now. Isabela is waiting for me. I know she is. I miss her. Bernadien too."

As she pulled on the maroon velvet curtains that closed off the Broekhofs' box bed, Nelleke's pleas became louder and more strident.

"I'm scared. Mrs. Broekhof. Mr. Broekhof."

Jos rolled over and groaned in his sleep.

The evening had gone so well. The Broekhofs had been granted permission for Nelleke to stay overnight with them for the first time, to go to church with them in the morning, and then accompany them on an afternoon outing to a farm.

With each visit, Myriam seemed to blossom. Until he noticed the color in her cheeks, Jos had not realized how pale she had become. Until he saw her wearing a new cap, blouse, jacket, and skirt, he had not acknowledged to himself how shabby she had been for months. He delighted in the return of her smiles and her energy, in her renewed interest in her boys and, tentatively, in Jos himself. Myriam also took pleasure in planning each of Nelleke's visits and knowing how Nelleke loved animals, she was especially looking forward to the farm outing.

When Myriam gave Jos a quick kiss on the cheek two nights ago, he was buoyed with hope, thinking that perhaps she might return to his arms. When she turned her back to him as usual, he knew he had to give her still more time. But he did make a decision.

He would share with her – in small steps depending on her reaction – his obsession.

This very night he told her about the six etchings and mentioned briefly his attempts to obtain the seventh. He did not tell her anything about their nature or that the artist was Nelleke's father. He said the etchings told a story – a joyful, amusing story of a couple who loved each other. Because the ending of the story was missing, he felt sad, even a sense of longing. Could he show her the first etching? The one he had labeled "Monday?"

"Of course," Myriam had replied. "I have always admired your taste in art, dear Jos."

"Wait here." Jos requested.

When he returned, Myriam was sitting up in bed, expectantly. First Jos showed her "MAANDAG" in his handwriting on the back. Then he turned the etching over. Myriam gave a little cry and then took it from him so she could study it. Jos held the candle closer. There was the young man sitting in a wooden tub of soapy water with his hairy bare chest and muscular shoulders drawn so perfectly that Myriam felt an impulse to reach out and caress them. The man's head was bent forward so that his face was not visible. The tips of the thick hair on his head reached into the water. In the background was the outline of his pants thrown over a chair. A fully dressed young woman leaned over the man and massaged his shoulders.

"A private, sweet, quiet moment, isn't it, Jos? I like it. May I see the others?"

"That is enough for tonight, my sweet. I will share the others with you in due time."

Myriam knew he was teasing her. She was curious, but she would be patient. She kissed him on the cheek again and they both fell asleep. Jos had placed the etching propped on a table against a wall, so that they could admire it when they awoke.

Until tonight, whenever she was with the family, Nelleke had always worn the black- and-red orphanage uniform. Because she would sit with them in church tomorrow and spend the entire day with them, Myriam had new clothes made for her – a sprightly new bonnet held in place with silver pins; a white blouse with lace around the collar and sleeves; a full dark skirt; and leather boots that came just above her ankle. And most importantly – her own pair of soft gloves just like Myriam's. Together they had laid out all the clothes so they would be ready for dressing before church the next day.

To prepare Catherina's room for Nelleke, Myriam had put away in the cabinet all of her daughter's clothes and toys. Lovingly, dwelling on each piece, Myriam placed Catherina's favorite – the dollhouse with its hand-carved furniture and embroidered linens, with the small iron oven, the fireplace and the miniature people – up high where Nelleke could not reach them. Each item contained a precious memory and Myriam was not yet ready to share those memories or objects with this new child.

After Myriam had shown Nelleke the new clothes and Nelleke had delightedly tried on the gloves made especially for her small hands, Myriam read her a story and kissed her good-night, promising a fun day tomorrow seeing the kinds of animals Nelleke enjoyed – horses, cows, sheep, chickens, ducks.

But Nelleke had never slept in a room all by herself. As an infant and toddler she slept in the round – mostly outdoors or in a makeshift tent – near a fire with her mother, grandparents, aunts, uncles, cousins, and dogs nearby. Often she would sleep between her parents, snuggled up tight between, feeling their warmth, feeling safe.

Later, after her parents died, she slept under Uncle Johannes and Aunt Griet's high bed wrapped around Jacob. During the cold winters, the family slept on a second-floor ledge, warmth rising from the animals on the first floor of the house just below them.

At the orphanage she slept in a bed with two or three other little girls and Isabela was always close by – just on the other side of the narrow room.

Being alone in a bed in a room – even a pretty one with blue lace curtains and a warm quilt with embroidered flowers, even in fresh-smelling clean night clothes – was frightening and lonely for her.

Myriam pulled back the curtain. From her position in the raised bed, she was looking directly into the tear-stained face of her little guest. For this first overnight, Myriam had ordered for Nelleke a sleeping dress – full-length, cotton with matching bonnet. Nelleke was wearing this nightgown now and clinging to the doll she always played with during her day visits, but she was dragging her orphan outfit behind her.

Myriam slipped down off the bed, draped the orphan clothing over her own arm, took the child's hand, and led her back to Catherina's room.

"You're spending the night with our family – here in our house, Nelleke, remember?" Myriam said, as she tucked the reluctant child back into the bed and sat down beside her.

"What did we say we would do together tomorrow?"

"Go to church together."

"Yes, and then what?"

"Wear my new gloves."

"Yes. We'll wear our matching gloves. Go to a farm. See the animals. Won't that be fun?"

"Yes. Thank you, Mrs. Broekhof. But I can't sleep here."

"It's the middle of the night, Nelleke. Mr. Broekhof is sleeping. Daniel and Simon are sleeping. Anna is sleeping. All of Amsterdam is sleeping. The gates to the city are closed. The night watchmen are making their rounds. Shall I sing to you?"

"Can you sing in Isabela's language?"

"I'm not sure what language Isabela sings in, but I can sing to you in French. A lullaby in French is called '*une berceuse.*' Shall I?"

"Yes, please, Mrs. Broekhof."

When Myriam began singing, Nelleke's eyes were as open and curious as if it were noon.

"*Fais dodo, Colas, mon petit frère.*»
Fais dodo, t'auras du lolo.
Maman est en haut, qui fait du gâteau.»

« I understood, Maman,» Nelleke said, fighting her drooping eyes.

"That's right. The child's mother is upstairs making a cake. The child will get some of the cake in the morning after a good night's sleep.»

"My mother sang to me. I sort of remember. But I didn't get cake."

"*Papa est en bas, qui fait du chocola . . . .*»

As Myriam's voice dropped to a whisper, she finished the *berceuse.*

"*Fais dodo, Colas, mon petit frère.*
Fais dodo, t'auras du lolo.»

Now, looking at the sleeping child in her daughter's bed, it was Myriam's face that was streaked with tears. Seeing her there brought a flood of memories of Catherina. Her feelings about Nelleke were terribly ambiguous. Her obligation to the child extended through tomorrow afternoon. After that, she just wasn't sure. But the child was in her care tonight and she did not want her to wake up frightened. Myriam tiptoed back to her own room, retrieved a pillow and blanket and fell asleep on the floor rug beside Nelleke.

The city had recently built a footbridge over the Heerengracht within view of the Broekhof home. It was a gracefully arched brick bridge with sides of circled iron painted a shiny black. Given the Dutch propensity for utilitarian, no-nonsense public works, the ironwork was surprisingly decorative. Being able to move quickly from one side of the canal to the other made Myriam's and Anna's daily marketing easier. It shortened the distance and time needed to lug the heavy baskets.

Just before dawn, Myriam saw the bridge in her dreams. At first it seemed empty as she admired it in the early morning mist. Then she noticed movement. A child was moving to the other side – away from Myriam. When the mist lifted, Myriam could see that the child was Catherina. She seemed to have grown. Her head could be seen above the sides of the bridge, framed by the ironwork.

Thrilled to see her child again, Myriam tried to run after her. She was convinced that she must reach Catherina while she was still on the bridge, before she set foot on the opposite side. Before she could catch up, Catherina stopped and waved at her mother – a jaunty, triumphant wave that seemed to say, "Look, Mamma, I can do this all by myself." Then Catherina descended the bridge, stepped down onto the street, and disappeared into the busy crowds. The city had suddenly awakened.

Myriam felt a sudden fear for her child. She was too little to go wandering alone. She would be lost. But when Myriam tried to run faster, she seemed to be frozen in place. Panic gripped her. Then terror woke her.

At first she could not remember why she was lying on the floor. Then she remembered and looked over at Nelleke. Even curled up and sleeping she looked so much bigger than Catherina. The two were nothing alike either. Not in appearance or in temperament. Catherina was so demure, so content in her quiet way to imitate her mother's activities.

Nelleke, on the other hand, was boisterous, demanding, exuberant – sometimes ridiculously so . . . and. Myriam's chest heaved as she realized what word described Nelleke best – alive. She was so very much... alive.

Now Myriam understood that she had made an error in acquiescing to these visits. The day had not yet begun and she already felt fatigued at the thought of meeting this child's needs for an entire day. She would waken Jos and tell him that he must return Nelleke to the orphanage immediately. They must cancel their plans for the day. She did not want to see this child ever again. When Nelleke stirred and held Catherina's doll closer, Myriam felt something akin to rage – at herself, at this... how had Nelleke referred to herself? At this "Gypsy child." Whatever had she been thinking? That this child could ever replace her own sweet Catherina?

Nelleke sat upright and greeted Myriam. She never needed time to transition between sleeping and waking.

"Good morning, Mrs. Broekhof. How are you today?"

Myriam did not answer.

Then, as if they were continuing a previous conversation, Nelleke said, "I was wondering about your family's last name, Mrs. Broekhof. It must have a lot of letters in it. I wonder if I could ever learn to make all those letters. Do you think you could teach me some day? Mrs. Broekhof, would you please draw the first letter on my back?" Nelleke turned around and waited expectantly.

Slowly, Myriam approached. She smoothed Nelleke's nightdress over her back as if she were stretching out a blank canvas. She could feel the heat from the child's body through the cloth. She could sense how hard Nelleke was concentrating. When she swept Nelleke's long ringlets to one side, she uncovered tight spirals springing along the little girl's creamy neck. The tendrils resembled the curly pattern on the bridge in her dream. With her index finger, Myriam made a straight line from Nelleke's neck to her waist. Then she added two "u's" on their sides on top of one another, attached to the right side of the line.

Nelleke turned and beamed. She began clapping with delight.

"It's a 'B,' isn't it, Mrs. Broekhof? The family name begins with a 'B.' Oh, I just knew it. I was so sure."

Nelleke was ready to leap down off the bed and go dancing around the room with the doll. She smiled at Myriam, expecting to see her excitement mirrored back to her. Instead Nelleke saw that same expression Myriam had the first time she met her – that time when Nelleke broke away from the orphans to pet the horse. This time she noticed the tears in Myriam's eyes.

Nelleke knew what to do about tears. When she was very little, if she cut her knee on a sharp rock or when villagers sometimes ran after her family calling them names, someone near her always scooped her up and held her. She did the same for Jacob. And then there was Isabela – the expert at dispelling tears.

You put your arms around the person. You rest your cheek against theirs. You stay like that until the person begins to move away a little. That means the sadness has lifted.

When Jos looked in the room to summon them for church, he saw two people on their knees – the child on the bed, the woman on the floor, both in white night dresses and caps. Their heads were on the same level and they were locked in an embrace.

* * *

Every time they passed a cow or sheep, Nelleke would ask, "Is this the one?" "Not yet," Jos would answer. "The farm we're visiting is much larger."

Finally, less than one hour's carriage ride from Amsterdam's outer walls, they stopped. Nelleke counted three windmills, two ponds, and six buildings surrounded by flat, low-lying peat bogs, lush green fields with forests beyond.

"I see their house," Nelleke said, "but it's so much bigger than Aunt Griet's and Uncle Johannes's and bigger than Dirck's and Sebastiaan's too. How many children do they have?"

A man and woman came to greet them. One of their sons took the horse and carriage.

"Hello. I'm Mr. Van Bast and this is Mrs. Van Bast," the man, said, shaking hands with Jos, Daniel, and Simon. His wife lowered her head a bit and curtsied slightly.

"We have twelve children, Miss," Mr. Van Bast continued. "You will meet some of them. Wouter and Gerbrand are expecting you. After we've served you a drink, they'll show you how they make clogs." He gave a little chuckle. With twelve growing children, it's easier for us to make our own shoes than to buy them in the village."

After Nelleke, Simon, and Daniel had drunk buttermilk, Myriam a mug of light beer, and Jos a locally brewed gin, they entered the clog building to find two boys hard at work, even though it was Sunday. The boys nodded as Mr. Van Bast explained that many willow and poplar trees grew on their land and that the logs from these trees were excellent for making strong wooden shoes.

One boy was using a sharp knife to carve the outline of a clog from a thin log. Another was sanding a pair of shoes to make them smooth. The air smelled of fresh clippings, oil, and polish. A pile of wooden shavings had been swept into a corner. But what startled and attracted Nelleke were the rows upon rows of finished clogs in a variety of sizes. Some were placed to catch the sun, apparently drying out. Others were waiting to be barrel-polished. Many were lined up, looking strong and expectant with their tips pointing upward, waiting dutifully for new wearers.

Nelleke began to count them out loud and soon arrived at 99. There was one more shoe, though. Nelleke tugged on Jos's jacket and looked up at him? "Sir?" she quizzed, anxiously.

"One hundred, Nelleke," said Jos, enjoying this instructor's role. "After 99 comes one hundred."

"One hundred. One hundred. One hundred shoes," chanted Nelleke happily.

Wouter showed Daniel and Simon how to carve out the rounded toe, and let the boys try it themselves. They laughed at their own awkwardness and returned the tools to the experts.

By now, Myriam knew Nelleke well enough to know that she would want to try everything the boys got to do and, believing she was too young to use one of the sharp knives, she quickly distracted her.

"Look at these small clogs, Nelleke. Aren't they sweet?"

"Here, try on a pair," said Gerbrand.

Looking down at her feet and pulling up her long skirts slightly in order to see them, Nelleke wiggled her toes and clomped forward and backward.

"These are bigger than the ones I had at my aunt's," she said.

"You've grown, Nelleke," said Myriam.

Then all the Broekhofs tried on clogs and Jos purchased five pairs.

Wouter painted three red vertical X's – the symbol of Amsterdam – on each of their new shoes. "These will be dried and ready for you to pick up when you leave," he said.

Next Mr. Van Bast took them to the cheese-making building.

Five of Mr. Van Bast's daughters, including a pair of twins, were engaged in various tasks. Nelleke closed her eyes for a moment and absorbed the aroma. It was as if she had stepped inside of a giant block of cheese and was surrounded by it, the smell blocking out all other odors.

The youngest rinsed buckets and barrels and placed them near a straw furnace to dry. Another was pouring a yellowish substance into a vat. As Nelleke peered into the vat, the daughter said, "Annatto coloring. From the Annatto plant. Would you like to stir it?"

The twins worked in tandem to press the curds into cheese molds and submerge them in a pickling vat of salt water. The oldest washed her hands and picked up cheeses that had been dried on a perforated wooden board. She rubbed them all over, explaining "This keeps them from getting moldy. Would you like to taste one of our cheeses?"

The oldest daughter then opened a door to a storage area and invited the guests to step inside. "These are ready to be taken to market," she explained. From floor to ceiling there were shelves laden with wax-wrapped cheese in all sizes, some in rectangle shapes, some squared, some round. Each shelf was carefully labeled with a date and with one of these three words: "young," "mature," "aged." The young woman chose a block from the "young" shelf, brought it back to the main room, unwrapped it, and cut it in bite-size pieces. Following the "tasting," Myriam selected a variety of packages to purchase.

After they bid the big sisters good-bye, Mr. Van Bast led them past fields of horses, cows, and sheep. "Look," said Nelleke, pointing. "That cow has a white patch on his forehead. It's shaped like my scar." Then, holding out her fist to show Simon, Nelleke said, "She has a diamond on her head. I have a diamond on my hand."

Later, sitting around the long wooden table in the Van Bast kitchen, the hungry guests feasted on fried pigeon, salted herring, fresh bread slathered in butter, and, of course, cheese.

That evening as they returned their child guest to the orphanage, Nelleke roused herself from Mrs. Broekhof's lap where she had fallen asleep. Jos lifted her down from the carriage. Her new clothes and clogs would stay at the Broekhof's. Once again she was the little orphan girl dressed in her red, black, and white clothing, wearing modest leather slippers. After she said good-bye, Nelleke reached into her apron pocket to grasp a fistful of the cheese samples she had saved to share with Isabela and Bernadien. She had so many stories to tell them. Maybe even one hundred stories, she thought.

Chapter Twenty-seven
Betrothal

sabela and Nelleke walked along the Heerengracht feeling self-conscious in their fine, new clothes, and unsure of what to expect when they arrived at the home of the Regentesse, Mrs. Comfrij. They could hear music and singing and shouting in the distance. The invitation to Mrs. Comfrij's daughter's wedding had arrived at the orphanage six weeks earlier with a note promising to send suitable outfits for them both. Now here they were approaching Mrs. Comfrij's home, wearing the pale-blue gowns she had sent them, with slippers tied with blue silk bows. The bonnets of pure lace covered only the back of their heads, leaving their thick locks exposed on top. The bonnets were held in place with shiny silver clips that brought out the deep-brown hue of Isabela's eyes and the sparkling black of Nelleke's. Around their necks they wore matching simple necklaces of small pearls.

Because of Mrs. Comfrij's governing position with the orphanage and the hours of volunteer service she dedicated every month, Housemother could not prevent the girls from attending, but she did require that Isabela complete her morning duties and arrange for one of the other girls to cover her afternoon and evening responsibilities while "you're out partying," as Mrs. Heijn put it. "And as for you, young lady," scolded Mrs. Heijn, speaking to Nelleke, "I expect you to behave and honor your upbringing here at our institution." "Yes, Mother," agreed Nelleke, although she had little idea of what was expected of her at such a celebration. Because the wedding took place in the late morning, they had missed the ceremony, but they would be able to participate in the banquet. Isabelle was disappointed about missing any aspect of this wedding, but relieved too about not having to attend the ceremony in the church. She knew nothing about reformed churches and she was sure she would have made mistakes, perhaps offended the parishioners or even her hosts.

In any case, Isabela was grateful and excited that an afternoon and evening of merriment awaited her, even if she were mostly an observer. She had not been to a party since the previous summer in England. The wedding celebration would be the culmination of a lifetime of preparation on the part of Mrs. Comfrij. Beginning almost the day her daughter was born, she began building her daughter's trousseau, collecting the linens, pots and pans, silver and china that her daughter would eventually need for her own independent household. Although several of her neighbors had arranged early betrothals for their daughters, usually by age twelve, often to a cousin, Mrs. Comfrij explained her philosophy to the orphans during her weekly visit.

"No early arranged betrothals for my daughter. Absolutely not. It is my belief that marriages are pre-ordained by the Divine. I am certain that God, in his infinite wisdom, will take my daughter's hand and lead her to her intended mate. God knows what is best. The Lord will arrange Saskia's fate for her."

"Of course," Mrs. Comfrij explained after placing her broad rump on a stool and setting up for the orphan girls' weekly instruction in embroidery and needlepoint, "I gave God a helping hand. By the time my Saskia reached age fifteen, I had instructed her in the fine art of what I call 'honest flirting,' that is to say not shaking her shoulders or showing a bit of ankle." As she spoke, Mrs. Comfrij shook her own shoulders and pulled up her own skirt to momentarily reveal her own ample ankle. Then she smoothed her skirts back into their usual modest position. "No, none of that." As she continued speaking, she took time to act out each motion she described. "I taught her how to smile slightly . . . listen . . . stand upright . . . fake an air of mystery if she must . . . but use her wiles and intelligence to engage the interest of a young man in such a way that would lead to a proposal. Of course, Mr. Comfrij and I know all the best families in the city and in The Hague as well," she told them. Then leaning toward the young girls, Mrs. Comfrij confessed that she even kept records of the ages and activities of the sons from these families – and she'd done so for years.

"My husband, Mr. Comfrij, was not born wealthy, you know," she told the girls, while circulating among them and observing their sewing progress. "But my, does he have a nose for business? That tulip craziness? He knew when to buy, when to sell, and when to abandon the nonsense altogether. Sold his last tulip bulb just two weeks before the market collapsed. And, oh, what a beauty it was too." She stopped and clapped her hands together. "*Semper Augustus*, they called it. Just imagine purple petals with white and crimson-colored tips on top. Sublime. Truly. 'Some people lost everything,' he explained to me, but 'my dear,' he said, 'me and my missus – we are set for life. Our girls don't need all those so-called "skills" you're teaching them – that "honest flirting" carrying on. The men will come a-courting. Lots of them. Our girls will have their pick.'"

Each week the story would continue and Mrs. Comfrij would entertain the cooks, the girls in the older school, the young ones – anyone who would listen.

"Well, one evening, a flower shows up tied to the knocker on our front door. You know what that means, don't you? Some young man is interested in our Saskia. Next night there was a whole bouquet. The third night a wreath filled with greenery and yellow tulips. Now what does my wise Saskia say? 'Mamma, I'm not going to react until I know who this young man is.'"

"Take your time," I told her. "God will speak to you."

"But guess what? A different kind of single flower appeared. Then a second bouquet and a second wreath. What's more" – and here Mrs. Comfrij stopped for a moment to be sure she had the full attention of her audience – "our maid told us about a scene the bread roll delivery man had witnessed early one morning. A nicely dressed young man tiptoed to our front door and, finding a wreath left by someone else, removed it, stomped on it, and left a new one – the one HE had brought in its place. Then he stalked off with the ruined wreath and tossed it in the canal."

"Saskia was not amused. She did not want a fight breaking out on our street," she said. What she wanted was a future husband. And she cried. Oh, did she cry. I could not console her."

"'Who are these men, Mamma?' she asked with alarm. 'That's all I want to know right now. Who are they?'"

"Excellent work, Bernadien. How about trying this yellow thread for your next design? It would go very well with the pale green leaves. What do you think?"

"Anja, I think you need a larger needle. That one is too small for your little hands. Here, try this one."

"Let's see what you're working on, Nelleke dear. Oh. I think perhaps that embroidery is not your forte."

"What is forte, Mrs. Comfrij?" Nelleke asked.

"It's a French word. It means strength."

"But I am strong," Nelleke protested. Nelleke dropped her embroidery, lifted Anja up off her toes and held her until they both tumbled down to the floor, giggling.

"Oh, yes you are strong, Sweetheart, and you have many talents," Mrs. Comfrij said, pulling Nelleke to her feet and giving her a squeeze. "Perhaps needlework is just not one of them."

As Nelleke bent once again over her sewing, which she did in fact find uninteresting and tedious, Mrs. Comfrij noted the white star shape covering her hand. Mrs. Comfrij remembered clearly meeting the child for the first time in the sick room and seeing that same hand submerged in a bucket of cold water. Learning that the accident had occurred just hours after her traumatic and upsetting arrival at the orphanage, seeing her spunk and liveliness in spite of the pain and confusion, had endeared Nelleke to Mrs. Comfrij. She looked forward to regular visits again with the little girl in her home once this wedding business was over. Saskia would soon be a married woman with her own household, but here was a motherless child who needed Mrs. Comfrij's guidance and affection. She was pleased that Nelleke and her beautiful English "Big Sister" Isabelle would attend the wedding feast in just a few weeks.

"Well, the gifts continued to arrive. Saskia did not even want to look at them. Then little notes appeared in two different hand-writing styles. 'Saskia, the girl with the lovely eyes.' Or 'Saskia, I want you for my own sweet love.' Or 'I will soon reveal who I am. I hope you will write back.'"

"Finally, on the same day, two notes were left and THIS TIME," Mrs. Comfrij nearly screamed before dropping her voice to a whisper, "there were names."

"'Darling Saskia, please leave me a sign. Do you care for me at all? Roemer Flinck.'"

"'Oh, lovely girl, I long to walk with you. Would you let me hold your hand?'

Your future beloved, I do hope. Jan Visscher.'"

"Now my poor Saskia. She cried harder than ever. 'Mamma, I do not want to marry Roemer Flinck. That awkward man with the spread-out nose and the mouth that constantly twitches. I do not want to marry Jan Visscher with his bony fingers and limp, thinning hair.'"

"But my dear daughter," I say to her, holding her while she sobs. "As if it's such a terrible thing to have TWO SUITORS! These young men are both from fine families. Either one will give you a home of your own, children, a fine life."

"'But, Mamma,' Saskia says, pulling herself away from me, her lower lip trembling, then falling back in my arms again. She was mumbling. Her words were muffled. I thought I heard her say, 'I love someone else.' Well, I heard correctly. Having said it once, Saskia straightened up, stuck out her chin, and repeated what she had said." Mrs. Comfrij imitated her daughter, separating each word, emphasizing the feeling, the total certainty. "I . . . love . . . someone . . . else."

All stitching activity stopped as the girls waited to see what followed next.

"Someone else? Well, couldn't she have told me that months earlier?"

Everyone laughed with relief, but only briefly because they wanted to hear the continuation of the story.

When the bells tolled 3:00, Mrs. Comfrij rose abruptly and began gathering her needles, thread, and handiwork samples.

"Oh my goodness, it is late. The seamstress is coming to fit Saskia and me. Saskia's dress . . . well, I'll have to tell you about that another time. I may not be back now for a few weeks, dear children. I will miss you, but there are so many details that the mother of the bride must attend to."

Mrs. Comfrij continued to chatter cheerfully as she tidied up and kissed each girl good-bye.

"The music, the food, the servers, the décor, readying the garden. It just goes on and on."

"But, Mrs. Comfrij," Isabela could not help asking, "Is Saskia marrying the man she told you she loved? Is this bridegroom the man of her choice then?"

As she exited the room, Mrs. Comfrij turned and called back over her shoulder. "Oh there's so much more to tell. Good-bye, children."

The little girls enjoyed Mrs. Comfrij because of her obvious affection for them, because she was teaching them a skill, because she was a dramatic and amusing storyteller. The content of the courtship stories was not important to them. If they listened intently, it was in order to follow the varied expressions on Mrs. Comfrij's face, her gestures, her changes in tone and volume, but they did not quite see the relevance of the stories to their own lives.

Isabela, on the other hand, had hung on every word, trying to make sense of the courtship rituals in this culture so different from her own. Always the same questions plagued her. How would she find a husband when her life revolved around the orphanage and her duties to the little girls whom she loved? Which was better – for the parents to choose mates for their children or for a girl to be able to choose for herself?

What does 'better' even mean? Did Saskia in fact choose the man she would marry in a few weeks? Did God lead her to him?

If someone did take a fancy to Isabela, how would he communicate that? Leave a flower with her name on it on the orphanage latch? Drop off messages with the watchman?

How could Isabela sort out all her questions and longings? With both parents dead and her maiden aunts far away, who would help her?

"I love someone else," Saskia had said. "I love someone."

How did she know she loved that man? Did she, Isabela, in fact love Pieter, she wondered? Because there he was, infused in every question. Floating in and out of her consciousness almost constantly. She could call forth effortlessly the touch of his hand when he helped her down off the city's outer wall where they had met, the light pressure of that hand on the small of her back when she walked with him across the courtyard to the orphanage gate after each of the one-hour sittings. She could see him looking down at her from that wall the first time she saw him. His kind amused eyes. That hand again – outstretched to help her – the hand she had refused that first time.

Oh and the sittings. Three of them now. Each only one-hour long – time Housemother allowed while the little girls rested. Beforehand, Isabela would steal a moment to step into a fresh orphan outfit and replace her every-day bonnet with her Sunday one. She would pinch her cheeks and practice her smile as she walked briskly to the orphanage reception room where she knew Pieter was already setting up the easel, removing the paints and brushes and rags from his carrying satchel. With each step the mix of odors became stronger, exciting her.

And then there he was, seated on a stool, calmly mixing colors. He would smile and greet her before becoming totally involved in his work. For the next hour, she stood still while his eyes alternated between her and the easel. Occasionally the twinkle broke through briefly, but mostly his eyes were serious, intense, impersonal. She felt like an object no different from a vase or a windmill. Conversation would have been difficult in any case. Orphans skipped about. Deliveries were left. Housemother poked her head in occasionally.

Mrs. Heijn had forcefully rejected all of Pieter's attempts to arrange for Isabela to pose in a studio. The cleaning girls scrubbed around their feet, more industriously than usual, Isabela noted. Once Straw, as Nelleke named him, leaped up onto Pieter, stretched, and tried to settle down on Pieter's warm lap. Before he wrapped his tail around himself, Straw had flicked that tail in Pieter's face. Pieter had to lift the brushes high over his head and to one side to avoid dripping red paint on the animal. They had both laughed then and Isabela broke her pose to shoo the cat away. When she took advantage of the momentary break to do a cat-like stretch herself, they laughed together again.

Pieter said artists do not share their work with their subjects until the work is finished, so she had no idea of his progress. What did he see really? Did he have any feelings for her? Would the painting reveal his thoughts and emotions? She thought sometimes of the self-portrait her father had brought her when she was a young girl, how alive and real the man seemed. She now knew that it was Rembrandt who had painted himself in that portrait. Now it was gone, drowned along with everything and everyone else on her father's ship, except for the rowboat, Cornelius and herself.

But this was an important work for Pieter. His plan he had explained to her at the beginning was to submit her portrait as his signatory work, first to Rembrandt for the master's critique, then to the guild. Without guild acceptance, approval, and membership, he would not be able to practice his trade. Once he did become a guild member, however, he could establish himself, accept his own clients, build a business and, he added, glancing at her in a way that made her weak and set her mind racing, "then he could have his own home and family...a wife," he said quietly. She wondered if decorum required her to look away but, in this culture, women could be bold, she had noticed. She held his gaze before he returned to his easel and she to her pose looking slightly to the left as he had instructed her.

Among all her questions and wonderings, there was one that was too troubling for her to contemplate for long. It was like a small pebble lodged in her brain that could not be removed, a thought that she kicked aside quickly, just as she chased away a small spider that might frighten one of her little girls. A stomp. A kick. Gone. Yet with each sitting, with each slow stroll to the orphanage gate beside Pieter, with each shared smile, with the memory of the look on his face when he emphasized that word "wife," the irritating pebble rolled back into her consciousness. Stomp. Kick. Gone. But not for long.

Her betrothal. She had a fiancé. Or did she? She had had one since the moment of her birth. Her adoring father wanted what he thought was best for her. He felt so strongly about the engagement that he made her promise she would honor it in exchange for allowing her to accompany him on one journey. How grateful she was to her father who gave her life not once but twice – once when she was conceived; again when he made arrangements for her safety should disaster strike his ship while she was a passenger. But must she follow the path he designed for her? And even if she wanted to, how could she return to Spain? Her aunts wrote regularly, but she knew only a few of their letters made it through. They missed her terribly. Tia Luisa was not well. She was needed there, she knew, yet they cautioned her not to risk a voyage while the long war between Spain and The United Provinces continued to rage.

Her father was no longer alive. She had a new life now far from her native village. She barely knew Diego de Vega. Didn't she have the right to choose a mate as Saskia apparently had? Wouldn't God lead her to the right man, as Mrs. Comfrij believed? Had God led her to Pieter?

Then suddenly Isabela and Nelleke came upon the source of the music and merriment – the wedding procession itself on its way from the Reformed Church to the Comfrij home. In the lead were half a dozen small children strewing bright flowers in every direction. Right behind the children were Saskia and her bridegroom, with what looked like hundreds of people following. Seeing her joyful face as she walked arm in arm with her new husband, it was impossible to believe that Saskia was once the sobbing young woman her mother had described.

Twice Saskia had come to the orphanage to fulfill her mother's volunteer duties. "I'm too busy with your marriage arrangements. You go in my place please. The little girls will love seeing you and you will enjoy them," Mrs. Comfrij had said.

As Saskia demonstrated how to embroider a large, perfect rose rising from the fabric as if nourished by sun and rain, her needle passing rapidly through the cloth from one side to the other, Isabela noticed the large ring on her finger. It was like a small sculpture with two parallel circles carved into it.

When Isabela asked about it, Saskia took it off, showed it to her and slipped it on Isabela's finger for a moment. It felt strange, heavy – like an encumbrance.

"Philip has an identical one," Saskia explained with a coy smile, looking lovingly at the ring as she reclaimed it from Isabela and placed it back on her own finger. Once we have both pledged our love and fidelity during the ceremony, he will remove his ring and place it above mine, once we have both answered 'yes' – first me, then Philip, to the minister's – oh, you know that question (but Isabelle did not) 'Do you . . . take, etc, to be your . . . ?' then I will wear both rings . . . for the rest of my life," she added with a dreamy look.

Casually, she switched from pink to green thread and began adding leaves to the completed rose, holding up her work for the orphans to observe.

"Once Philip and I exchanged rings, registered our engagement and published the bans – not once, but THREE times – mind you, as required, mother instantly began sending out invitations. Oh, I'm almost weary from all the preparations, excursions and parties," she sighed.

But what interested Isabela was the continuation of Mrs. Comfrij's story. She could no longer hold back her need to know.

"Tell us about your betrothed, Saskia," Isabela said, trying to sound casual. "How did you meet him?"

"Oh, I had suitors, you know, leaving me hints, and gifts, and notes. But I already loved Philip. 'Mother,' I told her. 'I want to marry that handsome young man who sits in church between his mother and father two rows in front of us each Sunday. I believe he's noticed me. Haven't you seen how he keeps turning around to look in our direction?'"

"Well, my dear mother got to work immediately, to learn who he was, all about his family."

"'His name is Philip de Vos,'" she reported. 'His father is a magistrate. Philip is expecting to follow his father's career. They are a respected family, but certainly not among Amsterdam's most wealthy. I think you can do better, Saskia.'"

"'But, Mother,' I pleaded, our family was not wealthy until recently. Neither you nor father's family had much money. I don't care about such things. He is the one I want.'"

"Mother had mentioned where Philip is studying. I volunteered to do errands so that I could pass him as he left the college. At first, we nodded, then smiled, and eventually we spoke – the first time for an entire hour, standing there on the street. Soon we were seeing each other almost every day. He proposed, and asked if he could speak to my father."

Saskia's storytelling lacked the dramatic fervor of her mother's. Her tone was one of contentment – a girl focused on her wedding, confident of her future, communicating the attitude that loving and marrying Philip de Vos was simply the way it was supposed to be.

Every time one of the little girls would begin to lose interest or interrupt Saskia –

"Show me how to make leaves." "I wish we were still playing outside." "I don't like embroidery." "Ouch, I pricked myself." – Isabela would comfort, help a child focus, or correct behavior as needed, and then gently bring Saskia back to the topic of courtship.

"How did your father feel, then?" Isabela asked. "Your mother obviously eventually agreed? Was that difficult for awhile?"

"Oh, once they met Philip, they embraced my choice. I wasn't always sure they would, but now they adore him."

Isabela would have liked many more details. What were the first words the couple exchanged? Who spoke first? How much time passed between the first meeting and the betrothal? Between the exchange of rings and setting the wedding date? These were questions a confidante might pose, but Isabela and Saskia were not even friends. Saskia did not see her as an equal, Isabela realized, but rather as one of the orphans probably, albeit an almost grown one, or as a servant. But Isabela had learned what she found most valuable: ultimately, the future husband had not been selected by her mother or father. The choice was Saskia's.

Suddenly, Nelleke cried out, "I see Mrs. Broekhof." She dropped Isabela's hand and without a "Good-bye" or "May I?" or "I'll be right back," she was moving through the throng. Isabela watched as the Broekhofs caught sight of her, Mrs. Broekhof leaning down to embrace her and exclaim delightedly over her dress, slippers, and bonnet. Isabela was stunned by the change in the woman. She had met her only once before at the time of Nelleke's first visit to their home. She had actually felt sorry for Nelleke having to spend time with the drab, pinched, distracted Mrs. Broekhof, but the woman now moving through the procession holding Nelleke's hand looked lovely in her fine clothes and almost radiant, moving along with the crowd, holding Nelleke's hand in the most natural way. There was Mr. Broekhof too, that small but handsome man, walking in his usual bouncy, neck-stretched way. The last glimpse Isabela had of them, Nelleke was now holding hands with the youngest boy – Samuel, was it? – and they were skipping happily.

Mrs. Comfrij had said that all their neighbors, friends, and relatives from near and far would attend, including the most prominent Amsterdam families – families with names like Coymans, Bicker, Munter, De Geer, Trip, Six. She had stopped her sewing then and moved her head slightly side to side, raised her shoulders, and lifted her eyebrows as she slowly repeated each family name.

But Isabela did not know what a Trip or a Six or a Munter looked like. She did not know anyone in this crowd of revelers. She searched for Mrs. Comfrij, but thought that perhaps she had hurried home immediately after the ceremony in order to make last-minute preparations, smooth her hair, and greet her guests. Isabela felt self-conscious and awkward standing there alone. She considered just returning to the orphanage, but Nelleke was her responsibility. She could not abandon her without conversing with the Broekhofs and they were now way up ahead. She felt like a complete intruder and could not force herself into the moving line.

Then, back about 20 people, she saw a familiar face. At first she barely recognized him. No splattered paint in sight. Only what appeared to be a brand new, clean cap – this one, too, set back on his head revealing that warm expression, those endearing eyes.

She wanted to call out to him, "Pieter. Over here. It's Isabela." As a child, Nelleke could do that, but for her it would be unseemly, drawing attention to herself that way. She would wait until he was even with her and hope that he noticed her. Perhaps she would venture a small wave as he came near.

He was certainly enjoying being part of the procession. The serious expression he wore when he painted – the expression she was most familiar with – was gone. He was laughing and singing . . . and then she saw what must be the source of his merriment. A beautiful girl was walking beside him. Close beside him. Their shoulders were touching.

They may have even been holding hands. They were engaged in lively conversation now, very at ease, familiar with one another.

She glanced back again, telling herself this would be the last time. She saw Pieter reach down and take both the girl's hands in his. A small opening appeared in the crowd as the two of them swung round and round, like a couple of children. They stopped to add a little girl of about nine and then continued, their heads back, their arms outstretched, spinning faster and faster, laughing, the girls beginning to scream. Pieter's cap flew off. They stopped. Someone handed the cap to the young woman, who reached up and placed it on Pieter's head. She set it straight. He pulled it back to its usual position. She pulled it forward. It was a game – perhaps one they had played many times.

Isabela's breath seemed to leave her body. Her chest began moving in and out rapidly. She was gasping. Her legs refused to hold her steady. Was she going to weep in front of all these people? Then he could have his own home and family . . . "a wife," he had said. So he had been engaged all this while. How utterly foolish she had been to think that he was thinking of her when he said that word – that word "wife" that she didn't think she could ever again pronounce out loud. She had never felt so alone, not even when she tried to climb over the side of the boat to join both her father and the man who had given her his last kiss, not even then pelted by heavy rain, dodging lightening bolts. At least Cornelius was there. Now there was no one. Just family after family passing by her, enjoying each other. She tried to calm herself by singing in her mind the song she had used to comfort Nelleke after her accident, the song her mother and aunts had sung to her as a child. Its image of the tadpole's tail changing, growing into a full-grown frog, always helped her see that whatever disappointment she was feeling was temporary, that it would heal.

"*Sana, sana, colita de rana.*
Si no sanas hoy, sanarás mañana."

Reverting to her native language – a language no one here spoke or understood – only reinforced her loneliness. Thinking in the language she had not used out loud for the past ten months made her want to flee this city and return to her loving aunts, back to the security of her small village. She turned to walk away from the boisterous procession, hoping to look dignified, trying not to run but beginning to run anyway, trying to find a private place in this irritatingly bustling city, to get away, before the sobs she knew were coming wracked her body and overwhelmed her.

Chapter Twenty-eight
Wedding Celebration

"Isabelle. Isabelle. Wait. Stop."

Through her mind's fog, trying to shut out the sounds of the joyful procession behind her, unable to control the tears, Isabelle imagined she heard a familiar voice dear to her. But that was just her muddled head, she thought, a wish from her ridiculous heart. "Isabelle." Pieter, slightly out of breath, put a hand – a light grip really – on her upper arm to stop her. He tried to turn her toward him. She resisted, kept her head turned away, eyes down. So this was real. How dare he chase her, catching her at her most vulnerable.

"I thought that was you, but I wasn't sure at first. This is a beautiful dress you're wearing. Were you going to celebrate Saskia and Philip's wedding, by chance? They're good friends of mine. I didn't realize you knew them too," Pieter said, the mystery of this young woman tugging at his heart as it always did.

"How could he be so cheerfully chatty?" Isabela thought with irritation.

Still clutching her arm so she wouldn't bolt, Pieter looked down at her sideways and saw the tears. Growing up among so many females, he was accustomed to occasional extremes of emotion, but that his lovely friend Isabelle should be in distress alarmed him.

"I'm sorry," he said in a softer tone. "I see something is troubling you. Can I help?"

He reached for the clean pocket handkerchief that Adriana had carefully folded for him and insisted he take. He had made a face at

Adriana and, to tease her, had balled it up and thrown it haphazardly so that it hung at all angles out of the front pocket of his fine vest. The maid grabbed it, refolded it, and arranged it so that only a small triangular corner showed. Now he was grateful for Adriana's insistent care.

Isabelle looked at the offering he was waving gently. It reminded her of the white flag her father kept on the ship, the flag he used to signal to ships at a distance that his was not a warship, but a merchant ship going about its business. The flag was left over from the days when he was involved in caring for the sailor victims of wars, before she was born and her mother insisted he find a less dangerous way to earn a living. Without looking up, she accepted the handkerchief, wiped her eyes and face, returned it, straightened her bonnet and, finally, stopped fleeing.

She had not said a word, but whether or not she actually was an invitee to the Comfrij/de Vos celebration, Pieter saw an opportunity, a whole evening spreading out before him, to be with her, perhaps to get answers to the many questions he had pondered for months.

Just as Isabela was gathering some composure and had thought of an explanation she could give Pieter for her behavior, his fiancée approached with the younger girl close behind.

"Pieter, all of a sudden you were gone. We've found you," said the pretty young woman. She seemed younger at this close distance than Isabelle had thought.

"Anneliese. Agnes. Come meet the beautiful English girl I've been telling you about. The one who is posing for my final project."

Isabela was flattered that Pieter would refer to her as "beautiful," but also dismayed.

How would the fiancée react to hearing her future husband refer so openly to another girl that way?

But the girl reached out her dainty hands and took Isabela's hands in both of hers.

"Oh, so you are Isabelle. We've heard so much about you. How you met on the city wall, how Pieter had to convince your Housemother to allow him to paint you at all. She's rather severe, isn't she? But you're upset. Can we help?"

So he had told his fiancée all about their meetings and the posings – those precious times so special to Isabela that she guarded them for the rare moments when she could ponder and relive them.

Sniffling and struggling to appear composed, Isabela explained. "The little orphan, Nelleke, and I were invited by Mrs. Comfrij to attend her daughter's wedding. She even generously sent us matching outfits. We were unable to attend the church ceremony and began walking to Mrs. Comfrij's home when we saw the procession. Nelleke saw a family she knows – the Broekhofs – and bolted away to greet them. I am responsible for her. I felt I had lost her and did not know what to do."

"Oh, don't worry one more minute, Isabelle," Anneliese said brightly, still holding her hands. The Broekhofs are neighbors of ours. They will take good care of her. We will help you find her when we arrive at the banquet."

Somehow, with the fiancée on one side of her, Pieter on the other, they had turned her around and were leading her back to the procession. What an efficient team, Isabela thought with irritation. This couple understand one another, even without speaking. Anneliese was holding the hand of the younger girl who skipped along happily and slipped her other arm through Isabela's. She felt like breaking away, but the fiancée had been so sweet, Pieter's concern so genuine, their promises to help find Nelleke so sincere, to flee would have been quite rude.

Anneliese was chattering now about the wedding banquet. She had helped Saskia and Mrs. Comfrij arrange the greenery and the wreaths along the walls, and hung the ceilings with wax angels and cupids. The town magistrates gave the Comfrij and De Vos families large goblets featuring their respective coats of arms. "I'll show you everything," she promised and then continued describing the gifts, the dishes, the decorations.

Isabela realized that for the first time since leaving England, a young woman close to her age was treating her as an equal – the equal she actually was if education, upbringing, and family status counted. If she had been wearing her orphan uniform that may not have been true, but now dressed as she was and with some kind of positive report from Pieter apparently preceding her, Anneliese simply took it for granted that they were friends too.

"So, you're from England," Anneliese said, as they reached the procession and moved along with the crowd. I've always wanted to go. Will you teach me English? I can speak quite a bit, but I want to learn it perfectly. If I do, perhaps I can convince Father to take me one day. Where in England did you live? Do you know other languages as well? French? Your aunt taught you? I wish I had such an aunt."

Sensing that her new friend was a tender soul who had suffered loss, Anneliese posed each question gently, but held back on the most obvious.

How did Isabelle get to Amsterdam? Why did she come here? Will she return to England? Meanwhile, Pieter listened to the conversation attentively and learned more about Isabelle in those few moments than he had in the few months he had known her.

"I want to go to England too," Agnes chimed in.

"Do you really think Father would allow both his daughters to take off at the same time? I'm the son. I'm the oldest. I'll get there before either of you," Pieter teased.

Daughters. Father. Son. The relationships took awhile to penetrate Isabela's consciousness. These three have the same father? These girls were Pieter's sisters. Anneliese is not his betrothed. She is his sister. Isabelle glanced at Anneliese's hands and at Pieter's. There were no engagement rings. His sister. How untrusting and ridiculous she'd been to assume that Pieter had withheld information from her. Yet she was not ready for her heart to return to loving him, if that's what she had felt, not yet ready to dream and hope like the foolish girl she'd been since meeting him.

The four of them were among the last to arrive. Once they entered there was so much to look at and so much noise that for a moment Isabela craved the order, simplicity, and relative calm of the orphanage. Then she saw the newly married couple in the center of the reception room, seated in two matching velvet chairs raised on a platform, like newly anointed king and queen greeting their subjects. Saskia was wearing her long bridal robe now, made with a splendid, rich heavy cloth, silver threads weaving in and out of moss green and claret panels. Philip was smoking the decorated pipe that Saskia had selected for him – the traditional gift from the bride to her new husband.

A carpet woven in a floral pattern hung behind the couple. Family and friends approached offering congratulatory kisses and placing at their feet furniture, porcelain, bedding, elaborate candle snuffs, even pots and pans – all for their new home nearby. The couple crossed arms and sipped wine from the goblets Anneliese referred to earlier, Saskia from the one with the De Vos Coat of Arms, Philip from the Comfrij one. The two families were joined.

The guests, hungry after the ceremony and the walk from the church, began to find their places at the long tables that ran from wall to wall in all three of the main downstairs rooms. Nelleke came running up to embrace Isabela who had just spied their names scrawled on the hull of delicate miniature carved wooden ships placed at the top of each

dinner plate. As they took their respective places, an elderly man fell
clumsily into the chair next to Isabela's and began talking to her loudly,
using a speech pattern that seemed distorted. Isabela understood only
an occasional word, nodded and continued to look around the room.

The walls were covered with paintings, floor to ceiling – some of
them of a religious nature, some still-lifes, others of simple family scenes
that contrasted with the elaborateness of the home in which they hung.
In one corner above a giant globe, a parrot stood on its perch, adding its
squawks to the din. A small orchestra was setting up in a neighboring
room.

On the table itself, straw cornucopias spilled forth an abundance of
apples, cherries, pears, plums and figs. Varieties of jams and biscuits,
cheeses and breads had been set beside bowls of creamy yellow butter
and gleaming silver knives. People were beginning to discreetly nibble,
waiting for the official blessing of the newlyweds that would signal
the beginning of the feast. Isabela looked around for Pieter and found
him whispering in Mrs. Comfrij's ear. Mrs. Comfrij smiled amusedly
and looked over her guests until she saw Isabela. Waving at Isabela
and patting Pieter's arm reassuringly, she approached her two orphan
guests with outstretched arms, greeted them delightedly, and turned her
attention to the mumbling man seated next to Isabela.

"Mr. Van der Voort. How nice of you to join us this evening. How
are you, Sir? I have something to tell you, Mr. Van der Voort. Your
friends, Mr. and Mrs. Roemer have been asking for you. Would you be
so kind as to accompany me to the next room where they hope you will
join them?"

Mrs. Comfrij nodded at Pieter who suddenly appeared behind the
man's chair. Pieter helped Mr. Van der Voort to his feet, offered his arm,
and led him away. Soon Pieter returned and claimed the empty chair
for himself. Still recovering from her fears, Isabela was taken aback.
She really did not know how to talk to Pieter in a social situation like
this. Pieter poured a watered-down beer for Nelleke, a generous glass of
wine for Isabela, and a few drops of wine for himself. He wished to be
completely alert on this unexpectedly delicious occasion.

When Mr. Comfrij slipped behind his daughter and new son-in-law,
the guests became quiet. After saying grace, he held upside down over
their heads by the stems several thick bunches of juicy, succulent purple
grapes. "May God bless this newly married couple. May they always
remain the proud, productive Christian citizens of our city which their

families raised them to be; may their devotion remain true and their fidelity live long; may their union be fruitful and joyful."

When he presented them each with a bunch of grapes and spread his arms around them both, Mrs. Comfrij yelled from the kitchen door. "That's right. Mr. Comfrij and I want grandchildren. Lots of them. "

The crowd laughed. The small instrumental ensemble began playing. On cue, a parade of women and men entered the rooms carrying steaming platters. For the next three hours, the servers cleared empty platters and brought fresh ones covered with sirloin, breasts of veal, mutton, and venison wrapped in pastry and flavored with butter and mustard. There were pheasants, capons, turkey pies and stuffed cabbage, sliced beef and minced ox tongue, roast pork and prunes, sausage and pile after pile of every manner of fish. The servants continually refilled casks of wine and pitchers of ale.

When the orchestra took a break, songbooks were distributed. The guests, satiated, but still anticipating sweets, joined in one rousing chorus after another.

The merriment was interrupted when a servant ran from the kitchen asking for Dr. Tulp. A number of curious guests went to investigate, further crowding the hot, steamy space. Two women, both carrying sweets that Mrs. Comfrij had ordered, had gotten into a tussle. Cakes covered the floor. Other servants were slipping in a sticky caramelized sauce. One woman, Elsbeth van Randen, claimed that the other, Elsje Levens, had tripped her and then, while she lay dazed on the floor, had attempted to open the bodice of her blouse. The second woman denied trying to trip the first. She did acknowledge opening the woman's blouse, however, but stated that she was only trying to help the fallen woman breathe more easily.

After the doctor examined the humiliated Mrs. Van Randen and found her to be unhurt, the others helped her to her feet. When she began retying her bodice, she reached in, as she had done several times a day for the past six years, to be certain that the by now ragged half playing card was in place. Before she began hiding it in her bosom, when Willem was five, he had found the card in a box that also included the blanket wrapped around him at the time he was found. Mrs. Van Randen suspected that Willem's natural mother had pinned the half card to the blanket and kept the other half in the hope of one day finding the child she had abandoned.

She had never been able to bring herself to destroy the card, even in spite of the portrayal of an alarming demon-like snake with a long forked tongue, large human eyes, and thick black lashes. Willem deserved the opportunity to learn the truth about his origins, she felt – some day when he was an adult. She had always suspected that the card was designed and printed by her brother, Nicolaas, and that he, who brought her the child before daybreak saying it had been left on his doorstep, was actually the natural father of her son.

Desperate for a child of her own, she claimed the baby immediately. She shared her suspicions with no one, not even her husband who loved the boy. Because of her fears that Nelleke was actually Willem's half sister, she had always been nervous seeing how much they enjoyed each other. After Willem began visiting Nelleke in the orphanage after her accident, Willem asked his mother, "Can people marry their cousin?"

From then on, she forbade all contact between them. Yet hearing the minister preach so often about the importance of truthfulness, and believing herself to be an upstanding Christian woman, she held onto the evidence. Perhaps it might one day prove useful for her son but, for now, she kept that evidence hidden.

Upright now and beginning to look for a broom to sweep up the ruined cakes she had labored over all day, Mrs. Van Randen reached more deeply into her blouse, rummaging, assuming the card had become dislodged. She explored around and below her ample breasts all the way down to her waist, first by touch, then by looking.

"Missing something, Mrs. Van Randen?" one of the male servants asked, embarrassing her further and eliciting chuckles from other servants who had noticed the strange behavior. She found the pin that had been holding the card in place, but the card was gone.

"That woman took something valuable from me. She did trip me deliberately, don't you see? She stole from me. Who is that woman?" Mrs. Van Randen called out. The servants ignored her and continued to arrange on platters the stacks of waffles, pancakes, currant fruitbreads, and cakes spiced with saffron, cinnamon, and cloves, helping themselves to the sweets before delivering them to the guests. But Elsje had carefully submitted her *poffertjes* and collected her fee before becoming entangled with Mrs. Van Randen. She was no longer in the Comfrij house.

At this very moment, as Elsbeth searched her bodice in vain, having fled the chaos she had created Elsje arrived at the next corner.

Acknowledging the waiting Rudolf, she slipped him several coins and a package of *poffertjes* dusted with sugar.

"You were right. It's a match. I've waited ten years. Now I know. Thank you."

The increasingly rowdy children had been taken home and put to bed, Nelleke among them. Isabela hesitated when Mrs. Broekhof offered to take the child to her home and promised to return her to the orphanage in time for school, but she reasoned that Nelleke had already stayed three Saturday nights with the family and seemed quite at ease there. The bridal couple had slipped out somehow when no one was paying attention, perhaps during the kitchen ruckus. The dinner orchestra had packed up and left, but a pair of fresh violinists brought the remaining guests – mostly young people – to their feet. Tables and chairs were pushed back. Dancing began and continued well into the night.

The next morning, Isabela awoke in her orphanage bed late, with an aching head. Mrs. Broekhof was in the room helping Nelleke change into her orphan uniform. "Several of the older girls took over your morning responsibilities, Isabela. Your little girls are all at breakfast. I'll deliver Nelleke to the classroom. She had a fine breakfast this morning. Oh, and she lost a tooth."

Nelleke kissed Isabela and, placing her hand in Myriam's, she happily left the room.

Isabela so wanted to lie in bed and luxuriate in the memories of her evening at Pieter's side, but she knew she must leap up and apply herself to her responsibilities immediately. As a Regentesse, Mrs. Comfrij would never tolerate her dismissal should it come to that, but, still Housemother could find ways to punish Isabela if she were angered. When she arrived at the breakfast room, the children were exiting. She glanced in and saw that Housemother was involved in spooning gruel into her husband's drooling mouth and did not catch sight of her surreptitiously peeking in.

Isabela walked with the children to the classroom as she did every weekday, but today she was able to assist very little. Conversation from the previous evening came to her in snatches. She thought she remembered telling Pieter everything about herself. He listened intently, the blue eyes coming close to her face in order to block out the party noise and concentrate entirely on her. She had laughed at times and was embarrassed now that she had also cried, telling about the shipwreck and the death of her beloved father. Out came the helpful handkerchief again.

She could hear Pieter saying, "I'm so sorry for your losses, Isabela. You have experienced a great deal in your young life. But you are resilient and so alive. You have adapted, learned our language, found meaning in a totally different place. I admire that about you."

"So you are Spanish, then, from Spain, not from England?"

Then more solemnly, "That means you are Catholic?"

"Your Catholicism, is it important to you?"

She could not remember her responses, only that she continued to talk endlessly.

This morning, though, she did recall that he referred again to her religion later and said that he would need to talk to his father about it. About what exactly? And why? she wondered. She did not understand why Catholics were forbidden to worship openly in this country. She had once walked by the Nieuwe Kerk and peeked in. Catholics were forbidden from entering. She found it bare and solemn, although the large white columns and the arches lent it an air of majesty.

But the minister conducted the service in Dutch, she had heard. How she loved the Latin the priests used, its lilting cadences. All the rituals soothed her: placing the mantilla on her head, the kneeling, the beads passing through her fingers, the familiar prayers. Weren't they all worshipping the same God? What difference could it make to Pieter's father if Pieter had a Catholic friend, a Catholic fiancée, or, she allowed herself to dream, a Catholic wife?

She must have explained to Pieter what the orphanage meant to her at some point. How, even though the woman was severe, Isabela was grateful to Housemother for taking a chance and hiring her.

Peter had replied, "Mrs. Heijn is a calculating businesswoman, an uneducated, but intelligent woman. I'm sure she recognized instantly when she met you that you would be a loving companion for the young orphans. Some day, you will also be a wonderful mother, Isabelle."

Isabela loved the hushed, intimate tone of Pieter's voice when he had said those words. She repeated them again in her head, wishing she could say them out loud.

The little girl pupils were all bent over their slates, clutching their chalk and practicing the letter "M." "M" the Schoolmaster repeated. "M. Mmmmmmm."

Every time she repeated those words to herself, hearing Pieter's voice – "Some day, you will also be a wonderful mother," – Isabela saw herself surrounded by beautiful, playful, contented, boys and girls, some with her dark eyes, some with Pieter's blue ones. She was seated holding an infant. Pieter was standing near with a chubby toddler clinging to him. She had seen many posed paintings of Dutch families, but this imagined painting was more joyful and lighter, full of movement.

Pieter told her how he had begun his apprenticeship with Rembrandt nearly six years ago. At first he was assigned menial chores – grinding pigments, stretching canvases, placing paint on the master's palette, even cleaning the studio at the end of the day. Gradually he learned to paint parts of the master's current projects – leaves, trees, fruit, then feet, eyes. Later whole heads and bodies, both nudes and in costume. When Isabela's portrait was finished – in another month or so – he would submit it to the artist guild – the Guild of Sint Lucas. If approved and accepted, he would set up his own studio, become a real artist. He would make a living from selling his own art and from the tuition of his own apprentices. Then he could afford a home and a family.

Oh, and then there was the dancing. Whether it was moving sideways in a large circle, holding hands with others, but always with Pieter at her side or twirling in his arms, holding her tight against him to avoid falling, laughing if she misstepped, sometimes feeling herself lifted and swung in time to the music, it made her delirious. No wonder her body and head ached this morning.

But this morning's mild nausea, fatigue and memory gaps did not keep her from being able to recall every sensation of the kiss. The second kiss of her life. Pieter's kiss. He was walking her back to the orphanage, hours and hours after the city curfew. The night watchmen had been alerted and were instructed not to fine or detain any of the celebration guests. In fact, as the watchmen passed by the Comfrij's during the evening and into the night, their time announcements ignored or not heard at all, they lingered, looking in the windows from the street. Adriana made sure the watchmen received generous helpings from the multiple platters before they continued their stroll through the city.

It was dark, but on every street there were at least three houses with a large candle burning in a special holder on the front door. Pieter placed his arm around her waist. After a few steps, he took her arm and placed it around his waist. All winter long on her way back from Our Lady in the Attic she had observed couples skating smoothly across the icy canals, in tandem, in this very position. Two glides to the right. Two to the left. As if they had one set of legs. She had always felt a stab of loneliness, of envy, always wondered what that felt like. Now here she was in stride with a man she adored and, given his absolute attentiveness to her during the evening, perhaps he loved her too. As they moved, their linked shadows appeared and disappeared, sometimes lit by a candle, sometimes fading back into the blackness. It was like a visual continuation of the dancing.

The strides became shorter and slower. "Good," she thought, "he doesn't want to say good-bye to me." But there was another reason, Pieter was slowing down. He was looking for the perfect spot, the right tree or wall. He was also listening intently to be sure there were no footsteps other than their own.

Then he found the magical space as if it had been waiting for them and led her to it – a handsome linden tree full on top, but with an arched opening underneath. Old, wide, wise and welcoming, the tree was close enough to one of those candles so that he could see her face, but not so well lit that any insomniac looking out a window could clearly perceive the couple.

Isabela thought a kiss was a kiss. Though she reveled in the memory of her first one in spite of the terrifying circumstances, she assumed that if she ever experienced a second, it would be the same. But if that kiss was her first, it was Jules's last. That kiss was sudden, furtive, hard, wet, desperate, delivered by a man with whom she had never exchanged a word, a man who knew he was within moments of his death.

Pieter took her face in his hands, kissed her forehead, her temples, her cheeks, her chin, the corners of her mouth, slowly and rhythmically, brushing the tip of her nose as he playfully moved from one side of her face to the other and back again. Kisses on each side of her nose, then on her nose, then pulling back for a moment, hesitating, he looked into her eyes, closed his eyes and kissed her lightly on the mouth several times. By the time her lips parted and she pressed herself against him, she felt totally cared for, completely trusting, desired. She truly believed she could remain there in that exact position until daybreak – no, for days, weeks, months. It felt as if she needed nothing else from life.

The next sitting was not until Monday. Three days away. How could she endure those three days without seeing him? How could they return to the silence the sittings required? Now that they had shared hours of conversation, there was so much more to ask, to tell, to learn.

Housemother was getting impatient, though. She had asked how many more posings the painting required. "Couldn't Pieter just finish it in the studio?" she inquired. Isabela now suspected that she was right and that Pieter was extending the sitting period beyond what was necessary to capture her likeness. She needed to free herself from Mrs. Heijn's tyranny and find a way to be with Pieter.

"And now the next letter, children. Watch carefully," the Schoolmaster was saying, as he held up his own slate and slowly drew three connected lines: "Up. Down. Up. Pick up your chalk. No, Bernadien. Not in your fist. You'll never learn to write that way. The way I showed you. Thumb under the chalk to support it, finger on top to guide. Thumb is your support. Finger is your guide." As soon as the Schoolmaster turned his attention again to his own chalk and slate, Bernadien scrunched up her nose, grabbed her chalk with her fist, and drew an angry, lopsided "X" that covered her whole slate.

In an instant, Isabela was at Bernadien's side. A kiss on her cheek and a pat on her arm chased away the child's frustration. Isabela gently arranged Bernadien's thumb and finger on the chalk and placed her own thumb and finger over the child's. Together they followed the Schoolmaster's example.

"N for Nelleke," Nelleke shouted out. She had learned to make that letter – all the letters of her name, in fact, almost a year ago. Now she wanted to learn to read words. Words to songs. Words that tell stories. Words that make you laugh.

Nelleke counted on her fingers the number of letters the Schoolmaster had taught them. A through N. Fourteen.

"How many more letters <u>are</u> there, Schoolmaster?" Nelleke asked, forgetting as always to ask for permission to talk. "Do they go on forever?"

"Twenty-six in all," he answered impatiently. But that did not answer her question.

Isabela knelt down, put her arm around Nelleke and whispered to her, "Twelve more. We're more than halfway through. How about if I teach you to read some words tonight at bedtime? You tell me five words you'd like to be able to read. Wouldn't that be fun?"

Nelleke shook her head up and down, hugged Isabela, and drew an "N" on her slate.

The Schoolmaster faced the children and held up his perfectly made letter.

"N. You see? Up. Down. Up. N. Nnnnnnnnn. N for Nnn...NO.
N for nnnn . . . NOT NOW. N for nnnn . . . NEVER."

Baring their teeth in perfect imitation of their teacher, the children
chanted,

"N for Nnn . . . NO . . . N for NOT NOW. N for nnn . . . NEVER."

Chapter Twenty-nine
Disappearance

The Broekhof household was the first to be alerted. Jos had just stepped down from the bed stool to the floor. Before gently pulling the curtains around her, Jos gazed at Myriam for a moment. The smile she wore while still sleeping swept Jos with a feeling of contentment and gratitude. His wife's listlessness and vagueness that had frightened and haunted him since Catherina's death had nearly been replaced by her former self. She had returned to the role expected of a good Dutch wife – dedicating her days again to scrubbing their home – furniture, floors, walls – to her daily marketing where she lingered on the way to chat with neighbors and vendors – and to her boys, aware once again of the need to balance praise and discipline, supervising their studies, interrupting when their playful fights became potentially hurtful.

At the Comfrij wedding celebration, she seemed, if still somewhat reserved, to be truly enjoying herself, joining in the singing, even dancing with Jos briefly before bringing Nelleke home with them for the night. The worrisome, unkempt appearance had been replaced by a coiffure that was carefully combed each morning and neatly tucked into a clean bonnet.

He had now moved on to sharing the Tuesday, then the Wednesday, etchings from the Strad Series with her – always in the privacy of their bedchamber and always returning them afterwards to the locked cabinet in his study. Each time she asked to see Monday's too, so she could get a sense of the entire story the etchings seemed to be revealing. She covered her mouth and exclaimed "OH!" upon seeing that the female figure had placed one leg over the tub, her bare toes pointing down to the surface of the bath water, the man lifting her skirt above her ankle.

"Where did you get these, Jos? There are seven in all? One for every day of the week? Were they expensive?"

"I will tell you the entire story once you've seen them all, my dear. That is, if you wish to," he teased.

"Jos, my mysterious husband," she would say kissing him on the cheek.

The biggest change, the change he was most hoping for, had not occurred. But she had become affectionate again. Rather than saddening her further because her own daughter was gone, the pleasure she experienced caring for the orphan seemed to have expanded her, made her more loving toward them all.

Just last Friday morning after the feast, Nelleke had awakened crying. Myriam ran to her immediately and found that blood on Nelleke's pillow had frightened her. Myriam investigated and found a little baby tooth on the floor. As he passed the bedroom door, Jos heard Myriam singing the traditional song she had used with both her boys to explain that the baby tooth would soon be replaced by a grown-up one. She used to sing to Catherina all day long, her repertoire of amusing or instructive children's songs seemed endless. But Catherina died with her baby teeth intact. Until recently, Myriam's songs seemed to have died with her.

"Why is little Jan crying?
He's lost his tooth.
Oh, it hurts when the tooth gets loose.
Little Jan can't sleep.
Poor little Jan.
Why is little Jan laughing?
He has a NEW tooth.
Now Jan is a little man.
He can bite carrots and cookies.
Happy little Jan."

The soothing sounds and silly words mixed with Nelleke's and Myriam's giggling followed him as he descended the stairs where his breakfast ale and warm honey bun were waiting.

This morning, Monday, as he was dressing, he retrieved a note from his pocket. He felt like tearing it into little pieces and burning it. Instead he reread it, "just one more time. It's just that Rudolfo up to his old tricks," he thought. "He's alert to the secrets and obsessions of all the townspeople, insinuates his way into their lives, and manipulates them into giving him money or food in exchange for information he claims that he and he alone is privy to."

There was a tinge of admiration, however, mixed into Jos's feelings of disgust and disdain. The dwarf was clever. Before he went blind, he had learned to read. He seemed to have retained everything – every poem and song, history facts. He had been especially drawn to botany and could talk about color as if he were still seeing plants and flowers right in front of him. There was a rumor that traders had consulted him during the tulip mania. He saw himself, not as a beggar, but as a businessman, providing something people wanted and were willing to pay for. Sometimes his riddles were outright ridiculous, an obvious attempt for attention, to prolong the exchange, demand more money. He could still write. Here was the note in Rudolfo's large scrawl, written with his oversized left hand, no spacing between the words, some lines overlapping, the lettering slanted so far to the right, it was almost vertical in places, no "T"s crossed or "I"s dotted – but still legible.

"Dear Mr. Broekhof, The object you desire is in the possession of someone who was in attendance at Thursday's wedding celebration. If you learn to love her, the object will be yours."

"Love HER?" The missing etching was in the hands of a WOMAN? Certainly not a respectable woman! No woman at that feast would own such a detailed depiction. LOVE her? He did not love, did not want to love, would never love any woman but Myriam. In a way, he had been wooing Myriam for nearly fourteen years, since the day he first met her. He won her once. Then lost her. Now, hopefully, he was winning her back.

Once, Jos would never have discarded any reference to his precious etching, no matter how obscure. Anything that might eventually prove to be a clue was carefully dated, recorded, explored, and filed. But this note seemed bizarre to him, almost desperate.

As he was about to dispose of it, there was a soft tapping on the door. What was this? The boys should have already left for school. The home's only live-in servants, Anna and Karel, never knocked on the door of their bedroom. During Myriam's prolonged sadness, she slept for hours every day. He believed in hard work and duty, but he could also see that sleep was restorative for her. She would awake soon enough. He did not want her disturbed.

Tap, tap, tap. Jos pulled on his trousers, tucked in his shirt, and opened the door.

Karel held out a note. Jos stepped into the hallway and closed the door behind him. "This was delivered moments ago, Sir. I thought you should receive it immediately."

The note was hastily folded. "To Mr. Jos Broekhof. URGENT."

URGENT? Had one of his sons been involved in an accident? Injured? Fallen into the canal? Myriam did not have the strength to recover a second time if she lost another child. Or was it his business? Had there been a robbery? Had it burned to the ground?

De Nes had recently suggested a new business direction, one that, given the people's endless desire to gorge themselves on sweets, could be quite profitable, he believed – mixing sugar with the intriguing spices coming from the East – cinnamon, nutmeg, cloves, ginger. A ready-made concoction that bakers, cooks, and housewives could add to their breads and cakes. This very morning he had an appointment with De Nes to discuss his report. Sources. Costs. Expenses of the new venture. Bulk storage required. Potential outlets. Pricing . . . Profit.

He unfolded the note and glanced at the bottom of the page to read the name of the sender. *"With concerned greetings, Dr. Voerman, Resident Physician. Amsterdam City Orphanage.*

"So it was Nelleke then. Something had happened to her. The child found her way into too many mishaps. She was impetuous and foolish."

"Dear Mr. Broekhof,

Please excuse my contacting you so early in the day. The children's wing of the orphanage is in mourning at this moment. The primary caretaker of the youngest girls, their "Big Sister," Isabelle, has disappeared. Although she read and sang to the children last night and tucked them in as always, she was not in her bed this morning and cannot be found. The little girls are upset, confused, and afraid. Isabelle and Nelleke were especially close and Nelleke is inconsolable. As you know, she is a resilient child, but the accumulation of losses in her young life, seems to have collapsed her spirit. She is asking for Mrs. Broekhof.

Sir, I know your wife is a busy woman with many responsibilities, but I wanted to share Nelleke's request with you.

Thank you, Sir."

When Myriam arrived at the orphanage a short time later, she met Mrs. Heijn hurrying through the courtyard. Myriam had never seen the usually cool, brisk woman so frazzled.

"Oh, Mrs. Broekhof. Thank goodness you are here. I'm on my way to warn the Schoolmaster that his pupils will not be quite themselves today. The other "Big Sisters" and I managed to calm most of them and dress them. We just want to normalize the day for them.

"Nelleke, however, upon seeing Isabela's empty, mussed bed and not being able to find Isabela anywhere, climbed into Isabela's bed, rolled over on her stomach, buried her head in the pillow, and will not budge. The arrival of the police upset her further. I told the police my fears and observations. At first I thought she might have run off with that student of Rembrandt's, that Pieter Hals. Pieter is from a fine family, but you never know what young people will do these days. In any case, the police have since reported that they encountered Pieter, carrying his painter's case, on his way to Rembrandt's studio. Pieter was as alarmed and horrified as we are."

"I also told the police that Isabela was a clean, neat young woman who never left her bed in disarray. Her nightclothes have not been found, leading us to speculate that she may have been carried away still wearing them. Her day clogs were still placed neatly under her bed ready to step into. Her freshly laundered uniform was hanging in the closet. As you know, our residents are allowed few personal belongings, but Isabela did keep her rosary under her pillow. It is not there, not under the bed either. The police asked to talk to the night guard, but could not locate him."

Just then the day guard came running up. "Mrs. Heijn, I reported to duty at my usual seven o'clock time this morning, but I did not see the night guard. Occasionally, he leaves a few minutes before I arrive and we pass each other coming and going. I did not see him on the street either. 'Perhaps, he took another route today,' I thought. "I took my post and just now, an hour later, I heard some thumping coming from the small room behind the guard stool. The door is locked from the outside. I searched in the spot where the night guard always leaves the key to that room, but it isn't there. When I call through the door, the thumping only becomes louder."

"A duplicate key to that room is kept in the kitchen. I will get it for you and together we will investigate, Sir. First I must guide Mrs. Broekhof to one of our distressed orphans. Secondly, I must warn the Schoolmaster of what has happened. You should know, too, that our Isabela is missing and may have been kidnapped. How they got past the guard is something the police will investigate. Be alert today, Sir."

"Thirdly, as long as no additional crises present themselves, I will investigate your thumping sound."

"Mrs. Heijn," Myriam offered. "The doctor wrote that Nelleke has asked for me. May I have your permission for her to spend the week with us? You have much to attend to here. If you agree, I will go directly to her room. I know where it is."

"Yes. Yes. Of course. Please go to her," Mrs. Heijn agreed with a wave of her hand as she continued her walk toward the school room.

Myriam was halfway across the courtyard, when Isabela's group of little girls began exiting the children's wing and walking toward her, the youngest ones holding the hands of the "Big Sister" temporarily assigned to them, the others clinging to each other, their eyes red, their cheeks wet.

When the group passed Myriam, Bernadien pulled on her sleeve.

"Mrs. Broekhof. You've come for Nelleke? Take me with you. Please. Take me home with you too," she pleaded. Myriam bent down and embraced Bernadien. In the little contact she had had with the child, she had found her sour and unpleasant, but she was still a child.

"We would like for you to visit, Bernadien," she said kindly. "But at a later time."

Bernadien sniffled and continued walking toward the classroom, but she looked back at Myriam with a frown that was almost threatening.

Myriam found Nelleke just as the Housemother had described her, face down in Isabela's bed. It was as if Nelleke believed that, as long as Isabela's scent lingered, there was a chance she would reappear, embrace them, and give them all an explanation. Myriam sat down on the bed and began rubbing Nelleke's back gently. Nelleke shrugged off the touching. When Myriam placed next to her face the doll Nelleke always played with at the Broekhof's, however, Nelleke turned her face slightly to see what was there and then rolled over completely and threw herself into Myriam's arms.

Myriam made an effort to remain strong for Nelleke, but Myriam knew too well, the complicated mix of feelings brought on by sudden loss: the fear, resentment, anger, confusion, even betrayal – and the aloneness. They cried together.

As they passed through the orphanage gate onto the street, Myriam noted that the thumping noise continued and that there was also a very faint grunting/humming noise coming from behind that locked door. It may have been an animal. It may have been human. But it was not her concern at the moment. She would dedicate this week to reassuring, comforting, and diverting her lovely, little guest.

"Let's go back to my house, get our shopping baskets, and go to the market, Nelleke. How does that sound? Will you help me choose the best vegetables? Shall we find some fresh fish for tonight's supper?"

When Myriam began singing, Nelleke laughed a little and joined in on the last line:

"Fisherman from a foreign land,
What have you in your net?
Two herring and two mackerel
All juicy and well oiled.
Put them in the kettle
and brown them in the pan.
Place them on a great big plate
and lap them right up, Ma'am."

After helping Myriam market, prepare, and serve, Nelleke sat down with the family to enjoy the evening meal. Because Jos had to attend an emergency Regents' meeting at the orphanage, he would be late. Myriam recited grace. As they were finishing, Jos arrived. Anna brought him a plate of food. After kissing his family and Nelleke and taking a few bites, he reported what he had learned.

"The night watchman's wife visited early in the morning, alarmed that he had not returned. Mrs. Heijn was wondering if he too had been kidnapped and whether she should alert the police about still another disappearance, when she remembered the thumping that the day watchman had reported. She had been so involved comforting children and integrating Isabela's daily duties into her own that she had forgotten, she said. She hurried to the kitchen and grabbed the key to the small storage room behind the guard post. The thumping had subsided. Cautiously, the day guard opened the door. There they found stretched out on the bare ground on his back the night watchman with a kerchief over his mouth, his hands and feet bound. The man had been asleep and was startled by the sudden light and the two people standing over him. He had to remain there a few more minutes while Mrs. Heijn returned to the kitchen to get a knife to cut the ropes."

"You can imagine his relief at being found and released," Mrs. Hijn reported to the Regents. The perpetrators had not struck him, nor had they robbed him, but he was stiff, hungry, tired, and angry that it had taken so long to free him. He was anxious to return home, but Mrs. Heijn would not allow it until the police interviewed him.

The night guard reported to the police and again this evening to the Regents how three Dutch soldiers had gagged him, grabbed the keys to the gate, tied him up and placed him in that tiny space. One of the soldiers did the talking. The guard recognized him. He saw the man once walking arm in arm with one of the young cooks from the orphanage kitchen, but he had never been dressed as a soldier before. All the soldier said was, 'Do not make a sound. We will not hurt anyone. We just have some quick business to accomplish. Cooperate and you won't be hurt.' He could not see the other two soldiers very well in the dark, but he had a vague impression that they may not have been Dutch soldiers at all, but foreigners. Very soon afterward, he heard the three of them return and exit through the gate. 'Leaving me without food or water or a pillow,' he added rubbing his sore head. He heard them close the orphanage gate behind them and he was grateful for that. They were inside for such a short time, he didn't think they could have done much mischief, but it was worrisome."

"Delicious soup, Anna. Another bowl, please."

"Nelleke helped pick out the vegetables, Jos," Myriam told him. She's a good vegetable scrubber too."

"And Mrs. Broekhof let me cut up some of the carrots, Mr. Broekhof. I was very, very careful with the knife."

"Yes, she was," Myriam confirmed.

Myriam was anxious about exposing the child to too many details about the story. She knew that Jos liked to draw out a tale and keep people a bit on edge. For her and Nelleke all that mattered was to learn if Isabela had been found, if she was safe. But Jos was obviously going to share everything he knew. Perhaps he should have been a policeman or a writer, Myriam thought. He loves mysteries and clues. Myriam placed her arm around Nelleke as Jos, after slurping half of his second bowl of soup, tried to restart the telling.

Nelleke was trying to be polite and not interrupt, not ask questions, but she could contain herself no longer. She did not really see how anything she had heard was relevant to the answer she hoped to hear.

"But is Isabela back now, Mr. Broekhof? Did the police find her?"

When she heard his answer, "They are still looking for her," Nelleke buried her face in Myriam's shoulder and did not look up until Jos stopped speaking. Jos was gratified that his boys were very attentive, however.

"Assuming that the three soldiers are somehow linked to Isabela's disappearance, the police searched the city and asked citizens to be alert for three men and a young woman who speaks Dutch with an accent and who may be either English or Spanish."

"Isabela is from Spain," Nelleke said, the words muffled since she did not lift her face from Myriam's arm.

"Of course, they searched the boats in the harbor too, but by then it had been hours since the three men had forced their way into the orphanage. The harbor authorities did report something that might be relevant. We just don't know. A small fishing boat had been among the first vessels to exit the harbor once the gate was lowered at dawn. The boat flew a Dutch flag and was manned by a Dutchman named Cornelius van Hensen who had registered the boat and requested a docking space for the previous night. There were two other fishermen on board. A young woman with dark hair – a wife of one of the fishermen, they assumed, was calmly sitting in the back of the boat, cleaning fish."

"Several sailors on nearby ships had seen three men board the fishing vessel in the middle of the night. One of them was carrying a woman, but men bring women to the boats all the time and the sailors thought nothing of it."

"Jos, please. The children," Myriam scolded.

"Well," he said defensively, "In any case, they could not see her well, had no idea of her age or appearance. She was wrapped in a blanket. They were adamant, though, in insisting that the woman seemed to be cooperating. She was not kicking or calling out."

"Perhaps you should share the rest of what you know with me later, Jos. Anna, I believe it is time for pudding. In honor of Nelleke's staying with us for an entire week, we've made a delicious molasses sauce."

That announcement brought enthusiastic "Mmmmm" sounds from the boys, but was not enough to divert Jos from continuing.

"One more bit of news. The police visited the Van Hensen family. They live in Amsterdam. He is not a soldier, but a sailor who works on a variety of ships from several companies. They had no idea why he might be wearing a soldier's uniform or where he could obtain one. He was an explorer in his own way, perhaps, they said, but would never harm anyone. They believed the night watchman had identified him incorrectly. Cornelius had been home for the past three days and had told them all good-bye the previous night. He had accepted a position on a ship that would take him to the East Indies, he said, and would be gone a long time. They, too, were concerned about Isabela's sudden disappearance. They had nursed her back to health eighteen months ago and then led her to the orphanage. 'She was a lovely young lady,' they said and they hoped she had come to no harm."

"What about the cook? Did the police interview her?" asked Myriam.

"Oh, yes. That's right. Good thinking, Myriam. The cook said that she and Cornelius intended to marry as soon as he returned from his next trip. The last time she saw him was the night before last. She had no idea why he would break into the orphanage in the night. In fact, she was adamant that the night watchman was wrong. The soldier could not possibly have been her fiancé. Even so, because of hint of a possibility of a connection between the cook and Isabel's disappearance, Mrs. Heijn fired the cook."

"The police will continue to investigate, but they have many matters to attend to. I fear we may never have answers. Meanwhile, the Regents made a decision in the guarding of the orphanage gate. Beginning immediately, there will be TWO night guards from 7:00 in the evening until 7:00 in the morning."

"Oh, and the doctor also reported to the Regents briefly. By the end of the day, the children seemed to be recovering somewhat."

"With all she had to do during this confusing day, Mrs. Heijn managed to hire a replacement for the disappeared Big Sister. This new hire led the orphans in prayer and put them to bed with a sip of warm milk to help them sleep. The Regents congratulated Mrs. Heijn on her handling of the crisis."

Chapter Thirty
Words Into Phrases

⟨⟩

"Jos, she can count to 1000 now. This child, who has no patience for sewing or embroidery, will sit for hours, observing moving ants and counting them. While I weed and water Catherina's memory garden, Nelleke studies the ants."

"'They have six legs,' she reported to me, 'and a body in three parts.'"

"Oh, she made endless observations."

"They're just so busy," Myriam continued, in an adult woman imitation of a little girl's voice. "All doing a job – like in a city. Look at these, Mrs. Broekhof. They're working together. I think they're hauling food back to the nest. I put a piece of bread – as tiny a piece as I could make near them, but it takes three of them to move it along. They disappeared with the crumb into a hole in the ground. Do you think they've got baby ants in there? Will they use my bread to feed their babies?'"

"Nelleke picked up a stick and poked it down the hole after the ants disappeared with her bread. She wanted to borrow my garden tool and dig up the site so she could see what they were doing underground, but I diverted her – for now."

"Of course, she wants to know everything, our curious guest, and asked me about the stone animals. She exclaimed over the rabbits, frogs, turtles, and bear cubs, petting them and talking to them as if they were live."

"'This is such a pretty little space, Mrs. Broekhof.'"

"So I told her, Jos, about the memory garden, about Catherina. Later I showed her Catherina's doll house, all the precious parts to it. You gave it to Catherina, Jos. I hope you don't mind. Nelleke would always rather be outside, exploring anyway, than playing pretend."

"I'm glad you could talk about Catherina with Nelleke," Jos told her. He could see she felt better just being about to speak Catherina's name out loud. Perhaps, he thought, so did he.

It was Saturday night. Nelleke would accompany them to church as she had been doing for several months now, and spend Sunday with them. They were scheduled to return her to the orphanage as usual by late Sunday afternoon in time for Sunday supper and Bible reading.

Isabela had not been found. The police had other matters to attend to, more important than the disappearance of a young orphaned woman. They might never know what happened to her.

"Jos, Nelleke, has not slept at the orphanage since Isabela disappeared. I'm fearful she will fall back into severe mourning. There, she is not allowed to keep the doll she always sleeps with here. The "Big Sister" in charge of her group is new, of course. There will be nothing and no one to comfort her."

"Jos, I would like to keep her with us longer. Perhaps much longer. You're a Regent. Can we get permission to do that?"

Late Sunday afternoon, Jos went to the orphanage alone. He found Mrs. Heijn in the dining hall spooning soup into her husband's dribbling mouth. The children had all gone up to bed.

"Everybody looks after his own share," Mr. Heijn yelled, in an apparent attempt at a greeting. Each word sent a mix of spittle and bits of food dribbling down his chin onto the large cloth covering him. Mrs. Heijn hushed her husband and dabbed at the mess.

"Mrs. Heijn, excuse me. I fear I am interrupting you."

"Please sit down, Mr. Broekhof. Mr. Heijn likes adult company during his supper."

"Good evening, Mr. Heijn."

"One cannot shoe a running horse, Sir."

"How true, Mr. Heijn."

"Mrs. Heijn, Mrs. Broekhof and I would like to keep Nelleke with us indefinitely. I'm afraid she has quite wormed her way into my wife's heart. We lost a daughter, as you know."

"One joy scatters a hundred griefs."

"I suspected as much, Mr. Broekhof. You must know the child well enough to have observed that she does have challenges with self-control and obedience."

"My wife seems to find those qualities enchanting actually, Mrs. Heijn. As the mother of two boys, she knows when to divert and when to discipline as the situation calls for."

"Set a beggar on horseback, and he'll outride the Devil."

"Enough of your outbursts, Mr. Heijn. You will get your honeycake only if you remain silent. I am conducting business with Mr. Broekhof."

Apparently, Mr. Heijn understood. Though his mouth was wide open, he remained silent. Mrs. Heijn placed a bit of honey cake on his tongue and he chewed it contentedly.

"As a Regent, you are familiar with our rules. In order for us to switch custody – and it sounds as if that is what you are talking about – to an unrelated family, we must first get the permission of the next of kin. In this case, that means, contacting Nelleke's two aunts. One lives nearby. The other lives in Ouderkerk. This will take time. And, of course, they must both agree. Meanwhile, you may keep Nelleke with you if you wish."

As Jos opened the door to his home, his thoughts were still on the new developments at his business. His manager, De Nes, had worked with local bakers to concoct sample products using the sugar/spice mixes he suggested. Next De Nes named and numbered each sample and asked the workers of Broekhof and Son to sample and react to them. "#7 too sweet," most agreed. "This one tastes like beef, not bread." "Me, I like my bread plain – with butter when I've got the coin for it."

So De Nes kept experimenting and refining the mixes until the comments were more favorable. "Mmmm a hint of something interesting. What is that?" "What's in this one? Cinnamon? Cloves? I like it."

Once they began marketing a few successful sugar/spice mixes, De Nes suggested that they mix a bit of sugar and spices into butter and see what result that gave. De Nes was conducting experiments on those now.

Jos thought he had not yet adjusted to the little orphan running up to greet him whenever he returned home, yet tonight when she did not, he realized he missed what had become a routine for them both. "Where were they then?" he wondered. Not in the kitchen. Not in the garden. Not in Catherina's room. Then he found them.

Myriam had purchased a smaller version of her writing desk and placed it next to hers. The two of them were bent over several slates, sounding out words, their white bonnets side by side. When he leaned over to kiss Myriam, Nelleke hopped off her small chair and offered it to Jos.

"Hello, Mr. Broekhof. Please sit down." As soon as he obeyed, his short legs splayed out in front of him, Nelleke sat on his lap.

"Mrs. Broekhof is teaching me to read any word I want, Mr. Broekhof."

She held up the slate, pointed at a list and read them all.

"Daniel,

Samuel,

Jacob – that's my brother,

Jesus,

Anna,

Doll,

Ant,

Tooth."

"Isabela," she read sadly.

"Where do you think she is?"

"And look at this, Jos. Nelleke can pick out the words in a phrase and read some of the phrases too. Show Mr. Broekhof, Nelleke," Myriam said, handing her another, larger slate. Find the phrase with 'tooth' in it, why don't you?"

Nelleke looked up and down the slate covered with phrases in Myriam's neat handwriting.

"It has two 't's in it," Miriam said encouragingly.

"And two 'o's too," Jos said, joining the game.

"I see it. I see it. I can read the whole thing."

"Poor little Jan lost his tooth."

Jos picked up a piece of chalk and drew a boy with a sad face and tears.

Daniel and Simon burst in the front door, heard the three of them laughing, and went to investigate.

By the time Anna called them to dinner, the five of them were still crowded into Myriam's writing nook, thinking up words to make Nelleke laugh, and writing them out for her.

"Sour milk. The boy spit it out," said Samuel, making a mock spitting noise."

"Pig in mud. It stinks," said Daniel, holding his nose.

"Okay, boys, take your little sister …," Jos stopped when he realized what he had just said, and backed up. "Take Nelleke to wash up. Supper is ready."

But the boys had heard. "Is Nelleke our little sister now?" Samuel asked.

In a preview of the crisp fall and raw winter to come, the late summer evening had suddenly turned cool. Myriam took from the linen chest the quilt that had been packed away most of the summer. White, soft, and downy with a wide garland of embroidered flowers at its center, it was one of their favorite wedding presents. Although she never looked forward to trudging through the icy streets, placing the quilt back on their bed each fall had always brought forth delightful memories of the first months following their wedding. This year those exhilarating nights of tenderness and discovery seemed to belong to another couple.

After they lost Catherina, during Myriam's "dark period," as Jos thought of it, the quilt had become gray and worn looking. Recently, though, Anna and Myriam had laundered all the bedding in the house. They scrubbed the sheets, pillow cases and coverlets, hung them in the sun, pressed them, folded them and carefully stacked them to avoid wrinkling. The quilt, pulled up to their chins, smelled of lye, fresh air, and sunshine. The summer smells also reminded her of Nelleke's pleasure, as she worked alongside the two women, stopping frequently to splash her little hands around in the suds.

"I noticed some leaves on the ground today, Jos. They scattered their bright reds and yellows around Catherina's memory garden. Nelleke quickly gathered them up, counted them, and arranged them in different patterns. But it started a thought. It will be difficult to contain Nelleke's energy inside the house. I'm delighted to continue to teach her whatever I can and we can go skating in mid-winter, of course, but I'm wondering if we should investigate more formal education possibilities for her. Our sons attend an all-boys school, but the possibilities for girls are more limited."

"You are a superb teacher, my dear," Jos said. Reaching under the quilt for her hand and then bringing it to his lips, he tried to warm it by covering it with kisses.

"She is still young and is enjoying all the learning you offer her. I suggest we inquire from our friends who have daughters and make a decision for the following fall. Would you find it burdensome to be Nelleke's instructor for another year?"

He could see that Myriam was already planning a year's worth of lessons in her head.

She turned to him and smiled.

"Thursday?" Jos then asked in a low, conspiratorial voice. It had been almost a week since they had viewed the etchings together. Looking shy and perhaps feeling somewhat guilty, even fearful of what Thursday might contain, Myriam nodded.

Jos opened the bed curtains, stepped down the bed ladder, reached beside the bed under a chair where he had hidden the etchings, and climbed back up. Myriam was sitting up, waiting expectantly

"Start at the beginning, Jos."

Slowly, one by one, Jos held up one etching at a time for Myriam to view. The ornate silver frames contrasted with the starkness of the scenes: one man, one woman, one wooden tub. Ordinary folk perhaps at the end of a day of hard work, after their young children were asleep. There would be no servants in this household. They may have been farmers or laborers, or tailors, shoemakers or printers running their own shop. "Or perhaps this couple wasn't married," Jos suddenly thought with alarm. He had always assumed they were.

"Monday's" innocent and caring gestures. The familiarity with which she leaned into him, rubbing his tired shoulders. The way he gave himself over to her care. It seemed too trusting, too normal to be illicit. He hoped that Myriam too assumed this couple had exchanged vows of fidelity, that the artist had captured them in private moments which confirmed and strengthened their bond. Still "Thursday" was hardly a repeat of "Monday." Baths were not a common occurrence in Dutch homes. This evening story was unusual and it was advancing.

Myriam never asked to hold the etchings herself. She was willing to look at them, even perhaps to relate to them, but she did not want to become so involved with them as to touch them. It would have pushed the invasive feeling she already felt to a point where shame would have negated any curiosity and voyeuristic daring she allowed herself.

With the three familiar etchings arranged in order, Myriam noticed something for the first time.

"Oh, look, Jos, I think there are letters in the lower right-hand corner of each etching. They're blended into the side of the tub. Is that an 'N' and an 'S'? Those are Nelleke's initials too. It had never occurred to Jos that Nelleke and her father had the same initials. He did not answer, drawing her attention to the numbers just below the initials.

"Do you see this, Myriam? 1/1. That's etched into each of them too."

"Is that a date? He couldn't have completed them all in one day."

"You're right. It does not refer to a date. With an etching, an artist can use the same plate he has cut many times. With each subsequent printing, however, the print becomes a little less sharp. Each printing becomes less valuable. On some etchings you'll find 5/20 for example. That means that 20 prints were made in all and that the viewer is seeing the fifth printing."

"So only one printing was made of these?"

"Right, my dear. We possess the only printings of this set that were ever made. FIRST printing – 1 – out of the ONLY printing – 1. 1/1."

"Jos, you are so clever."

"Are you ready for Thursday then?" Jos asked, holding back, teasing her, but also forcing her to agree to react more fully to what she was seeing.

"If you think it's not too much for me, Jos, go ahead." Then as a delaying tactic, not sure she was ready for the next step in the series, Myriam switched her curiosity to all the unanswered questions surrounding the etchings.

"How long have you had these, Jos? Did you buy them as an investment? How much time have you spent with them?"

"Two more etchings, my dear, and I will answer all your questions."

"Friday, Saturday, and then the missing Sunday, the identity of the artist and so much more to explain," Jos thought. "I promised her, but I will take my time."

Myriam nodded and slid down into the bed slightly as if she were putting distance between herself and these works of art her husband so treasured.

Layering the four etchings on his belly, Jos separated out the new one, held it up, and brought the candle close so she could see it clearly. This one did not elicit the "Oh" that "Wednesday's" had. Instead, after one quick glance and a second longer stare, Myriam covered her eyes.

"I've pushed her too far," Jos thought, frightened. "I've disgusted her. Alarmed her. Alienated her."

Myriam had slid way down under the quilt now. Only the top of her sleeping bonnet showed.

"Why did I share them with her in the first place? Why did I keep going? I could have just showed her 'Monday,' so sweet and innocent. What was I thinking?"

Then a snuffled giggle arose from under the quilt.

Jos couldn't move quickly enough. He slid off the bed, placed the etchings on a chair, blew out the candle, climbed back up in the bed, lifted the quilt, and slipped in beside her. All that seemed to have taken an eternity, but she was still giggling. Jos pulled her against him. It had been over a year since she had allowed him to caress her. With visions of the nameless couple in their heads, the man reaching for the woman's bare breasts bursting out of her bodice and floating on top of the water, Myriam and Jos renewed their love for one another.

As they were falling asleep, Jos murmured into the back of Myriam's neck,

"Myriam, I forgot to tell you. One of Nelleke's aunts – the one who lives in Amsterdam – she agreed to sign over full custody to us."

Myriam heard but was too weary and too content in her husband's arms to ask about her other aunt – the one on the farm.

Chapter Thirty-one
Return to Ouderkerk

"One year is a long time in the life of a three-year-old, Nelleke. He will get used to you again," Griet said, trying her best to turn the butter churn with Jacob clinging tightly to her knees. Nelleke's little brother eyed her warily from behind the folds of Griet's skirt.

"Langenek knew me," Nelleke said. "He came right up to me."

"Probably just looking for food."

Nelleke pouted. She felt like running outside, but Aunt Griet had made it clear that chores must always come before anything else.

"You are old enough to help the family now," Uncle Johannes kept repeating firmly.

"There is much work on a farm and we expect you to contribute."

Her current chore was to shell the peas she had picked that morning. Her back was sore from bending over the plants. Now, seated at the table, she had shelled one bucket, but there were two left. Splitting one pod after another and scraping the small hard balls into a pan was tedious. The only fun was counting them. She was up to 376.

"All that counting slows you down, Nelleke."

It was at the weekly Regents' meeting that Jos had learned about the Verhoevens' decision. Mrs. Heijn included it in her report, almost as an afterthought in what she called "changes of note."

"Anselma Maarten has recovered from a severe sore throat and fever, but the doctor and I are monitoring her closely."

"Our newest orphan, Georgina Xander, refused to eat for the first three days. I am happy to tell you that she is now eating normally."

"You may remember Nelleke Stradwijk who was enrolled at the orphanage one year ago. The aunt and uncle with whom she lived previously have requested that she return. They were recovering from losses sustained during a major flood on their farm. Their situation has improved. They are better able to care for her now. They inquired about her behavior. Her wildness and disobedience were constant worries then. I assured them that, after a year in our care and the strict daily regimens we follow, she has become more respectful and subdued."

"I wish to acknowledge the generosity of Mr. Broekhof and his wife who have cared for Nelleke since Isabela's disappearance."

Turning to Jos, Mrs. Heijn said, "Thank you, Mr. Broekhof. You have been most kind to our little orphan. Her uncle will come for her on Saturday. If you can bring her back to the orphanage by Saturday noon?"

Jos barely heard the request – or rather, in the voice of Mrs. Heijn what sounded more like an order. Surely the other Regents heard his heart thundering in his ears. They must have noticed him gulp down an entire goblet of wine in an attempt to quench his suddenly dry throat. When a cough seized him and would not let go, he pushed himself out of the large chair and walked shakily to the corridor.

To his horror, tears had welled up in his eyes. He tried to blame the coughing, but had to acknowledge that it was loss he was feeling, the kind of sudden, unexpected loss he should have acknowledged when Catherina died. Instead, he had concentrated on being the comforting husband and father. Now, although his first thoughts again immediately settled on Myriam's reaction to this news and the unhappiness of his boys, he had to admit to himself that he too would suffer enormously without Nelleke in their home. As he got the cough under control, he became aware that he was trembling. It had never occurred to him that he could so enjoy, yes, even love, someone else's child.

He felt ashamed that his original interest in the child was related to the missing etching. The twin mysteries of the etching's whereabouts and Nicolaas's murder no longer occupied him. Myriam refused to view "Friday" and "Saturday." The unfinished set remained locked in his hidden cupboard. He had not looked at them since the joyous night Myriam returned to him.

As Jos stood alone in the corridor, he could hear Mrs. Heijn's voice continuing her report. At this moment he reviled her. He wanted to slam the door and never hear her voice again, never again set eyes on her smug, self-satisfied face. How dare she disregard the Broekhofs' feelings for Nelleke and make this announcement so indifferently – at a meeting!

The orphanage was a business to her, a place of employment. One orphan was like any other. She formed no attachments to any of them. She thought of the Broekhofs as servants, for Heaven's sake, assisting her with her duties. Yet, they had indicated their desire to assume permanent custody of the child. Did Mrs. Heijn assume that was a gesture to prove to the community that they were solid Calvinists and upright citizens? Did she believe they would display the child in order to flaunt their goodness and sacrifice? Is that what she thought?

He wiped his face, stretched his head upward and took two steps in his usual bouncing way, feeling more keenly than ever the challenge of his small stature.

"Gentlemen. Mrs. Heijn. I seem to have taken ill. Please excuse me."

He considered taking the long way home, but decided instead to go directly. He did not want to encounter anyone. What he wanted was Myriam's comfort. During these past summer months, he had felt so buoyant, so proud of his happy, lively family, so proud of himself for having coaxed Myriam back, for having brought a daughter into their lives. Now he felt that he had failed them miserably. He was a Regent of the orphanage for Heaven's sake. He should not have entrusted the decision about Nelleke's future to Mrs. Heijn. All she cared about was enforcing the rules. When the Amsterdam aunt agreed to relinquish custody, he had assumed the other aunt would also. How stupid, inept, and incompetent he felt. How powerless. He would speak with the Verhoeven couple personally. His first visit with them had not gone well, but he was determined that the next meeting would be successful. This time he would secure their cooperation and acquiescence.

"702," Nelleke pronounced. "Two buckets full. I need to use the privy, Aunt Griet."

"Oh, all right, but hurry back, Nelleke. And don't go anywhere near the pond!"

Nelleke leaped up and ran out, kicking over a bucket of milk on the doorstep. The pigs approached with glee and began lapping at it before it all seeped into the ground.

"Nelleke, that was all the milk we have left for today. Milk for the boys and for the butter we need to sell. Please watch where you are stepping. Uncle Johannes will be unhappy. He works so hard to take care of us."

"I'm sorry, Aunt Griet," Nelleke said. She came back inside and kissed her aunt on the cheek. She tried to kiss her brother too, but he turned his head away.

She used to have such strong loving feelings toward her only sibling. The way he would laugh uncontrollably when she played peek-a-boo, hiding behind a chair, then jumping out, calling his name. How they warmed each other on the freezing winter nights, their two child bodies curled into one under Aunt Griet's and Uncle Johannes's bed. As soon as he could walk, she taught him to jump. She would go leaping around the house, making up silly rhymes and he would follow, trying to imitate her, alternately bending and straightening his sturdy legs that sometimes actually left the ground. Their own little parade.

In the months she was in Amsterdam, Jacob had become shy and withdrawn. The Verhoevens did not have many visitors and there was so much work that most Sundays they did not even make it to the village church. He seemed to have forgotten how to play and to have forgotten Nelleke herself. Since arriving back at the farm, Nelleke had tried coaxing him away from Griet. Twice he had become interested long enough to join her – once watching her spin a top she found in a corner, once sticking his tongue out and wrinkling up his nose following her example, but he made faces in a serious manner. No smile. Whenever they seemed to be making progress, Aunt Griet or Uncle Johannes would call her away to wash the dishes or help drag the laundry out to the line.

Griet had nearly brought the butter to the turning point when Frans awoke from his morning nap and called for her. He was still a sickly child with thin, weak limbs and she herself was recovering from still another miscarriage. She rubbed her overused arms, spread honey on bread for the children, and sipped some thin ale. She had planned to churn the milk in the bucket that Nelleke just spilled, but there were many additional pressing chores to choose from.

Griet had hoped that reintegrating her now seven-year-old niece to their household would be a support for her. Nelleke may be a year older and taller, but her unpredictability kept Griet on edge. She still had that sweet, affectionate nature that made it difficult for Griet to discipline her consistently. She could not stay angry with her for long. But that meant that Nelleke found it easier to continue her careless behavior. Uncle Johannes was a gentle man, but he too was exasperated with her at times.

Griet carried Frans to the door and looked out over the field. The privy was only a few yards from the house. Nelleke should be finished by now. But there was the door left wide open, the round wooden opening visible, the odor almost reaching the kitchen. Nelleke had wandered off and she had not put lime down the privy.

Griet strained to see her and caught a glimpse of her in a section of undeveloped land that used to divide the two family properties – one that had belonged to Griet's father, the other to Johannes's mother. That was before their parents died, they inherited the properties, married, and joined both small farms together into one larger one. Nelleke's head alternately bobbed and disappeared. Griet felt obligated to stand and watch to be sure . . . . "She's probably picking wildflowers or chasing spiders," Griet thought. "Just as long as she stays away from the pond."

Nelleke stayed out until the fall cold drove her back into the house and she knew she could not ignore Aunt Griet's third cry for her to return. She sat down at the kitchen table reluctantly and began shelling the third bucket of peas. Aunt Griet sent her to wash her hands first.

After making a great show of washing, rinsing, and drying – probably a delaying tactic, Griet thought – Nelleke sat back at the table again.

"Where was I, Aunt Griet? I know. 702. This pod has 6 peas in it. 703, 704, 705, 706, 707, 708. Each hard pea made a plunking sound as she dropped it into the pan.

"I could teach her addition," Griet thought. She insists on counting and the addition would speed up the process. But when would I find time to teach her that? It seems the more she learns, the more she wants to learn. I can't keep up."

After about two minutes, Nelleke began scratching her legs. They got so itchy that she lifted up her skirt, scratched harder and began slapping them. Griet noticed and came to investigate.

"Oh, Nelleke, what did you get into out there? There are red welts all up and down your legs. Are they bug bites? Nettles? Hives? Your forehead is a little warm too." When Johannes arrived home, he found Nelleke lying down with a cold cloth on her head, Jacob clinging to Griet, Frans in Griet's arms, one churn full of butter when there should have been two, two-thirds of the peas shelled, many of them scattered on the floor, and supper not yet ready.

"What would you call this color, Aunt Griet? Dark lavender or purple? And this one? Orange, yellow, or bronze? I think it's a mixture of all three."

Jacob and Frans had fallen asleep long ago, but Nelleke showed no signs of fatigue.

Griet and Johannes had learned not to force her to bed. She would toss and turn, make noises, sing, call down to them. "When will the sun come up?" It meant they had very little time alone together to discuss the children or the farm business, to make decisions. It was difficult to wear Nelleke out.

Nelleke lay wild flowers out on the table lined up like little soldiers. She treated them like pets, caressing their petals, poking at their centers, sniffing them, even talking to them.

"I'm going to call these four 'cousins,' Aunt Griet. They seem to belong to the same family, but they're each a little different in size and shape. "

"Did you ever notice how many varieties of red there are? I'll bet each red has a different name. Mrs. Broekhof would know."

Nelleke sighed. "Mrs. Broekhof knows the names of all the flowers and plants. If there's something she forgets, she looks it up right away in a big book on the shelf in the salon. I miss her. I miss Samuel and Daniel. I even miss funny little Mr. Broekhof."

It had been two weeks since Nelleke returned to the Verhoeven household now. In spite of the Housemother's reassurances, Griet thought she really hadn't changed that much. "It's her nature,'" Griet realized.

Her nature. Daughter of a Gypsy, she spent her early years with no roots, her extended family performing in villages, sleeping outdoors in forests. She and Johannes believed that the confines of the orphanage would tame her, but she had found ways to escape it.

"Uncle Johannes, I know one thousand. Is there a two thousand? A three thousand?"

"Yes, Nelleke. There's even a hundred thousand and a 900,000."

"That BIG? What would anyone need it for? To count stars maybe?"

"What is the biggest number ever, Uncle Johannes?"

"When you're ready for bed, Nelleke, I'll tell you the highest number ever. Then you can dream about it all night."

Nelleke was excited. She slipped off her indoor slippers, her apron, her outer skirt and top, washed her hands, and splashed her face. Now, wearing a shiny face and the nightdress that served as an undergarment during the day, she approached Johannes.

"I'm ready," she said with a little bow as if presenting herself to the king's court.

"I think you forgot something."

"Oh, I know what."

Nelleke returned to the water bowl and picked up the stick that Uncle Johannes had cut into thin bristles for her, leaving a handle that was just the right size for her hand. As she lingered over each tooth, she contemplated what she knew about numbers.

Returning to where Johannes was entering information in his account books, Nelleke asked, "Is it nine hundred ninety nine thousand nine hundred ninety nine? That's it, isn't it, Uncle Johannes? That's the largest number."

She chanted the number over and over. Nine hundred ninety nine thousand nine hundred ninety nine. Nine hundred ninety nine thousand nine hundred ninety nine. It was like a tongue twister. She had to slow down to say it right. It could be the first line of a poem.

"So many words rhyme with nine. Did you every notice that? Fine, kind, line, mine, pine, rind, sign, vine, wine."

"I could write a long, long poem using nine hundred ninety nine thousand nine hundred ninety nine."

"How many nines is that, Uncle Johannes? I want to see the number."

Johannes wrote the number at the top of his ledger: 999.999

Nelleke counted. "Six nines."

"But Nelleke, that's not the biggest number. No one knows what the biggest number is. The numbers continue forever. I don't even think they all have names. They do not stop. When there's no end to something, we call it 'Infinity.'"

"In . . . finty," Nelleke tried to repeat.

"No. Infinity."

"In . . . fin . . . it . . . ty. I don't get it."

"No one really does. It's hard to imagine."

Infinity. The word made Nelleke feel weary, small, and lonely.

"I like counting things better. Things I can see and touch. May I count all the animals on the farm, Uncle Johannes? Tomorrow, I mean. Not tonight. Not to infinity, either."

"You may count the animals after you've helped Aunt Griet tomorrow, Nelleke."

"I know. There is much work on a farm and you expect me to contribute."

Johannes gave her a sharp look. She was repeating his exact words. Was she being disrespectful? It was hard to tell when her tone was so chipper, her little-girl voice so innocent sounding.

"What are you writing?" she asked.

"You offered to count the animals, Nelleke. That is a good idea, but I already keep careful track. Every time a calf, piglet, or lamb is born I make note of it. Every time an animal dies, I write that down too."

"May I see?"

Johannes slid the large book over and the candle too.

The date was written at the top of each page.

There were columns of animals with numbers after them. In some places he had added notes.

"Pigs," she read – "7."

"Sheep – 10."

"Does that say 'chickens'?"

"Yes, that's right."

"Chickens – 15."

"Cows – 5."

"Uncle Johannes you make your fives backwards. The half circle at the bottom – like a pudgy tummy – goes to this side," Nelleke said, drawing a large imaginary circle in the air, that moved to the right. "Your fives go in the other direction." She demonstrated with more air circles moving to the left.

Nelleke picked up the piece of thin charcoal that Johannes used to enter the information. She put a cross through his 5 in 15 and redid it correctly. She began looking at other pages and correcting the fives on those pages.

Before he realized it, Johannes' careful notes and records were a smeary mess of crosses and large-size fives.

"Nelleke, I can't even read my own records any more. Go to bed. Now."

"I want a ledger too."

"We're not talking about what you want. We're talking about turning this farm into a successful business. Good night, Nelleke."

Nelleke kissed Aunt Griet and climbed up the ladder to the loft. The two little boys slept under the adult bed now. Nelleke had her own small bed in a corner.

"Nine hundred ninety nine thousand nine hundred ninety nine," she sang over and over, softly so as not to wake her brother and cousin like she did two nights last week. She invented a tune that went way up on the first part of the number and came back down on the second half. Nine hundred ninety nine thousand . . . nine hundred ninety nine." Her musings drifted down to the lower level of the house.

After a few minutes of quiet, Johannes, who had been recopying the ledger pages with dark smears, and Griet, who was knitting wool socks, exchanged a relieved glance.

Nelleke sat up and yelled.

"Infinity."

The couple froze, hoping the boys had not been jarred awake by her outburst.

Chapter Thirty-two
Surprise Visit

I n their quest to diversify their sources of income, Griet and Johannes had begun keeping bees and selling honey. Nelleke was fascinated. They allowed her to study the bees for a few minutes each day and praised her when she was careful to cover herself with the net and gloves as they had shown her to do.

By "study" they had meant sitting and observing. Johannes moved a flat rock and placed it at a safe distance from the bees. "This is your 'bee seat,' Nelleke." "Study" to Nelleke meant getting as close to the hives as possible, considering the bees reaction when she poked them with a stick, and following a single bee to see how far away it flew, how it behaved, what it did when it returned to the hive. She kept her eye right on that bee, noting where it stopped, which flowers it preferred, the little dance it did. She did not pay any attention to where she placed her feet or in what direction she was going.

The first time she followed a bee, she ended up in the neighbor's field three farms away. The neighbors brought her back. In spite of numerous warnings, she followed another bee a week later. This bee remained on their property, but brought her perilously close to falling in the pond. With envy, she watched the bee fly on out over the water and escape her view.

When Griet heard Nelleke giving little cries of dismay, followed by "Hey, come back you," she leaped up to see Nelleke right at the edge of the pond leaning forward.

The image of seeing the child's bonnet floating on the surface of the pond the previous year brought back all the terror and helplessness Griet had felt at the time. Dragging both little boys out into the cold, she moved as quickly as she could toward Nelleke and angrily ordered her back into the house.

By mid morning the family had already put in four hours of work. Johannes had milked the cows and conferred with their closest farmer neighbor. The two of them were planning some breeding projects that they hoped would increase milk production. They also discussed the possibility of coordinating on experiments to grow flax, hemp, or hops.

Johannes' next task was to clean, sharpen, and repair his many tools: the small carpenter tools, but also large ones like scythes, spades, and hoes. He had only one of each and they all needed to be kept in working order. Now he was in the field guiding the wooden plow pulled by their only horse.

The fieldwork was delayed the previous week when the horse's hooves were injured.

With great delight, Nelleke had rediscovered a pouch she had kept hidden in the barn before she was taken to the orphanage. The pouch contained her shell collection. For two days, she spent stolen moments poring over those shells, putting them in piles – the pink ones here, the largest there. Other piles – those that had a hole in them, those that curled. All the tiny ones together. After the third day, she was through with them. 'Those shells were fine when I was six," she thought to herself. "Now I want a new shell collection."

Griet called for her to come to the house and hold her cousin, Frans, so Griet could prepare the mid-day meal. Nelleke picked up a rock. In a minute she had broken all the shells into small sharp pieces. When Johannes returned the horse to the barn that evening, the pieces caught on the horse's hooves. Some of them cut and bled. The next day Johannes had to lead the horse into the village to the blacksmith. He did not want to risk damaging the horse further, so he walked beside the horse the entire way there and back. This errand took a whole day.

Griet and Johannes were fearful that their sickly son would never be much of a farmer. They had great hopes for Jacob, though. He was a strong child who enjoyed riding on the horse in front of Johannes. Johannes showed him how to hold the reins.

Johannes had recently begun allowing Jacob to carry small buckets of milk from the barn to the house. Jacob held the handles in both hands and, with his tongue between his teeth, he concentrated hard on not losing a drop. It wasn't much of a help now. But Jacob liked imitating his uncle and feeling that he was doing something useful. They believed that in four years, when Jacob was seven, he would be able to significantly contribute to a number of tasks.

They had hoped that Nelleke, who was already seven, would become more and more proficient at women's work, at relieving Griet from some of the gardening, cleaning, peeling potatoes, mending, and all the other dozens of needed chores. But the child tried to avoid all such work, intent on following her own pursuits. Griet could think of one time when Nelleke saved them unnecessary effort. They had not yet clipped the wings of two new turkeys they had just purchased and the turkeys had escaped their pen. Nelleke saw them and shooed them back into their enclosure. But that was the only significant contribution Griet could think of. It seemed that the expense of feeding and clothing their niece was simply not paying off for them.

When the Broekhof carriage pulled up to the farm about noon, Johannes was still plowing. Griet was inside, comforting Frans, who had just fallen. Jacob and Nelleke were making a small stir among the chickens. Knowing he liked chores, Nelleke had enticed him to join her by placing a small basket over his arm. "Now you have your own basket, Jacob. I'll bet the chickens have given us some eggs. Want to look? How many do you think we can find?"

At the most recent weekly Regent meeting, Jos had learned some information that might prove useful in their quest to win Nelleke back. Myriam leaped at the chance to join him on the impromptu visit.

When Griet saw that it was Mr. Broekhof climbing down from the carriage that had stopped in front of their home, she was not pleased. The little man who had come searching for an etching of her brother's months earlier was not a pleasant sort. It was as if he were accusing them that day of hoarding something that was rightfully his. When the orphanage contacted Griet and Johannes and asked if they would consider relinquishing Nelleke permanently to the care of the Broekhofs, she was startled and suspicious. "That weasel Mr. Broekhof must think he can use Nelleke to somehow find that work of art he was so keen on." She barely gave the idea another thought. The Housemother had assured them that Nelleke had grown up. Frans's illnesses were more manageable. Jacob was a year older. They had nearly recovered from the flood losses. It seemed clear that it was time to take Nelleke back.

Still holding Frans, she watched through the small window as Jos walked around to the other side of the carriage, extended his hand, and carefully helped a woman descend the two steps to the ground. When the woman patted Mr. Broekhof on the shoulder and slipped her arm through his, Griet realized the woman must be Mrs. Broekhof. The woman stopped, looked at Jos, and bent her head. He put his arm around her and said something to her quietly. She nodded and they proceeded together toward the front door.

Observing these intimate, comforting gestures, and seeing them exchange a smile, softened Griet's opinion of the man somewhat. He was a gentle husband, probably also a father, not just a greedy, demanding ogre. But why were they here?

Nelleke had heard and seen the carriage. She came running up to the visitors before they had a chance to knock on the cottage door. Griet watched as Nelleke threw her arms around Mrs. Broekhof. The grown woman with the lace collar and cuffs, the woven fringed shawl, the leather gloves. The child with the mud-covered boots, the soiled gray apron, the smudged face. They held each other for a long time. Nelleke gave Mr. Broekhof a warm, but shorter hug. Jacob came toddling around the house, upset at being left behind.

"Nell. Nell. Where are you?"

He began to wail after his knee bumped one of the eggs from his basket and it splashed on the ground, leaving a runny mess of yellow yolk and white shell pieces.

"Don't worry, Jacob. You've just given the pigs a snack. They'll be happy." Nelleke reassured him, as she took his hand and led them all into the house.

"Aunt Griet. Aunt Griet. Look who's here. Mrs. Broekhof is here. Mr. Broekhof too."

When the two women shook hands, Griet saw tears in Mrs. Broekhof's eyes.

"Could it be that they loved her niece? That they truly wanted her as their own child?"

"Please sit down, Mrs. Broekhof. Mr. Broekhof. May I offer you some bread and freshly made butter? Some ale?"

Mr. Broekhof accepted, but Nelleke took Mrs. Broekhof's gloved hand, stroked it and pulled her toward the back door.

"Come see the farm, Mrs. Broekhof. I feed the chickens. I gather the eggs. I pick the peas. I chased a bee and got lost. I'm gathering shells for my new collection. I want so many seashells that I can't count them anymore. Until they are infinity."

Griet and Myriam exchanged an amused look. Jos felt awkward at the thought that he was going to be alone in the kitchen with Griet and the two little boys.

"Thank you for the lovely offer, Mrs. Verhoeven. On second thought, if I may, I would enjoy Nelleke's farm tour too."

When Johannes disengaged the plow and brought the horse to the barn for a drink, he washed his hands and shook hands with the Broekhofs. This was Jos's chance to talk with the Verhoevens – while Nelleke and Myriam were walking around the property.

"Mrs. Verhoeven," Jos said, following Johannes into the house. "I've changed my mind. I can't resist your offer after all. My wife enjoys your niece so much, I'll just let them get reacquainted."

"I can see that Nelleke is very fond of Mrs. Broekhof too, Mr. Broekhof," Griet responded.

"We lost our little Catherina over a year ago. She was only three. My wife was quite despondent for a long time. Nelleke brought her back to life, really. We all – my boys too – had grown quite fond of your niece. The past month has been difficult for us. I hope we're not intruding. I know you are very busy. We won't stay long."

"How about a piece of ham with that bread, Mr. Broekhof? Johannes is taking a lunch break. You might as well join him. You must be hungry."

"Very generous of you. Thank you."

Although he wanted to jump to the main point of this visit, Jos controlled himself.

He waited until Johannes had eaten half his lunch. Meanwhile, he attempted to make conversation with the quiet couple without sounding as if he were probing.

Trying to control the tremor in his voice, Jos finally began.

"Beyond our wanting to visit with Nelleke, Mr. and Mrs. Verhoeven, I do have another purpose for being here today. You may not be aware that I serve on the Board of Regents for the orphanage? In addition to being the overseers for the running of the day- to-day operation of the orphanage, we also handle all the finances."

"Finances, Mr. Broekhof? My father made certain that my brother and his wife, in spite of their wanderings, were registered citizens of Amsterdam. It was our understanding that, as such, should their children be orphaned, they could be housed in the City Orphanage at no charge. We are grateful for the care given to our niece during the past year. We did not expect there to be any fees."

"Oh my, no. There are no fees. You are quite correct about that. The expenses of the orphanage are paid for from the city coffers. It was another aspect of finances I wished to discuss with you."

"Two of the Regents are assigned the duty of determining and safeguarding the assets of each orphan. Although they have no family members who can raise them, several of the orphans come from wealthy families. Many have no assets at all. Most fall somewhere in the middle. As you well know, your father was quite meticulous. His will stated that you should inherit the farm – this farm. Nicolaas would inherit the Amsterdam house along with the printing business. His oldest daughter, Elsbeth, would be given all cash assets."

"Nicolaas, however, left no will. At least none has been found. While Nelleke was at the orphanage, the Regents continued to investigate. They approached the manager of Stradwijk and Son, Mr. Karelson, who, after your brother's death, moved his family into the house. Unless Mr. Karelson could produce a legal document that indicated otherwise, the house and the business belong to Nicolaas's legal heirs, Nelleke and Jacob."

Johannes listened carefully and took another sip of ale. Griet could not understand where this was leading. She knew that Karelson had taken over the business and the house, but it had not occurred to them to question his right to do so. He had been running the business for years, growing it in fact, with little input from Nicolaas that she was aware of.

Immediately, after Nicolaas's funeral, Griet and Johannes took from the home everything that appeared to belong to the children, and brought them to the farm with the intention of becoming their substitute parents. Since then, with the demands of combining two farms and raising three children, they had simply thought no more about the small house and business on a narrow street in Amsterdam.

"Mr. Karelson did not produce a will nor did he know of any, but he did produce a contract signed by him and Nicolaas soon after your father's death. It was notarized. Essentially, the two of them agreed that Karelson would take over full-time management of Stradwijk and Son, while Nicolaas would use the shop on evenings and weekends for his own projects. They agreed on a salary for Mr. Karelson and agreed to split the profits that remained after all expenses were paid. Of course, Nicolaas continued to live in the house behind the shop with his children."

"So you are saying that as Nicolaas's heirs, Nelleke and Jacob are entitled to Nicolaas's share of those profits?" Johannes asked.

"That is correct. The system worked well while Nicolaas was living, but arrangements must now be made to switch what would have been Nicolaas's share to his children. What's more, his children are entitled to a monthly rent from the Karelson family since they are now living in the house that Nelleke and Jacob own. And, of course, should the property be sold . . . ."

"And as guardian of the children, Griet will be entrusted with those funds?" Johannes asked.

"Is that why Mr. Broekhof wanted custody then," Griet wondered. "So that he could get his hands on Nelleke's property? He is a successful merchant. Why would he do that?" Her first impression of him as a greedy obsessive was correct after all.

Jos heard Myriam and Nelleke chattering near the barn. He needed to set forth his proposition quickly before they returned. Given the very likely possibility that the Verhouvens rejected his offer, Nelleke should not hear of it or perhaps ever know of it until she was an adult. He and Myriam would fade in her memory. She would continue to be a farm girl, possibly with little education beyond what this couple – intelligent enough – could provide her. "Did they love Nelleke, though," he wondered?

Jos's head stretched toward the ceiling. He swallowed. He took a last swig of his ale.

"Mr. and Mrs. Verhoeven, Myriam and I are devoted to Nelleke. If you agree to transfer custody to us, we will give her every advantage. You can visit with her and she with you as often as you both wish. I am a successful businessman. Nelleke would become one of our heirs, along with our two sons. We have no need of the assets Nicolaas left her. As part of the custody agreement, we would forswear any right to those assets. They would go to you instead. I see how hard you work here, how determined you are to build a success of your combined properties. Although not a fortune, the combined additional income from Stradwijk and Son plus the modest rent of the living space behind it would be useful in helping you meet your goals. You could hire extra help, for example. Buy better seed. Purchase an improved tool. Extend . . ."

"Mr. Broekhof, there are many needs on the farm, of course," Johannes interrupted. "I understand your offer. Griet and I need to discuss it before reaching a decision."

"By the way," Jos interjected, "This is not just about assuring that the children's assets are secured moving forward. Mr. Karelson is in debt to Nelleke and Jacob. He owes them their share of the business profits plus rent dating back to Nicolaas's death."

Nelleke's voice could be heard quite close by. "Do you believe I found strawberries growing on the far side of the barn, Mrs. Broekhof?"

"And, of course, you counted them, didn't you, Nelleke?" Mrs. Broekhof said playfully. "So, tell me. How many were there?"

"Only three. I ate them."

Nelleke and Myriam stepped through the back door, laughing, hand in hand.

"The next time I find a strawberry, I'll save it for you, Mrs. Broekhof."

Jos was dismayed that he had not had time to include his last part of the offer.

A pink, short-legged, snorting piglet followed Nelleke and Myriam into the house. With a "husha, husha" sound and waving her arms, Nelleke chased it out the door into the back yard. Myriam followed.

"Go find your Mamma," Nelleke told the piglet.

"Look, Mrs. Broekhof. The mother pig has six babies. This one is the tiniest."

She tried to pick up the squealy creature, but he had smelled his mother and slid out of her arms.

"He has trouble fighting his brothers and sisters when he's hungry. They're constantly feeding. Maybe when he runs off he's looking for food elsewhere."

"I will sign a statement now, if you agree," Jos said quickly. "Our respective lawyers' notaries can write up the legal documents later. We would like to take the child with us when we leave today."

Chapter Thirty-three
Pillow Monologues

"Jos, my clever husband, you have brought her back to us. We continued the storybook right where we left off. She slipped into Catherina's bed, cuddled up to the doll, and fell immediately to sleep as if she had never left. When I gave her a light kiss, she opened her eyes, looked startled momentarily to see me and said, 'Mrs. Broekhof, do you think Mr. Broekhof would let me dig a pond in the garden?' She closed her eyes again, but as she was falling back asleep she mumbled something about frogs and tadpoles."

"The only difficult part of that parting for Nelleke seemed to be saying good-bye to Jacob again, but you know our little girl, Jos. She's able to brighten herself up even with all the changes she's endured and the losses she's suffered. 'I will miss Jacob, Mrs. Broekhof,' she told me, 'but Daniel and Samuel are like brothers to me too.' Besides, with promises on both sides to visit each other, Jacob can always be part of her life."

"I want to hear what seductive argument you used to convince them, but, although I am exhausted from the day's journey, there's something else that has nagged at me since we said good-bye to the Verhoevens. We had packed up Nelleke's few belongings and lifted her into the carriage. I was sitting beside her. You were making some final legal explanations to the Verhoevens. The last thing Mrs. Verhoeven said to you was, 'Mr. Broekhof, did you ever find the missing etching?' I couldn't have been more stunned, Jos. In spite of the happy afternoon and evening, I've been haunted by her question. Please tell me how that young woman, living a four-hour ride away from us, on a farm, could possibly know about your etchings?"

"I had always thought, Jos, that your sharing them with me was something intimate, something just between us, husband and wife. I feel betrayed, horrified really that the young Mrs. Verhoeven may have seen them. I simply cannot imagine it. I cannot think under what circumstances you would have shown them to her. You explained to me that there was only one print made of each etching, that you are the owner of those etchings, that you keep them on the third floor of our home in your study, locked in a cupboard. I know you and I had an agreement that after I viewed numbers 5 & 6, you would tell me how you acquired them. I still refuse to view those remaining etchings. I have seen enough. But I do want you to tell me how you acquired them, Jos. Tell me now."

* * *

"Jos, I've thought about it for a whole month now. With the initials that Nelleke and Nicolaas share – with N.S. carved into the tub and given the nature of the etchings, I'm concerned. She is an extremely curious child. Jos, I know they are locked away, but what if she should find your keys and the secret cabinet? After you've told me how many people know about the etchings, how many people you involved in your mad, frantic quest to complete the set, I'm afraid that one day she'll learn about them and want to see them for herself. Whatever memories she has of her first parents, I don't want them to be tainted by discovering that her father spent the last year of his life creating those bawdy, so-called "works of art." I do not want to risk her ever setting eyes on them. I want them destroyed, Jos. All of them."

Chapter Thirty-four
Gift and Letter

The letter arrived early afternoon. That same day – in the morning – Nelleke climbed the stairs to the third floor and casually stepped into Jos's study. "Pappa, I have something for you," she said.

For the first time in the three months since they had changed her last name to Broekhof, Nelleke had explored her old belongings – kept in the small wooden box that had accompanied her from Amsterdam to Ouderkerk, back to Amsterdam, back to Ouderkerk, and back to Amsterdam once more.

The box was tucked onto the lower shelf of a cabinet in her bedroom behind Catherina's dollhouse. Whenever she played with the dollhouse, she saw the box. She already knew what it contained and was not particularly interested in it. She remembered the items she and Bernadien had found there after Marja died and they had stolen the key to the orphanage storage room. She understood that she had two new parents now. When she forgot and called her new mother, "Mrs. Broekhof," Myriam corrected her with a gentle, "Mamma. You can call me 'Mamma' now."

Sometimes saying "Mamma" made her think about her first mother. She knew her name was Rona, that her father had first seen Rona performing in the streets of Amsterdam. The members of the troupe that were to become Nelleke's grandfather, uncles, and cousins played violins and clarinets and drums while Rona danced. There was a crowd of people watching and they gave the troupe money. Nelleke did not have to imagine the scene because she had seen it many times later in villages and, until they returned to her other grandfather's home in Amsterdam behind the print shop, she herself danced in public sometimes. The sound of villagers' coins dropping into a bucket suddenly came back to her. She still sometimes sang the songs and hummed the tunes that surrounded her during her first four years of life.

She remembered the skirt in the box too. The ankle-length, layered skirt. A mix of many fabrics, it swayed, clung, and billowed as it followed Rona's graceful and occasionally provocative motions.

Nelleke pulled the box out from the cabinet, sat on the floor, opened it, and found the skirt. The colors were still bright. She held it to her face. It smelled musty. The bottom of it appeared to have been brushed in dust. When she shook it, twigs and dried leaves fell to the floor. Nelleke stepped into it and pulled it up over her clothes, but the waist was too large and the skirt dragged on the floor. She let the skirt drop and turned her attention to the folded baby clothes. A tight, wool baby cap with a ribbon to tie under the chin. Several long-sleeve blouses. A skirt, that although tiny, probably came to her ankles at the time. Long, warm stockings. She had a sudden image of her grandmother, sitting at the base of a tree, along a river, knitting. "She probably made these clothes for me," Nelleke said out loud to herself. "She probably made all the children's clothes."

Nelleke ran her finger over the raised flowers on the plate that the Regentesse, Mrs. Comfrij, gave her after her hand got burned. She could hear Isabela's voice reading haltingly with her funny accent – reading Mrs. Comfrij's note – the one that accompanied the plate carefully wrapped in bright colored cloth: "To make your food taste better, so you'll get well soon." Where could Isabela be at this moment?

"Mrs. Broekhof – Mamma – would like this pretty plate," she thought. "I'll give it to her."

And then there were the maps rolled up and tied with string. Those old maps. Her first father had made them. Sometimes he sold them. Sometimes the troupe consulted the maps as they trekked from village to village, from forest to forest. "I'll give one of these to my new Pappa," she thought. She chose a roll that was a little thicker than the others and climbed the stairs.

The cloudy light pushed through the lead windows. Jos was at his ornate desk, bent over his ledger. It was still not clear to Jos that De Nes's suggestions for diversifying the business would be profitable. "Let's just stick with what Broekhof and Son has always done best, Timotheus," Jos told him during their most recent discussion: "Importing and trading in grain."

"Pappa, excuse me."

Jos's children knew not to bother Jos when he was in his study. It was regarded as his sanctuary, that mysterious place where he contemplated business dealings and earned the money that enabled them to live a comfortable life. Nelleke knew he would forgive her, though, for breaking the rule if she didn't interrupt him for too long.

"I have something for you. It's a map my first father printed. He designed it too."

She placed it on his desk on top of his ledger.

"Nelleke, my darling daughter, that is very sweet of you, but I think you should keep this. It will be a remembrance of the first father who loved you as much as I do."

"I have lots of them, Pappa. You keep this one," Nelleke said. She gave Jos a quick kiss. He could hear her footsteps descending two flights of stairs.

"Mamma, I have something for you. Anna, are you preparing our mid-day meal yet? I want to help."

Jos picked up the roll and glanced over at the painting that hid the secret cupboard. It was true what he had told Myriam. He had placed the painting there so that the afternoon sun would shine directly on it. But that would not happen often now until spring. Besides, there was no longer anything to hide behind that painting. He stood up, set the painting, aside, and opened the cupboard. The gesture contained none of the drama or feelings of expectation he had felt for so many months. Except for the Strad Journal and the seven ornate silver frames, the shelves were empty.

Jos had not opened the cupboard since he and Myriam removed the six etchings from their frames. Before sunrise one morning they lowered the prints face down one by one into the canal. While Myriam watched, Jos, using a broom, pushed each one into the murky water and held it under until they could no longer see any sign of it. When they had all disappeared, Myriam walked back into the house. Jos stood there for awhile. As the sun began to rise, he thought he saw a corner of one of the etchings. Perhaps it had floated to the surface so he could have one more glimpse? Or perhaps it was just a dead leaf. A cloud covered the rising sun and he could no longer identify what it was he saw, or even where on the water's surface he had seen it. It may have been nothing but a shadow.

Jos started to place the rolled map on a shelf but, instead, out of curiosity or homage to Nicolaas, or a suppressed longing for the etchings themselves, or perhaps feeling reluctant to return to his ledger, he tried to untie the string. This was no easy bow. The string was wrapped around the roll multiple times and tied in complex, overlapping, tight knots. Jos reached for the knife in his pocket and cut at the string in several places until it gave way.

Jos had seen several of the maps when Nelleke moved back into their house for the final time. Most were of villages along rivers, with the fields and forests beyond them. This map was further proof of Nicolaas's considerable skill. A portrayal of all seven of the United Provinces, it was more ambitious than the village maps.

There was the sea along the left side with outlines of ships. In the upper left-hand corner two men stood on either side of the Stradwijk and Son business sign. Shields with symbols of the seven provinces hung from the sign. Two pert cupids lay on top of it. On the bottom right was the proud coat of arms of the United Provinces – the fierce lion, standing upright, showing its might, keeping enemies at bay with its long, threatening tongue, sharp claws and raised tail.

The coastline was smooth in some places, but interrupted by clusters of islands in others. The Zuider Sea took up about a tenth of the map with rivers and tributaries leading to and from it.

Jos turned the map over. A second piece of parchment was attached to the large map. Although he could see only the back of it, he assumed it was another map that supplemented the main one or showed a detail of the larger map. The smaller piece had become loose at one of the corners. Jos pulled gently with thumb and forefinger. When it didn't give way, he tried loosening it very slowly with his knife. Slipping the knife under the opening, and without cutting or ripping the print, he worked his way all around the edges of the second map. Nicolaas had used an adhesive, but only along the outside of the map. He had left the center unglued.

Laying the larger map aside, Jos turned the newly freed piece over. At first he was stunned. He stared and blinked, closed his eyes, opened them, and stared again, not believing what he was holding in his hands. There was the familiar wooden washtub with the initials N.S. There were the numbers 1/1. And there was the couple at whom he had gazed for so many hours, the sensuous couple he had seen move from Monday's relatively chaste shoulder massage through increasing stages of undress, including the Tuesday, Wednesday, and Thursday etchings he had shared with Myriam. He had accompanied this man and this woman for months, first as if he were peeking through a window, eventually as if he were standing next to them.

He had observed as the expressions on their faces turned from fatigue to surprise to teasing, to hilarity, to joy, to pleasure. He knew every gesture this woman made, every fold and curve of her body. At times it was as if he were caressing her himself, as if it were his mouth, his own skin touching hers.

Clutching the parchment to his chest, Jos walked to the door of his study, closed it, took out his keys, and locked it from the inside.

And now "Sunday." In his possession. The final etching. The one he had sought all over the city and beyond. At first his attention was drawn to the mass of intertwined arms and legs intersecting the water, then to the breasts he knew so well, pressed nearly flat against the lover, but with the smooth, rounded side of one of them still visible. The couple's faces were pressed tightly against each other, buried in each other. For the first time, Nicolaas had hidden those faces – as familiar to Jos as his own. But for anyone who had followed what preceded this scene, as Jos had, it was not difficult to imagine their expressions of ecstasy.

The woman's thighs could be seen just below the surface of the water, the rolls of flesh resting on the man's thighs as she straddled and surrounded him. There was no longer any separation between them. Jos beheld the etching for a long time. When he heard Myriam call him to the noonday meal and then Nelleke calling him in perfect imitation of her Mamma's inflection, he dipped a pen into black ink, turned the etching over, and wrote in his careful script, *Zondag*.

As he was starting an elaborate "7" beneath the word, he heard Nelleke summon him again. "Pappa, what are you doing? We are waiting for you," she called, each word a little louder as she made her way up the steep stairs.

"I'll be there shortly, Darling. You say grace for me and begin."

"No, I won't," she said a little breathlessly from right outside his study door. "The Pappa is supposed to say grace. I am waiting for you right here."

She was correct, of course. He could imagine her sitting on the top step, forcing herself to be still, her pretty lower lip in a determined pout, smoothing her skirts over her knees and ankles the way Myriam taught her, the light from the window falling on her crisp white bonnet.

Hurriedly, he placed the etching gently against a cupboard wall so the ink could dry. He glanced at the seven empty frames scattered about, closed the cupboard, replaced the painting, unlocked the door to his study, stepped into the hallway, and took his daughter's hand.

* * *

Jos had just said grace and the family had taken their first bite of lamb when they heard a knock on their front door. Karel, who sometimes joined them for meals, answered the knock and quickly returned holding a letter. "It's addressed to Nelleke," he said, uncertain exactly what to do with it. "A delivery from the orphanage."

"*My darling Nelita,*" Nelleke read out loud. "*My Dutch writing never was good. As I sit to write whatever I maybe know, I seem no longer to know. I back now in my small village where I was born, high on cliff over the sea. From my window, I see path. I ran down path to greet my father when his ship arrived. That was long ago. I was small like you. But maybe you grow? How I wish . . .*

I'm switching to English now. Please ask Anneliese to translate for you."

"Mamma, it's from Isabela. She's alive! May I go ask Anneliese to translate for me? Please. Please."

Glancing at Jos, Myriam, answered, "Finish your meal first, Nelleke. Then I will walk you to Anneliese's house."

"But, Mamma, no. I need to know what she's saying NOW. I can't wait."

Nelleke stood up, buried her face in Myriam's lap, and began to sob loudly.

Caressing the child's curls, Myriam looked at Jos. Jos nodded.

The Hals family was just finishing their midday meal, when Nelleke lifted the heavy knocker on their front door and banged three times loudly before Myriam could stop her.

"*When they came for me in the middle of the night, I knew who they were. I understood I had to go with them. I did not cry out. I did not want to alarm my little darlings. But, oh, it was so hard not to say good-bye to any of you, not to be able to explain to you, to Anneliese, to Pieter.*

Cornelius – the Dutch man who saved me after the shipwreck, whose family nursed me back to health. They paid Cornelius a large sum to find Dutch soldier uniforms for them, to find a fishing boat. Cornelius did all the talking, arranged space in the harbor for their ship, gave them a Dutch flag for that ship. Those are such serious crimes that Cornelius can never again return to his own country.

Cornelius had courted one of the orphanage cooks who told him exactly where I was sleeping. Later, I learned, they punished her by taking her job away. It was not her fault. She thought she was just conversing casually with a suitor, but he was a false suitor."

When Nelleke burst into the Hals' household waiving the letter, Myriam apologized profusely. Anneliese and Pieter excused themselves from the family table and leaped up. Now the four neighbors were seated in a tight circle in the parlor, waiting with great impatience as Anneliese read each sentence silently before translating out loud into Dutch.

"They wrapped me in a blanket and carried me to the fishing boat and then to their ship. In the morning we set sail for Spain. It was my destiny. I always knew it. I accepted it, but still I cried. How I cried. Tell Pieter he could never offer me enough handkerchiefs for all my tears."

Pieter hung his head between his knees. Anneliese, anxious to continue reading, reached over and placed her free hand on her brother's back.

"Diego talked to me very little during the voyage. He told me just three things – that he and I would honor the pledge our fathers made to each other when I was born; that we would marry as soon as we arrived; that he is sorry I lost my father, but that his family thinks my father was foolish and careless to take me on that trip to England.

They took turns watching me, though. The entire trip their eyes were on me. I barely remember it, but Cornelius told Diego that I tried to climb overboard and drown myself after the shipwreck. They must have been afraid I would try that again.

Aunt Lucia sent books and needlepoint with them to help me pass the time, but with the constant jostling from the waves, they weren't much use. Just days and days with no real company, their eyes checking on me constantly.

I no longer live in the big house that was my home until that fateful journey with my father. My Aunt Anacleta died during my return voyage. I knew she was ill and felt so guilty that I did not get to see her. Perhaps I could have saved her. My Aunt Luisa lives there alone. She has always been a sad person, but she enjoys seeing me every day and she is excited about the baby."

Anneliese stopped reading and took a breath. There was silence while she reread the last sentence to herself and translated it out loud for the second time.

"*She enjoys seeing me every day and she is excited . . . about the baby.*"

"The baby!" Nelleke cried out and jumped up, trying to peer over Anneliese's shoulder. "What baby? Is Isabela going to have a baby?"

Pieter stood and began pacing.

"I live with Diego's family now. Diego left one week after the wedding. He is following the profession of his father and mine. After his father's accident several years ago, he took over his father's shipping business. Diego does not even know yet that he will become a father soon. When he returns I will ask him if I can name the baby Nelita, if it is a girl.

Diego's father, Captain Miguel, entertains me with stories of my father's prowess and daring on the seas. He has always assumed that I would marry his son. Captain Miguel now owns all of the property from our two families. I would like to name my second girl Anneliese. And my first boy – Pedro – the Spanish name for Pieter."

Pieter sat back down, bent his head, and began moving his fingers through his hair, pressing on his scalp from front to back, front to back, over and over.

"It is hard to write when I become upset. Penning these words to you, Nelita, imagining you sitting with Anneliese as she translates, perhaps with Pieter listening – I feel so far from all of you. I must try to post this letter. It could be months before you receive it, if you receive it at all.

Please tell my little girls I love and miss them. I hope you have a new Big Sister who sings to you. And you, my precious Nelita, I imagine you in your red-and-black uniform, your thick blond girls bursting out of your bonnet just as you burst into every new day with wonder. I wish you were here to be my little sister, to play with my baby, to sing to her in Dutch and make her laugh. Perhaps one day."

Pieter listened to his sister's voice with increasing agony, anger, and helplessness. After the delicious evening spent in Isabelle's company at Saskia's wedding celebration, the walk home, the languid kisses, he saw her one more time. They arranged to meet two days later on Sunday when Isabela was returning to the orphanage after Mass in the secret chapel.

Pieter had brought his drawing materials. Isabela asked him how he could make far-away objects look so distant and close ones look as if they were right in front of them. How could he do that when the sketch pad was perfectly flat? He gave her a mini lesson on perspective and depth. Did she want to try? She smiled shyly and reluctantly took up the charcoal he held up for her. He showed her how to hold it and placed his hand over hers, guiding her lines.

"See how the canal narrows the farther away it is? Try that."

She laughed at herself, but she enjoyed trying and was mildly proud when she did indeed succeed in a primitive way in distinguishing between the canal right in front of them and the canal several meters away.

Pieter had been pondering how to share with his father the deepening feelings he was experiencing for this intriguing young woman. His parents must have noticed that he had spent the entire Comfrij wedding celebration at her side. He feared his father would never support a marriage to a foreigner and would forbid his marrying a Catholic. He could see how much Isabelle's Catholicism meant to her. What if they moved to Italy, he had been thinking. Giving up the support of family and community would be difficult, but they would have each other.

That day on the bench he had wanted desperately to tell her he loved her, that he wanted her at his side the rest of his life. He thought he had time. Now he was furious with himself for not speaking. The thought of her with another man, carrying another man's child – it was unbearable. He hated himself for not protecting her.

Unable to even glance at the nearly finished portrait of her and uninspired to begin a new project that could lead to his becoming a member of the guild, Pieter had been assisting with the master's projects, but taking no initiative to develop his own. Isabelle's smiles. Isabelle's eyes. Isabelle's tears. Isabelle. He was languishing.

But Nelleke was full of questions. "Will we ever see her again, Mamma? How far away is Spain? Can we visit? I want to hold her baby. I wonder if . . . "

Pieter stood and left the room.

"I know what we'll do," said Myriam, taking both of Nelleke's hands in hers trying to steady her. "Let's go home, sit at our mother/daughter desks and write her letters. She doesn't even know yet that you have a new family."

"Oh, yes, Mamma. There's so much to tell her." Nelleke pulled on her mother's hand, impatient to get started. "I'll tell her that Daniel lets me play with his toy ship now, that I hoist my skirts up and run with the kite Samuel gave me . . . and I almost never fall. I'll tell her how I can read and write now – how you teach me, Mamma, every day. I'll tell her I can count nearly to infinity. I'll tell her about your memory garden. I'll . . . "

Anneliese folded the letter, placed it in the envelope and tucked it in Nelleke's hand. The gesture, along with the tears in Anneliese's eyes, interrupted Nelleke's stream of accelerating chatter.

"Thank you, Anneliese, for the expert translation," Myriam said, as she patted her young neighbor on the arm. "I hope it is comforting to learn that your dear friend is safe, that she has returned home. And now, Nelleke darling, it is time for us to return to ours."

Epilogue

"Mamma. Mamma. I found it. Look. That's me, isn't it? Up there with all those men?"

"Slow down, Nelleke, please, I'm coming. Where's your father?"

"He's fetching a chair for you, Mamma. I'm heading in the wrong direction. See that, Mamma? All the men are facing one way. I'm going in another."

Myriam felt the life within her give a furtive kick with its tiny foot.

"This child always reacts to the sound of Nelleke's voice," she thought. "It will spend its life following after its Big Sister, trying to keep up, just as I am trying now with my slow waddle."

As Nelleke pulled her through the crowds in the Banquet Hall of the Musketeers' Headquarters on the Amstel River, Myriam tried to glimpse over all the heads at the seven paintings. Various artists portrayed different civic guard companies. She paused to rest in front of one of them. "Nicolaes Eliaszn. Pickenoy," she read "*Civic Guardsmen of the Company of Jan van Vlooswijk*, 1642." The men were posed, still, formal, serious, all in a row, dressed mostly alike, holding their muskets, looking directly at the viewer. "Strange that they are all exactly the same height," she thought.

"You could behead them all with one blow," someone called out creating laughter from those around him.

"Why is our painting at the very end on the farthest wall? Excuse me. Excuse me, please, Sir. Ma'am. Mamma, Mamma, I'll just run ahead."

"No, you will not, Nelleke," said Myriam. "And you will behave like a young lady. No pushing." Myriam placed her hand under her belly, supporting it for the final steps. "We will get there soon enough."

But Nelleke had already dropped Myriam's hand and moved forward. The crowds were even thicker in front of the painting she wanted most to see. She could see the master standing just off to the right side of his huge work of art – the largest one she had ever seen. His long, wavy, reddish hair – combed, for once – fell on both sides of his craggy face from under a white beret. He looked older than when she first saw him. Now there were flecks of gray in his unruly eyebrows and unkempt moustache. Over a brown wool tunic, he wore a long-sleeved jacket, and on top of the jacket a full-length cape trimmed in beaver fur. The wide black-leather belt with a large, square gold buckle was placed low as if to hold up his own protruding belly.

"He looks like an actor who has just stepped off the stage to meet his audience," Nelleke thought. Just then he caught sight of her.

"Is this my little orphan girl? My firefly? I hardly recognize you when you're not wearing your black-and-red uniform. Aren't you quite the young lady now, Miss?"

"I'm nine years old now, Sir. And I'm not an orphan any more. I have a new Mamma and Pappa and two new brothers and I'll be a big sister in three months."

Jos appeared with a chair just as Myriam, panting, arrived at this end of the hall. He helped her settle in and together, they, along with dozens of others, tried to absorb the chaotic scene on the wall before them. There was their daughter dominating the left side of the canvas, all lit up. She certainly fit in with such an expectant and excited group of people – all of them on their way to somewhere else. The artist had caught her intensity and determination, that look she had of never being quite at rest, of always needing to move, explore, seek answers. Like the militia, Nelleke was ready for action. Her blond curls were set free and cascaded down her back, held in place on top by a cap of woven gold.

All around them, people stood contemplating the painting. Some turned and walked away, back through the long hall, mumbling, shaking their heads. Others surrounded the artist and offered praise or asked questions. A few made audible comments.

"I've never seen anything like this."

"I don't know what to make of this approach."

"They're moving out, aren't they? Rallying for duty? To guard the gates? To greet a visiting dignitary maybe?"

"I see who is giving the orders, but who is obeying? They're all going their own way. There's no unity."

"I believe it's quite natural. It's the way such an event would actually unfold."

"Mamma, Pappa, I counted everyone. There are 31 men in my painting, 2 girls – see there's one hiding behind me – and one boy running off here, see him? I heard someone say he's the powder boy. When Jacob sees me, he'll make fun and call ME the chicken girl. I hope that bloody thing doesn't ruin my yellow dress. Isn't that the most beautiful gown ever? And just look at the pearl earrings Rembrandt gave me, and the gold money pouch. I'm wearing the colors of the militia. My job was to carry their goblet for them. The artist told me."

"Oh, and a dog – a little white dog. It looks like Pieter's dog, Runt. It's slouching away. I don't think it likes all the noise. I can hear the sounds in my head. The drum. The muskets firing. The shouting. Oh, I think it's marvelous. That cape on my shoulders is the most exquisite fabric I've ever seen. Mamma, I could stare at this painting until infinity and never see it all."

"This is a public space, Nelleke," Jos said. "You can come back whenever you want. Ask Samuel and Daniel to bring you. They haven't seen it yet. But your Mamma is tired. We have to go home now. I'll bid good-bye to the artist."

Jos joined the throngs surrounding the master and gradually worked his way into a position where he could speak with him.

"Very interesting piece of work, Rembrandt. I congratulate you. I'm not entirely sure of your purpose or vision here, but I know our family will return many times to view what Nelleke is calling 'my painting.'"

"A most lively and curious child. I knew the moment I saw her that I wanted to paint her. By the way, Broekhof," Rembrandt continued, lowering his voice, "Did you ever find anyone to complete that remarkable set of etchings?"

"No, I did not."

"I'm still interested in purchasing them. They would make an excellent addition to my collection."

"I'll keep your offer in mind, Rembrandt."

Acknowledgements

I wish to thank Maarten de Haan, Monique Hutten, Martha Kline, Sylvia Rose, Anna Strauss, and Kate White, early readers of my manuscript whose enthusiasm and suggestions helped shape this work; Faye Camardo for her sharp editor's eye; Lodewijk J. Wagenaar for contributing to the story's historical accuracy; Marga Dieter for sharing her publishing experience; Carla van Delft and Jos Lombarts, my wise Dutch language teachers for their patience and their knowledge of Dutch culture; the Amsterdam Museum for its extensive and varied historical exhibits, especially those pertaining to the City Orphanage; the Rembrandt House; the experts at the Amsterdam Archives; the dozens of novelists, historians, and art researchers whose writings plunged me into the world of Golden Age Amsterdam; and Allen White for his steadfast belief in me.

Discussion Questions for Readers Of
The Seventh Etching

1. Who are the probable father and mother of the baby who appears on Nicolaas's doorstep in the Prologue? Where is that child ten years later? Describe his relationship to Nelleke. How do you react to Elsbeth van Randen's reasons for keeping the children apart?

2. In what ways does the Prologue foreshadow the novel's events, secrets, and revelations?

3. During Amsterdam's Golden Age when this story takes place, it was the wealthiest city on earth. What evidence of that wealth do you see in the novel?

4. Were there dangers in extreme wealth? What role did the church attempt to play in curbing its excesses?

5. The wealth was not evenly distributed. What social problems existed and how did they affect the story? Even among the most opulent, child and maternal deaths were common. Why could they not protect themselves against these losses?

6. One reader described Part I as "good people forced to make difficult decisions." What does that description refer to? Do you agree? Are there villains in this story?

7. Reactions to Nelleke's character have ranged from endearing to irritating. Do you believe either or both of these apply? How many adjectives can you come up with to describe her?

8. What explains Jos's obsession with completing the set of etchings? Do you find his determination compelling? How is his obsession similar and different from modern-day obsessions?

9. Which character do you think undergoes the most change? Discuss the arc of that change. What influences the alteration?

10. There are several secondary stories. Identify them. Do they contribute to / reinforce / hinder the flow of the main story?

11. When asked, "Who is your favorite character?" most readers identify the same character. Do you have a favorite? If so, what is it about that character that appeals to you?

12. Were you surprised by Myriam's reaction upon viewing the first etchings in the series? By her refusal to view more? What did you think of her insistence on destroying the set?

13. Did you believe the seventh etching would be found? If so, where did you think it might be located?

14. One reader commented: "As I approached the final chapters, I was afraid the author would leave me up in the air. But, no, she tied up all the loose ends." Do you agree? If so, are the resolutions convincing? Satisfying?

Excerpt from
The New Worlds of Isabela Calderón de Vega

ometimes – quite often in fact – Isabela reaches down, curls her wrist and comes up with a fistful of sea water. In order to steady her hand, she keeps her elbow tight against her body. Her attempts to retain the heavy liquid in her palm are usually successful for only a few moments.

Before it all drips through her fingers, she carefully lifts the water up to her nose and sniffs its brine, its fishiness, secrets, and mysteries. Then she licks the drops that remain, along with the tiny, chewy bits of seaweed. Resisting the urge to swallow, she savors the salty taste on her tongue until it fades.

All her life she has observed this unpredictable, deceptive monster. One moment the ocean is a calm, stately beauty, the sunlight or the moonlight plunging its depths and reflecting off its surface. A composed, flirtatious lady bedecked in layers of green and blue flecked with diamonds and rubies. But you can never trust this *grande dame*. The next moment, clouds might hide her loveliness. A wind could excite her. She will become a holy devil reaching up with all her force to pull down, capture, surround, kill.

Once Isabela nearly succumbed to the raging sea. During a confused moment, she wished fervently to lose herself in its blackness – to find solace in its depths. She wanted to join her father there. And the wounded sailor, Jules, too, who gave her a desperate kiss – her first kiss ever – before diving from her father's sinking ship and disappearing. But it was Cornelius who pulled her back into the rowboat and into reality. Cornelius handed her a bucket. "Bail," he bellowed. And bail she did while Cornelius pulled the oars and rowed. Hours later Isabela – a nearly drowned creature wearing a silk nightgown, now in tatters and twisted around her limp body – arrived at the shore of a strange city. Gutteral sounds of its language approached and receded as she regained consciousness. She came to love that city. The city where she met Pieter.

"Mama, Mama, give me the cup, please. Pedro's made a castle. I want to fill up the moat."

"Not yet, Nelita," Pedro says with older brother irritation. "I'm not finished. Mama, come see. Here's where the horsemen approach. They're still far away, these soldiers. See, Mama?" Pedro places his wooden carved toy figures on a sand path some distance from his miniature castle's entrance. You can tell how far away they are. When they look ahead, the path looks narrow. I made it that way. That's perspective. Like you taught me, Mama."

"Per..pec..tif," Nelita struggles to repeat. She reaches up to her mother. "Cup please, Mama?"

With their dark hair and eyes and their olive skin, her children look thoroughly Spanish. They speak no Dutch. They have never visited Amsterdam. Yet, every day something in her life with them in the small village where she was born reminds Isabela of the twelve months she spent in that city. Nearly a dozen years ago now. So far north. So far away. So much a part of her. So dear to her.

Perspective. That one word sends her back in time to Pieter who has placed a piece of charcoal between her fingers. She feels the warmth of his hand as he guides her drawing. The only art lesson she's ever received. "You can do it, Isabela. See how the canal gradually narrows the farther away from us it flows?"

But she must not dawdle in the past. Diego has stated that he will soon take Pedro on his first voyage – a celebration of his tenth birthday. There's no persuading him otherwise. "He will follow the path of his grandfathers and father, Isabela. You think he's still your little baby?" Nightmares of the shipwreck pursue Isabela. The terror of losing her precious son to the sea overwhelms her. She must find a way to protect her child.

About The Author.

Photo by Marc Jeanneteau

Judith Kline White is the oldest of six children and the mother of three. She also has three granddaughters and has survived countless family dramas. While living in Amsterdam, she became fascinated with the city, especially with its Golden Age history, tumult, and art. Judith is fluent in Spanish and French, and takes great pleasure in using her expanding knowledge of Dutch on return visits to The Netherlands. Her careers span linguist, educator, entrepreneur and non-profit fundraiser, and include: Peace Corps volunteer trainer; Founder/Director of Foreign Language for Young Children Inc.; and Co-Founder/Co-Director of Global Child, Inc. Her previous publications include *Phrase-a-Day French for Children*; *Phrase-a-Day Spanish for Children*; and *Phrase-a-Day English for Spanish-speaking Children*. Judith lives in Brookline, Massachusetts with her husband, Allen L. White. *The Seventh Etching* is her first novel.

Lightning Source UK Ltd.
Milton Keynes UK
UKHW040848140120
356927UK00001B/72/P

9 781475 908114